She was a police analyst. He couldn't believe she'd commit cold-blooded murder…but he also couldn't get past the evidence.

Scarsdale pulled a photograph of Zarko out of his notebook and showed it to Loper. "Have you ever seen this man before?"

Loper studied the picture. "Yes, as a matter of fact, I have," he said, nodding as he handed the photo back to Scarsdale. "He came in last Tuesday, inquiring about a vacancy in Building 3. On the third floor, as a matter of fact."

"About what time was that?" Harris asked.

"Oh, I'd say umm…just before dusk. Six or seven."

So, did you have a vacancy on three?" Scarsdale asked.

"We did. Apartment 310. We showed it to him and he said he'd let us know."

Scarsdale and Harris walked back to the car.

"Zarko never wanted to rent that apartment," Scarsdale said. "He wanted to see the lay-out."

"Are you thinking what I'm thinking?" Harris asked.

"Yeah. Dani Mueller was the woman in Lasiter's closet. And Zarko wants to get rid of her."

"So what the hell was she doing in his closet ?"

Scarsdale recalled something Amanda had told him. "You remember that old man across the alley from Lasiter's? You thought the taillight sketch he drew fit a Mercedes?"

"Yeah."

"Well, guess who sold her Mercedes recently?"

Harris stopped and looked at Scarsdale before his eyes dropped to the pavement and his mouth tightened into a straight line. For Scarsdale, if Dani was involved, it complicated things. Deep down, he hoped she had a plausible explanation. Like Harris said, she was too classy to be mixed up with the likes of Lasiter and Zarko. But if she was the one, he didn't want Shannon hanging out with her. After all, she *had* left town kind of suddenly. *If* she came back, they'd have a serious chat about Lasiter's murder.

His focus is on solving the murders—until the unthinkable happens…

Recently widowed, Austin Police Detective Jason Scarsdale works to solve the murders of two pedophiles, while trying to be both mother and father to his five-year-old daughter. During his investigation, Scarsdale is forced to navigate between the crosshairs of two police commanders out to get him. Drawn to Austin Police Crime Analyst, Dani Mueller, who has also suffered tragedy, Scarsdale fights both his attraction and his suspicions that something just isn't right…

She is hiding a secret, one that could not only cost her a job—it could end her life…

Dani hides a deadly past. After her daughter was brutally murdered, Dani exacted her revenge then changed her name and fled to Austin. But if her secret ever gets out, she knows there is no place she can hide from the murderer's vicious family.

Pulled into a web of malice and deceit, Scarsdale and Dani discover the value of breaking the rules. Then just when they thought things couldn't get worse…they do.

KUDOS for *Price of Justice*

Price of Justice grabs you from the opening page and tells a riveting story. ~ *Suzanne Lakin*

A page turner with many unexpected twists and turns. ~ *Joan Adamak*

It's the characters, both sympathetic and unsympathetic that have to drive a good detective story these days. *Price of Justice* definitely has both, which makes it a good solid mystery, with some dark undertones, that a solid fan of the genre is sure to enjoy. ~ *Shannon Yarbrough, Amazon Top 1,000 reviewer*

Price of Justice by Alan Brenham is a police procedural/who-done-it with a twist—the guilty may be innocent and the innocent guilty…Brenham crafts a complicated story with intriguing twists, turns, and subplots that foil both the heroes and the villains—an intense, fast-paced thriller that defies you to put it down once you pick it up. ~ *Taylor Jones, reviewer*

I found the characters well-developed, three-dimensional, and endearing, the story line riveting and thought-provoking. Brenham gives you a good, honest look at how frustrating a cop's job can be and how tempting it is to want to mete out justice yourself if you are in a position to do so. It also points out how dangerous it is to assume you know who is really guilty. Price of Justice is a hard-hitting, gritty crime thriller that is truly hard to put down. ~ *Regan Murphy, reviewer*

A gripping, fast-moving, and emotionally charged drama centered on well-drawn characters with genuine motives. ~ *Kirkus Reviews*

ACKNOWLEDGEMENTS

I want to thank the following people whose help and advice was essential to this novel: first and foremost, my wife, Lillian, whose perseverance, support, and patience are most appreciated. I can't thank you enough.

Thanks to my brother, Kevin Behr, Chairman of the Criminal Justice/Law Enforcement Department of Coastal Bend College for his practical advice on modern police investigative procedures; to Tom Walsh, retired sex crimes detective with the Austin Police Department and Sergeant Scott Ehlert with the Homicide Unit of the Austin Police Department for their advice and assistance; to Jerry Pena with the Austin Police Department Forensics Lab for his help with forensics; and, to David V. Rossi, Senior Crime Scene Analyst now retired from the Harris County Sheriff's Office, for his assistance with crime scene operations.

PRICE OF JUSTICE

Alan Brenham

A BLACK OPAL BOOKS PUBLICATION

DEDICATION

*To the law enforcement officers and criminal investigators
who work tirelessly to protect our children
from violent predators.*

*In memory of my brother, Roger L. Behr,
Austin Police Department, retired.*

CHAPTER 1

"There's no way out of the desert, except through it."
~ *Old African Proverb*

Looking down the black barrel of his service weapon, Detective Jason Scarsdale saw the promise of peace. Just pull the trigger, flick out the lights, and rest. He couldn't sleep, he didn't eat, and he couldn't work. The fingers of his right hand were poised on the trigger guard, his left clutching the grip. With deliberation, he shifted his hold to adjust his wedding ring so that the three diamonds were showing. She had bought it for their first anniversary and, after the priest blessed it, had placed it on his ring finger in a reaffirmation of their vows. She told him the three diamonds signified the Holy Trinity. She said the Trinity would protect them, keeping their union intact as they grew old and feeble.

Now Charity was dead. Killed four weeks ago. Dead at twenty-eight. Dead because of him.

When they first met, he knew right away he wanted to be with her for the rest of his life but it took a while to win her over. He was older and she had reservations about being a cop's wife. But in the end he had won her heart.

He tried to imagine the future without her. Family and friends said time heals, but time was his enemy. All he could see was an eternity of black emptiness. To him, each minute of each day for the past four weeks had felt the same: empty, except for the pain. Daytime or nighttime—it didn't matter.

He lifted the gun and opened his mouth, jerking violently as his cell phone rang. His eyes went to the dashboard where he kept it. The display read *Home*.

He stared at it, wrapping his head around that word

Home. Taking a deep breath, he laid the gun in his lap and picked up the phone.

"Hello, Sarah,"

His eyes were riveted on the gun, his voice a flat mono-tone.

"Jason, are you okay? You didn't eat anything. You walked out of here like a zombie."

"Wasn't hungry."

Sarah was his sister, three years his junior. Despite every terrible thing he had done to her when they were kids, from putting frogs and lizards in her bed to blowing up her favorite doll with a cherry bomb, she was always there for him. She wasn't stronger, but she was kinder. She never held onto things like he did.

"Trust me," Sarah said. "Things will get better. It'll just take time."

He traced the contour of the gun. "Maybe, maybe not. I don't know anymore."

A few seconds of silence passed.

"There's someone here who wants to talk to you."

"Who?"

"Who do you think? Does a certain little five-year-old named Shannon ring a bell?"

"Is she all right?"

"Of course. She just wants to ask you something. Hang on."

Shannon. He hadn't been there for her. "Honey, your daddy's on the phone," Sarah said.

A beat.

"Hi, Daddy," Shannon said. "Aunt Sarah read me a story about Narnia."

Shannon's image filled his mind. The day in the hospital when he first laid eyes on his new-born daughter, when he first held her in his arms. "She did? That's great."

"When are you coming home, Daddy? I miss you."

"I miss you too, princess, but I can't make it home right now. I'm working on a case. But I'll be there as soon as I can."

His police cell buzzed. He glanced at the screen. It was his partner, Sean Harris.

"Sweetheart, I have to hang up. I'll see you tonight."

"Daddy, will you read me more about Narnia tonight?"

"Of course, I will."

"You promise?" she asked.

"I promise," he said and knew that he meant it.

He laid his cell down and pressed the *Talk* button on the police phone.

"Yeah?"

A moment of silence on the line and then Harris spoke up, his voice tentative. "Where are you, buddy?"

Scarsdale looked around. In front of him was the Zilker Park pool, closed for the season. He turned to see a single jogger pass by. His lips tipped in the tiniest wry smile at the sight of an older couple strolling along a walking path, smiles on their faces, her hand holding his arm while her head rested on his shoulder. Life just went merrily on. He looked at the gun now resting in his lap.

"Zilker Park."

"You feel up to working a kiddie diddler case with me?"

A long silence.

Scarsdale shoved the revolver into its holster and pressed the thumb break tabs together. "Yeah. Meet me at the station."

ᴄᴈᴄᴈ

Harris leaned across the seat and opened the passenger door for Scarsdale. Harris was a heavy-set man with gray stubble around the sides of his shaved head and eyes that viewed the world with a wary kindness reserved for the proven few.

As they drove away, Scarsdale sat, slouched in the seat, staring straight ahead, his clenched fists planted on his thighs. With a tremendous effort of will, he focused his thoughts on Shannon. Charity had taken the lead being a parent and role model for their daughter. Now it all fell on his shoulders, and he didn't have a clue how to do it. But starting now, no more guy's nights out, no more football Sundays. From here on, Shannon was the reason, the center of his universe.

"Almost ate your gun, didn't you?"

It was more statement than question and Scarsdale felt a weight lift at the plainly spoken fact.

They drove a while in silence. Scarsdale stared out the side window. The whole afternoon played in his head again, like it had so many times since patrol officers came to his door with the news. It felt strange to him because he always figured, being a cop, he'd be the one to die, not Charity.

"It wasn't your fault," Harris said.

He shot a quick glance at Harris. "It *was* my fault. She asked me to—" Scarsdale took a deep breath and let it out. "—go to the store." He looked out the front window then out the side. "I begged off. Too damn busy watching a game," he said. "She gave me a kiss on the cheek, asked who was winning, then left." He looked down at his ring. "I should have been the one driving that car."

"How's Shannon doing?" Harris asked as they drove south on First Street, passing over Ben White Boulevard.

"She cries a lot at night. But she's getting better. Sarah's going back to Waco Thursday evening, so I've got to find a babysitter. Know any good ones? Really good ones?"

"Mary and I haven't needed one for quite a while but I'll check with her. Have you asked around the department? A lot of stuff's posted on the bulletin board. You might try that."

Scarsdale nodded, etching the task into his memory. He'd need someone available to pick Shannon up from kindergarten on those days when a case prevented him from doing so. Someone to come in on short notice when he had one of those late night investigations working.

"How many cases did Mitchell pile on your desk?" Harris asked.

"Too many. You recall that citizen's complaint about kids buying porn from Blue Cloud Adult Books and Videos?" He looked at Harris.

Harris cast a sideways look of surprise at him. "He gave you that piece of crap? Patrol should have handled that."

"Yeah, tell me about it." Scarsdale sat up straighter. "How old is the victim in this case?" he asked as Harris pulled up to the curb before a rundown duplex. Three patrol cars were parked on the street in front.

"All of three years old." A scrawny brown dog barked at them, circling around behind them, and approaching tentatively as they walked across the dead grass toward the front door. Scarsdale reached down, causing the dog to skitter away and bark furiously. He picked up a Barbie doll lying in the yard, brushing off pieces of grass and a small glob of dirt. Two uniformed officers, providing scene protection, stood about ten yards away from the duplex. The officers nodded as Scarsdale and Harris headed for the front door.

The on-scene supervisor, a uniformed sergeant named Daryl Fields, briefed them before they entered the duplex. "The perv lived here. Was the mother's boyfriend. When she got home from work at seven, she caught him in the kid's bedroom with his pants down around his knees. According to the neighbor—" Fields nodded toward a gray-haired stoop-shouldered woman standing on the adjacent porch. "—Ruth Short. Said she heard the mother screaming like a banshee. Stuff smashing against the wall. When Ms. Short got over there, the perv flew out the door. Almost bowled her over."

"The perp's name is…" Scarsdale asked.

He heard the bellowing Texas twang of a woman, he assumed was the mother, coming from inside the house, threatening violence against the perp.

Fields read from his notes. "Olsen. Terry Wayne Olsen. White male. About fifty. Bald over brown, about six foot, around one-hundred-forty to one-hundred-fifty." Fields nodded in the direction of the door. "The voice you hear is the mother, Dory Mabry. The victim is Beth Ann Mabry, three years old."

Scarsdale opened the door—a lightweight screen door trimmed in green that wouldn't close completely. Once inside the duplex, he saw the mother and the three-year old victim—

her daughter Beth Ann—standing a few feet away. Neither looked his way.

The blonde-haired Dory gestured, using a lit cigarette to emphasize her story. "That bastard better hope you people find him before I do." She pointed with the cigarette toward the kitchen. "I got me something in there that'll fix that son of a bitch real good."

She paused long enough to take a drag off a cigarette and blow the smoke out her nostrils before continuing her rant. She drowned out a female officer who was trying to ask questions.

Dory was a big woman, not fat, light-complected, and dressed in a pale-green waitress uniform. From the wrinkles and creases on her cheeks and forehead, Scarsdale guessed her age to be about thirty to thirty-five.

Beth Ann seemed small for a three-year-old, but healthy. Cute, with big blue eyes. Little rosy cheeks. Her jeans and T-shirt had some stains. Not too bad for a child her age. Shannon always seemed to find a mud hole in the backyard and wade right into it.

He looked around the room. The inside of the duplex smelled like stale cigarette smoke. Maybe a trace of pee. A large flat screen TV—brand-new, about forty-six to fifty inches—covered the far wall and made the room seem small. The room was clean, a few toys scattered around. No roaches scurrying up the walls. No trash littered around the room. Some dust caked around the window sills. An ordinary room with simple furnishings, except for the TV. He couldn't help fixating on the TV. It was a lot better one than he had.

Scarsdale moved in front of Dory, drawing her attention away from the officer, who had given up trying to ask any questions, realizing the futility of her efforts.

She stopped talking and stared at him, taking another drag off the cigarette, and gave Scarsdale an apprising once-over.

He smiled at Beth Ann as she clung to her mother's leg, half-hiding behind her. She stared up at Scarsdale. Her eyes were wide—a frightened look.

"I believe this is yours," he said, handing the doll to her.

When he knelt down, she moved behind her mother around to the other leg. Dory snatched it out of his hand.

"Don't." One word, in a tone that portended an ominous warning. "It ain't good for her to be taking things from strangers no more."

And Scarsdale knew better than to say anything.

The female officer looked at Scarsdale. An ever-so-slight curling up at the corners of her mouth. A rolling of her eyes as she backed away. "She's all yours, Detective."

The baton had been passed. Flipping his pocket notepad open, he introduced himself.

She looked down at Beth Ann and handed her the Barbie doll. "Baby girl, why don't you go over there and play with your doll while me and this here cop visit."

Beth Ann protested. "Mama—"

"You go on now. Put some clothes on your doll before she catches a cold." A minute or two after Beth Ann walked away, Dory turned to face Scarsdale. "I swear to Holy Jesus if I catch that shitass, I'll slice and dice him," she said, her voice subdued. "She's only three, for crissake. I hope the prick rots in hell."

Scarsdale sighed. He couldn't blame her. "Okay, Ms. Mabry. Tell me exactly what happened."

Dory gave him all the lurid details and Scarsdale questioned her about small gaps in her recollection of events.

"Where's Beth Ann's room?" Scarsdale asked.

She motioned with her hand for them to follow her. "Down this way."

He followed her down the hall and into the diminutive bedroom. Light-blue walls complete with crayoned stick figures. Pieces of a lamp were scattered around the floor. A few spots of blood sprinkled the floor near the door.

"Was Beth Ann hurt?"

Dory looked at him dumbstruck. "Hurt? Ya mean like broken bones? Bleedin'?"

Scarsdale pointed at the spots. "Bleeding, like that. Whose blood is that?"

Dory leaned over, looking at the blood spots. "Aww, hell no. That's from him."

He readied himself to take some good notes. "So you found him in here?"

"Yeah. When I come in, he had Beth Ann right here," Dory said, slapping the unmade bed. "He was fixin' to—" She took another drag off the cigarette. "It makes me wanna puke to even think about it." She blew out a long cloud of whitish smoke toward the ceiling. "That's when I took that there lamp and busted his skull with it." She pivoted around as if she were swinging the lamp. "I caught him right smack on the head. That jackass took off for the door." She pointed in the direction of the living room. "He lit outta here, runnin' faster than a bee-stung stallion. I done grabbed a butcher knife off the kitchen table and chased after that no-good sonofabitch. But he got away before I could catch up to him."

She nudged the pieces of the lamp into a pile with her shoe. "His head was for sure gushing blood. I hope I cracked his damn skull real good. He ain't gonna ever come within a mile of Beth Ann or me again. I damn sure guarantee that."

"Who babysits Beth Ann when you're at work?"

"He did. My next-door neighbor, Ruth Short, is gonna do it now."

"Do you have a photograph of Olsen?"

He followed Dory to living room where she grabbed a framed picture off the coffee table and handed it to him. "That's him," she said. "Keep it."

"Do you know where he may have gone? Any friends? Relatives in the area?"

"No. He don't have no kin around here and I never seen him with any friends but he did talk about a guy named Fergie and no, I ain't never met the guy."

Satisfied that he had all the information, he and Harris left, heading back to the office. Scarsdale had an appointment later with a prosecutor to go over his testimony.

And tomorrow, in district court, he'd testify about his investigation and arrest of a murderer named Scott Lasiter. By

Friday, he figured the jury would sentence that defendant to death.

CHAPTER 2

"Women do most delight in revenge."
~ *Sir Thomas Browne*

On Tuesday, I found myself seated in the third row of the Travis County courtroom for the trial of Scott Dewayne Lasiter.

My name is Dani Mueller and I used to be a defense attorney and crime analyst in Sacramento, California, under another name—Karla Engel. But all that life was gone now. Seven years practicing law and a life—a once happy life I shared with my ten-year old daughter, Katarina—wiped away by a maniac's sick frenzy, a maniac named Doyle Burton.

Before I left California, I filed a petition for a name change under California's Safe at Home Act. The Act permitted a confidential name change if I could show I was a victim of a stalker. In my case, it was the entire Burton family—Doyle's mother, Mattie, his half-brother Phoenix Wilson, and a demented sister they called Bunny. His other brother, a psycho named Parnell, mailed threatening letters to me from prison until the warden put a stop to it.

Everywhere I went—the grocery store, my office, the courthouse, even my home—they were there, bumping into me or making obscene and threatening gestures at me. I kept Fix-A-Flat cans in my trunk and became an expert at changing tires, fixing busted taillights and headlights. The court granted my petition, allowing a confidential name change, from Karla Engel to Dani Mueller, and sealed the records.

As I got ready to move to Texas, I set up a few rabbit trails so the Burtons would never find out where I ended up. Using the internet, I created a law office for Karla Engel near

Chicago. If they discovered the name change, they'd find Dani Mueller had relocated to Del Mar, in southern California. That would at least slow them down.

Using my prior experience as an analyst for the Sacramento police, I landed a similar position with the Austin Police Department about two and half months ago. Utilizing various databases and software to analyze and interpret crime data, I developed crime series, patterns, and suspect profiles at the request of detectives working cases around the city. My personal specialty was child molesters.

But I was not here today because of my job. I came to see if the legal system in Texas functioned better than it did in California. Taking some vacation days, I sat here to see if this defendant got what he deserved. Or would this be round two of the theater of the absurd? I hoped not.

Lasiter was the lowlife on trial for the murder of a young girl. That pervert sat at the defense table to my left, directly in my line of sight. He wiped the back of his hand across his brow and glanced at the victim's mother, Susan Crowell. He looked in my direction and shifted in his seat.

Nervous, Lasiter, you sick monster? I dug my fingernails into my purse every time I looked at him. I wished they were digging into his eyes instead.

Today Susan's worst nightmare would become a horrible reality, and I knew exactly how she felt when she walked past me on her way to the witness stand. The jurors' eyes scrutinized her every step as she neared the witness chair just like the jurors in Burton's trial did to me. That chair sat behind a white pine modesty panel, next to the judge's elevated bench. Susan would be center stage like I had been two and a half years ago. She seemed to be trying hard to maintain her composure, but I could tell by the way she shifted in the witness chair, the way her hand alternately covered her mouth and toyed with the gold cross dangling around her neck, that she was anything but composed. Testifying was a nerve-wracking experience. No, actually, it was a terrible experience—it had been for me and it would be for Susan, too.

I figured Susan's heart must be in her throat by now. Her stomach churning so bad she probably wanted to vomit. The loss of a child was a terrible hurt that a mother never recovered from, and having to relive it in front of a room full of strangers, staring and hanging onto her every word, would make it a hundred times worse. I hoped for Susan's sake the system worked this time. It hadn't for me.

When I took that long, frightening walk to the witness stand fourteen months ago, my entire body had shaken with a rage I'd never felt before. My heart had beaten faster knowing I would finally confront him. My face had felt very warm; I couldn't see it but I knew it was flushed. At that moment I wanted Burton hacked up just like he'd done to my Katarina.

I had felt like a zoo animal on display. Every tear, every quiver, each breath I took was studied by every pair of eyes in that room. Every word I spoke was sucked up by eager ears.

Looking around the room now, I saw Susan's husband sitting on the cushioned bench in the front row to my right—directly behind the prosecutors. His hard eyes, tightened lips, and taut jaw line told me that a terrible anger churned deep inside him too. I watched him glower at the defendant, his coal-black eyes boring holes right through the man, loathing his very existence. Yes, the air in that courtroom was thick with virulence—the Crowells' and mine. I wondered if Lasiter felt it too. I hoped he did.

I studied Susan as she leaned forward. Her eyes focused on the assistant district attorney, Rusty Tidwell. Her lips moved in sync with his question as if she was repeating it. Tidwell appeared to me to be in his mid-twenties, a baby lawyer. A second prosecutor, Madge Blackmon, sat with him.

"Would you please tell the members of the jury how you were related to Amy Crowell?"

I saw Susan's lip quiver before she took a deep breath and looked in the direction of her husband. When I had been asked a similar question, I'd broken down and cried. Katarina had been my life, and that pedophile Burton had taken her from me. I knew Susan Crowell felt the same way about Amy.

The quick, hateful glance she cast at Lasiter before turning to face the jury reminded me of the same hateful glance I shot at Burton when I testified. Unlike Susan, I didn't stop with the scowl. I had pointed at Burton, calling him a butcher and saying he should die for what he did. I'll never forget his sleazy expression. When the jury acquitted Burton, that snake slithered out of the courtroom, laughing at me the whole way. Justice lost that day.

"Amy was my—" I could feel the hot tears Susan wiped from her eyes but she stiffened and faced the jury. "She was my daughter." Susan looked at Lasiter again, this time through tear-filled eyes. "She was *only* nine years old."

She said, it as if asking Lasiter a question. Katarina had just turned ten when that monster Burton raped and then mutilated her with a knife.

I watched Tidwell as he picked up Amy's photograph from the table and, with the judge's permission, handed it to Susan. I could feel her anguish when she bit her lip while staring at the picture. I think that was just her way of keeping her focus and not breaking down—of coping with a horrible situation.

I hadn't fared as well when the prosecutor handed me Katarina's photograph. The prosecutor told me later that I had sat there, staring at Katarina's picture in abject silence. She didn't know what I was feeling—I mean, how could she? She'd never lost her child.

I held my breath when Tidwell asked Susan if she recognized the person in State's Exhibit Number One.

When the California prosecutor had asked me a similar question, I remembered my response—it was swift and directed right at Burton, instead of the jury. "She's my daughter. She was just a little girl."

"Yes. It's my daughter, Amy," Susan replied, her reddened eyes fixed on the photograph.

I didn't know if it was possible to despise Lasiter any more than I already did. I envisioned him on his knees, begging for his life, as my blade sliced deep into his body. He and

Burton were sub humans—both were perverts and murderers.

Tidwell walked Amy's photograph over to Lasiter's attorney and laid it on the table. "The State offers Exhibit Number One into evidence."

I watched Lasiter glance at the picture then look away. *What's the matter? You don't want to see the girl whose life you snuffed out?* I wondered how he could sleep at night, knowing what he had done.

Tidwell placed Amy's photograph on the easel right where the jury could see it. From where I sat, I had a clear view of it, too. She was a beautiful girl, dressed in a green, polka-dot shirt and jeans. She favored her mother.

Katarina's photograph had been the one of her in fifth grade, dressed in that plaid skirt she loved so much and her favorite top—the T-shirt with the hot-pink-and-white stripes and "Superstar" printed on the front. She was my little superstar.

"Would you tell the jury about the last time you saw Amy?" Tidwell asked.

When the prosecutor had asked me that question, it became the roughest part of my time on the witness stand. The absolute pits. My emotions rocketed all over. I sobbed and cursed Burton under my breath. It had been a struggle for me to hold it together.

I fought the urge to cry. Burton would not get the pleasure of seeing me break down. But my voice had cracked when I said Katarina left with her two girlfriends and a parent to watch soccer at North Laguna Creek Park around ten in the morning.

Susan answered, "It was Saturday, June fourth. Right after our lunch together. Amy went to visit her best friend, Jenny. She was supposed to call me when she got there, but I never heard from her again."

I looked at Lasiter, sitting there somber-looking, jotting notes down on a yellow legal pad with his left hand, casting glances at Susan. *Keep looking at her, you worm. You know what you did to her. You need to feel her pain.*

Neither Susan nor I were given the opportunity to tell the jury how we felt when we saw our child's lifeless little body. How we felt standing in the doorway of our daughter's bedroom, knowing we'd never hear her musical laughter again, never see her playing with her Barbie, no more questions about why things happened the way they did. No more little fingers slurping cake batter right out of the bowl. No more "Mommy."

The day Katarina died, my life ended, too. I had carried her for nine months. I nursed her and did all those things a doting mother does for her baby girl. When Katarina had the measles, I cared for her. When she was hospitalized for a severe respiratory distress from Croup, I parked myself by her bedside for the two days she laid there. She had been as much a part of me as my own body. When Burton murdered her, he killed a part of me.

Tidwell asked a couple of questions about Susan's interaction with the police. She did much better than I had. She told the jury about the dreaded knock on the door and discovering grim-faced police officers standing there. The jury heard Susan describe her despair, her first day in hell—the same despair I felt when they knocked on my door.

My first day in hell began right around 3:30 p.m. when I answered the door and saw the two police officers there—a male and a female, serious and morose. My heart sank to my feet. Something was very wrong. When they said Katarina would never be coming home again, I refused to believe them. God wouldn't let anything happen to her. She had been a gentle, loving child.

I just stood there, denying she was gone. I kept telling them they were wrong. It wasn't her. It couldn't be her. She went to the park with her friend's family and would be back by four o'clock. But they persisted. When the female officer handed me Katarina's seashell necklace, my legs turned to rubber. I stood in the doorway, holding her necklace, bawling, and screaming. The female officer tried to put her arm around my shoulder to comfort me, but I shook it off.

When Susan left the witness stand, my eyes followed her

back to where her husband waited. He draped his arm around his wife's shoulder, drawing her close to him. Susan was lucky.

No husband had been there to console me. My miserable excuse for a husband, Tim Williams, had taken off a month before Katarina had even been born.

The state called Helen Jackson to the stand. She reminded me of my namesake grandmother—a frail older woman with silver hair done up in a bun.

I listened as Helen talked about standing in her front yard on Fritz Hughes Park Road when she saw a man take something wrapped up in a blanket or rug from the trunk of his car and carry it into the woods. When he emerged a few minutes later, he didn't have anything in his hands. She saw him as he drove past her—a distance of about ten feet away. But she couldn't positively identify Lasiter as that man.

Lasiter's attorney went after her like a junkyard dog. He crucified her. I felt so bad for Helen. By the time he finished, she admitted Lasiter only looked similar to the man. I wanted to scream at those prosecutors for not prepping her. Casting a quick glance at Susan, I saw her look down and shake her head.

I hoped the next witness—a gangly teenager named Darryl Grey would do a better job of nailing Lasiter.

After a few predicate questions, Madge Blackmon got to the meat of his testimony. "Mr. Grey, please tell the jury what you observed on Saturday June fourth."

"Me and my friend, Stacy Kimble, we're hiking along a trail right by Fritz Hughes Park Road when some dude crosses the trail up ahead, something slung over his shoulder. We saw him dump it in the brush and then kinda jog out to the road. We figured it was a body 'cause of the way it sounded when he dropped it. In a blanket and all."

Good so far. I remembered this boy's statement from the police file. I hoped he wouldn't buckle under on cross-examination by Lasiter's attorney.

"Then what do you see?" Blackmon asked.

"We followed him out to the road and seen him get into a green Pinto and drive off. Me and Stacy, we wrote down the license number. We went back to see what he dumped, um—" He glanced at Susan and looked at Madge. "I mean we went back to see if we could help the girl."

It's okay, Darryl. This is hard on all of us. Just tell the jury what you discovered, just like you told the detectives. I caught a glimpse of Susan sitting forward in her seat, nodding each time Darryl related a helpful fact. From Burton's trial, I knew the damning facts didn't always carry the day.

After Blackmon asked him what he found, his deer-in-the-headlight look told me he'd hesitate. His eyes flitted from the jury to Lasiter to Blackmon. I could barely hear what he said next.

"A dead girl all covered in blood. She looked like she was all butchered up. It grossed us out."

Grey's testimony flicked on my internal TV. Images of Katarina lying bloody in the tall grass of Laguna played like a horror movie. I tried to fight the tears but I lost. I saw Susan, bent over, with her face buried in her hands. Then she raced out of the courtroom, crying. I brushed my tears away with the heel of my hand and almost chased after her, wanting to console her, wanting to tell her she wasn't alone in this hellish situation. Then I saw her husband follow her out.

Grey said he couldn't ID the man when the police showed him a lineup. The man wore a cap low over his face. But he looked similar to Lasiter. *Good*, I thought. *Grey put Lasiter's license plate number in front of the jury. Just bring a detective in to tell them whose plate that was.* I glared at the back of Lasiter's head. *You bastard!*

I saw Susan return right before Tidwell called his next witness—Detective Jason Scarsdale. An eerie silence fell over the courtroom until I saw the doors open. Then a few people whispered words I couldn't make out. He walked past me on his way to the witness stand—shoulders slumped over, lips drawn together in a straight line.

I'd heard through the departmental grapevine about the

death of his wife. It took the fire department almost an hour to extract her from the car even with the Jaws of Life. He had a young daughter—didn't know much about her. I did know that the next few months would be hard on him, a fact I was all too familiar with. I'd wanted to help. Maybe I could talk to him sometime in the next few days.

As he swore to tell the whole truth, I glanced over at Susan. She wiped her eyes and smiled. Her husband seemed elated at Scarsdale taking the stand. From my reading of the file, I knew he'd nail that rotten snake.

Sitting on the stand, he looked like he'd lost some weight in the face since I last saw him. Sort of drawn-looking. A little haggard, like he hadn't been sleeping well. With what happened to him, it was understandable. I could relate to the pain and heartache he must have been feeling. I understood loss.

Scarsdale knew the facts. His responses were crisp, direct, and enunciated in a clear manner, and he addressed his answers right to the jury. I checked off his investigative steps one by one in my mind after each answer he gave.

He testified that the license plate number came back to a sedan registered to the defendant. My heart leaped when he pointed right at Lasiter. One of the highlights for me and, I'm sure, for Susan too was when he told the jury that the car bearing those plates was seized at the Lasiter residence. He observed dried leaves in the front floorboard of the car. Blood spots on the front seat. Hairs found in the trunk.

When he wasn't answering questions, he sat there staring grim-faced down at his lap. His thoughts, I'm sure, centered on his loss.

The trial resumed at 1:15 p.m. when Tidwell called Monica Turner of our crime lab who had done the DNA analysis. I couldn't have been happier when she testified that the blood found on the seat of the car and the hair fibers in the trunk matched samples taken from the body of Amy Crowell. I almost jumped up and did a fist-pump. I hoped that maybe, just maybe, this time the criminal justice system would work.

The State's last witness took the stand—one of the

pathologists from the medical examiner's office, Doctor Samuel Rushman. He testified about the autopsy of Amy Crowell.

My thoughts went back to the testimony of the coroner who had performed Katarina's autopsy. Dr. Frances Moyer had described in meticulous detail the multiple stab wounds Burton inflicted on Katarina. Her skull fracture. The broken bones in her face, jaw, and arms. She even had bruising to her neck that Moyer had said was consistent with manual strangulation. But he attributed her cause of death to blunt-force trauma.

Images of the stab wounds and blunt-force trauma done to Katarina flashed across my mind. A wave of nausea mixed with anger bubbled up inside me. I gripped the edge of the bench and took several deep breaths.

The judge recessed for a break and I followed the Crowells out of the courtroom, keeping my distance while stopping to sip some water from the fountain.

They stood together by the wall across from the courtroom doors, a few feet from me, just talking with each other. She was a pretty, fair-skinned woman. She and her husband turned to look toward Lasiter who just a second ago had walked out of the courtroom and headed for the exit door.

I wondered if he would become one of Austin PD's fugitives.

"I wish the police had found Amy's bracelet," Susan said.

I followed her line of sight as she stared at Lasiter.

"Can I just ask him about it?"

"No, honey," her husband answered. "If you talk to him, his attorney will accuse you of harassing him."

"I want her bracelet back," she said. "It belonged to my mother and he *took it* from Amy when he killed her."

I felt so sorry for Susan. I knew about Amy's bracelet from the police report. Susan told police Amy was wearing it when she left for her friend's house. According to the report, Susan had inquired everyday whether it had been found. Her anguish over the bracelet made chills shoot up and down my back. I remembered the German silver rhinestone heart bracelet I had given Katarina for her eighth birthday. It had been a gift to me from my mother, Petra. It was a symbol of my deep love for my daughter as it had been since Katarina's great grandmother—her namesake—first passed it down to my grandmother. I knew Amy's bracelet meant the same to Susan.

When I came out of the restroom, the Crowells were gone, perhaps back in the courtroom. I saw Lasiter standing outside the courthouse, smoking a cigarette. I wondered if he planned to abscond. Surely he gave it serious thought.

Despite my disgust with cigarette smoke and perverts, my curiosity piqued me into strolling toward him. I wanted a closer look. Maybe he'd sense the incredible hatred I felt for him.

Lasiter appeared sullen. His eyes stared into the distance like he was seeing into another world. I watched his hand move mechanically—raising the cigarette to his lips and back down. The smoke spewing from his nose disgusted me. But then so did he.

"You're that child-killing defendant, aren't you?" Words weren't strong enough a weapon to use on him, but they were the only weapon I had at the moment. If I had a gun or a knife, I would have used it right there. He had no right to live, not after what he did to Amy.

He looked at me with sad puppy-dog eyes as he chewed on his lower lip. He nodded before answering in a subdued tone. "I'm the defendant. Yes, ma'am. But I didn't kill anyone." His attorney came out the door and moved between Lasiter and me.

"Scott, come over here," Welsh said. He glanced at me, giving me the once over from head to toe.

I flashed one of those super-quick smiles, the ones which show a very minimal degree of friendliness, and lingered nearby, wanting to hear what they discussed.

"None of the state's eyewitnesses identified you as the man on Fritz Hughes Park Road," Welsh said. "Do you have any idea who used your car to dump the body?"

"No. If I did, I woulda told the cops." He blew out more smoke. "What do you think the jury will do?"

"No one really knows but I like your chances." He put his arm around Lasiter. "C'mon. Let's go back inside."

I seethed. *Chances? Give me a knife and five minutes, I'll show you what your chances are, Lasiter.*

Lasiter crushed the cigarette beneath his shiny black shoe. Turning, they started for the doors. Then Lasiter stopped and looked back at me with a tight-lipped smile. "Ma'am." He held the door open as a gesture, inviting me to precede him back inside.

"No," I said in the coldest tone I could muster. If it had been anybody else, I'd have accepted the offer, but a murderer was the last person I wanted walking behind me.

I watched him pass through the door toward the courtroom. His head hung down, and his shoulders slumped as he stuffed his hands into his pants' pockets. He shuffled his gait. His steps seemed weak and tottering like those of a condemned man. In my mind, he already was one. But if the system didn't work this time, if the jury let him go, I'd kill him myself.

Just like I had killed Doyle Burton.

CHAPTER 3

"Justice cannot be for one side alone,
but must be for both." ~ *Eleanor Roosevelt*

From Tom Zarko's view, Clay Ferguson looked paler than the face of death. A tall scarecrow of a man, he trembled while a big muscular man, wearing a black ski mask, walked around him like a jackal circling his prey.

"So you don't like the way I'm running this outfit," said the man.

Ferguson swallowed hard. "I didn't say that." He turned his head like an owl, watching the man. "All I said was we wanted a fair share of the profits from the stuff. We take the chances and do all the work." He looked over at Zarko, Phillip Agosti, and Rico Sanchez, seated on the sofa to his left. "Right, guys?"

Sanchez appeared to concentrate on the pocketknife, rolling from finger to finger over his hand and back again. He said nothing.

Zarko bobbed his head. "Yeah." He wondered, like they all did, who the man was. No one had ever seen him without the mask. He, Agosti, and Ferguson figured he was some big-shot banker or political muck-a-muck. Somebody used to always having things done his way. Zarko had given him the moniker of "The CEO" because the man always took control, always bossy. He ran the group like it was a company and he owned it.

Zarko checked Agosti's reaction. To him, Agosti was a mealy-mouthed wimp.

Agosti hesitated, his eyes open wide like a scared fawn, glancing back and forth between Ferguson and the CEO. Finally he nodded before folding his arms across his chest.

"We could vote on a fair amount," Ferguson said. "But Olsen—"

"Olsen has some problems right now, so he can't be here. Taking a vote without him wouldn't be fair," the CEO said, standing in front of Ferguson. "So I'll decide."

He glanced at Agosti as he removed a pack of smokes from his shirt pocket, tapped the pack so one cigarette stuck out. He raised the pack up to his mouth, dragging the solitary cigarette out with his lips. The CEO's loose fitting sleeve fell back exposing part of a black and green tattoo, but Zarko couldn't make out what the inked drawing represented. He saw the CEO stick the pack back in his pocket while the man glared at Ferguson. The CEO lit the cigarette, then blew a large cloud of smoke, right in Ferguson's face.

Agosti scooted closer to the other end of the sofa, as if distance would shield him from the CEO. Ferguson stepped back, then pivoted toward the kitchen. The CEO's meaty hand grabbed him by the throat, jerking him back like a ragdoll. He lifted Ferguson up and pinned Ferguson against the wall then blew a puff of whitish smoke in his face. Ferguson's face turned a purplish-red. His hands tugged furiously at the CEO's fingers. His mouth opened wide as he gasped for air.

"He can't fuckin' breathe," Agosti said.

The CEO's mouth curled up in amusement when he looked at Agosti. He snorted in derision before letting go.

Ferguson fell in a heap on the floor. He propped himself up on one elbow, massaging his throat with the free hand. He yelped when the CEO jammed the cigarette against his head, grinding it into his scalp until it was out.

When the CEO headed for Agosti, Ferguson jumped up and raced for the kitchen.

Zarko eyed the CEO as he grabbed Agosti's jaw and jerked him forward. "Would you like to take his place?"

Zarko smirked as Agosti's head wagged back and forth. *You no-balls sissy.*

"Nothing changes, guys," the CEO announced while

clenching Agosti's jaw. "Nothing." He eyed Zarko before slamming Agosti's head Into the sofa. A noise drew Zarko's attention toward the kitchen.

Ferguson emerged, brandishing a hatchet and a butcher knife. He charged the CEO, screaming, "I'm gonna kill you."

Wheeling around, the CEO grabbed Ferguson's knife hand at the wrist, twisting the arm behind Ferguson's back.

"Drop both of them or I'll break your arm," the CEO said.

The knife fell to the floor, followed by the hatchet.

"Let me go."

The CEO twisted his arm until the elbow popped. Ferguson shrieked. The CEO shoved him to the floor. He picked up the hatchet. "Turn that radio up, loud."

With the music booming, the CEO grabbed Ferguson's injured arm and held it on the coffee table. "This'll stop it from hurting." He raised the hatchet up like an executioner's axe.

Ferguson held his hand up. "No, don't. No."

A dark spot blossomed from the crotch area of Ferguson's pants. The pungent smell of urine filled the air.

The hatchet slammed down hard on Ferguson's arm. Music masked most of Ferguson's scream. The hatchet rose up then swung down one more time. The severed forearm tumbled to the floor. The CEO's eyes flitted from Zarko to Sanchez, then to Agosti.

Zarko glared back at him but said nothing.

Agosti gagged as though ready to vomit.

Sanchez only shook his head before averting his eyes. The CEO laid the hatchet on the table and picked up the butcher knife. He slashed Ferguson across the back.

"Okay, you made your point," Agosti yelled. "Jesus Christ! Don't kill him."

Zarko kept his mouth shut and his focus on an imaginary spot on the floor.

More screams filled the room as the CEO slashed Ferguson's chest again and again. Entrails spilled out.

The three men scrambled off the sofa as blood sprayed in all directions.

"Get it over with, goddammit," Zarko said, glaring at the CEO from the other side of the room.

"As you wish," the CEO said, the corners of his mouth curling up. He yanked Ferguson's head back by the hair and drew the blade straight across his throat. When he let go, Ferguson's body collapsed in a lifeless mass. "Anyone else want to have a go at it?" he asked, wiping the blade on the arm of the sofa.

None of the three men said a word.

He faced them with the butcher knife hanging at his side. "Do any of you think I'm not fair with the profits?"

Several seconds passed. Nobody voiced an objection.

"Didn't think so." He gestured with the knife at Ferguson's corpse and the blood-stained carpet. "Clean this shit up."

 espes

On Thursday, sitting in his six-by-six blue-walled cubicle, Scarsdale stared at the stack of nine cases that his supervisor, Lieutenant Eugene Mitchell, had dumped on his desk. He had no desire to read any of the files. Other people's tragedies seemed far away.

Instead, he picked up the photograph of Charity, taken on their second wedding anniversary. The one of her in a sky-blue bikini, laying on the beach in the Caymans. A huge grin on her face as she held her rum punch aloft. The seashell he'd found with a starfish imprint on top, from when they'd gone snorkeling, still sat on the mantle. A reminder of happier days.

A hand gripped his shoulder, startling him. Swinging his chair around, he saw Mitchell standing there, a ragged wood toothpick sticking half out of his mouth, a thick manila folder in his other hand.

"You get the word on the Lasiter jury verdict?" Mitchell asked.

"Yeah. Explain to me how the DA can blow a slam-dunk case?" Scarsdale asked, running his hand over his hair.

"How are you holding up?"

"I'm here."

"I can only imagine how tough it is," Mitchell said with a consoling tone in his voice. "You'll never get over what happened if you don't force yourself to focus on what needs to be done. I dumped a lot of cases on you. They'll keep you busy and help you get your mind off all that's happened."

Mitchell dropped the file folder on Scarsdale's desk then jerked his chin at it. "This case is a homicide but, since it involves a pedophile, we got it. I'm assigning it to you and Harris since you used to work Homicide. Let me know if there's anything you need."

"A quality babysitter for my daughter would be nice.

"I'll ask around." Then he walked away. Scarsdale laid his head back. Mitchell wanted to get him motivated. Even Sarah pushed him to reengage both at work and with his friends. But it wasn't that easy. The woman of his dreams had died, and he knew it was his fault, notwithstanding what anyone else said.

Was there a way to make things right? He'd thought so Monday morning, out there at Zilker Park. But Shannon needed her father. She missed her mother. He couldn't wallow in self-pity any longer. Shannon needed his love and protection. She needed the security of knowing her father would always be there. He had to get it together.

Scarsdale opened the case file, wondering why Robertson really assigned the case to Sex Crimes. Homicide had twelve detectives, three times the number in Sex Crimes.

He and Robertson knew each other from their time in the Patrol Division. Robertson had been a day shift lieutenant who reviewed officers' reports for completeness. Scarsdale recalled the time he rejected one of Scarsdale's reports for a couple of simple spelling errors, forcing Scarsdale to stay past his end of shift time to re-write the report. Scarsdale put in for overtime pay, but Robertson denied it. When Scarsdale appealed the denial, the Patrol commander reversed Robertson's decision, resulting in a counseling session that was documented in Robertson's personnel file.

Two years ago, the chief promoted Robertson from Commander of Support Services to Commander of Violent Crimes. During a division meeting of all the detectives, Robertson told them to re-learn all the department rules because each one would be enforced without favor. When he added that anyone who violated any rule would be dealt with immediately, he seemed to focus his attention on Scarsdale.

The new file concerned the murder of a known pedophile named Clay Ferguson. Scarsdale opened the lower right desk drawer and considered dumping the file in there—his packrat drawer where he stored other low-priority items. But something—a hunch or a cop's gut instinct or just plain guilt—made him keep reading.

According to the offense report Ferguson's body, or what was left of it, was found by his parole officer on Wednesday at 10:20 a.m. in a closet in Ferguson's house. The preliminary autopsy report stated Ferguson bled to death from one of two wounds—a slit throat or an amputated forearm. A neighbor living across the street heard loud music and a few screams around ten p.m. A half hour or so later he saw a person running south from the house. The witness described the runner as a husky male.

The report detailed police findings during the search of his house. Several adult magazines, a laptop computer, a video camera and a few blank DVDs were found in the living room and one bedroom. Ferguson's body had multiple stab wounds, his right arm amputated at the elbow, a slit throat, and several deep lacerations on his chest and abdomen. The report stated that no signs of forced entry were discovered which indicated to Scarsdale that Ferguson knew his killer.

"Whoever killed him did the world a big favor," Scarsdale muttered.

ᔕᗞᔕ

Scarsdale and Harris finally got a break on the guy who'd been caught molesting his girlfriend's kid. Someone called in on the TIPS line around nine a.m. on Thursday. Olsen, or a man fitting his description, had been seen in a strip-mall shopping center in northwest Austin. Communications notified Scarsdale, relaying information that a man believed to be Terry Wayne Olsen was seen on foot a few minutes ago near an emergency medical clinic in the vicinity of Duval Road and Highway 183.

Ten minutes later he and Harris drove into the clinic parking lot.

"Pull up there. We can eyeball the entrance through the rearview mirrors," Scarsdale said to Harris.

More than a half hour passed before a skinny male fitting Olsen's description came out of the shadows at the end of the building, walking straight toward the clinic entrance. He kept looking around like he feared discovery—another red flag waving in Scarsdale's head.

He held up the photograph Dory gave him of Olsen. "Looks like our guy."

"Let him go in. That way we'll have him cornered."

When the man got to the door, he gave the parking lot one last sweep before pulling the door open and disappearing inside.

"He's in," Scarsdale said, pushing the car door open. "Let's go."

The two detectives trotted to the clinic door.

"Ready?" When Harris nodded, Scarsdale grabbed the door handle. "Let's do it."

Scarsdale went in first. It took a few seconds for his eyes to adjust to low lighting. One door into the lobby from the outside. Another door to the right of the front desk. No windows.

A row of chairs lined up along the front window. A kid's play area occupied the middle of the room. Four children—three boys and a girl—sat on the floor by the table.

Scarsdale counted two older women, a young woman, and two men seated on chairs closest to the reception desk. Olsen occupied a seat on the far end.

They approached Olsen, hoping he'd surrender without a fight. With Scarsdale standing on his right and Harris standing between Olsen and the children, Olsen bolted for the door.

Scarsdale knew if Olsen made it out the door, he was gone. He chased him, dodging the women scrambling to get out of the way.

Olsen beat him to the door, shoving it open and hooking a hard left.

Darting out the door, right on Olsen's heels, Scarsdale stayed close enough in the first few yards of the pursuit to grab him. But as he reached out, Olsen accelerated.

Scarsdale had one chance left. Diving at Olsen's legs and belly flopping on the sidewalk, he managed to grab one ankle, yanking it out from under Olsen. He fell face first into the pavement. One of his shoes struck Scarsdale in the right eye.

The pain shot through Scarsdale's head, dull like a bad headache then sharp as if someone jabbed a nail in his eye. Olsen kicked at him with his free foot. Scarsdale held on. He heard Harris yelling, "Hold onto him. I'm coming."

"Hurry up!" Scarsdale shouted, his grip slipping.

If Olsen got free, they'd never catch him. Then Olsen's shoe slipped off.

Before Olsen got up, Harris pounced on him.

໒ຉໃ

An hour later, Scarsdale opened the door and walked into the small room. The Sex Crimes interrogation room had a video camera mounted high up on the wall close to the ceiling. The only furniture in the room was one table with two chairs. An omni-directional microphone rested in the middle of the table.

No one-way window for other detectives to view the interview.

Scarsdale slammed the door shut behind him. He tossed a file folder on the table. Turning the chair around so the back touched the table, Scarsdale straddled it, opening the folder. He whistled the tune "I Fought the Law" while he read the reports.

Olsen sat on the opposite side of the table in handcuffs. A large bandage covered a major portion of the right side of his face. His lower lip puffed out like a marshmallow. A purplish contusion swelled his left cheek.

He remained quiet for a few minutes until after Scarsdale slid a Waiver of Rights Form across the table with a pen. "You guys really fucked up, this time. I'm gonna sue all ya'll for false arrest." Olsen leaned forward to read the form. "I didn't do nothin' to that girl. You got nothing on me. That woman's a crazy bitch. Whatever she said I did, she friggin lied." He looked at Scarsdale as if waiting for a response. When none came, he yelled, "Get me a lawyer. I know my rights." He tugged and pulled against the handcuffs. He stopped after a minute or two, obviously realizing the futility.

His protests reminded Scarsdale of a pouting child who didn't get his way. "Your criminal history says here you've been convicted of indecency with a child twice. Served two stints in prison." He peered across the table at Olsen. "Third time's a charm, right?"

Olsen smirked as he looked at him. "I did a helluva job on your eye. Too bad I only got one."

During his years with the Austin PD, Scarsdale had received a lot of taunts and he dealt with this one the same way. He ignored it. Closing the file, he stood up. "Dory Mabry and her daughter aren't the only eyewitnesses."

Olsen's grin faded as he looked at Scarsdale. Scarsdale recognized the faraway stare in Olsen's eyes, as though he was trying to remember who else may have seen him. Olsen blinked. "You're trying to screw with me. There ain't nobody else."

Scarsdale laid his palms flat on the table. "Soon you'll be reunited with your old prison buds, Leroy and Billy Bob. Don't drop the soap in the shower." He picked up the file and headed for the door.

"Wait a minute"

Scarsdale turned around. "What do you want?"

"Let's talk."

"We can't. You want a lawyer. We both know I can't talk to you anymore until your lawyer is present."

"Screw the lawyer. I wanna make a deal."

Scarsdale walked a few steps toward the table. He waved the file in the air. "You're going to prison for the rest of your life. Why should I want to make a deal with you?"

"'Cause you want to know who offed Fergie."

"Fergie?"

"Yeah. Clay Ferguson."

Ferguson's name rang a bell. Then he remembered—the new homicide case. "He was a pedophile like you. What makes you think I give a damn who killed him?" Scarsdale ambled toward the door.

Just before he stepped through the door, Olsen spoke loud and clear. "It was a big man—with a black and green colored tattoo on his arm."

"So?" Scarsdale shrugged, as he reached for the door handle. He wasn't in any hurry to solve that case, but if he ignored Olsen's information, he'd be derelict. And Robertson was just waiting for an excuse.

"I know what the tattoo is. I seen it."

Sure you did, he thought as he walked back to the table.

❧❧❧

Scarsdale walked into the department lunchroom a little before one o'clock. Ten round metal tables took up much of the space. Five vending machines lined the wall, offering various sodas, coffee, pre-packaged pastries, and assorted snacks. A telephone hung on the wall next to the doorway.

Five female employees sat at a table closest to the vending machines. He recognized one as the Sex Crime Unit's analyst—Dani Mueller—from Sex Crime Unit briefings just before Charity's accident.

She had to be around twenty-eight to thirty. He tacked his babysitter notice up on the bottom edge of the bulletin board. Then, sensing stares from those in the room, he looked in the group's direction. They looked away as if they didn't want to be caught staring at him.

All except Dani. Her honey-colored eyes locked with his. She smiled at him—a genuine sort of smile.

Scarsdale only nodded before turning away.

⁊⁊⁊

After lunch, Scarsdale leaned back in his office chair as he finished reading through each of the new cases. One murder, one sexual assault, two indecencies, two teacher-student sex cases, an adult video store distributing porn to a child complaint, and three improper photography complaints.

He checked his watch. Three more hours until he went home to Shannon.

A female voice, soft and gentle, almost melodic in tone, startled him. "Detective Scarsdale."

He snapped his head around to see who called his name. Dani Mueller. She stood there holding a file. She was taller than he'd realized. He nodded. "Yes, ma'am?"

"Ma'am makes me sound so old." She smiled. "Please call me Dani."

He detected a European accent. "Okay, Dani."

"I hope the other guy looks worse," she said.

"Excuse me?"

She pointed at his eye. "Your black eye. Hopefully the other guy looks worse."

He touched his eye. "Oh yeah." Scarsdale forced a smile.

She handed a file to him. "My boss said to give this file to you since you're working Ferguson's murder. It's my analysis of Ferguson's sex crimes case."

"Thanks."

"There wasn't much to work with. If you develop any additional information, let me know and I'll take another stab at it."

He read the report. "Sure, you bet," he said without looking up.

"She's very pretty."

"Who?" he asked, following her line of sight to Charity's picture. "Yes, very pretty."

"I'm very sorry for your loss. I know how hard it must be for you."

Scarsdale nodded. He'd grown sick of hearing that phrase, having heard it so many times over the past five weeks.

She smiled. "No, I really mean it. I know how you feel. I've been there."

"You lost your spouse?"

"My daughter."

"I'm sorry. What happened?"

She glanced back toward Mitchell's office. "It's a long story. I saw the notice you posted downstairs. How old is your daughter?"

"Five."

"They're a lot of fun at that age." She stepped inside his cubicle. "You should bring her to work sometime." A slight flush appeared on her face. "I mean…not so much in here but around the building. I bet she'd love to see how her father spends his day. Every other Friday is a 'Bring Your Children to Work' day."

"Yeah, five is a great age," he said, remembering the time Shannon made him laugh so hard he almost rolled onto the floor when she paraded around the living room wearing the white crocheted sunhat Sarah gave her, the red sundress Charity had gotten for her, and a pair of Charity's high heels with her head tilted back, her nose up in the air, acting like a little snob.

"I don't know about bringing her here." He didn't want to bring her to the department then have to leave her alone in a building full of strangers if he got called out. Besides, Robertson would try to discipline him. "I don't think my boss would approve."

"Well, if you do, bring her by my office. I'd love to meet her." She started to leave then looked at him. "Having someone to talk to in a time like this helps. So if you ever want to just talk, I'm an excellent listener. Right down the hall." Dani waved and walked away.

He dropped the file she gave him into the Ferguson sex case file. Seems before he died, Ferguson had been a suspect in a failed abduction attempt near the Cedar Grove Elementary School. *Won't be needing that information now*, he thought, wondering for a brief second why Dani hadn't just e-mailed the information to him.

Scarsdale typed up his Cleared by Exception report on Ferguson's sex case, showing that Ferguson had been the victim of a homicide. Ferguson's criminal history showed four priors—two convictions for burglary of a habitation with intent to commit sexual assault, one for kidnapping, and the last for enticing a child. He wondered how Ferguson ever made parole with his history. "Abatement of a nuisance seems like a better offense classification than murder. Either way, one more pervert off the street, he thought, dropping the file in the Out basket. He unlocked a side drawer and pulled out a manila folder. Inside was a dog-eared Texas accident report. The report listed Charity as the operator of vehicle number two.

In the brief narrative, the investigating officer stated that vehicle number one ran a stop sign, colliding with the left side of vehicle number two. The measurement of skid marks from vehicle number one indicated excessive speed.

He remembered what Charity's car looked like after the collision. The whole driver's side looked like a tank had smashed into it. The autopsy indicated Charity died instantly as the result of a torn aorta and a broken neck.

As soon as he heard Mitchell's voice bellow his name, he shoved the manila folder back in the drawer and closed it. Mitchell didn't need to catch him poring over that report again. The man meant well but Scarsdale didn't want to hear the sermon that it wasn't his fault.

"That witness in the Ferguson case called. He remembered something else about the man he saw running away. Go talk to him, and see what he's got." He took a step then turned back to Scarsdale. "Any luck finding a babysitter?"

Scarsdale shook his head. "No, not yet."

Since Harris was on a stake-out, Scarsdale drove out to Ferguson's house alone. It was a white frame house in need of a paint job in places. The neighbor who had seen a male running across the yard lived across the street. The report identified him as Cecil Anderson. Scarsdale stood in front of Anderson's house, studying Ferguson's place. The nearest streetlight was ten yards south. He guessed it had taken the man maybe ten to twelve seconds to make it to the light. His car must have been parked up the street.

He ventured over to Ferguson's house, not sure what he'd find, if anything. Tall Johnson grass covered the yard. It scratched against his pants legs as he waded through it. Closer to the sidewalk, the Johnson grass and weeds had been trampled down—a few bald areas devoid of any grass or weeds. Then he saw it—about five yards from the sidewalk. A heel print in the dirt. The direction indicated that whoever made it came from the house. Unsure if the print was missed by the crime search team or was a recent impression, he called for the crime scene techs.

While the crime team re-worked Ferguson's yard, Scarsdale interviewed Anderson. "Tell me about this additional information you have."

"I plumb forgot about this when I talked to the police that night. Getting old, I guess. Anyway, when I stepped out here for some air that night, I told them I saw that big man come out from behind that house," Anderson said, pointing at Ferguson's house then moving his finger to the left. "And trot down that way."

Scarsdale didn't recall a height given by Anderson for the man. "How tall was he?"

Anderson paused and looked down. His hand massaged his chin as if thinking back to that night. "Hard to say. Not quite as tall as you. "

"Did you notice anything else?"

"Yes, this is the part I forgot. A short while later, maybe ten or fifteen minutes later, I saw three guys run from around back." Anderson pointed to the right. "They ran like bats outta hell right up that way."

"Could you see them well enough to ID them?"

Anderson shook his head. "Uh-uh."

"Anyone else?"

"Nope. About that time, my missus hailed me back inside. You know how fussy some wives can get," Anderson said, nodding at the wedding ring on Scarsdale's left hand. "Maybe yours is too young to be like that, but give her time."

Taking a deep breath, Scarsdale looked down at his hand, glancing at the ring. "Yeah, I wish."

Scarsdale went straight home from the Ferguson crime scene. He made it to the front porch when Shannon came tearing outside.

"Daddy," she shouted. A big grin stretched across her face.

Scarsdale swept her up, nestled her against his shoulder, and kissed her on her forehead. "Hi, princess."

She wrapped one arm around his neck as he carried her inside. "Aunt Sarah and I cooked dinner."

After he set her down, she raced into the kitchen, emerging a minute or two later, carrying a plate of fried chicken and set it on the table. She dragged a drumstick off it and deposited it on his plate. "I cooked that one just for you, Daddy."

"You better like it," Sarah said, sitting down. "She really did cook it herself just for you."

He bit off a chunk while Shannon watched in eager anticipation.

"This is super good," he said.

While they ate, Sarah inquired about his day.

"A truckload of new cases including a murder." He thought about Ferguson and Olsen before casting a quick glance at his daughter. *What happened to Beth Ann Mabry will never happen to you, Shannon. Never.*

After dinner, Shannon crawled up on the sofa next to her father, handing him a book titled *The Time Garden*. "Aunt Sarah got this for me today." Opening it to the first page, she read a few sentences to him. Then she placed the book on his lap. "Now it's your turn, Daddy."

He wondered what happened to the Narnia book but decided not to say anything. Instead, he read several pages of *The Time Garden* aloud before closing the book. "That's enough for now. Time for you to get ready for bed. Now go put your pajamas on."

After tucking her in, he sat on the edge of her bed and opened *The Time Garden* again.

She rolled toward him, propping her head up on her hand.

"All right, let's see now. Where did I leave off?"

"The part about when Roger makes a wish," Shannon said.

After about two minutes, she interrupted his reading. Her voice was subdued. "Daddy, do wishes really come true?"

"Sometimes, sweetheart, but it depends on what you wish for."

"Is Mommy an angel?"

He forced a smile. He couldn't let himself lose it in front of Shannon. "Yes, an angel with bright white wings." He pointed up. "She's in Heaven, looking down on us. She'll always be watching over us."

That sense of loss he felt during the past few weeks washed over him again. Deep inside, he was torn between two opposing sentiments. On one hand, he wanted the emotional roller coaster ride to stop, yet, on the other, he refused to let go, treating it as a kind of punishment.

"I wish Mommy would come visit us so we wouldn't cry no more."

He gazed at her soft brown eyes. "Me, too, baby girl." He searched the page for where he'd stopped.

She extended her arms around his chest as far as she could reach and hugged him. "I love you."

He smiled back at her and put his arm around her. "I love you, too."

Later, he spent the evening talking with Sarah about his progress in finding a babysitter. "I posted a notice on the bulletin board at work, but no interest so far. I take that back. Our analyst, Dani Mueller, wants to meet Shannon this Friday. Something about a 'Bring Your Kid to Work' day."

He still had reservations about bringing her.

"Shannon would love that. To spend the whole day with you would make her week." Sarah paused, gazing down at her lap. "She misses Charity a lot. This afternoon, I found her in your bedroom, clinging to one of Charity's pictures, sitting on the floor crying. She's still trying to cope with her death."

"I know. We all are." He sighed. "Maybe taking her with me might help both of us. But I don't know what my division commander would say about family hanging out there."

"I could bring her home with me to Waco. Just until you find a babysitter," Sarah said.

Coming home to a house without Charity hurt bad enough. The thought of coming home and Shannon not being there made his stomach churn.

CHAPTER 4

"Revenge is a confession of pain." ~ *Latin Proverb*

I heard through the grapevine that the jury found Lasiter not guilty. It was like déjà vu. Totally unbelievable. A verdict of not guilty. Just like the Sacramento jury did for Burton. Were they listening to the same testimony I heard? Didn't they realize what kind of animal Lasiter was? Well, he wouldn't get the chance to touch another child or destroy another family. I'd make sure of it. I knew where he lived. His weather-worn house would be on the market after tonight.

I sat in front of my dresser mirror and lowered the blonde wig over my short black hair. I tucked in a couple of stray ringlets and brushed the wig lightly. As a finishing touch, I dipped my finger into the white contact lens holder and slid the soft lens out. Leaning closer to the mirror, I slipped it in place, squeezing my eyes shut before repeating the process for the other eye. Then I applied a little blue eye shadow. Gazing in the mirror, I admired my new look—a perky blonde with peacock blue eyes.

Before I left on my quest, I booted up my laptop to check the California parole status for Parnell Burton. The man had threatened to kill me. I had to keep tabs on him. The website showed him still incarcerated with no date set yet for a parole hearing. I arrived at Lasiter's house around eight that Wednesday night, but he was driving away in his truck as I pulled up. Not knowing when he'd be back, I followed him. Maybe he was going to find another victim; maybe he wasn't coming back home for a while. When I'd hunted Burton, I'd had only to follow him to the park, circling behind him as he lurked in the trees.

❦

The country music blared loud from Dave's Pub and Tavern while Lasiter drank and danced. *That sorry bastard is celebrating.* I watched him as he danced the two-step with two different partners on the bar's worn-out wood floor.

I felt comfortable that nobody would recognize me, blending right in with my Levi jeans, a long-sleeved western shirt with a white rose imprinted above the pocket, and a pair of kicker boots.

When he wasn't dancing, Lasiter hung out near the bar, leaning against the waist-high wooden counter, guzzling one beer after another.

A waitress with purple streaks in her hair carried a brown tray of beer bottles as she traveled from table to table until venturing up to me. "Can I get you anything from the bar?"

"No thanks," I said, holding up my nearly full beer.

As soon as she meandered off, one of the guys from the next table approached me. He glanced back at his grinning buddies, who nodded encouragement to him. He held out his hand and gestured with his head toward the dance floor. "C'mon. Let's dance."

"No, thanks." I smiled and looked in the direction of the men's room. "My boyfriend will be right back."

His mouth opened like he wanted to say something but nothing came out. He turned to walk away, frowning while rubbing the back of his neck. After he went back to his friends, I sauntered up to the far end of the bar. There were enough people up there that Lasiter wouldn't notice me. The huge mirror at the back of the bar allowed me to watch him undetected.

Lasiter seemed so smug. I wanted so badly to walk over and slap him. Things got interesting when another man joined him. This guy wore a gold-colored earring in his left earlobe. It was shaped like a heart. Blue, green, and red tattoos galore ran up and down his forearms. His hair was longer than Lasiter's. His most notable feature was a crooked nose.

From Lasiter's gestures and tight-drawn lips, it appeared

the two were discussing something serious—maybe even arguing. I inched closer to eavesdrop.

Lasiter's voice at the courthouse had been subdued, but right here, right now, I had no problem hearing him. Maybe the several beers dissolved his inhibitions. Or maybe his quiet tone in court had been a ploy to con the jurors. Too bad it worked.

"Like I said, this mess would never have happened if you had gone fishing with me that week. You could have vouched for me in court," Lasiter said, jabbing his finger against the guy's chest.

I glanced around the bar area, wondering if he was spouting this garbage for someone's benefit. *Your mess, as you so succinctly put it, Lasiter, wouldn't have happened if you had acted like a real man.*

"I said I'm sorry, okay?" the man said, his eyes staring hard back at Lasiter. He pushed Lasiter's finger away from his chest and took a swallow of beer.

"Hell, you didn't even come to my trial, you sorry sonofabitch," Lasiter remarked as he turned to the bartender. "Give me another beer."

"Hey, asshole, I said I had to work," Lasiter's friend said.

I watched as Lasiter swigged down a mouthful of beer, scanning the room. "So did I, dude. You could have been there."

The guy took a long swallow of beer but didn't reply to Lasiter's comment. Instead, he gazed around the room with an occasional sideways scowl at Lasiter.

"I still want to know who the hell used my car," Lasiter said, swigging down more beer.

"Don't even look at me, shithead. Anybody could have taken it. You leave it unlocked all the fuckin' time." The guy gulped down some beer. "I betcha you never told the cops that one of Claude Mayben's mechanics might have taken it? Biggest bunch of douche bags that ever walked the Earth." He stared at Lasiter, waiting for a response that never came. "Thought so," he said, taking another swallow of the beer.

The bartender approached me, placing his mitts on the edge of the bar. He had a walrus mustache and hands the size of college textbooks. "Ready for another one, lady?"

"Sure," I said, finishing off what was left in my bottle.

"There ya go," he said, looking at me with his eyebrows arched as he set the beer on a dingy coaster and pushed a bowl of peanuts in my direction. "I ain't seen you around here before, so let me explain the house rules." He leaned on the edge of the bar. "I allow a bar tab up to three beers. Then I expect you to pay up. Understand?"

I nodded. "How much do I owe?"

Lasiter stood there, gazing around the room, drinking beer, one gulp after another. "Somebody set me up." He set the empty bottle on the bar and asked for another one.

The guy chuckled. "The jury cleared you. You got no problem," his friend said. "Now talk about something else."

No problem? Don't bet on it.

"Yeah, I got off, but it wouldn't have gone that far if you'd had some balls and talked to the police. Now I get those crappy sideway stares like I'm some kind of pervert." He looked out at the crowd. "Hell, people I thought were my friends cross the street or walk the other direction when they see me coming."

They avoid you because you're a child killer. Maybe you hoodwinked those twelve jurors, but the rest of us know better. Tonight you'll plead for your life, just like one of your victims.

Lasiter jabbed him again. But this time, the guy shoved him away. "Don't ram your fuckin' finger in my chest unless you want it broken."

I was hypnotized by the action. And I wasn't alone either. Some of the people near them began moving away, looking back as they did. Maybe I wouldn't have to kill Lasiter. Maybe this guy would do it right here.

"Why didn't you help me?" Lasiter asked.

His friend looked around the room. "Just shut the hell up, asshole." His tone was somewhat hushed. "Someone's gonna hear you."

The bartender returned with my tab, and I laid a ten dollar bill on the bar.

Lasiter waved his hand in the air. "Hey, everyone, this dude right here said he's my friend." He pointed at the man with the earring. "You know what? He coulda testified for me but he had to *work*. Yeah. Whatcha all think about that? Some friend, huh?" Lasiter bellowed. Staggering and loud. He was drunk.

A young woman approached Lasiter and, taking his hand, guided him out on the dance floor. Doing the two-step, Lasiter stumbled a few times.

I stole a quick glance at Lasiter's antagonist as he stood there stewing, his chest heaving, his face red, glaring hard at Lasiter. He slammed his beer bottle down on the bar. A peanut bowl nearby bounced. "Give me a tequila shot," he said, scowling in Lasiter's direction.

Another guy sidled closer to me. "Hi, I'm Carlisle. I'm the judge for the hot chick contest." He gestured at three guys standing at the other end of the bar, drinking beer and laughing. "We voted you the winner."

"Tell your friends 'thanks' but that line won't work. I'm in a relationship." I turned away, drank a mouthful of beer, hoping he'd get the hint.

He didn't. "Wanna dance?"

I took another swallow and set the bottle on the bar. "No thanks. Time for me to leave. Six o'clock comes early." I pointed at the clock on the wall. It was almost midnight. As I walked toward the door, I gave Lasiter one last glance. *See you soon, pervert.*

My car clock showed 12:06 a.m. when I drove past the front of his house, a single-story frame house situated between older and better-kept frame-and-brick homes in north Austin. All the neighboring homes were dark except the one next door.

I pulled into the alley behind his house, shifted into neutral, and coasted to a stop close enough to his backyard fence so my car wasn't blocking the alley. Snapping on a pair of neoprene gloves and shoe covers, I crept up to the wood fence.

The gate stood open. Using my flashlight, I made it across his yard without banging into or tripping over anything. The backdoor was locked so I went around to the front, figuring he'd be the type to hide a key nearby.

I found it inside an old black metal mailbox mounted on the wall next to the front door. How original. Men like him are so predictable.

I walked into the living room. It was nasty looking. Empty beer cans everywhere and several magazines strewn on the sofa, the coffee table, and the floor. I inspected the covers of a couple of the magazines, expecting to see porn. I wasn't disappointed—two *Hustlers* and a couple of *Playboys* along with a few sports magazines. An ashtray, overflowing with butts and ashes, sat on the coffee table next to the TV remote. A few dried-up chicken bones lay inside a crumpled KFC box on the sofa. One worn-out fabric chair sat in the corner. A medium-sized television rested on a small table opposite the sofa.

I looked around the living room. Where would he hide Amy's bracelet? I searched through the drawers in the end table and under the seat cushions of the sofa and chair. All I found were lot of old food crumbs, loose change, and a few scraps of paper.

The bedroom was just as filthy as the living room—bed sheets and a blanket hanging over the side of the bed. A pillow lying at an angle. Clothes draped at its foot and scattered on the floor. Beer cans on the nightstand. A tall dresser stood against the wall three or four feet from the door. A clock on his nightstand ticked loud.

I ransacked each dresser drawer and the bedside stand— no bracelet. I even pulled the drawers out and felt underneath, figuring maybe he taped it there. Still nothing. It had to be in this house somewhere. Someplace the police didn't look. Perverts like him always kept a trophy from their conquests. Did he have a safe deposit box? If he considered the bracelet a trophy, he'd have it secreted somewhere.

The door to the bathroom a few feet away was one of those old wood-panel doors with round doorknobs. I saw two more porn magazines lying on the floor near the toilet. I was sure the police had searched this snake pit and confiscated all his reading material, if one could call it reading material. So he got some more.

After checking all the possible hiding places in the bathroom, I took one of his bath towels from a stack in the bathroom closet and tucked it in like a bib. Probably the cleanest thing in this dump. I figured it would soak up any blood spraying on my clothes. I'd had to burn the clothes I wore after killing Burton.

It was almost one o'clock when I heard the sound of a car out front. Then a car door slammed. Then another one. Some loud yelling.

I hurried to the front window, my knife in hand. Two days from now would make it two years since I'd last wielded it—at the Reichmuth Park nature area, near the south side of Sacramento. Maybe Lasiter would tell me where the bracelet was when I started cutting on him.

I peered out the window and saw Lasiter stagger up onto the porch followed by his guy friend from the bar. Lasiter tripped and fell face-first on the porch. His pal stood there, hands on hips, looking down at him, laughing.

Dammit! I couldn't subdue both of them. I didn't have time to unlock the back door, so I hid in the bedroom closet.

It wasn't a spacious closet. I tucked my five-foot eleven-inch frame as far back as I could, deep among the musty-smelling shirts and coats that made my face itch. I stood there, hunched over so my head wouldn't bump against the shelf.

The front door squeaked when he opened it, and two sets of heavy footsteps made the wood floors groan. I heard Lasiter speak first.

"Go home, Tom. I'm going to bed." Lasiter's words were slurred.

Somebody or something slammed into the wall. I heard some glass break. The whole house shuddered.

"Don't tell me what I need to do," Tom said. His was a raspy voice and deeper than Lasiter's.

"What the hell's wrong with you?" Lasiter yelled. Another crashing sound and the walls shook again. "Don't be a dick, man. Just get the hell outta my house."

"I'll go when I'm damn good and ready," Tom yelled. "You got that, asshole?"

"Put the frigging bat down."

A dull thud, followed by two more in quick succession. I heard someone grunt and yell. I thought it was Lasiter. Then another crashing sound.

Tom screamed at Lasiter. "You hard of hearing? Is that what your problem is? Let me say it slowly so you'll get it. Shut up. I'm sick of hearing about the damn girl. She's dead and you're in the clear. Everyone is in the clear. So shut the fuck up about her."

Both of them were yelling and cursing, only louder now, like they'd moved into the bedroom. More crashing and banging sounds really close. The closet wall shook.

"How's that feel, you prick," Lasiter said, his voice breaking. "You did it, didn't you? You killed that little girl."

Lasiter said something else but I couldn't understand what it was.

"Shut up!" Tom shouted. "You fuckin' shut up, you sorry son of a bitch."

"It *was* you all along, wasn't it," Lasiter accused. "Ya gonna cut me up now?"

"I'm gonna fuckin' rip you apart."

Then a loud groan.

I heard a thud that sounded like a body crashing into something. Then a screeching sound like furniture sliding across the floor. More grunts and the distinct thud of bodies slamming into things. I burrowed deeper back into the dark recesses of the closet. The last thing I wanted or needed right now was to be discovered by two drunk guys in full road rage.

Tom yelled. They were right outside the closet door. "You sonofabitch. You wanna run your mouth some more?" A thud followed by a crunching sound.

Then silence. All I could hear was someone—presumably

Tom—breathing heavy like he'd just finished a mile run. From his breathing, I knew he was near the closet door. I prayed he didn't open it.

"Scott?"

A few seconds of silence that seemed more like a few hours to me. Then Tom spoke but in a scared kind of way. His voice was a few octaves higher and cracking.

"C'mon, Scott." Silence. "Scott, get up, man. You ain't hurt. Just a little bump on the head." Another pause. "Oh shit."

I heard the hollow sound of something metallic hit the floor and bounce to a stop, then footsteps right outside the closet. I could see his shadow under the door. He bumped the door then moved away. My heart pounded as I heard his steps pacing back and forth. Drops of sweat dribbled down my cheeks.

Tom's voice got louder.

"It's *your* fault, Scott."

I heard him sobbing.

"Why couldn't you just shut up? But no, not you. You had to shoot your mouth off. Everyone at Dave's heard you," he yelled. "You fuckin' happy now?"

Footsteps moved closer to the closet door. I inched back as far as I could go. My head banged hard against the shelf, causing a box to fall. A pair of boots spilled out on the floor. My wig came off, stuck to the shelf.

Oh my God. He knows I'm in here.

Pulling the wig free, I held my breath and adjusted it on my head as fast as I could.

What am I going to do?

I raised my knife in the direction of the door.

Footsteps got closer.

The door creaked as he opened it.

"Who's in there?" he yelled.

His shadow appeared in the doorway, creeping deeper into the closet. My heart thumped like hailstones on a roof. Sweat dripped into my eyes. The butt of the knife pressed against my waist. Footsteps clicking on the wood floor.

Then I heard footsteps running. The front door opened and slammed shut. I exhaled in relief then waited a few minutes to be sure he was gone before I crept out.

The bed sat at a weird angle. A pillow had fallen onto the floor. When I walked around to the foot of the bed, I saw Lasiter. His eyelids were half-moons, eyes fixed in a death stare. Several gashes around his mouth, cheek and eyes and his nose was bloodied. A pinkish froth dribbled from his mouth. His head lay at a funny angle on the floor, tilted to the left yet facing toward the right. I didn't feel a pulse.

According to my watch a half hour had passed since I first entered his house until I stood over his corpse. Now I had serious doubts that Lasiter killed Amy Crowell. A huge sense of relief that I wasn't the one who killed him enveloped me. But if Lasiter didn't murder Amy, who did? Tom?

My hand shook as I held the knife at my side. For those few seconds looking down at him, I realized how close I had been to being caught. Sitting alone in that Sacramento police interrogation room two days after I killed Burton was the last time I felt this scared. *Do I really need to be doing this*?

I spent the next few minutes backtracking through every room, double-checking for anything that would indicate I had ever been there. It was time to get out of here. If Tom came back or—worse—if the police showed up…

I slipped out the front door and headed around back to the alley. My heart was still beating fast. A gnawing feeling told me this episode was far from over.

My disposable gloves went into a plastic bag along with the towel. Then I drove my car a few yards up the alley and stopped. Using a board I found nearby, I dragged it over my tire tracks, erasing them. All the while taking occasional glances around to be sure I hadn't been discovered.

All of a sudden, the backyard neighbor's rear porch light came on while I was removing the shoe covers. A bald man appeared in the doorway dressed in pajamas, highlighted by an interior light.

Looking in my direction, he raised his hand over his eyes

as if shielding them from the porch light. "Who's out there?"

As I drove out of the alley for home I worried that he'd seen enough of me and my car to be able to make an ID to the police.

CHAPTER 5

"The Law of love could be best understood and learned through little children." ~ Mahatma Gandhi

Zarko sat in his truck a half a block away from Lasiter's, wondering who was in the closet. When he saw somebody walk out of Lasiter's house and go around the corner toward the alley, he drove in that direction with the truck's headlights off.

Stopping just short of the entrance, he looked left up the alley and saw the tail lights of a Mercedes along with the silhouette of someone standing by it. A street light at the other end of the alley highlighted the person's form. The full head of hair and the person's shape convinced him the person at the car was a female. Then he saw her doing something behind it.

"Who are you and what were you doing in Scott's house?" he said to himself.

When the Mercedes drove out of the alley, he fell in behind it, staying as far back as he dared. Camouflaged by other traffic he followed it all the way to the Walnut Grove Apartments in Pflugerville, a bedroom community just northeast of Austin.

Parking in a space near the Mercedes, he watched the blonde-haired woman hurry up three flights of stairs to an apartment. He saw the dark windows light up after she closed the door. He got out of his truck, looked around before moving toward the stairwell. Once there, he again surveyed the parking lot then went up the concrete steps, one at a time, stopping to glance up the stairs and around the area. Once up on the third floor, he sauntered past her apartment, noting the number—Apartment 312.

When he got back to his truck, Zarko sat there, watching her apartment and weighing his options. He'd have to keep her from going to the cops. How? A set of headlights lit up his truck so he slid down in the seat. Peeking out his window, he saw a cop car creep by. Somebody musta called 'em. Did she see him pass by her apartment? As soon as they drove behind the building, he cranked up the engine and drove out of the parking lot. "I'll be back for ya, bitch."

♥♥♥

The following morning, Scarsdale squatted down by the foot of Lasiter's four-poster bed, peering at the body. An aluminum softball bat lay on the floor about five feet away, covered in blood and hair. Lasiter's battered face had dried blood at the base of the nose and on the ear. A pinkish froth filled the mouth. Broken teeth. The side of the head appeared to have been struck by a blunt instrument, presumably the bat. A halo of blood surrounded Lasiter's head. His hands had already been bagged by the medical examiner's investigator. From the position of the body and the injuries, Scarsdale assumed whoever killed Lasiter was right-handed.

He examined the bed. The mattress sat at an angle like it had been bumped. He made a mental note of one bedpost that appeared to have some hair and blood spatter on it.

The ME's investigator handed him Lasiter's wallet. It contained about one hundred and twenty-five dollars, two credit cards, a union card, some photos, and his driver's license. Scarsdale crossed robbery off as a motive. He handed the wallet to one of the crime scene team to secure as evidence before heading into the living room to talk to the reporting person, Tom Zarko.

Scarsdale stood by the front door, appraising Zarko, while a uniformed officer wrote down Zarko's name and address off his driver's license. Zarko seemed relaxed, sneaking peeks in the direction of the bedroom. "Tom Zarko," Scarsdale asked, inspecting the driver's license. "I'm Detective Scarsdale."

"Any clues about who killed him?" Zarko asked.

"Not yet. You told the officer you found Lasiter in the bedroom?" Scarsdale gestured with his head at the uniformed officer standing inside the living room.

Zarko nodded, taking an occasional peek around Scarsdale in the direction of the bedroom.

"Tell me what happened."

"Well…we'd been out drinking last night. He—"

"Where?"

"Dave's Bar. Anyway, he didn't show up for work this morning, so the foreman sent me over to check on him. No one answered the door, so I let myself in. That's when I found him. You know the rest."

Scarsdale figured they had celebrated Lasiter's victory in court. "How did you let yourself in?"

Zarko hesitated, clearing his throat. "He never locks it when he's home."

"When did you last see him alive?"

Zarko paused as if he was trying to remember. "Umm, last night…maybe just after midnight. We stayed at the bar until it closed. Scott walked home alone. I stopped by later to check on him and some blonde chick was here with him."

"Describe her."

A blonde chick being the last to see him alive piqued Scarsdale's interest.

"I didn't get a good look at her." Zarko shrugged then chuckled. "Hell, man, she was half naked. Long blonde hair and a nice rack." He cupped his hands in front of his chest to indicate her breast size.

One thing Scarsdale prided himself on was his ability to notice the little things. In this case, it Zarko's bruised knuckles and hand. That landed Zarko on Scarsdale's suspect list, right behind the blonde chick. "How tall was she?"

"I dunno." He shrugged. "Maybe an inch or two shorter than me."

"And you're what? About five ten?"

Zarko grinned and pointed at Scarsdale. "Good guess."

Scarsdale made some notes of Zarko's description.

"I did see a car parked in the alley when I left," Zarko added. "I guess she gave him a ride home."

"Did you happen to see a license plate number?"

He shook his head. "Nope. Sorry."

"Was she his girlfriend?"

"Girlfriend?" Zarko chuckled. "Oh, hell no. Scott dated around."

"Would you recognize her if you saw her again?"

He shook his head. "I was checking out Thelma and Louise."

"Excuse me."

Zarko grinned as he cupped his hands in front of his chest. "You know, Thelma and Louise. Her rack."

"How long have you known Lasiter?" Scarsdale asked because he didn't recall seeing Zarko's name on the Lasiter witness list, and he'd never interviewed Zarko about the Amy Crowell killing.

"We ran around together. Partied together. Maybe a year or so now."

"A year or so. Were you aware he had been arrested for murder?"

"Sure, yeah, I knew."

"Would it be fair to say you two were close friends?"

Zarko shrugged. "Yeah, I guess so."

"But not close enough to stand up for him at his trial."

Zarko glared at Scarsdale for several seconds. "He didn't need me."

Scarsdale stared back. "Did he ever confide in you about that charge? You know, tell you any details? Show you any trophies he took from the victim?"

"The jury found him innocent," Zarko said.

Scarsdale closed his notepad. "That's not what I asked you." He clipped his pen into his shirt pocket.

"He didn't do it so how could he have any trophies?" Zarko checked his watch. "Is that it? I have to go back to work."

"Know anybody who had a grudge against him?"

"Maybe that blonde. Maybe he didn't like the way she did him and kicked her ass out. Look, detective, if I don't get my butt back to work, I'll be fired."

"One last question, Zarko." Scarsdale pointed at Zarko's hands. "What happened to your hands?"

Zarko's face paled as he looked at them.

"I saw them when you were describing Thelma and Louise."

Both were red and raw. Some skin scraped off the knuckles on the left hand.

"Happened at work. I scraped them against some two by four posts. Humph. Guess I messed them up worse than I thought."

Scarsdale called the technician over to photograph Zarko's hands.

Zarko backed away, tucking his hands behind his back. "What's this for?

Scarsdale extended his open hand in the direction of Lasiter's body. "Your *former* best friend looks pretty beaten up. And you have fresh injuries to your hands. You can do it here or downtown. Your choice."

"Are you shittin me?" Zarko asked.

Scarsdale gave him a cold stare. "Do I look like it?"

"Don't you need a warrant to do this?"

"Is there some reason you don't want to cooperate? And, no, I don't need a warrant. Your hands are in plain view."

Zarko held out his hands for the picture. "This is crazy. If I killed Scott, why the hell would I call you guys? Check out the blonde. She was the last one to see him alive."

"We will. But you should go to the ER and get your hands checked." Scarsdale pointed at the right hand. "Looks swollen. Might be broken or infected," Scarsdale said. What he wanted was a DNA sample but he needed a search warrant for that. A doctor's report would help with the probable cause for a warrant if the diagnosis found the injuries resulted from a fistfight.

"Come down to my office by four o'clock today and after

you see the doctor. I need a statement from you. And some elimination prints, too, unless we already have them."

Zarko walked away without answering.

Scarsdale watched him climb into a ratty green Ford pick-up parked out front. He noted that the truck needed a muffler and, when he heard the gears grind, a new clutch.

After a technician finished lifting the partial print from the closet door, Scarsdale looked inside the narrow room. Shirts and trousers hung from a wood pole stretching the length of the closet. A couple of coats lay in a heap on the floor. A partially crushed shoe box propped on its side was on the floor with the box top a few inches away. A pair of new work boots rested on the floor, half in and half out of the box. Looking out the bedroom window, Scarsdale scanned the homes on that block—older single-family types. He wondered if anyone had seen or even heard anything suspicious, including a loud pick-up truck.

Harris came up to Scarsdale. "I checked the place. Other than the living room and in here, nothing appears disturbed."

Scarsdale briefed Harris about Zarko seeing a blonde female being here late last night.

"Maybe they got into an argument. It escalated then ended poorly for Lasiter," Harris said.

"Could be." Then Scarsdale glanced around. "But I seriously doubt it. If Lasiter did leave the bar drunk and alone and ended up with a female here, he must have found her along the way."

"Prostitute?" asked Harris. "Drunk guy alone would sure make a nice target for a robbery or theft."

"I doubt there's anything here worth stealing. Besides Lasiter's wallet was untouched."

"Okay, someone pissed about the trial outcome—other than us, that is," Harris said.

"I doubt the Crowells had anything to do with this," Scarsdale said. "But we need to interview them and get their statement." He shot Harris a quick glance. "My money is on Zarko. His hands were all messed up. Fits with the damage to

Lasiter's face." He opened the front door then looked back at Harris. "Want to go knock on some doors with me?"

"Go ahead. I'm gonna continue looking around in here."

Before Scarsdale left the house, a crime scene technician called him over to the closet. The technician, Billy Waddell, showed Scarsdale the inside of an evidence collection envelope. A few blond hairs.

"Where did they come from?"

"They were stuck in the edge of that shelf." Waddell pointed at the spot with a laser pen. "Right above that trampled box. Whoever left the hairs had to be tall to bump into that shelf. The shelf is exactly seventy inches off the floor."

Then Waddell showed him a button in another envelope with black threads still attached. "That was found on the floor about two and half inches from the box and toward the rear of the closet." Again he pointed the laser pen. A red dot pinpointed the location. "Right about there. From the pastel color, I'd say it was a button off an article of female clothing."

Scarsdale stood there. *That makes no sense. Why would she be in the closet? Unless she was here first. Hiding. But Zarko saw her half-nude.* Scarsdale did a second walk-through, stopping at each out-of-place piece of furniture, each damaged spot on the wall, each broken item, and each fallen picture.

Several minutes later, Scarsdale talked with an elderly lady named Janice Lambright who lived across the street from Lasiter. She remembered him from when he interviewed her about Lasiter in the Crowell case.

"Have you caught the man who killed that poor little girl?"

Scarsdale smiled, pretending he didn't hear that question. "Other than Mr. Lasiter, did you see anybody at his house last night?"

"I saw a scruffy-looking man, the same one that just left, go in there around noon today," she said, bobbing a bag of tea in a cup of steaming water. "He's been coming there for a quite a while."

"Did you see Scott Lasiter come home last night?"

"No." Her eyes danced around like she was trying to remember. "You know, now that you ask, I think I did I did see that other young man last night. Couldn't sleep so I got up to fix me some chamomile tea. It's a good elixir for sleeping."

"So what time was it you saw him?" Scarsdale jotted down some notes.

"Yes. Yes, of course," she said, taking a sip of tea. "Must have been around midnight or so when I saw him or someone run out the door." She nodded toward the front window. "I was standing there, sipping my tea, looking out."

"And where did that person go?" Scarsdale asked as he moved to the window, parted the curtain and peered out.

"I'm not really sure. I don't make it a habit of spying on my neighbors." She giggled. "Don't want to be known as a busybody."

"Yes, ma'am. Did you see any vehicles parked over there?"

"Oh, just his truck. He really should get it fixed. Sounded like gunshots going off when he drove away."

"Did you happen to see a blonde female over there last night?"

"No. No blondes. But I have seen other young women there."

"Any last night?"

"No."

He checked the house right next door to Lasiter's. A middle-aged couple lived there with their daughter—a nurse named Nicole Landry. He had talked with Nicole back when he investigated Lasiter for Amy Crowell's murder. Nicole's mother, Anna, recalled her daughter mentioning something about hearing a commotion next door and seeing someone running away.

She told Scarsdale that Nicole left early this morning for a nursing convention in Dallas. She would have her phone him when she got home.

❧❧

Before visiting with Susan Crowell, Scarsdale and Harris drove to Dave's Bar. It was four blocks from Lasiter's house. Scarsdale said little during the drive, chewing instead on his lower lip while staring out the window.

"Still running all the possibilities through your head?"

"Not that. Sarah wants to take Shannon back to Waco until I find a babysitter."

"If it was me, I wouldn't let her go," said Harris, staring straight ahead out the windshield. "The little munchkin is trying to cope. And she needs to do it with her father by her side."

"I've been reading a book I got at Barnes & Noble about daughters raised by single dads. They need a female presence in their lives," Scarsdale said, staring off into the distance.

"You talking about Shannon's life or yours?" Harris said.

Scarsdale shot a hard look at Harris and saw the smirk. "Shannon's life, smartass." He turned toward the side window. "I don't know what to do. She belongs with me. She's my responsibility, not Sarah's but she's close to Sarah."

"We'll find someone." Harris parked the car in the bar parking lot.

If he couldn't find a reliable babysitter fast, Scarsdale would have little choice but to let Sarah take Shannon to Waco. "I want someone experienced and reliable," he said, getting out of the car.

The bar by day, like so many others, looked trashy. Using a mug shot of Lasiter, Scarsdale got the bartender, Fred Adler, a plump man with a shaved head and a walrus mustache, to confirm Zarko's story. Adler stood there scratching his balls, a cigarette dangling from his lower lip.

"Was anyone with him? A white male about five ten with curly brown hair and a broken nose?"

Adler pondered the question for a few seconds. "Yeah. Seems like there was. What'd he do?"

"Just checking his story. Any idea when they left?" Scarsdale asked.

"Nope."

"Was there a waitress working last night?" Scarsdale

asked. He figured the waitress might know since she floated among the customers. Maybe she knew even more.

"Yep. Alice. Alice Brewer." He turned to glance at the clock. "She'll be in here in about an hour. Ya wanna wait?"

"We'll be back later," Scarsdale said.

He and Harris drove to Lasiter's work site and located the fortyish-year-old foreman, Jeff Winkler. They knew him from their investigation of Lasiter in the Crowell murder. "Did you send Tom Zarko to Lasiter's house yesterday?" Harris asked.

"Sure did. Lasiter was always on time, so it kinda surprised me that he didn't show at all. Then Zarko told me about their celebration." Winkler grimaced. "Any idea who did it?" Winkler's eyes shifted back and forth from Harris to Scarsdale.

"Not yet." Scarsdale had a good idea who but didn't want to make any accusations without more evidence. "Did Lasiter have a girlfriend?"

He shrugged. "Not to my knowledge but then what they do in their free time is their business."

"Ever see a blonde female hanging around here with Lasiter? Maybe she showed up at lunch time or at five?"

"Nope."

"What does Zarko do here?"

Winkler nodded in the direction of the third floor. "He's a steelworker."

"And what was he working on yesterday?"

"Rebars. Up there" Winkler gestured with a head nod. "On the third floor."

"Any two-by-four construction up there?" Scarsdale asked.

Winkler shook his head, eyebrows still furrowed, as if he was trying to figure out what Scarsdale was getting at. "All steelworkers, no carpenters. Why?

"Zarko told us he injured his hands at work. Do you how that happened?"

"I didn't know he had." He turned around and yelled up to the third floor. "Hey, Stu. Tell Zarko to get his ass down here now."

A few minutes later, Zarko approached the three men. "What's up?

"Hey, dumbass. I preach and preach about reporting on-the-job injuries immediately," Winkler said, pointing at Zarko's hands. "How come you didn't?"

"Sorry, boss, I forgot," he answered, scowling at Scarsdale.

"How'd you do that?" Winkler asked.

"Um, I musta done it when I tripped carrying some reinforcing bars."

"Hold on, Zarko. You told me you scraped it reaching in between some two-by-fours," Scarsdale said.

Zarko snorted. "I'm an iron worker, not a friggin carpenter. I handle rebar and metal sheeting, not wood." He turned away from Scarsdale. "Get your fuckin' ears checked, cop."

"Get yours checked, too, dumbass. Now get in there and fill out the workers comp paperwork," Winkler said.

"What did the doctor say? Or did you forget to go?" Scarsdale asked.

"Don't need a doctor," Zarko said, over his shoulder, while walking toward the foreman's trailer.

"See you at my office at four today. Don't forget," Scarsdale shouted.

Turning to Winkler, Scarsdale asked, "Last year, on Saturday, June sixth, I believe you told me your workers were here that day, except, of course, Lasiter. Was Zarko here that day too?"

"Think so." Winkler squinted. "I'll have to check and get back to you."

❧❧❧

Back at Dave's Bar, Scarsdale and Harris introduced themselves to Alice. Scarsdale noticed her missing front tooth and a left eye that didn't track with the other one. "Do you remember this man?" He handed her Lasiter's mug shot.

"Yeah, a nice tipper. What did he do?" she asked as she wiped down a table.

"Do you recall another guy, a white male with curly brown hair, about five foot ten, broken nose, talking with him?" he asked.

She stared down at the floor like she was trying to recall anybody matching that description. "Oh yeah." She gave the two detectives a quick glance. "He was a real jerk." She arranged the single page menu, salt and pepper shakers at the center of the table. "They was arguing over something. Didn't catch what it was." She wiped down another table. "I remember that dude there," she said, pointing at Lasiter's photo, "jabbing his finger at the other guy's chest."

"Did they leave together?" he asked.

Alice looked from Scarsdale to Harris and back. "Wasn't paying much attention to them when they left. Cleaning up so I could go home."

"Nothing else?" Harris asked, giving Scarsdale a questioning look.

"Yeah." She pointed at Lasiter's picture again. "He was totally wasted."

"Why do you say that?" Harris asked, smiling.

She gave Harris a look of disbelief. "'Cause after he tipped me, he gave me a kiss on the cheek. Guys lookin like him don't give women like me the time o' day. So he had to be drunk."

"Did you see either of them with a tall blonde female?"

"Hmmm…nope. There was one fittin' that description in here about that time. When I seen her, she was sittin' right over at that table." She pointed toward a four-chair table next to an eight-chair one. "But not with either of them."

"Describe the woman," Scarsdale asked.

"Well, she sure turned heads. I wish I had her complexion. Smooth as satin," Alice said, wiping another table. "And her figure too." She slid her hands down her wide hips.

"Her age?" asked Scarsdale.

Alice scratched the back of her head. "I dunno, maybe twenty-seven or so."

"What about eye color?" asked Harris?

"I dunno. Kinda sky blue."

"Ever see her in here before?" Scarsdale asked.

Alice shook her head. "Nope.

"Do you remember anything else about her? Scars? Marks? Tattoos?" Harris asked.

"Nope. Nothin' like that. Just that she was tall." She pointed at the bartender. "Ask Fred. She stood up at the bar."

The two detectives asked Fred the same litany of questions about the blonde.

"Oh yeah. I remember her now. She looked finer than frog hair," he said, arranging peanut bowls on the bar. "And, no, I ain't never seen her in here before."

"That it?" asked Harris.

"Seem to recall she didn't talk like she was from around here," Fred said, stacking napkins along the bar.

"What do you mean?"

"Just sounded different, that's all."

"Did she leave about the same time as this guy?" Scarsdale asked, showing Fred the mug shot of Lasiter.

"Didn't pay much attention to when she left. Had other customers to take care of."

"Could you'd pick her out of a photo line-up later?" Scarsdale asked.

"Probably. Long as it's not during my working hours."

❧❧❧

"Let's go talk to Susan Crowell," Scarsdale said, unlocking the driver's door. "Then we can eliminate them."

"So we have a blue-eyed blonde Playboy Bunny at the bar that may or may not be the one at Lasiter's," Harris said, a grin spreading across his face. "We should have asked Fred about her boobs."

"He would have mentioned them." Scarsdale laughed. "Anyway, we can't rule her out but I doubt she's the same one. She had no contact at the bar with either one and nobody knows when she left. Besides, if she was finer than frog hair, why would she go after some drunken bum like Lasiter? She could have hooked up with a guy much higher in the food chain."

"Then why would some sweetheart like that go to a crappy bar like Dave's?" Harris asked.

"Maybe she was checking on a philandering husband or boyfriend. I don't know but we'll damn sure find out."

Scarsdale pulled into the circular driveway at the Crowell residence—a two-story brick home with a two-car garage. He marveled at how their front lawn seemed so pristine-looking—mowed and edged. "Must use the greens keeper from the local golf course to do their lawn." He pointed at the hedges. "Trimmed with a ruler."

Scarsdale checked his watch—it was ten after two. He scanned the neighborhood as they waited for someone to answer the door. After a few minutes and two more doorbell rings, they left.

"She must be working full-time now. Anything to stay busy and keep her mind occupied," Scarsdale said.

He remembered how distraught Susan had been during the investigation—seemed like she camped out at his cubicle, waiting for any news. She showed up at nine every morning and hung around, sometimes with her husband, asking a lot of questions, jumping at every phone call, wanting to read each statement, each report, for information about Amy's killer.

He allowed her to be there because he felt sorry for her, keeping her updated as much as he could. At the time, he didn't really get what she was going through. He could only imagine how it felt to her. Shannon, then, had been only four and was safe at home under the sharp, watchful eye of Charity. Now, having lost Charity, he understood better what Susan went through. The guilt trips, the roller-coaster ride of emotional turmoil, the anger. He got it.

He and Harris drove past the wooded park where Amy's body had been found. The sight of the park reminded Scarsdale of his recent nightmares. In that all too vivid dream some man chased Shannon through the woods. He heard her pleading cries for Daddy to help her. Him screaming her name, always just a few yards away but couldn't ever quite catch up to her. Like some force held him back—until he woke up. He'd venture to her bedroom door, flipping on the light to make sure she was there, safe and asleep.

"I hope they drive a different way out of this neighborhood. Seeing that park has to be a living hell for them," Harris said.

Scarsdale's cell phone rang. The screen showed the crime lab. "Detective, this is Ted Barnsmith. Those blonde hairs are synthetics from a wig. We can submit them to FBI if you want to know the wig maker. I can't guarantee they can determine the manufacturer or even how long it'd take them."

"Go ahead." He knew the FBI lab would take forever to send him useful information on the wig fibers, but he had to do it.

Scarsdale punched in the phone number for the latent print section.

"I'm calling about the prints recovered from the Lasiter crime scene," Scarsdale said. "Did any of them match up with anyone?"

The examiner put him on hold while he located the report. "No. The partial off the door didn't have enough points."

"Anything off the baseball bat?" Scarsdale asked.

"Nope. It had been wiped clean."

After he hung up, Scarsdale turned to Harris. "We struck out with the latents."

They arrived at the thirty-story Franklin Towers office building. It was the newest office building to dot the Austin skyline. Scarsdale gazed around the lobby as they approached the guard's desk, their shoes clicking on the glazed porcelain tiles. The tinted glass windows, pale-blue walls, and modern-style furniture gave the interior a bright, spacious feel.

The guard directed them to the elevators. Once off the elevator on Five, they approached the receptionist's counter. The lobby had shiny smooth, dark green tile floors, snow-white stucco walls, leather furniture, and nice artwork.

A few minutes later, Susan walked toward them, smiling. "Detective Scarsdale. What can I do for you?" she asked, extending her hand first to Scarsdale then to Harris.

Scarsdale liked both Susan and her husband. He considered them to be "good people."

Her face had a few additional creases since he'd last seen her. He assumed the stress of Amy's death and the trial had taken its toll on her.

"I'm sorry about the outcome of the trial." Scarsdale said. He wished he was somewhere else now. Anywhere else.

"And I'm very sorry about your wife," Susan said, a doleful expression on her face.

Harris spoke up. "We're here about—"

"I understand why you're here," she answered, gazing at Scarsdale. "My brother-in-law told me this morning about Lasiter. It's a horrible way to die, but then it was for my Amy, too. Reporters have called wanting our comments about his death." Her pencil-thin eyebrows narrowed. "I want to ask you something—something nagging my husband and me. Since the jury let him go—does that mean Amy's killer is still out there?"

Scarsdale dreaded this question. "All the witnesses and the evidence pointed to Lasiter as the one. The car. An eyewitness or three. The stuff we found in his house. All of it pointed to him."

Her eyes searched his. "Do you believe he was the one? I mean, *really* believe he murdered my Amy?"

"Yes, ma'am, I do," Scarsdale said. "But now I have to ask where you and Robert were last night?"

Susan frowned. "We were home all night." She looked away, as if considering what Scarsdale said about Lasiter.

"Is there anyone who can corroborate you? A neighbor. A friend?"

She cast a quick glance at him, then at Harris. "Both. Jill and Frank Riley from next door."

"At any time during the trial, were you or your husband approached by anybody you didn't know, offering help or expressing ideas about revenge?" Scarsdale asked. In the back of his mind, he believed Zarko killed Lasiter, but he had to show his superiors and the DA's office that he'd exhausted all reasonable leads and suspects.

She paused, her eyes darting back and forth as she looked right at him. "No, I don't recall anyone like that." She folded her arms across her chest. "Do you think Lasiter's murderer attended the trial?"

"Possibly," he said.

Harris smiled at Susan. "He could've had some enemies who'd want him dead or people out there who disagreed with the decision and felt he should pay for what he did."

She nodded in agreement. "Well, I can certainly understand how they felt. I, too, disagreed with the outcome. But it worked out all right. He's dead. I know I shouldn't say that but I couldn't be happier."

Scarsdale turned to walk away. "Sure. Have a nice day."

"Detective?" Susan said.

They pivoted around. Susan stood about ten feet away. She glanced down at the floor again before looking up at them.

Scarsdale saw the deep creases on her forehead, right above the bridge of the nose.

"Do you think you'll ever find Amy's bracelet?"

Scarsdale took in a deep breath, letting it out slow. "I hope so."

CHAPTER 6

"Truth may be eclipsed by a thrilling lie."
~ Aldous Huxley

Scarsdale's cell phone buzzed. A female voice spoke. "Is this Detective Scarsdale?"

"Yes. Who's this?"

"Nicole Landry. My mom said you wanted to talk to me. I'm home now if you want to stop by."

Twenty minutes later, Scarsdale and Harris pulled up in front of Lasiter's house. Scarsdale did a head nod toward the two-story house next door. "Let's go talk to Nicole Landry."

Nicole's mother, Anna, met them at the door. "Please have a seat." She gestured at the sofa in a large open room next to the front door. "I'll get her," she said, rushing out of the room and heading down the hallway.

They sat in the living room, waiting for Nicole. The room had French-provincial furniture with a very large blue and gold woven rug in the center of the room. Nicole strolled into the room, beaming. She hadn't changed much in the two years since he'd last talked to her. Still looked twenty-five with a freckled face. Today she wore a T-shirt adorned with caricatures of dogs and a pair of faded jeans that outlined a shapely body. "Hello, Detective Scarsdale."

Both men stood up. Scarsdale flipped his notepad open. "You remember. Still working in pediatrics?"

She nodded. "Yes. I'm still there," she said with a note of optimism.

"Once again, we're here to ask you some questions about Lasiter." Scarsdale said, pointing with his thumb in the direction of Lasiter's house.

"I was shocked to hear about what happened. Right next door. But I have to say I'm not surprised. The way he lived and all." She cocked her head to the right. "Do you think what happened had anything to do with the trial?"

Scarsdale resigned himself to the fact that question would be on everyone's mind now, even his. "Anything's possible. Let's talk about what happened last night. Your mom said you heard a commotion and saw someone running away."

He heard the patter of footsteps coming close. Anna appeared in the hall, reaching for the front doorknob. "Nicole, I'm late for work. There's a casserole in the fridge. Have a nice night. See you in the morning." Then she was out the door. He checked his watch: 5:07 p.m.

"I was getting ready to take a bath when I heard a commotion outside," Nicole continued. "When I looked I saw two men walking up to Scott's front door, arguing. One of them was Scott and he fell down on the porch and the other guy began laughing like a hyena. I blew it off as Scott being Scott. You know, drunk."

"Did they fight?"

"Not that I saw, although it sounded like they would."

"From the time you heard the commotion until they went inside, how much time passed?"

"I didn't time them, but I'd venture to guess about three or four minutes."

"Then what happened?"

"I jumped in the tub. When I came back in my room, I heard a noise like a door slamming, really hard. When I looked, I saw the same guy running from the front porch, jump into his truck, and speed off."

"So you've seen this guy there before?"

"Sure. Like I said, he's been at Scott's house many times.

Many times before? Scarsdale felt like strangling her. *Why the hell didn't you tell me that when I was investigating Amy's murder?* "What did this guy look like?"

"I never really saw him close up but I recognized his truck. Like I said I don't hang out with them."

"What about the vehicle?" Harris asked.

"A green pick-up truck."

"Okay. Anything else happen?" Scarsdale asked.

"Maybe twenty minutes later, I heard the door slam again, just not as loud as before. That's when I saw her.

"Saw who?"

"At first I didn't know if it was a guy or girl. But when she rounded the corner of his house, I saw the blonde hair."

"Can you describe her?" Scarsdale asked.

"Kind of slender. Shaggy blonde hair."

"Height?"

Nicole shook her head. "I couldn't tell. Looking down from up here, I'd say she seemed tall but I had no frame of reference."

"Did you happen to see when this woman arrived? Was it about the same time as Lasiter or the other guy?"

"I didn't see her arrive. Like I said, I was in the tub." Nicole shook her head. "After the truck left, I brushed my hair until I heard the door slam again."

"So you never saw this woman enter Lasiter's house? Only run out?" Harris asked.

She nodded. "Only coming out. And she didn't run. She walked fast."

Scarsdale gave her his card. "If you happen to think of anything else, anything at all, give me a call."

❧❧❧

Later, while standing on Lasiter's front porch, Scarsdale glanced at Nicole's bedroom window. "If I had just killed somebody, I wouldn't be walking fast. I'd be hauling ass." He walked to the far end of the porch and peered around the corner in the direction Nicole said the woman went. "When we finish here, I want to check that alley. Zarko said Lasiter always kept his house locked when he wasn't home. Crime Scene checked all the doors and windows. No signs of any forced entry. Look for a spare key," he said, bending down and lifting the doormat. He ran his fingers along the white trim across the top of the doorway then scanned around the porch.

Harris examined the underside of the wood porch railings. "Maybe there wasn't one."

"Or maybe the female subject kept it," Scarsdale said as he opened the mailbox. "Bingo." He looked over his shoulder at Harris, pointing at a house key. "Get me an envelope from the car."

Scarsdale picked up the key with his pocketknife and dropped it in the envelope.

"Either our mystery woman knew where the spare was, let herself in, and put the key back or she came in with Lasiter," Harris said, sealing the envelope.

"Doesn't make any sense to park in the alley if she drove Lasiter home." Scarsdale sucked on his teeth as they walked around the house to the alley. He wondered who the mystery woman was. Tall and slender could describe a quarter of the female population in Austin.

"Then she either knew where he kept the key or she got lucky."

"This woman had a plan. She didn't run so as to call attention to herself. She parked back here to avoid detection," Scarsdale said, peering up and down the alley, before walking down the alley toward the street, stopping about midway. He knelt down and examined the gravel. "No tire tracks. Looks like she had the presence of mind to drag something to obliterate them." He walked over to the side of the alley, eying a board lying in the grass. He picked it up and ran his fingers along both ends. Then he felt the grit as he rubbed his fingers together.

"Lasiter came straight home. Our mystery woman and Zarko were the only ones in that house with him."

Harris said. "I vote for the girlfriend surprise theory."

He nodded. "Or some surprise theory. She hid in the closet because she wasn't expecting two guys. And she had to be tall, close to six foot for her wig fibers to snag in that closet shelf."

Scarsdale looked at the back of a house across the alley and saw an elderly woman raking leaves in the backyard. He walked toward the chain-link fence separating her yard from the alley.

"Ma'am. I'm Detective Scarsdale. This is Detective Harris." He displayed his credentials and pointed at Lasiter's house as she approached him. "We're investigating a death that occurred there. Did you hear or see anybody in this alley last night?"

"I didn't, but my husband saw a car out there late last night. He's inside."

A few minutes later, the two detectives stepped up on the front porch of the woman's house. It was an old frame two-story with a wrap-around porch. Scarsdale pulled the screen door open and rapped on the front door. He turned around and peered out in the street as Harris stood on the sidewalk talking on his cell phone.

"If you're selling anything, I ain't interested," the male voice barked from inside the house.

"Police officers," Scarsdale said.

The door opened. Scarsdale faced an elderly man about seventy or so with a short white beard.

"Are you here about that car I saw out in the alley?" he asked.

"Yes, tell me about it," Scarsdale said, flipping his notepad open.

The old man sighed. "Let me get my brain working." He gave Scarsdale an appraising look. "It was a dark-colored sedan. Maybe green. Maybe blue. Couldn't tell. Don't know the type of car. Too damn many kinds."

"Did you get a look at the driver?" Scarsdale asked.

"Not real good. I think it was a woman. Couldn't make out what she looked like. Was doing something behind her car."

"What do you think she was doing out there? Did you see her pulling or dragging anything?"

"Nope. Just standing on the other side of her car, doing

something. After I yelled at her, she got into her car and drove off."

"Did you happen to see the license plate?"

"License plate? Nope. Never thought to look at it."

Scarsdale handed him his business card. "Call me if you think of anything else you recall about her or the car."

"Wait a minute. There is something else about that car. It had funny taillights. Like they were split. Red on top and on the bottom with something in the middle. And they was slanted on the inside edge. I wished I knew more about these danged new cars."

Scarsdale took it all down in his notebook. Then he sketched a taillight based on the old man's description and showed to him. "Look like this?"

"No, no. It was more slanted down." He stepped out onto the porch. "Here let me do it. You can't draw squat."

Scarsdale glanced back at Harris, who seemed quite amused.

When the old man was done, he handed the pad back to Scarsdale. "There. That's what they looked like."

Harris looked over Scarsdale's shoulder. "Looks like several different ones—Acura, Lexus, Mercedes, or maybe even a Toyota. But I'm more inclined toward the Mercedes."

Scarsdale called Mitchell to find out if Zarko was there waiting on him. Mitchell's answer was succinct. "No."

The two detectives drove back to Zarko's job site. Finding Winkler in the foreman's trailer, Scarsdale asked to speak to Zarko again.

Winkler sighed then frowned before asking one of the workers in the trailer to bring Zarko down. "I hope you guys get all the information you want this time. I can't keep pulling guys off the site." He pivoted around to the table where he began reading some blueprints.

Scarsdale and Harris stood around, peering out the window as Zarko walked toward the trailer. Inside the trailer, Scarsdale pulled a small card from his shirt pocket and read Zarko his constitutional rights.

Zarko said he understood his rights but didn't want an attorney. "So am I being arrested?"

"Not yet. Since you didn't come downtown like I told you, here we are. Now you care to revise your story about being in Lasiter's house when he was killed?" Scarsdale asked.

Zarko's eyes shifted back and forth from Scarsdale to Harris. "I already told you what happened."

"We have a female witness who identified you running out of Lasiter's after midnight," Harris said.

Zarko shook his head. "So? I told you I stopped in to check on him. But I damn sure didn't run."

"You're positive about that?" Scarsdale asked.

Zarko nodded. "Yeah, I'm positive. I oughta know what I did."

"You don't remember the woman in the closet?" Scarsdale asked, making a few notes before glancing up at a now silent Zarko "She gave us a statement about everything she heard and saw. Now we want to hear your side." It was a lie but he wanted to gauge Zarko's reaction.

The color drained out of Zarko's face. He remained silent, staring at the floor, his eyes dancing back and forth.

Scarsdale had seen his share of those expressions. Did Zarko know who the woman was? Maybe, maybe not. But from his reaction, Zarko knew she was in the closet.

"We want you to go to the hospital with us so we can obtain a saliva sample," Scarsdale asked, hoping to avoid the need for a search warrant. "It's the fastest way to get us off your back."

Zarko shook his head. "I better talk to a lawyer."

❧❧❧

It was almost five o'clock when Scarsdale got back to the office. He pulled up Zarko's criminal history. Two arrests: one in Austin for assault. The disposition screen showed that Zarko got credit for time served and paid a fine in Travis County Court at Law Number Three.

The second one was in Round Rock Municipal Court for public intoxication. The screen showed he paid a fine there as well.

His phone rang. The caller ID indicated it was Lasiter's mother. The two of them had locked horns several times during his investigation into Amy's murder. Ms. Lasiter had even filed a complaint on him, claiming harassment and planting evidence on her son. A subsequent investigation by Internal Affairs Commander Dorian Winters cleared him but left a bitterness in him over Winters's style.

Winters's steely blue eyes and trademark puckered smirk seemed to indicate everybody except him was guilty, forcing the officer to prove his innocence. Scarsdale remembered his session with Winters as if it was yesterday. He had told Scarsdale if he refused to answer questions or submit to a polygraph, Scarsdale would be suspended from duty. Winters reminded him of a modern day version of Hitler's Gestapo chief—Himmler—minus the spectacles

"How can I help you, ma'am?" Scarsdale asked.

"I want to know if you caught the man who killed my son. Not that *you* would really try to find who did it."

Scarsdale bit his tongue to stop himself from saying something he'd regret so he spit out a stock answer. "We've been conducting some interviews but haven't identified his killer yet."

"I'll have Commander Winters put another detective on this case. You don't want to find out anything. In fact, you're the reason he's dead. You ought to be tried for his murder." She hung up before he could respond.

Later Scarsdale walked down the hall to Dani's office. Even though she'd worked as the Sex Crimes analyst, he had never been to her office.

He stood in her doorway. Area maps of Austin appeared on her several computer screens. Stacks of documents lay scattered on her desk and computer table. Files and books lay on the floor. Her analyses had helped him and the other detectives clear several cases.

She sat with her back to him, hunched over, flipping through pages of a report, laying unwanted ones face down on the desk to her left.

He wanted Dani to work her computer magic by running the manner and means—modus operandi—of both the Lasiter killing and the Ferguson murder through her databases, including the FBI's Violent Offense database, known by its acronym "ViCAP."

He rapped his knuckles on the door frame. "Hey, Dani."

She swiveled her chair around and looked up at him. Tendrils of black hair hung down across her forehead. The corners of her Cupid's bow lips curled up.

He never saw her wear any makeup—not that she needed it. Just like Charity. One of the guys said she had come from California after her divorce became final. Someone else said she hailed from overseas somewhere. Another officer said she used to be a behavioral analyst with the FBI. The department's rumor mill churned out all sorts of tales about anybody. One even had the resident Gestapo Commander Dorian Winters with a pierced ear and an earring.

"Ah, Detective Scarsdale. How's your day going?" she asked, a relaxed smile on her face. Then her expression changed to a more serious look. "Did you ever find a babysitter?"

"I think I have one from my church. Have to talk with her Saturday."

"Well, let me know if she doesn't pan out. There's an older lady at my church who does babysitting. By the way, are you bringing your daughter to work this Friday?"

"I still haven't decided. If I have to go out to the field, I can't bring her with me. And I don't want to leave her in my cube alone." He remembered that Harris's wife, Mary volunteered to keep her until he found somebody if the church lady didn't work out.

"Leave her with me. I promise I'll take good care of her."

He stood there, silent, pondering her offer. *Would Shannon be okay with that?* He'd love having Shannon close by.

The two of them could even stop off at Chuck E. Cheese for pizza on the way home. "You sure it's okay? She can be a handful at times."

Dani smiled, a kind of playful grin. "Trust me. I have lots of experience."

He saw her glance at a desktop photograph of a young girl.

"Your daughter?" he asked, remembering Dani told him her daughter died. "She was very pretty. What happened? Was she ill?"

"She was killed."

He saw her lips quiver just before she clenched them tight. "I'm very sorry."

"So what can I do for you today?" she asked, appearing to have regained her composure.

He looked down at his legal pad, asking, "Can you get me a list of any calls for an officer in the 800 block of West 37th Street in the past two weeks?" He flipped a page on the pad. "And would you run the manner and means of the Lasiter and Ferguson killings through your databases? In Ferguson, I'm particularly interested in this guy they call the CEO."

"Okay. Any suspects in the Lasiter case?"

"So far, just a tall blonde female driving a dark-colored car, maybe green or blue, possibly a Mercedes, Toyota, or a Lexus. I was hoping you'd work a little of your magic and…" He shrugged, not knowing what else to say. "Whatever you can do, I'd appreciate it." Taking one last look at Dani, he pivoted and walked toward the door.

CHAPTER 7

"Resentments are burdens we don't need to carry."
~ *Anonymous*

I waited until he left my office and then let out a ragged breath. All I could do for the next few minutes was stare into space and try to calm my pounding heart. I had a ton of work to do—cases and analyses piling up—but they would have to wait. First things first. I had to get rid of that car. *Now*.

Other green cars parked in the parking lot, but I had the only Mercedes. So I took a few hours off and traded my car in.

I told my boss, Pat Greenwood, that I had a doctor's appointment. He needed the results of my analysis of a series of jewelry store robberies on his desk by tomorrow, for a meeting he had at ten o'clock with the chief, so I told him I'd be back to finish it tonight.

I had some very well honed negotiation skills. After all, I was a trial attorney. I had clear title to the Mercedes and a fat bank account. It didn't take long to strike a great deal for cash.

I was back in Austin around seven that evening, now the happy owner of a new metallic-gray Acura TL. I went straight to my office. I didn't know what was more stressful—Scarsdale's suspicions of a woman in a Mercedes at the Lassiter crime scene, or buying a new car in less than three hours. Either one or both had given me a splitting headache. Two aspirin didn't put a dent in the pain. I finished the research and analysis around nine o'clock, slid the file under Greenwood's locked door, and headed home.

When I got on the elevator, Detective Amanda Colbert was in the car on her way down. She thanked me for the work I did on the Donaldson case—the serial rapist. Amanda worked sex crimes and I'd never met a cop more passionate about bringing down the bad guys. She had more knowledge in her head about the behavior of pedophiles and perverts than I could call up on my computer in a week. I respected her, but her sharp eyes could be disconcerting. When we got to the door leading out to the parking lot, she insisted on walking me to my car. My assurances that it wasn't necessary fell on deaf ears.

She followed me to my new car and what happened next was just the nightmare I'd hoped to avoid. I thought nobody knew about my Mercedes.

She marveled at the new Acura, asking all kinds of questions, such as how long I'd had it, where I bought it, and why I got rid of my green Mercedes. I wanted to crawl into a hole and pull the dirt over me.

With adrenalin rushing through me, I leaned on the trunk, hoping to obscure the date on the temporary tag. I told her I traded my old car in last week. That predated the Lasiter killing.

Amanda said all the nice things about my car, even sat in the driver's seat and stroked the light-brown leather interior. She lavished praise on my choice of car while I stood there with a smile plastered on my face, my head throbbing and my heart pounding so hard I was sure she could hear it. I was on the brink of exploding when she finally said good night.

On my way home, I saw Fred's Liquor Store. I didn't drink hard liquor…well, except for that night when my ex proposed to me—the vodka relaxed me. But tonight I wanted something to take this awful edge off, just wasn't sure what.

The store clerk was an older man with a short beard and a big, red bulbous nose. I smelled a mild odor of alcohol on his breath and connected the dots when I saw the roseola pink in his cheeks. I wondered how much of his stock he had tasted today.

"I'd like a nice, smooth-tasting liqueur. Maybe something with a fruity taste. What do you recommend?" I asked, looking from one brand to another.

"Well, how about this?" He displayed a bottle of Grand Marnier, cradling it in both hands. "You seem like a lady who appreciates the finer things in life. This is a really great French liqueur."

When he handed the bottle to me, I read the label. An orange liqueur. Perfect. "How do I drink this? Do I mix it with something?"

"You could mix it one to one with whatever fruit juice you liked, but it's also good if you pour a small amount in a liqueur glass and sip it."

Then I heard her voice coming from behind me. Amanda! *I don't believe it*! *With all the liquor stores in Austin, she has to stop here—or did she follow me*?

"Great minds think alike," she said, setting a bottle of Jack Daniels on the counter next to a six-pack of Budweiser. "Grand Marnier, huh? I've never tried it. What's it taste like?"

I gave her my best polite smile. "I don't know. It's a gift for a friend." I caught a glimpse of the clerk out of the corner of my eye. He smiled but didn't say a word.

Her voice was loud. "Well, girlfriend, are you in a hurry to get somewhere? C'mon over to Baby Acapulco's. Some of the guys from sex crimes and homicide are getting together for a drink. The bartender makes Margaritas to die for."

"I don't really feel too good. Could I take a rain check?"

"Okay. But you must let me drive your car sometime. I love that fresh leather smell new cars have, don't you?"

"Oh yeah, sure."

When I set the bottle on the floor behind my seat, Amanda walked up from the rear of my car.

"So now's as good a time as any..." She held out her hand, expecting me to hand her the keys.

"I can't. Not today. I really need to get home. Next week, I promise."

When I drove away, I saw her standing there, watching me—the temporary tag in full view.

Amanda had to be blind not to see the date on the tag. What if she put two and two together? I've been to meetings the detectives and their sergeants had in the conference room they called the "Bullpen." What if she mentioned my Mercedes and the new car to Scarsdale during one of those sessions?

The permanent license plates would arrive in a week. If I rode a Capital Metro bus to work until then, maybe Amanda would forget all about it. Out of sight, out of mind maybe? I couldn't dwell on it.

I'm usually not so happy to get home but it felt like a sanctuary tonight. Despite the battle to open my warped door—I kept forgetting to ask the apartment manager to have it fixed—it was such a relief to wrestle it closed and breathe the air of solitude. I poured myself a glass of Grand Marnier and orange juice like the man suggested, got two Tylenol, and collapsed in my recliner. I took one fair-sized sip and the pills, laid my head back, and closed my eyes for a few minutes.

Feeling better, I went into my bedroom, knelt by the nightstand, and slid the removable baseboard open. I had rigged the board with clips so I could pull it off. Inside the space was a white box where I hid my diary and the California news clippings.

Sitting on the carpet with my back against my bed, I opened it to the next unused page. After entering today's date, I wrote out a summary of the day's events. Before I put the book back, I unfolded one of the *Sacramento Bee* news clippings. The headline blared *Young girl found murdered in North Laguna Creek Park*. The article was dated November 8. It had been over two and a half years since Katarina was killed. I cried as I read the clipping.

Police were called to a wooded area in North Laguna Creek Park where the body of a young girl was discovered by joggers yesterday afternoon. The child's name was withheld pending notification of next of kin. Police and detectives declined comment. 'We are following up on several leads right now, but have no specific suspect at this point,' a police spokesperson said.

A day after the jury let him go, Burton called to tell me

why. We both knew he couldn't be tried again for Katarina's murder so he bragged about taking Katarina's rhinestone bracelet—the same one passed down from mother to daughter in my family. I begged him to give it back to me but all I got were his taunting words. "You'll get it back when you pry it off my wrist." I had hung up on him when he started describing in sick detail what he did to her.

The next folded clipping was dated September 18th. *Body found in park.* I read the story for the thousandth time.

Police responded to a call at Reichmuth Park on Wednesday to investigate circumstances surrounding the discovery of a dead body. A city worker told reporters he found the mutilated body of a man lying in a wooded area of the park but wouldn't provide any additional information. The victim's identity was not yet known to police. A police spokesperson declined to make any further comment about the case at this time.

I didn't want to look at the third clipping so I put the diary and the clippings back in their hiding place. I switched on my laptop and returned to my recliner. From the table beside me I picked up the framed photograph of Katarina and me and traced the outline of her beautiful face. I thought about the times we'd go off for the weekend to the beach and have a contest as to who would find the prettiest seashell. Wanting her to build self-confidence, I always made sure she found the prettiest one. I still had her favorites. "I miss you so much, baby girl." I kissed the picture and set it back down.

When my laptop was ready, I went to the California Corrections and Rehab website to check on Parnell Burton's parole status. His name wasn't listed so I breathed a sigh of relief. I'd check again in a couple of weeks.

My thoughts turned to the Lasiter debacle. Sipping my drink, I questioned what I had almost done. Other than Burton, Lasiter was the first pedophile I wanted to kill. Now it appears he didn't kill Amy Crowell. His so-called friend Tom may have been the one.

I felt a stirring of doubt about eradicating those degenerates. If I kept to my mission, I'd have to be extra sure my target really did it. I'd never forgive myself if I, or my actions, harmed an innocent person.

Then I wondered how long before Scarsdale focused on me as a person of interest in the Lasiter killing? And how long would it take before Scarsdale identified me as the woman in the closet? Did I want my life reduced to moving, reinventing myself, and getting a job, again and again? I'd have to be very careful.

The nature of my job with the Austin PD gave me certain privileges. The detective's reports came across my desk a day or two after the facts had been discovered—a day or two that could mean the difference between leaving or getting caught. I'd already acquired access to Amanda's working notes but I needed access to Scarsdale's. He kept them in a password-protected file I hadn't been able to decipher yet. I tried all the usual passwords—his birthday, his wife's name, sports teams, even Shannon's name. Almost got caught doing it once.

I needed to know what he knew, what he was thinking about this case. If I couldn't access his notes, maybe I needed to get close to him. Get him to talk. Whatever it took.

ᕉᕗᕉ

Friday morning I carried the documents Scarsdale had requested over to his desk. *Wonderful.* He and the rest of the detectives were out. Having his permission to be in his cubicle, I searched his desk for anything that might contain his password. If I didn't find it, I'd befriend Scarsdale and gain his trust.

I stopped when I saw his wife's photograph on the desk. She had beautiful brown hair. I cleaned the smudges and fingerprints from the glass covering her picture. As I set it back down, I saw the photograph of his daughter. She looked like a very young version of her mother, just as pretty, but with blond hair. She appeared to be a very happy child.

Looking at his daughter, I wondered if I'd ever find happiness again. Had I forfeited that chance when I killed Burton, leaving me with only bad memories from my past? I had been a good mother once, or at least I'd tried to be. I'd like to be one again. Despite what I did to Burton and would have done to Lasiter, I didn't consider myself a bad person. But then again maybe I sealed my fate that day in Reichmuth Park.

I opened the middle drawer. Nothing but pens and pencils, paper clips, and a few small notebooks. I leaned around the corner to see if anyone was approaching. All clear. A few minutes passed as I went through each notebook.

Then I opened a pedestal drawer. It made a loud scraping noise which I hoped no one had heard. But someone did.

A gruff voice bellowed. "Hey, Scarsdale? Are you in there?"

I stuffed things back in the drawer. In my haste, I knocked a can onto the floor. It banged on the linoleum. Pens scattered everywhere. *Oh crap*!

"What the hell are you doing in here?" Mitchell growled.

I looked up at him while squatted down picking up the pens. He had graying hair and a thin frame that reeked of a minty smell of tobacco. His taste in clothes was poor. A cobalt blue and red clip-on bowtie. I saw the brown stain on his lower lip. Probably from chewing tobacco.

"I brought some research documents he wanted. He asked me to put them on his desk," I said, standing up, then moving out of the cubicle. I gestured toward his desk. "See for yourself."

"Well, if he wanted the papers on his desk, why is that drawer pulled out? Or did it just magically open?" he asked. He crossed his arms and stood there, legs spread apart, waiting for an answer.

"Lieutenant, I don't have a clue. Maybe he left it open. Maybe my hand hooked it when I knocked the pens over and I bent to pick them up. Your guess is as good as mine. I didn't open it on purpose if that's what you implying." A bald-faced lie. I struggled to keep from wincing.

He squinted at me like he was trying to place me. "Aren't

you the one I caught messing with his computer a couple of weeks ago?"

"Like I said then, if entering necessary information equals messing with his computer, than, yes, I messed with his computer. He was out on bereavement leave. Besides, it's how I do my job."

He glared at me as if he thought staring me down would force a confession.

The situation needed diffusing. Making enemies at work, especially with a detective lieutenant, would be plain stupid. "I'm sorry I made such a mess, Lieutenant. I think everything has been picked up," I said as I surveyed the area around Scarsdale's desk. "I should get back to my office now."

"Yeah, go ahead."

What an abrasive man. I could feel his eyes on me as I walked down the hall. When I turned into my office, I glanced back. He stood there, hands on his hips, watching me. Why? Did Amanda tell him about my new car? Did she mention my Mercedes?

CHAPTER 8

"Children make you want to start life over."
~ Muhammad Ali

The round-shaped clock with its white face and black numbers hung high up on the wall overlooking the detectives' cubicles. Scarsdale glanced up at it as he went straight to his desk. 7:05 a.m.

Shannon held tight to his hand as the two of them walked past the various detective cubicles. She wore a pink shirt with a large picture of Hanna Montana on the front.

"Where's your office, Daddy?"

"Right up here, sweetheart."

He'd decided to bring her today, skipping the morning kindergarten session and the need for a babysitter. Sarah had caught the early morning flight for Waco and home. Her family needed her, so she wouldn't be coming back like before. But there was another reason—a huge reason—he wanted her with him. He needed to spend more time with her, and she needed his reassuring presence, now that Sarah had left a gap.

Scarsdale didn't really know his daughter—not like Charity had known her. He realized Sarah had come to know Shannon better in the past five tumultuous weeks than he had since Shannon was born. And it was time for him to play catch-up in a big hurry. He even bought a book at the mall so he could learn about helping Shannon grow up to be a winner.

He had been a lousy father and he cursed himself for it. Except for family outings every so often, he had squandered hours and days and weeks engaged in work and his own selfish interests—like being with the guys and collecting autographed sports memorabilia. Time wasted that he should have spent getting to know her—establishing that father-daughter bond the book stated was crucial to her developing into a confident young woman.

His resolve was solid and unshakeable. He would be the father she needed and the pseudo-mother she no longer had. He had seen children her age and younger in the course of his investigations that would never have that chance, living gray and pathetic existences. He vowed Shannon would never end up like that. The book he'd bought stated that it would be a challenge like a gauntlet thrown down—a challenge he gladly accepted.

He hoped today wouldn't be one of those days when he roamed around town checking leads, finding witnesses, and spending a better part of the day out of the office. But fate sometimes dictated its own agenda.

In his cubicle, Shannon spied her mother's photograph right away. "That's mommy before she became an angel."

Scarsdale stared at it. "That's right, sweetheart." He swallowed the lump that rose in his throat.

She pointed at her own photograph. "That's me." She turned to look up at him, grinning. "Where's yours, Daddy?"

"Don't have one here, baby girl."

Mitchell's bellowing voice reminded him he should take Shannon over to his office for show-and-tell.

"Why is that man yelling, Daddy?"

Because that's vintage Mitchell, he thought. "C'mon with me. He's someone I want you to meet." He walked her down the hall, smiling at her curiosity as she gave everything they passed a visual once-over, asking what this or that was, why something looked like this way or that.

"Where's Uncle Sean's desk?"

"Over on the other side."

"Will we see him?"

"Of course," he said, rubbing her head.

She pulled away, scowling at him. "Stop it, Daddy. You're messing my hair up."

"Sorry." He smiled. *Just like her mother.*

After they visited with Mitchell, Scarsdale took her down the hall to meet Dani. On the way, Shannon tugged at his hand. "Daddy, why does Mister Mitchell's office smell so awful?"

Scarsdale resisted the urge to laugh. "Probably from the tobacco he uses."

"Why does he use tobacco? Mommy said tobacco is very bad." She paused as if she was trying to understand Mitchell's habit. "Why does he do bad things?"

"It's an old habit he can't change." Scarsdale thought about some of his own bad habits—like disappearing from his family on football weekends instead of spending it with them. He promised himself he'd change. He hadn't watched a football game in five weeks.

Dani had asked to meet Shannon if he brought her to work, so he kind of felt obligated to introduce them. They stopped in her doorway. "Hello, Dani," Scarsdale said.

She glanced over at them, and a big smile crossed her face as she stood up, every inch of her. "Hi."

He glanced down at Shannon and saw her eyes widen as Dani approached her and leaned over. He felt her small fingers grip his hand tight.

"And who are you?" asked Dani.

"Shannon," she said, raising her fingers to her mouth.

Dani squatted down in front of Shannon before glancing up at Scarsdale. "She's so adorable." She looked back at Shannon. "How old are you, sweetie?"

"I'm five," she answered with a growing smile.

Dani stood up and held out her hand to Shannon. "Do you like cookies?"

Shannon looked up at Scarsdale as if seeking approval. When he smiled and nodded, she took Dani's hand.

She led Shannon toward two metal containers sitting on her desk—a brown one decorated with stag horns and one with horse-drawn sleighs on a snowy background. Leaning close to Shannon before casting a sideways glance at Scarsdale, she told her in an almost whispered tone, "I have German chocolate cookies, or you can have chocolate chip cookies."

"Umm, chocolate chip." Shannon cast a wide grin at her father as Dani opened the brown container.

She held the container low under Shannon's eyes, letting her pick one.

"What do you say?" Scarsdale asked from the doorway.

"Thank you," Shannon said, eyeing the cookie. "My mommy used to make cookies too. She'd let me lick the bowl after she put the cookies in the oven." She took a bite.

Dani set the container back on the desk. "I bet she made really good cookies, too."

"She went to Heaven. She's an angel now. Daddy tries to make cookies but he doesn't do so good. I have to help him." Shannon pointed at the framed photograph on Dani's desk. "Who is she?"

"That's my daughter," Dani said, looking at the photo.

"Did you bring her here today?" Shannon asked, looking up at Dani.

"No, I didn't."

"Why not?"

Dani's mouth tightened into a narrow line. "It's a long story, honey."

Scarsdale reached for Shannon's hand. "Okay, Shannon. It's time to go." He looked at Dani. "I'm sorry."

"It's okay. Why don't you let her stay here with me?" She smiled at Shannon and said, "If that's all right with you."

"I don't know," Scarsdale said. "I don't want her to be—"

Dani reached her hand out to Shannon. "She won't be any trouble. We'll have fun. Besides, you have some cases to investigate."

He hesitated. He was reluctant to allow Shannon to stay with someone not family. *Should I leave her here? Just how well do I know this woman?* "Are you sure you don't mind?"

"Sure. We'll get along fine, won't we, Shannon?"

Shannon grinned. "It's okay, Daddy."

He headed toward his cubicle but stopped a few yards from Dani's office. He glanced over his shoulder toward her office. *She lost her child.* He shook his head before continuing on. One of the things he prided himself on was being a good judge of character. In his job, it was a necessary trait. *No, no way she'd do that.*

ַַַ

When Scarsdale sat down, he spotted the documents Dani had left on his desk. He studied her Lasiter analyses, flipping through all five pages. The criteria she used to perform the research and analyses were listed in the right-hand margin: Mercedes, male, female, fists, night, residential, male sex offender victim, and Southwest region. He carried her report over to Harris's cubicle and handed it to him.

"I don't believe it. No similar offenses anywhere?"

"Nope. Looks like our field of suspects is narrowed to Zarko or everyone who believed Lasiter did kill the Crowell girl. When we get the autopsy report back, it'll set a time frame for Lasiter's death," Scarsdale said.

"I'd run Zarko on a polygraph but he isn't that dumb."

Scarsdale picked up Harris's phone and called the lab. "This is Detective Scarsdale. Anything on the submissions from the Lasiter crime scene?"

"From the design and color pattern, the button came from female attire. It was a two-hole metal shank button, a type commonly found on women's denim jackets. The threads appear to have been frayed recently."

Scarsdale hung up. "I'm gonna check on how Shannon and Dani are getting along."

ַַַ

Scarsdale stopped a few yards short of Dani's office. Her door was closed. He didn't see a light shining from under the door. His heart began beating faster as he hurried to her door and rapped on it with his fist.

No answer.

He tried the door.

Locked.

He turned to face Harris. "Where the hell are they?" he asked.

Harris shrugged. "Beats me. Little girl's room, maybe?"

After searching the entire floor, they made it back to Scarsdale's desk in record time.

"Maybe that's from her," Harris said, pointing at the flashing red light on Scarsdale's phone.

Scarsdale punched the speaker button and listened to the recording while chewing on his fingernail.

"Detective Scarsdale, this is Dani. I hope you don't mind, but I'm taking Shannon to the third floor break room. Some of the ladies in Records are hosting a party for the younger kids. I think Shannon would really enjoy it. If you want, you're welcome to come on down."

"Guess we can cancel the Amber Alert and the call to the FBI," Harris said, tongue-in-cheek.

Scarsdale stood there, looking down at the floor, took a deep breath, and let it out. What a stupid thought. He'd been having plenty of those lately—the dumbest being his trip out to Zilker Park.

"I want to see how she's doing. Want to tag along?" Scarsdale asked.

"Are you kidding me? And miss out seeing my favorite little munchkin? Let's go."

When they got off the elevator, they followed the sound of children's laughter. A crowd of people stood in the doorway. Being so tall, Scarsdale saw over top of them. The tables had been pushed against the wall. Balloons with long dangling strings floated up against the ceiling. On the table was a huge chocolate layer cake already cut into small squares and plastic cups filled with some red liquid that Scarsdale figured was Hawaiian Punch.

He saw Shannon pull down a balloon and hand it to a girl who had been trying to reach it but was too short. *That was a nice gesture.*

Dani stood at the back of the room, arms folded, chatting

with two women he recognized from the Records Section—Doris Levine and Tillie Garza. He watched her track Shannon as she roamed the room with the other children. Seeing her attention to his daughter eased his nervousness. It was a fleeting sense of contentment. Dani had other commitments, and he still needed a reliable babysitter.

Shannon seemed to be really enjoying herself. The last time he saw her have this much fun was when Charity and he had taken her for a weekend trip to the beach at Port Aransas this past summer.

Scarsdale's cell phone dinged. A text message from the Sex Crimes Unit secretary stated that Tom Zarko's attorney, Devon Jackson, called. If Scarsdale wanted to talk to his client, he'd have to arrange a date and time through Jackson's office.

"So much for the Zarko interview. The SOB got himself a lawyer," Scarsdale said to Harris. He gave Shannon one last look before turning to head for the elevator. She'd tell him all about her day over a pizza dinner.

Back at his office, Scarsdale telephoned the medical examiner's investigator, Jonas Short. He knew Short from when they worked together in Homicide.

"When will the Lasiter autopsy report be ready?"

"The preliminary is done. Several facial fractures but the cause of death was due to a fractured cervical spine. Waiting on the drug screen. A lot of foreign epidermal tissue and blood was found on the victim's clothes, face and under his nails. If you have a suspect, you might want to get some samples from him or her."

"Figured as much. Now tell me this, did those skin and blood samples belong to one other person or two?"

"Just one. Why?"

"A witness saw a second person leaving Lasiter's house. A female."

"Well, she'd have to be built like an Amazon to do this kind of damage. But I guess anything's possible."

"How about a time of death?" Scarsdale asked.

"Coupled with witness reports, the pathologist computed

death anywhere between eight to twelve hours before the body was discovered. That probably doesn't help much at all."

"It does a little. And every bit helps." Scarsdale wanted every piece of evidence he could obtain to make a rock-solid case against Zarko.

Remembering that the crime scene team had performed a glue fuming exam of Lasiter's body at the scene, he telephoned Emily Hansen. She was the technician in charge of the Lasiter crime scene team. With over fifteen years' experience, she worked a lot of violent crimes with comprehensive skill procedures that made all the detectives very happy to see her set up shop at their crime scene.

"Any fingerprint results from the tests you did on Lasiter?" he asked. He knew the basics of glue fuming. He'd learned about the procedure at a homicide school put on by the FBI. They said it was a fairly new procedure performed at crime scenes to develop fingerprints on corpses. A portable device blows glue fumes onto the skin. Magnetic powders are then applied, and any latents are lifted for later comparison.

"Yes. Just finished the last step this morning. We got some good ones off the inside of Lasiter's right forearm. I found two unusable smudge prints on the body's neck area. Right over the carotid. Like someone wearing gloves may have checked for a pulse. I'll have a fingerprint examiner run the latents through the FBI's automated fingerprint database." Emily said.

He didn't share her enthusiasm about computers—too many different passwords. He was always opening the book to find the password for whatever database he wanted to access. And the computer kept locking up on him, forcing him to reboot it. "And you'll let me know as soon as you get a response?"

"Of course."

Scarsdale went to work on a rough draft of his arrest warrant affidavit, leaving a blank spot for the expected fingerprint confirmation.

He knew an air-tight murder case had a way of persuading arrestees to talk. If Zarko knew the person who had fled Lasiter's house, he'd spill his guts in exchange for a plea deal.

"Humph," he muttered, thinking about Olsen's attempt to get a deal by claiming he knew the name of the man who killed Ferguson.

Olsen had refused to disclose the name without a signed and sealed deal from the DA. Did Olsen really know or was he trying to game the system?

∽∾∽

After closing the door, Commander Acker Robertson sat down in Winters's office. "I got your email," he said, brushing lint off each sleeve of his white dress shirt. "So what clever words of wisdom do you have to impart to me today?" Robertson knew his question sounded facetious—he meant it that way.

Winters leaned back and propped his feet on his desk. He picked at his fingernails with a small pocketknife. "Detective Jason Scarsdale."

Robertson drew in a deep breath and let it out. "Oh yeah, him."

"Ms. Betty Lasiter claims he murdered her son."

"Well, the DA's office screwed the pooch on that one. And her *innocent* son paid the price. So I understand her complaint. Now it's a finger-pointing game. And as much as I'd like to hang it around Scarsdale's neck, I signed off on his final report. Nevertheless, the department is facing a potential public relations nightmare so somebody's going to have to be the sacrificial lamb."

"Yes, of course," Winters said, casting a quick glance at Robertson, while continuing to clean his nails with the knife. "And I'm familiar with the history between you and Scarsdale." He reached over, flipped open a file and read from it. "In April 1993, he successfully appealed an overtime request which you had denied." Winters looked at him. "I believe you were his lieutenant at the time."

"What's your point, Dorian?" Robertson asked, taking a peppermint candy from a bowl on Winters' desk.

He turned to another page. "Earlier this year, your wife divorced you over an affair. Rumor has it the affair involved an out-of-town female officer in the back seat of a city-owned vehicle. Other rumors have you blaming Scarsdale as the one who leaked the details to your then wife."

Robertson shifted in the chair. "What are you doing, Dorian? Keeping intel files on people "a la" J. Edgar Hoover? Rumors run rampant in a police department. You of all people should know that."

Winters smiled in a way indicating he knew something Robertson didn't. "And I know some rumors also have a basis in truth. That's the beauty of divorce petitions and other lawsuits like the one your mistress filed seeking child support. They set out enough information to enable a skillful investigator like myself to ferret out the rest of the story. I'm wondering, Acker, did the mother of your bastard son ever find out your real name?"

"Don't fuck with me, Dorian. Just remember you don't exactly have clean hands," Robertson said, giving him a cold, hard stare.

"Take it easy, Acker."

"I know about the Shelly Ambrose case. How she spent the weekend with you on the Riverwalk and, poof, her IA case disappeared."

"That would be very damaging for me if it were true." Winters smiled. "But it's merely an urban legend."

"That's the great thing about rumors. You probe deeper and all sorts of nasty little secrets crop up," Robertson said, popping another mint in his mouth. "Secrets I can prove. "

Winters chewed on his lower lip while staring back at Robertson. "Regarding Ms. Lasiter's complaint and this potential public relations nightmare, what steps do you plan to take?"

"What I plan to do? Isn't that your shop?" Robertson asked, seeming a little puzzled at the question.

"Not necessarily." Winters shrugged, folding the blade of the knife back. "He's your detective. And sooner or later someone, likely Scarsdale, may well blab the whole truth about what you did in that backseat. Do you really want to pass on this golden opportunity?"

"If I removed him unilaterally, I'd be open to a charge of retaliation. I'm not venturing down that road. At least not alone."

"Fair enough." Winters sat up, tugging at the cuffs of his gray shirt. "Remove him from the Lassiter case and leave the rest to me. That way, you get your revenge and I get another scalp for my collection."

Robertson sat there, giving Winters's suggestion serious consideration. "And what are *you* going to do?" Aware that Winters's reputation for duplicity was well-deserved.

"Acker, you doubt my word?"

"I have a better idea. You build a case on him first."

"And what exactly has he done to warrant an IA case?"

"Scarsdale's wife died. He's got no woman. I've seen him talking to that sex crimes analyst—Dani Mueller. Mitchell tells me he's found her in his cubicle a couple of times. Plus he brought his kid and left her with Mueller," said Robertson.

"Inference. Not enough to open an IA case."

"Interpretation says differently."

"Interesting," Winters commented, writing some notes on a pad. "Okay. Here's what I need you to do."

Robertson listened, as Winters outlined a plan, then he consented to it

After Robertson left, Winters slid the recorder out from under his desk. He popped the microcassette tape out, wrote "Robertson" and today's date on the edge. Then he unlocked the bottom drawer of his desk and pulled it open, revealing a collection of microcassettes, each with somebody's name on the edge. He slipped the Robertson tape in place and locked the drawer.

CHAPTER 9

"The only thing that overcomes hard luck is hard work."
~ *Harry Golden*

About one-thirty in the afternoon, Mitchell summoned both Scarsdale and Harris to his office. At fifty-two years of age, Mitchell's thin drawn face had more wrinkles than a Shar Pei pup. He wore a rumpled tweed jacket and a blue-and-white striped bowtie. "Sit down," Mitchell said as Scarsdale and Harris trudged in.

The room had one window with yellowing blinds, and the air was redolent of Mitchell's mint-flavored dipping snuff and days-old coffee. It made for an odd and not entirely pleasant combination. Scarsdale couldn't stretch his legs out since the desk was only two feet away. He couldn't even distract himself by staring at titles in the bookcase; they were covered. He glanced over at Harris and wondered how he could tolerate the stench coming from the plastic cup Mitchell used as a spittoon. Scarsdale covered his nose and mouth. *Let's get this over with so I can get back to fresh air.*

He noted the concern in his lieutenant's eyes as he picked the chair closest to the door. The pouches under Mitchell's eyes were bigger and darker, as if he hadn't slept in a few days. He sat there rubbing his forehead as he looked down at a document on his desk. Mitchell raised the cup to his lower lip. Scarsdale looked away but not before the brown juice flowed over Mitchell's lip into the cup. It disgusted him to watch someone spit tobacco juice. He'd seen more than enough of it land on his windshield while driving the local freeways.

"Betty Lasiter filed a complaint against you," Mitchell growled before spitting into his cup again.

Scarsdale knew Mitchell liked smooth, unruffled days. But a complaint on one of his detectives meant Winters got involved. And, for Mitchell, dealing with Winters meant the day would be anything but smooth.

Winters had been a patrol captain when Scarsdale was a cadet in the academy. He recalled a sketch some officer circulated showing Winters seated at a desk dressed in a suit and tie, except that the head of a penis had been substituted for his face, which made Scarsdale smile, a smile he covered with his hand.

"She wants you off the case."

"Yeah, I know. She thinks I—"

Mitchell pointed his index finger at Scarsdale's face which he understood to mean "shut up." Mitchell's eyes had turned cold and hard. "I spent the past half hour on the phone with Commander Robertson and another half with Winters. Robertson's inclined to grant her request," Mitchell said.

Robertson ruled the Violent Crimes Division with an iron fist. His management philosophy was simple: My way or the highway. That dictatorial approach didn't sit well with Scarsdale or many of the other detectives, but since the division was Robertson's figurative "ball," Scarsdale and the rest of the detectives had to play by his rules.

"You've got to be kidding me," Scarsdale said. "Since when does some scumbag's mother dictate case assignments?"

"She threatened to sue the department and you for violating her son's civil rights and for wrongful death." He spit in the cup then wiped the dribble from his lip with the back of his hand. "Winters plans to open an IA case on you after Robertson removes you."

"Me?" Scarsdale leapt to his feet. "For violating his civil rights? Since when did Herr Winters give a damn about anyone's civil rights?" He chortled. "What about Amy Crowell's civil rights? The Crowells should have sued her since she's Lasiter's executor." He remembered sitting in the Crowell's living room when Susan and her husband had discussed the merits of suing Lasiter's estate for wrongful death.

"They probably didn't since she's judgment-proof." Mitchell pointed at the chair, a gesture Scarsdale understood to mean "sit down."

"So am I." Scarsdale took a deep breath and snorted before sitting down. *What bullshit*, he thought.

"And Robertson wants to avoid a public-relations nightmare. We spent quite a few man-hours working up a case on her son and, boom, he ends up walking free," Mitchell said. "Only to end up murdered."

"It's not our fault the damn DA's office couldn't prosecute a slam dunk," Harris said, his arms leaning on the front edge of Mitchell's desk.

Mitchell cast a quick glance at Harris as if to acknowledge his comment. "Now we have the same detectives working his murder. Robertson believes it'd be better to assign it to another team."

"That's bullshit!" Harris bellowed.

Scarsdale put his hand on Harris's chest, pushing him back into the chair. "We know Lasiter backward and forward. We know the Crowells and everyone else involved. Robertson's so worried about man-hours? Well, it stands to reason another team would have to spend a lot of *man-hours* just getting up to speed. Besides we're close to arresting the bastard."

"Well, Robertson isn't happy about her complaint or the wasted hours. He translates those lawsuits into tax dollars spent by the city attorney's office having to defend them."

"I understand that," Scarsdale answered. *When was he ever happy with anything the detectives did*? "What about *Herr* Winters?"

"I'll see what I can do with him." Mitchell leaned back in his chair, putting his hands behind his head.

"Good luck." Scarsdale said. "He's wanted my head on a pole for the past year." He recalled Amanda's disciplinary hearing when Winters tried to have her suspended for allegedly threatening a suspect in a child abduction case. Amanda's attorney credited Scarsdale's testimony as a major reason she had been cleared. He remembered the menacing look he got from Winters when the two men passed each other in the hall later.

"Go out there and do your job. Just be more sensitive to Ms. Lasiter's ordeal, both of you."

"We know how to kiss ass," Harris said. "We just don't make it a habit to practice it every chance we get."

"Well, try it. You might like it, Harris," Mitchell said. "Robertson is big on public relations."

"I thought we're trying to solve murders, not be some Madison Avenue PR firm," griped Harris.

"Then go back to patrol," Mitchell fired back. He slammed his fist down on the desk so hard the shudder of the impact knocked the spit cup over. Brown liquid oozed into a puddle on his desk, then began dripping onto the floor. He jumped up, brushing his hand down his trousers. "Dammit! And I have a meeting in an hour with the chief."

Scarsdale saw the dark brown stain on Mitchell's pants and shook his head. "If he removes us, he's making a major-league mistake. We're this close to an arrest." He held up his thumb and forefinger, an inch apart.

"Then I'm sure he'll leave everything alone. If not, it'll be his mistake," Mitchell said, soaking up the puddle with a handful of Kleenex. "If he, in fact, does it. But you two better clear this case as soon as possible. I shit you not."

❧❦❧

When Scarsdale was about ten yards from his office, he heard Shannon chattering and laughing. As he turned the corner, he saw her seated on the small chair. Dani sat in his chair, smiling at something Shannon said.

"Daddy, Dani and me went to a party," Shannon said, holding a Drawing and Learning Board laptop. Her eyes gleamed when Scarsdale picked her up. "Look what I won. I can draw pictures and play music on it." She held up the board so Scarsdale could see the drawing. "That's me and Dani."

The toy laptop showed a rough sketch of a smaller female

in a dress holding hands with a tall woman. "Wow, that's really good."

"We had cake and ice cream."

"I can see that," Scarsdale said, noting the faint brown stain on her pink shirt. "Looks like you enjoyed yourself." He smiled at Dani. "Thank you for babysitting her."

Amanda Colbert swung around the corner of his cubicle. "Well, well, look who's checking up on Daddy." Amanda high-fived Shannon. "How ya been, young lady?" She looked at Dani. "How's your new car compare to the Mercedes?"

Dani's eyes opened wide, her gaze swinging between Amanda and Scarsdale. "Good," she said, almost whispering. She gestured at the flashing red light on Scarsdale's voice mail. "Looks like you have work to do." She got up and reached her hand out to Shannon. "Let's go get a cookie, Shannon."

Shannon took a step toward the cubicle opening then turned to Amanda, showing her the laptop prize. "See what I won today?"

Amanda leaned over to inspect it then stood up. "Cool." She looked at Scarsdale. "Gotta run. See ya later." She turned to go in the opposite direction from Dani and Shannon, spun around and pointed at Dani while walking backward. "Remember girlfriend, you promised I could test-drive your new car."

"I have to make a run to the DA's office sometime this afternoon," he said to Dani. "Would you mind keeping Shannon a little while longer? I really hate to impose. I know you have plenty to do, too."

"I don't mind at all. She's so sweet." She held out her hand for Shannon. "Let's go to my office, honey."

"I'll be back soon, sweetheart." He bent over and kissed her on top of her head. "How does Chuck E. Cheese pizza sound for dinner?"

"Yeah!" Shannon grabbed Dani's arm with both hands. "Can Dani come, too?"

He glanced at Dani. 'Sure, if she wants to." *Why not? It*

wouldn't be like a date. Just three friends. Besides, she's taking good care of Shannon.

Dani nodded. "I think I can find some time for that."

He watched them walk away, hand in hand, Shannon skipping and chattering away. She was happy, which made him happy. Then he tended to the flashing red light on his voice mail.

It was a message from Assistant DA Chandler Coffield III asking Scarsdale to bring the Lasiter file over and convince him there was sufficient probable cause for a search warrant to draw a blood sample from Zarko.

Coffield worked in the DA Case Intake Section reviewing felonies to determine if the cases rose to the level of sufficient PC. Scarsdale had met him once before. He was an arrogant, obnoxious prick and Scarsdale felt sure nothing had changed since their first meeting.

Thirty minutes later, Scarsdale sat across the desk from Coffield. He felt nothing less than contempt for the young prosecutor and his long brown shoulder-length hair. Coffield's black-rimmed glasses were too big for his beady little eyes. And his anorexic frame reminded Scarsdale of a meth addict.

Coffield's law school diploma and the Texas Supreme Court plaque certifying him as a licensed attorney hung on the wall directly behind him. He wondered who's ass Coffield kissed to get it.

"Let me see what you have, Detective."

Scarsdale slid the file across the desk to Coffield.

While Coffield took his time reading the file, Scarsdale let his thoughts drift to the upcoming Thanksgiving holiday. Less than two weeks away, it'd be the first one he and Shannon spent without Charity. It used to be a great day—with Charity assigning certain dinner prep tasks to him and Shannon. Charity would prepare all the veggies and desserts. His job was to cook the turkey. Shannon would set out the plates and utensils. She also doubled as the official taster of the desserts—a job she never turned her little button nose up at.

This year, his parents had invited them up to Dallas to

celebrate with the rest of the family. His grandparents, both brothers, and Sarah and her family would be there. He didn't know—maybe Shannon would enjoy it more with her cousins. Less time to think about a holiday without her Mom.

He rubbed his chin, feeling the whiskers he missed shaving off this morning, and turned his mind to the case and the Lasiter mystery woman. She was the key to nailing Zarko. Who was she? Why was she in there? Where was she now?

He glanced over at Coffield who leaned back in his chair, pushed his glasses up, and snorted. Coffield closed the file folder and tossed it across the desk in the direction of Scarsdale. "There isn't enough PC for a search warrant or an arrest warrant for Zarko."

Scarsdale shook his head in disgust. He'd gotten search warrants from other prosecutors for a lot less evidence than he had in this case. "Why not?"

Coffield picked up a magazine and flipped through it while answering Scarsdale's question. "Nicole's description of the person you think is Zarko is too vague. That person could have been anyone. If I were you, I'd go back to her and nail down a positive ID."

"She's seen this guy many times before. Zarko told me himself he'd been running with Lasiter for the better part of a year."

Coffield continued reading. "Zarko's hand injuries could very well have been caused by an accident at work, like he claimed."

Scarsdale paused. He felt the heat in his cheeks. "Maybe you've never been in a fistfight. I have. Zarko's scraped knuckles are consistent with a fistfight."

Again Coffield shrugged and kept his eyes on the magazine. "If I were Zarko's attorney, I'd explain the fuming prints from Lasiter's forearm as Zarko's efforts to check for vital signs on his friend."

Scarsdale could barely contain his growing anger. "Nobody checks vitals on the forearm. Try the wrist or the carotid. No latents found on either of the wrists." He shook his head.

One of those I-can't-believe-this-shit types. *I guess they don't teach common sense in law school—or at least not where you went, you little moron.*

"Ah yes, the carotid. Apparently the unidentifiable prints found on Lasiter's carotid belonged to a third person and…" His voice trailed off as he focused his attention on something in the magazine. After a couple of seconds, he resumed. "That brings us to the button in the closet. That button came off a denim jacket that could have been worn by a male as well as a female."

"I understand about the button and the wig hairs," Scarsdale said.

Coffield continued as if Scarsdale hadn't said a word. "The blonde wig could have also been worn by either a male or a female." He glanced up at Scarsdale. "Assuming the wig hairs and the button are even connected to this murder, you will need to identify this unknown actor. Then interview him or her so we know the extent of their involvement, if any. That person may be your killer."

Scarsdale grabbed the file and stood. He gave Coffield a hard stare while flashing a cold smile. "You do know proof beyond a reasonable doubt isn't necessary right now, don't you? All that's needed is PC for a warrant." Scarsdale stepped toward the door before turning to face Coffield. "Let me see if I got this straight. We've got the killer's DNA and a witness who knows Zarko by appearance. She sees someone who looks just like him, driving the same type of vehicle, coming and going at midnight, the approximate time, according to the medical examiner, that Lasiter died and you're telling me I don't have enough PC for a warrant to get a sample off Zarko?"

Coffield looked up at Scarsdale, a smug grin on his face. "That's right, Detective."

"I'll be sure to tell his mother we know who killed her son but the DA's office refused to give us approval for a search warrant for his DNA." Scarsdale didn't wait for a response before storming out of the office.

∽✐∽

"That sorry little jackass," Scarsdale muttered as he approached Harris's cubicle to update him and vent. *Coffield wouldn't recognize PC if it smacked him in the face. Worthless little son of a bitch.*

He wanted the anger and frustration out of his system before he met up with Shannon. But Harris was out, so he went to Mitchell's office. After Scarsdale told him what Coffield said, Mitchell stared at Scarsdale, then spit in his cup, and wiped his mouth with the back of his hand.

"Close the door," Mitchell said.

The thought of being in a closed space with the stench of that snuff almost made Scarsdale wretch. "Is that really necessary?"

Mitchell's eyebrows arched up. "Yes."

Scarsdale stood in the doorway and took a couple of deep breaths. Then he closed the door. The minty smell of the snuff filled the small office.

"After the Lasiter trial, the DA ordered a close scrutiny of all your cases, current and future."

"What? Those sonofabitches are blaming me for their screw-up?"

"In short, yes, they are." Mitchell leaned forward, his arms folded on the desk. "Do you really expect them to shoulder the blame? The DA is an elected official. Screw-ups, as you succinctly describe it, will get him unelected." He leaned back. "Ergo, you're the designated scapegoat."

Scarsdale pointed in the general direction of the DA's office. "They lost the Lasiter case because they didn't woodshed Helen Jackson. She fell apart only because they didn't prep her. I told Tidwell she was timid."

Mitchell looked at him with a slight smirk. "You know what you have to do. Go do it."

Scarsdale opened the door.

"By the way," Mitchell said, "the chief blocked the IA investigation and ordered Robertson to keep you two working the Lasiter case—for now." Mitchell jabbed his finger on his desk. "So you're still under the gun. Clear the damn case and do it fast."

Scarsdale's phone rang just as he walked into his office. The caller ID indicated it was Winkler.

"Detective, you asked me to verify whether Zarko worked on the day the little girl was killed. I've got the time cards, but our legal counsel said not to release them without a court order."

Great! Scarsdale thought. *What's next*?

CHAPTER 10

"To be in your children's memories tomorrow,
you have to be in their lives today."
~ *Anonymous*

That night, Scarsdale lay in bed, hands interlocked behind his head, thinking about the pizza party with the three of them—Shannon, Dani, and himself. Shannon had a great time, making him and Dani take turns playing video games with her. He enjoyed the time he spent sitting and talking with Dani about her life in Germany while Shannon devoured pizza. He had forgotten how much pizza a five-year-old could put away.

But he felt a little guilty being with Dani, kind of like being on a date, so soon after the funeral. Someday he might go out on dates, but for now his world revolved solely around Shannon. He reached over and picked up the book—the one on how a single father should raise a daughter—and opened it. He re-read the second chapter which focused on the need for telling and showing Shannon that he would always be there for her and he loved her unconditionally.

On Saturday morning, he stood in front of the stove, cooking breakfast for Shannon and himself. It had been five weeks since Charity's funeral. Today he and Shannon would be together without friends or family staying over. He wanted to believe he was getting a handle on widowhood. As he ladled scrambled eggs onto two plates with strips of bacon, he wondered how much longer the emotional roller coaster ride would last. Things were slowly getting better. The good days and the bad days were about even.

"Daddy, is breakfast ready?" Shannon asked as she

pushed a kitchen chair across the floor to the pantry.

He noticed her voice sounded funny. "Yeah, but what are you doing?"

"Getting the ketchup. I can't eat eggs without ketchup," she said as she mounted the chair and pulled the bottle off the shelf.

He walked over to her. "Are you feeling okay? You sound a little congested."

"I'm fine," she said, pushing the chair back to the table.

He felt her forehead—not hot. Her nose was red, like she had been wiping it or rubbing it. Then he saw the clear watery fluid dripping from her nose. Before he could grab a tissue, she wiped it with the back of her hand.

"Let's not wipe like that. Use a tissue. Here." He handed her a couple of tissues, which she used immediately to wipe more nasal drip. He got another one. "Blow."

"Oh, okay."

He studied her for a moment when she coughed. *She's coming down with a cold.* Last night at Chuck E. Cheese's, he recalled, Shannon played a video game with two kids, making him wonder if one of those kids passed something on to her.

He didn't remember either one of the boys coughing or sneezing but maybe he missed it while he and Dani chatted.

While they stood by the table, he said, "You're not fine." He pressed the back of his fingers against her cheek.

She pushed his hand away. "I'm fine," she answered, irritated as only a five year old can be.

"How are you doing about Mommy being gone?" He set the plates of food on the table. The book said to talk with her about what happened to Charity. To help her work through the grieving process too, just like he had to do himself.

"I miss her. I wish I could see her again," she said as she poured some ketchup on the eggs. She took a bite. Then she pulled her plate closer. "Dani said it takes time," she said, biting off a piece of bacon.

"Time for what?" He knew—just wanted to find out what she thought.

She gave him an exasperated stare. "Time to heal after Mommy went to Heaven."

The third chapter in the book was about the need to get Shannon to talk through her feelings about Charity's death and about how much time she would need to grieve. "So how do you feel about Mommy not being here?"

"Dani said there's no right way to feel about Mommy going to Heaven. She said she knew how I felt and I could talk to her anytime." Shannon glanced up at Scarsdale. "She said you could come to."

"Really? When did she tell you that?"

"In her office. Having facetime."

He smiled. "Facetime?"

"Yeah. We talked about girl things and about Katarina," she said as she put a forkful of egg in her mouth.

"What did she say about Katarina?" he asked, sipping his coffee.

Shannon glanced up at him. A serious expression on her face. "She's in Heaven with Mommy." She wiped her nose again with the tissue and resumed eating.

Later on Saturday, Shannon became a bit more irritable and coughed a lot, so Scarsdale called the duty nurse for his health plan. He described Shannon's symptoms and she instructed him to give Shannon plenty of bed rest and fluids, and Tylenol as needed, but not to administer any aspirin. The nurse cautioned that if Shannon's condition worsened, he should take her to the nearest ER.

He followed the nurse's instruction to the letter, even feeding Shannon bowls of chicken soup, some vitamin C, and several glasses of orange juice—a home remedy recommended by his mother. Sunday evening Shannon seemed to make a dramatic improvement.

On Monday, Shannon felt better, though still a little irritable, and ate a small bowl of oatmeal. Erring on the side of caution Scarsdale didn't take her to kindergarten, dropping her instead at the house of his new babysitter—Fran Tisdale. He'd found her through one of Charity's lady friends at church.

He, Shannon, and Fran had visited in the parish hall after church that Sunday. He'd delved into Fran's background, asking casual questions about her experience and personal history. She had babysat her granddaughters for a number of years.

He interviewed her as if he were conducting a background investigation. Scarsdale even ran her name and date of birth through the department's databases to be sure she had no criminal history even though departmental rules didn't allow searches for personal reasons. It was harmless and he figured no one would ever know.

Fran lived in one of those single-story wood frame homes with a brick veneer and a concrete birdbath in the front yard. An older model shiny green Mercury sedan sat in the driveway.

Shannon acted a little cranky as she walked with Scarsdale into the house. Fran presented herself in a plaid dress with a white apron bordered with a blue diamond pattern tied snug around her waist. Her graying hair had been pulled back into a bun. She reminded him of his grandmother.

Once inside, Scarsdale thought he'd stepped back in time. All the furniture was wooden—the kind of pieces he'd seen in the Amish homes he'd visited during a murder case he worked on the west side of Austin several years ago. Simple yet built with an old world pride and workmanship. Furniture built to last. He opened a backpack decorated with pictures of Disney characters: Mickey Mouse and Donald Duck. "Shannon's got the remnants of a cold so I put a bottle of Tylenol, a couple of packages of tissues, and two of her favorite books in here."

"I want to go to kindergarten," Shannon demanded.

"We're a little cranky today," Scarsdale said.

"Don't worry about it," Fran said, smiling at Shannon. "I've dealt with a lot of runny noses and minor ailments with my grandchildren back when they were Shannon's age. What are her favorites? Cupcakes? Pie?

"Cookies," Shannon said. "German chocolate ones."

Fran smiled at her. "How about chocolate chip? We'll whip up a batch just for you, dear."

"Okay. Shannon, I have to go to work. I'll see you later today." He bent over and kissed her on top of her head. "Give me a hug."

Shannon hugged him. "I'm supposed to be in kindergarten."

He turned to Fran and handed her a card with his office and cell phone numbers. "I should be back around five or so. I'll call later to check on her."

❦

Scarsdale and Harris drove to Zarko's work site—their third visit there in a week.

"Now what?" Winkler asked.

"We want to interview everyone who worked with Zarko last Wednesday and Thursday."

Winkler mumbled a few curse words as he walked to the door, loud enough for the two detectives to hear. "Wait here," he snapped before going out the door.

Ten minutes later, Winkler returned with two men, Randy Doss and Irv Stewart.

"Okay," Winkler said without looking at either detective. "Here they are. Have at 'em."

Scarsdale took Doss outside to the unmarked police car.

"Did you work with Zarko last Wednesday and Thursday?" Scarsdale asked. His cell phone buzzed but he ignored it. Then he heard the signal that a voice message had been left. He'd check it later.

"Yeah. We're teamed up since his buddy Lasiter got killed." Doss squinted at him like he recognized Scarsdale from somewhere but couldn't remember from where. Then his eyes seemed to relax. "Ain't you the cop that arrested Lasiter?"

"Yep. Back to Zarko, when he came to work on Thursday, did you notice anything unusual about him?"

"Everything about the man is unusual. Care to be a little more specific."

"How about his hands? Were they banged up like he'd been in a fight somewhere?" Scarsdale hated to phrase the question like that, but he figured Doss need some priming.

Doss shook his head. "Naw. But it wouldn't surprise me. Zarko, he's got a nasty temper. He gets real pissed lately whenever anyone asks him what he does on his time off." Doss raised his eyebrows. "I ain't scared of him or anything like that. I just figure no sense in startin' anything with the man seein' how I got to work with him."

"Did you happen to get a look at his hands on Wednesday?"

"Nope."

"You sure?"

"Positive."

"Could he have hurt them when he tripped over something, maybe like carrying a bunch of rebar? Is that possible?"

"I guess anything is possible." Doss said. "Shit, man. Around here, ya just do the job. That's what I get paid for. I don't check out what some other dude got on his hands—maybe if he got it on his face—maybe then."

Scarsdale shrugged. "Did Lasiter and Zarko run around together?"

"Oh, hell yeah. Well, I mean they wasn't like joined at the hip or nothing like that. Lasiter said they'd go guzzle a few beers after work." He chuckled. "Maybe go fishing. Zarko was more of a loner type than Lasiter. He'd go off by himself and eat lunch. Sometimes over at that park by the school." Doss gestured across the street.

"Really? Did Zarko seem upset or sad after Lasiter died?"

He shook his head. "Nope. Just kinda quiet. You know, kept to himself a lot."

"Were you working here on June 4?" Since Winkler wouldn't give him the time cards, he'd find out from Doss if Zarko worked the day Amy was killed.

"Umm, lemme think. Was that a Saturday?"

Scarsdale nodded once. "Yeah."

Doss stood there, staring off into space. Then he nodded. "Yep. Think so. Why?"

"I just was wondering if Zarko worked that day too."

Doss shook his head. "Not really sure. Maybe he did." Doss hung his head, looked down at the ground like he was thinking. "Maybe in the morning. That might have been the day he left at noon and never came back. Check the time cards."

"Thanks for your help." Scarsdale glanced toward the partially finished building. Zarko stood on the third floor, staring down at him. He gave Scarsdale an exaggerated salute.

Scarsdale stared back at him. *Go ahead and gloat, you worthless bastard. One day real soon—maybe not today or even next week, but soon—your ass will be sitting in County waiting for trial.*

ೕೆೌ

After lunch, Scarsdale and Harris found Nicole in the pediatric ward of Liberty Shores Hospital in north Austin. For about twenty minutes they stood by the circular nurse's station until Nicole finished her rounds dispensing meds to the children.

Scarsdale took a moment to call Fran. "How's Shannon doing?"

"She's all right. She hasn't needed anything. You have a very well-behaved daughter. She's sitting up on the sofa reading. Very quiet child."

He laughed. "Quiet now, but when she's feeling better, she'll talk your ear off."

"Don't worry. I'll call you if anything is amiss."

When Nicole approached them, Scarsdale told her they needed to ask her a few more questions about the blonde she saw leaving Lasiter's that night.

Nicole cast an over-the-shoulder glance toward the nurse's station. "Okay, but I have to record my med round before the doctors show up."

"Before we get into her, are you positive the man you saw around midnight ran from Lasiter's? Could he have been trotting?"

"I'm a runner. I know when someone is running and he was, for sure, running and fast. I just think it was that guy that's always hanging around there. Drives the crappy old pickup."

"What about the blonde?" Scarsdale asked.

"She went around the corner. All I could see was the back of her. She seemed tall now that I think about it. And I do remember now that she kept adjusting her hair, like it was a wig. Sorry I didn't remember that before, guys."

☙☙☙

Tuesday morning, Scarsdale had to roust Shannon out of bed. At breakfast she didn't eat much, seeming lethargic and sleepy.

"Sweetheart, I don't think you're in good enough shape to go to kindergarten today."

Her elbows rested on the table with her fists propping her head up. She glanced up at him from under a pair of droopy eyelids. "Will you stay home with me?"

He smiled. "I wish I could, but I have to go to work so I can buy you a whole bunch of toys and clothes and take you places when you get better."

She slid off her chair then meandered toward him, looking at him the whole way. "Promise?"

He nodded as he wiped her runny nose. "Absolutely."

He dropped her off at Fran's. As he walked out her door, he glanced back at Shannon, who stood there frowning at him. She held out her arms toward him. "Daddy, don't go."

☙☙☙

At the office, Scarsdale got on the phone with Short, the medical examiner's investigator.

"I e-mailed you the complete autopsy report on Lasiter and the one on Ferguson, as you requested," said Short.

"Thanks. I hope there's some new information in both of them."

"Nothing new on Lasiter. Regarding Ferguson, he bled to death, severed carotids," Short said. "The knife was wielded by a right-hander. Lots of wounds but you already know that. And the hatchet had a jagged edge that matched the wound on the amputated arm."

Scarsdale opened the Amy Crowell file on his computer. He wouldn't admit it to anyone right now, but a nagging doubt crept into his thinking. Did Lasiter really kill her or was he set up?

He read her autopsy report: Amy had sustained numerous lacerations to the face which were caused by blows from a blunt object. Based on the location and nature of the blows, the medical examiner believed the object was likely a fist.

Scarsdale opened the e-mail attachment from Short: the Lasiter autopsy. According to the medical examiner, Lasiter, like Amy, sustained numerous lacerations to the face caused by blunt-force trauma. The next sentence was almost identical to Amy's. Based on the location and nature of the blows, the medical examiner believed the instrument for the blunt-force trauma was a fist. Scarsdale pushed away from his desk and leaned back.

Harris strolled into Scarsdale's office. "Anything new?"

Scarsdale told him about the similarities of Amy's and Lasiter's injuries. "I know Zarko did Lasiter. I'm wondering about him and Amy."

"You think we should visit with Lasiter's mother?" Harris asked.

"My masochist side says yes," said Scarsdale. "My day isn't going too good now. Why not make it worse?" He cast a dismayed glance at Harris. "Shannon is still sick. I should be home with her."

"You told me she just had a cold. Has she gotten worse?"

"I don't know if I'd characterize her as worse…maybe no

improvement." He punched in Fran's number. "Ms. Tisdale, its Scarsdale. How's Shannon doing?"

"I'm glad you called. I was just getting ready to call you. The poor little thing threw up and had a bout of diarrhea. She's asleep right now."

Scarsdale imagined all sorts of terrible things happening. Maybe it wasn't a cold. Maybe it was something worse. Much worse. *I should have stayed home with her.*

"When she wakes, I'll try to feed her some broth."

He thought long and hard about taking Shannon to the ER. "Maybe I better come get her."

"I don't think that's necessary. She may have had a little stomach virus. Those things run their course pretty fast. My grandkids, years ago, came down with the same thing. If any problems arise, be assured I'll call you."

⁊⁊⁊

Thirty minutes later, Harris and Scarsdale stood at Ms. Lasiter's front door. Scarsdale heard the meowing of many cats. He heard footsteps nearing the door. Just before the door opened, he braced himself for the overpowering ammonia-like odor of cat urine. The first time he'd talked to her, almost a year ago, he'd gagged from the smell. "Oh jeez," he exclaimed as he covered his mouth and nose. Out of the corner of his eye, he caught a glimpse of Harris moving away from the door.

"You got a lot of nerve showing up here, you lowlife murderin bastard," Ms. Lasiter said as she glared at Scarsdale. "Get the hell off my property."

He looked into her eyes. They were like icy chunks of green. Her face was hard. It was the reception he figured she'd give him. "Ms. Lasiter, we have a suspect in your son's killing. We'd like to talk to you. May we come in?"

"No! You're not settin foot in my house. Just speak your peace and get off my property."

"Do you know a man named Zarko? Tom Zarko?" Scarsdale asked.

"Yeah. So what?"

"How long did he run around with your son?"

She chortled. "Scott wasn't enough? Now you want to ruin his best friend's life, too? I'm calling Commander Winters and my lawyer. Now get off my property. And don't you *ever* come back neither." She slammed the door.

ꕥꕥ

Back at the office, Scarsdale called Fran. "How's Shannon doing?"

"She's sleeping again. I had to wake her a little while ago because she was screaming her mother's name."

"I'll leave here in a few minutes, pick her up and take her to the doctor."

"Okay. I'll call you if anything serious arises in the meantime."

He made a couple of short notes about the day's investigative findings, updating the Lasiter file before he shut down his computer. He leaned back in his chair and stretched, his eyes on Charity's photograph, wondering what she'd do about Shannon. He grabbed his jacket as he cast a quick glance at Shannon's picture. Heading for the detective's sign-out board, a wave of apprehension washed over him. *Lethargic*? *Vomiting*? *Sleepy*? That didn't sound at all like his little girl. Just then his cell phone buzzed.

"Mr. Scarsdale, this is Ms. Tisdale. You better come quick. Shannon is having some kind of seizure."

Scarsdale sprinted for the door.

Harris yelled, "Hey. Where ya going?"

He didn't answer so Harris chased after him. As Scarsdale cranked up the engine, Harris jumped in the passenger side.

"What's up?" Harris asked, clicking his seat belt in place.

"Shannon's having a seizure," Scarsdale said, flipping the red and blue emergency lights on.

ꕥꕥ

Scarsdale pounded on Fran's door with his fist. He barged inside as soon as the door opened, almost knocking Fran to the floor. "Where is she?"

A sobbing Fran pointed to Shannon's limp body lying on her side on the sofa. "She said she had a headache. I gave her a baby aspirin."

His heart almost stopped beating when he saw Shannon. "Sonofabitch."

"I don't know what happened," Fran said, standing by the door. "One minute she was sleeping then all of a sudden, she was having some sort of seizure. I didn't know what to do so I called you and 911."

He glanced down at his daughter. He spoke her name. "Shannon?"

No response. He whisked her off the sofa and raced for the door. "Let's go," he yelled, barreling out the door.

Her eyes were shut. Her clothes were soaked in sweat. Her breathing was labored. Her arms and legs dangled.

"Stay with me, Shannon," Scarsdale said, pressing his cheek against hers. She felt hot.

He cradled her in his arms, tight against his chest, as Harris drove hell-bent-for-leather to the Liberty Shores Hospital ER. Harris told the dispatcher to notify the ER they were inbound with an unconscious five-year-old female.

The thought of losing her drenched Scarsdale with fear. His heart pounded against his ribcage. During the wild ride, Scarsdale brushed her wet hair back then mopped her face and brow with his shirtsleeve. He wished he had boned up on childhood illnesses.

He whispered in her ear, "Hang on, baby girl. We're almost there." He gazed at her, wishing she'd open her eyes.

When they pulled to the curb, ER nurses took Shannon from him. "Let go. We've got her."

He leaned down and stroked her cheek while the nurses loaded her on a gurney. Scarsdale and Harris followed them as they raced into an exam room. He stood there as two doctors rushed past him and pulled the curtain closed around Shannon's gurney. A third doctor approached Scarsdale. "Tell me what happened."

"She threw up at the babysitter's and got sleepy. She had a seizure and then lost consciousness."

"Anything else?"

Scarsdale nodded. "She's been kind of listless. No energy.

"Did she have any kind of a viral infection recently? A cold or flu symptoms?"

"Yeah. She had a cold over the weekend."

"Did anyone administer any aspirin to her yesterday or today?" the doctor asked, raising an eyebrow.

Scarsdale stared at him. "The babysitter gave her a children's aspirin before she had the seizure."

The doctor darted behind the curtain.

He heard terse words coming from the curtained off area, most of it in hushed tones. He couldn't make out what they were saying, but he realized from the doctor's expression and his hasty departure that something was very wrong.

Harris tried to usher him out to the waiting room, but he wanted to follow the doctor into the room.

Scarsdale looked at Harris, searching his eyes for reassurance. "She's gonna be okay, isn't she?" he asked as another doctor rushed past him toward her room. Two more nurses shoving a towel-covered cart followed him inside. Scarsdale heard certain words shouted out: "IV stat" and "normal saline" and a few he didn't know.

"She'll be fine. The doctors'll fix her right up," Harris said in a soft consoling tone. "Let's go sit in the waiting room and let them do their job, buddy."

Scarsdale paced around the ER waiting room, stopping every so often to peer through the small window, trying to see what was happening.

"Any news on my daughter?" he asked the medical clerk at the front desk.

Each time he got the same reply: "A doctor will be right up to talk with you as soon as they get her stabilized, sir."

When he saw a portable machine rolled behind the curtain

where Shannon lay, he rushed for the door. "What's that thing?"

Harris tried to hold him back, but Scarsdale jerked his arm free and stormed through the ER door. "I want to know what's happening with my daughter?" he said in a loud voice. He dodged a nurse and barged into the curtain-shielded area where Shannon lay. He saw the IV tube hooked up to her small forearm. An oxygen mask covered her face. A technician adjusted a device over Shannon's head.

"What's wrong with her?' he demanded.

One of the doctors, Samuel Tollerson, managed to calm him down enough to move him out of the room. "It's too early to know for sure, but we suspect either Reyes Syndrome or encephalitis. A lot more tests have to be run before we'll know for sure, Mr. Scarsdale."

Scarsdale glanced at Harris, who was tugging on his partner's arm in an effort to escort him out of the ER once again.

"There's a cafeteria right down the hall to the left if you'd like to get some coffee," Tollerson said. "I promise you as soon as we know something I will come and explain it all."

For the next hour, Harris and Scarsdale sipped coffee in the cafeteria.

"Shannon's a tough little cookie," Harris said. "She'll make it. You'll see."

Later, Scarsdale paced back and forth from the cafeteria to the ER window. Still no news. It felt like déjà vu. He had paced this same waiting room and hallway while Charity lay on a gurney in one of those same curtained-off rooms.

The book he had been reading about helping Shannon grow into a beautiful young woman didn't address this situation. He ran his hand over his head as questions popped up: *What should I have done for her? What would Charity have done? Shannon asked me to stay home with her. Why didn't I?*

He paced, unable to answer his own questions. He felt like he'd failed her when she needed him the most.

His muscles tightened when he felt a hand grip his upper arm. It couldn't be Harris. The touch was too gentle and light.

He glanced down at the hand. He saw the nail polish, the manicured nails, and the delicate fingers. He turned in the direction of the hand and saw Dani, a sympathetic smile on her face.

"I came as soon as I could," she said as her eyes searched his.

He didn't answer. Instead he pulled her close and embraced her. It was an instantaneous reaction. When he realized what he'd done, he let go and stepped back. "I'm sorry. I— I'm—"

"Don't apologize. Sometimes a hug helps in times like this," she said, looking into his eyes. "Any word on her condition?"

He shook his head as he stared down the hall toward the ER, hoping to see Doctor Tollerson coming his way. "They think it might be either encephalitis or Reyes Syndrome."

"Let's go back to the cafeteria. Everyone is in there."

It was after five when Doctor Tollerson came to the cafeteria. Dani gripped Scarsdale's hand as Tollerson delivered the news.

"Shannon has Reyes Syndrome." He sighed. "She's in stage two."

"What's that mean?" Scarsdale asked, kicking the chair back and standing up.

"Her brain and liver are swollen. We think we've stabilized her with anti-swelling meds. But the next thirty-six hours are critical. Her prognosis is guarded. She's in very serious condition. We've admitted her to Pediatric Intensive Care."

"I want to see her."

"Certainly. But she's still unconscious."

❧❧❧

Ten minutes later, Scarsdale stood by Shannon's bed, his hands gripping the railing tight. A large portable monitor displayed four blue lines indicating her vital signs and numbers he didn't understand. He saw the leads connected to her chest, arm, and finger. Another monitor on the other side of the bed displayed the electrical activity from her brain. "Shannon? Daddy is right here. Everything's going to be all right." He glanced up at Dani and Harris. Only one family member was supposed to be in the room at one time, but Doctor Tollerson had made an exception.

"Tell me she's going to make it. Somebody tell me," he pleaded, "that she's going to be okay."

Dani moved to his side. Putting one arm around his back and the other on his right arm, she spoke in a whispered tone to him. "She *will* be okay."

"That little munchkin is going to come through this with flying colors, Jason," Harris said.

It wasn't until around ten o'clock that night that Dani and Harris were able to persuade him to go downstairs to get a sandwich. When he returned to the ICU, he saw a host of doctors and nurses going in and out of Shannon's room.

"What happened?" he asked, craning his neck to see into the room. "Is she okay?" He tried to push his way into the room, but two male nurses ushered him out. "I want to see my daughter."

"The doctors are working on her," one nurse said before darting back into the room, closing the door behind him

Scarsdale peered into the room through the window in the door. Two doctors, one on each side of her bed, leaned over her, glancing up every few seconds at the monitors. A nurse injected something into Shannon's IV. When the doctors came out, he went right up to them.

"How is she? Is she going to be okay?" Scarsdale asked. He felt his heart sink when one doctor looked at the other before responding.

"Her vitals worsened and her intracranial pressure increased. We had to administer a different group of drugs to combat the swelling."

"Is she going to be all right?" he demanded.

The doctor sighed then pursed his lips as if pondering the answer. "I don't know, Mr. Scarsdale. The next eight hours will be critical."

CHAPTER 11

"Children will not remember you for the material things you
provided but for the feeling that you cherished them."
~ *Richard L. Evans*

I went to work on Wednesday but I spent most of the time thinking about Shannon and her father. After work, I went to the hospital to find Scarsdale standing at Shannon's bedside, looking as if he was lost in thought. His red and puffy eyes had dark circles underneath.

His face reminded me of the anguish I'd felt after the police left my house. I'd sat on Katarina's bed, fingering each shell on her seashell necklace. At least his child was alive, even if in the ER and hanging onto life. No one had brutalized her.

It must have been doubly painful for him. First his wife, now his daughter. I wondered how much more the man could take.

I stood across the bed from him and saw his empty stare. I sensed the pain and heartache he must have been feeling. Words would have been useless. They had been for me.

I stroked her smooth, pretty face as she lay there so still, wondering how she ended up with Reyes Syndrome. I didn't really know Scarsdale, but I didn't want him to endure any more grief.

Scarsdale stood there, caressing her face with one hand and holding her hand with the other. He was a nice-looking man, seemingly a good man who truly loved his daughter. In that moment, my feelings about him shifted.

I genuinely liked this man and felt bad about using him. But I had to stay abreast of his progress in the Lasiter case. I'd just have to find another way to do it. I walked around to where he sat and put my hand on his shoulder. "I can stay with her if you want to go downstairs and eat something."

His face looked like a plastic mask. His eyes were slits, fixed on Shannon. "No. I'm not leaving her bedside."

"Would you eat something if I went and got it?"

"I'm not all that hungry."

"C'mon." I gripped his upper arm, tugging him toward the door, but he wouldn't budge. "You have to eat something."

"She's absolutely correct, Jason," Harris said, walking into the room with his wife Mary.

"You guys go ahead. I'll be all right."

"Let's get something for him," Harris said, reaching his hand to Mary.

She balked. "Go on, Sean. My knee still hurts from all that walking. I'm going to rest it."

So I went with Harris. On the elevator ride downstairs, Harris asked me a lot of questions. "Somebody said you came here from California. So what brought you to Texas?"

Knowing he'd compare notes with Scarsdale, I only told him what Scarsdale already knew. "My daughter was murdered. I wanted a fresh start." I forced a smile. "So here I am."

"I'm sorry about your daughter."

"Thank you."

We rode down in silence.

Figuring Amanda may have told him about my Mercedes, I prayed he wouldn't ask about it, so I shot him a question. "How long have you and Jason been partners?" I didn't really care. I just wanted to get him talking about something other than me.

"Uh, let's see. It'll be three years the first of next month."

I fired off the next one. "Doesn't seeing those abused children make you angry?"

"It would if I let it. Now if I was in Scarsdale's shoes, with Shannon, I couldn't handle it. I'd have to transfer. But all mine are in college or married."

"Do you think he'll transfer?"

"Scarsdale?" He laughed out loud. "No friggin' way. He's got a stubborn streak a mile wide. Hell, he's worse than an Irishman."

The elevator door opened. *Thank God*. The cafeteria was just around the corner.

With our hands full of coffee cups and sandwich boxes, we headed back to the elevator bank. I dreaded the ride up but when a group of people boarded with us, Harris kept quiet.

The next day, on my lunch hour, I bought a bunch of roses for Shannon. With two of each color, a bunch of balloons and a get-well bear, I drove to the hospital. If she was anything like Katarina, she'd love them.

I arrived at the hospital just after one o'clock. Scarsdale was snoring in a chair by the window. I tiptoed across the room and set the mixed rose bouquet on the windowsill next to two other plants. I tied the "Get Well" balloons to the foot of her bed and laid the bear—complete with make-believe leg cast and crutch and a Band-Aid on its arm—on the pillow near Shannon's head.

She stirred a little when I accidentally bumped the bed. Her eyes fluttered a wee bit then closed again. Leaning over her, I kissed her on the forehead and with one last glance at her sleeping father, left the room, tiptoeing out so as not to wake them.

When I talked to Harris around three o'clock, he said Scarsdale's sister Sarah, and her family, arrived at the hospital an hour ago. He and Mary planned to visit Thursday evening. Since the hospital had rules about how many could be in the room at one time, I didn't go to see her. I didn't want to cause a family member to have to step out. Besides, Harris promised to keep me up to speed on Shannon's progress.

On Thursday, Harris told me Shannon had woken up. She recognized everyone, but slept a lot. He added that Sarah and her family would be staying at Scarsdale's house through the weekend.

I drove over to the hospital after work and walked all the way to the elevator bank, stopped and reconsidered. Sarah and

I had never met and now was not the time for introductions.

Instead, I went to the airport to make flight reservations for Germany. I hadn't seen my parents in over two years. Every time I called, Mother asked when I'd be coming home. With Thanksgiving just a few days off and everyone else probably hosting family, now was the perfect time.

The car clock showed 8:15 p.m when I got home. Coming from the airport on Highway 183, Austin rush hour traffic proved to be a nightmare. An accident blocking one lane didn't help. I was beat as I trudged up the steps to the first landing. Standing under the light, I stopped to fish my apartment key from my purse then climbed the last flight of stairs to the third landing. My mind was on how my parents would react to my visit and I wondered if six days was long enough after a two year absence.

I was almost at my door when someone slapped their hand over my mouth, wrapped a forearm around my neck, and pulled me backward. From the strength in the hands, I knew it was a man. I tried to pull his hand away so I could scream but his grip was like iron.

My first thought was Burton's brother, Parnell. I knew he was coming up for parole but hadn't checked his status lately. He had threatened to kill me right after the grand jury issued its no-bill in his brother's death.

I fought as hard as I could, twisting and squirming, even jabbing my elbow into his gut. But the more I struggled, the tighter his grip and the more he laughed. His laughter sounded like the braying of a jackass.

A skunky odor invaded my nostrils when his face touched mine. When he pulled my head to the side, I recognized his acne scarred face from the Lasiter file. Zarko.

"What took you so long to come home?" I felt his head turn to the side. "Nice-looking ride. What's the matter, didn't like your Mercedes anymore? Oh, by the way, back there in the alley, that was a neat trick draggin that board over your tracks." He tightened his grip on my neck. "Now we're gonna take a little walk to your place, go inside, and have us a little chat. If you scream or try anything, you'll end up just like Lasiter. You got that?"

I nodded, but other thoughts raced through my mind. Did he have a weapon? If so, where was it? He had nothing in his hands. My knife was tucked in the recliner, right where I'd left it last night. Could I get to it?

If he spotted it first, I'd have no chance. I had to do something right here. My keys. His body pressed snug up against me, which meant his feet were right behind mine. *If I could do this*—I jammed my heel down hard on the ball of his foot.

Zarko yelped, let go of me and stepped back.

I spun around, slashing my key across his face.

He grabbed his cheek, hollering, "Dammit."

I grabbed his shoulders and rammed my knee hard into his groin.

He crumpled down onto the landing, screaming and curling up into a ball, his hands tucked between his legs. "Oh shit. My nuts." He started gagging like he wanted to throw up. His dark eyes glared at me. "You fuckin' bitch. When I get up, I'll kick your ass."

I stood there, debating whether to kick him down the steps. But the thumpity-thump of his body and his probable cussing would wake up the whole building, if hadn't already. And inevitably someone would call the police. Then one of the second floor residents switched on their outside light.

Sprinting for my door, I got the key in and turned, but it wouldn't open. Stuck again. *Dammit.*

I glanced back at Zarko rolling in agony on the landing, hands still between his legs. I banged against the door with my shoulder until it opened. Once inside, I lifted it up and threw all my weight into shutting it, then turned the dead bolt. My chest heaved as I leaned against the door. My shoulder stung. My heart thumped like hail on a car roof. I found my knife, went back to the door, and listened.

I peered out the peephole to see Mr. Turner step outside. His door faced mine. He darted back inside, slamming his door behind him.

I hoped he wouldn't call the police. They'd expect answers that I didn't care to give. If they got Zarko, he'd surely lie his way out, telling them whatever came to mind. He certainly didn't want them involved any more than I did.

Damn you, Zarko.

Chills ran up my back and goosebumps covered my arms. I looked through the peephole again. I could see the stairs—no Zarko. My stomach turned cartwheels. I'd heard him drive away from Lasiter's house but I hadn't dreamed he'd follow me.

Holding the knife, I waited on the sofa, thinking. *He'll come for me again and he won't screw up next time.* My options? Stay in Austin or run away again.

Or I could kill Zarko.

✑✺✑

Another perk of my job was the ease with which I could get any address. Right before midnight on Friday, I drove past Zarko's house. No lights on. All the neighboring houses were dark except for one. And it was far enough away I didn't think I could be seen. I parked a short distance from his house, opting not to use the alley and risk a repeat of the Lasiter fiasco. With a hood pulled over my head, my knife tucked in at my waist, I headed for his rear door. Of course, it was locked so I crawled into the kitchen through an unlocked window. My running suit made me too warm and I flipped the hood off my head and unzipped the jacket.

Surprisingly, the house smelled nice, like fresh pine. No dirty dishes piled in the sink. All of the counters were clean. Dishes stacked in the cupboard—plates, saucers, bowls, cups. Even the trash can had been emptied. I opened the cabinet under the sink, shining my light in time to see two huge roaches scurry deeper into the recesses of the cabinet. *Oh my God*! I fell backward on my butt, crab walked backward away from the cabinet before bouncing up on my feet. I hated roaches.

In the living room, I shined my flashlight around. The

furniture appeared to be clean. Magazines were stacked on the coffee table in a perfect column, overlapping each other.

I went into the bedroom. The bed was made. No clothes strew around like at Lasiter's. A single dresser. I ransacked each drawer but no bracelet. I checked the nightstand, under the mattress and under the bed—nothing, not even a dust ball.

Standing in the doorway of his closet, I couldn't believe a degenerate actually lived here. His clothes hung meticulously in the closet—long-sleeved shirts together, short-sleeved shirts in their group, trousers draped neatly over wooden hangers. Shoes lined up on the floor like little soldiers. *This is too weird.*

In his bathroom, I saw his toiletries lined up against the back of the countertop. Towels hung evenly on the wall racks. Opening the doors under the bathroom sink, I saw a herd of roaches on the side of the cabinet as though they were having a family reunion. I slammed the doors shut and shuddered.

My watch showed 2:20. He ought to be coming home any time now. Today was a workday. Minutes passed but I had no trouble staying alert. While I waited behind the door for him, I shined the flashlight around the room, making sure no roaches ventured my way. *Stay away. Your roommate should be home soon.*

I leaned against the wall, knife in hand, and looked the room over. His house was too neat and, except for the army of roaches, too normal-looking. I looked down at the knife and took a deep breath. I'd come here for revenge. He had attacked me at my home. He was the one who killed Lasiter so no one would know Zarko murdered Amy Crowell. He was an evil man but waiting in that eerily tidy house I began to doubt if my killing him could be justified.

What if someone saw me leaving after I killed him? Zarko saw me leave Lasiter's house. Didn't I learn anything from the Burton matter? It was a mad quest for revenge and I realized it would never make anything right. Why was I here, waiting in the dark to kill a man? Peering around the silent house I saw a slippery slope that led to a place I didn't want to go. I felt a chilling tension in this regimentally neat home, alive with the sound of skittering roaches, and it came to me that I stood at a fork in the road—I could have a normal life with someone like Scarsdale and Shannon or end up in a mouse-colored room the size of Lasiter's closet for the rest of my life, peering out through black steel bars and being told when to get up, when to eat, when to shower.

Headlights beamed through the window and I peeked out. Just a passing car. Aiming my light at the bedroom door, I saw a roach running fast across the wood floor. How many of those creatures lived here? The thought of one climbing up the leg of my running suit made my skin crawl.

What am I doing here? I'm not an exterminator. It's Scarsdale's job to get these creeps. Let him do it. I've got to get out of here.

I made it out the back door in a minute flat, not because of the roaches but because killing child molesters like Zarko had lost its attraction. I wanted something better for myself. A normal life. A family of my own.

Pulling the hood over my head, I forced myself to walk, not run, down the sidewalk to my car. Dogs started barking as I got closer to my car. A couple of front porch lights lit up parts of the sidewalk.

A pair of headlights came around the corner ahead of me. Gears grinding. Backfiring. A loud muffler. Zarko's truck. When it got closer to me, it slowed down. I cast a quick glance before ducking my face down and walking on. If he stopped or backed up, I'd run like hell. A face to face confrontation with him out here in the open would not end well for me.

The truck kept moving, but slower.

I broke into a dead run when I heard the truck screech to a stop. Running past my car, I ducked behind a darkened hedge and peered over the top.

Zarko stood by his truck, backlit by the interior light. He looked in my direction with his hand on the door, as if he debated coming after me.

Another dog started barking. That triggered even more

dogs to howl and yap. Another porch light came on at the house across from my car. Then a porch light lit up the yard where I knelt down. *Wonderful.* The whole neighborhood was awake.

I heard heavy footsteps on the porch behind me. A gruff male voice, "Hey, what the hell are you doing in my yard? Madge, get my shotgun."

Taking a fast glance behind me, I saw open ground. I turned and bolted across the yard toward the intersection. The man's voice bellowed, "Better never come back here either."

I knelt down behind a large bush at the intersection. Zarko stood by my car, staring my way. *Go home, Zarko.* I'd had enough of this. I needed to go to bed and get some sleep. *He must recognize my car. Surely he knows I'm the one hiding behind the hedge. He'll be paying me another visit. I know it. Maybe I should stay with my parents for a lot longer than six days.*

A good hour passed before I got in my car and drove home, hoping Zarko wasn't watching, praying nobody took down my license plate number and reported it to the police.

CHAPTER 12

"When you get into a tight place and everything goes against you, never give up then, for that is just the time that the tide will turn." ~ Harriet Beecher Stowe

A murmur, a faint cry, or a word spoken softly. Scarsdale wasn't sure what it was that woke him. In fact, he didn't realize he had fallen asleep. He grunted as he straightened himself in the chair, twisting his neck to stretch the muscles. Blinking several times, he managed to clear the haze from his eyes.

He looked over at Shannon and the several tubes crisscrossing the hospital bed. A nurse stood over Shannon's bed, smiling at him. The head of the bed had been raised. A slight movement caught his attention.

Shannon gazed at him over the top of the bed rail. She slowly reached her hand toward him. "Daddy," she said in a soft tone.

He flew out of the chair like a sprinter off the blocks. "Hey there, princess," he said, taking her hand. He stroked her cheek with the back of his fingers then brushed a strand of hair off her forehead and tucked a golden lock behind her ear.

He looked over at the nurse. "She's going to be just like before, right?"

"Her vitals are stable," the nurse answered as she checked the IV. "That's always a good sign."

"Good morning, everyone," Doctor Tollerson said cheerfully, closing the door behind him. "Well, now, Sleeping Beauty is awake." He removed a penlight from the pocket of his lab coat. "You gave us quite a scare, Shannon," he said, shining the light into each of her eyes. Winking at Scarsdale, he said, "I think you made your father age ten years in the past few days."

Shannon managed a weak smile.

Now that she was awake, Scarsdale asked when the tubes and monitor leads would be removed. Doctor Tollerson stood there, gazing at Shannon for a few seconds, as if he was pondering the question. "Well, now, she's not out of the woods yet. Maybe later today. We'll see how she does," he said, looking at Scarsdale. Then he looked back at Shannon. "I'll bet you're as hungry as a bear, aren't you?"

She nodded before turning to look at Scarsdale, reaching her other hand toward him. "Home," she said in a whisper.

On Saturday afternoon, Doctor Tollerson gave the good news to Scarsdale. "She's a strong little girl. She appears to have made a complete recovery. The tests indicated no long-term issues," he said, smiling. His eyes moved back and forth from Scarsdale to Shannon.

"When can she go home?" Scarsdale asked.

"She'll be ready to go home later this afternoon. *But* you will need to monitor her progress at home." He handed Scarsdale two prescriptions. "I want her to have one of each twice a day. No spicy or fatty foods and no sweets for a few days." He glanced at Shannon. "Okay, maybe a little ice cream." He raised his thumb and forefinger, indicating a *little* ice cream. "Keep her quiet. Limit her strenuous physical exertion. No running or jumping." Tollerson made a face at Shannon and wagged his finger. "No cartwheels. No swinging from the chandelier."

Shannon smiled then looked at her father.

Tollerson faced Scarsdale without smiling. "And as much bed rest as a five-year-old can handle."

Close to three o'clock, Scarsdale was packing up Shannon's flowers and the bear when Father Joe strolled into the room. He was Scarsdale's priest.

"Well, well, so how's our young lady doing?" He patted Shannon on the shoulder and smiled at her before looking over at Scarsdale.

She smiled back. "I'm going home," she said, beaming.

"Well, that's certainly good news," he answered, gazing down at her. "Is there anything I can do for you, Jason?" he asked while holding Shannon's hand.

Scarsdale sighed. "About the only thing I can think of is a really good babysitter that's also a nurse."

"Mrs. Hargraves." Father Joe gave his *the-Good-Lord-provides* smile. "She's a former nurse. You remember her. She's all alone now since her husband passed a few months back. I'd bet she'd love to take care of Shannon," he said, smiling at her before letting go of her hand and walking toward Scarsdale. "It'd give her a purpose in life."

Scarsdale paused from the packing and chewed on his lower lip then looked at Father Joe. He knew how empty the woman must feel now and Father Joe was right—babysitting Shannon would help her and him. "She's perfect. Do you have her number?"

⌘

The next morning, Scarsdale scrambled some eggs for breakfast and added a dash of ketchup when he dished a small portion onto her plate.

"Just eat a little, and drink the juice. Dr. Tollerson said you need fruit juice."

"Daddy, can Dani come have Thanksgiving with us? She doesn't have family here. She's all alone."

"I think that'd be a great idea, sweetheart." He saw the sparkle return to her eyes.

"I can help you cook the turkey. Mommy always let me help her. We'll need stuff from the store." After breakfast, Shannon went to her room ostensibly to rest. A few minutes later, she sauntered into the kitchen where Scarsdale was washing dishes. She handed him a scribbled list of "stuff" he had to buy for Thanksgiving. The only problem was that he couldn't read her writing. So he faked it. "All this stuff?" He showed her the list, pointing to one entry. "What's that?"

She snorted in displeasure. "Cranberry sauce." She pointed at the other entries on the list. "That's apple sauce. Stuffing. Pumpkin for the pie." Then she looked at him as if to insure that he understood. "Mommy always made pie."

"How about if I buy a pie already made?"

She looked at him with a bit of displeasure, resting her hands on her hips. "If you have to."

Scarsdale spent the greater part of the day either reading storybooks to Shannon or watching cartoons on the Cartoon Network with her. After lunch, he made her take a nap. Of course, she insisted he take one too.

On Monday morning, Mrs. Hargraves, who he hired to stay with Shannon while he went to work, arrived precisely at seven o'clock sharp. He set out the prescription bottles, his office and cell phone numbers by the house phone, and gave her the nickel tour of the house. He hoped this time Shannon would be safe.

഼ഽ഼

Early Monday morning, he stopped at Dani's office to thank her for her support and the flowers and the bear. When he came to her doorway, her elbow was propped up on the desk with her face resting in her hand.

"Hey, Dani."

She jumped, then slowly turned and looked at him.

Her eyes were bloodshot like she hadn't slept much. "Is something wrong?"

"Are you okay?" he asked.

"Yeah, sure. Didn't sleep too good." She yawned. "Excuse me." She grinned sheepishly. "I heard Shannon's home. That's wonderful. How's she doing?"

"Much better. Thank you so much for being there, for the roses, the balloons and especially for the bear. She goes to bed with it every night now. She asks about you a lot."

Dani covered her mouth and yawned again. "You're welcome. I'm glad she's okay. She's a very sweet little girl."

Scarsdale saw the Delta Airline ticket lying on her desk. "Going somewhere?"

Dani glanced back at the ticket, took a deep breath, and then looked at him. "I'm going to Germany to visit my parents for a while," she said, stretching her arms up and arching her back, pushing her chest out. When she noticed him eyeing her breasts, she crossed her arms in front of her.

Scarsdale's smile faded. "How long's a while?"

"Just for the holidays. Maybe longer. I haven't decided yet."

His heart beat harder as the adrenaline coursed through his veins. "What time is your flight?"

She checked her watch. "In three hours." She yawned again. "I was just leaving."

Shannon will be crushed. "Shannon was hoping you'd spend Thanksgiving with us…you are coming back, right?"

She shrugged. "Probably. I don't know for sure when, though. The Christmas market festival begins at the end of November this year."

"Why now? Can't it wait?" he asked, as though perturbed at her timing.

"Jason, your family—everybody's family will be together beginning this Thursday. I want to be with mine now. I haven't seen them in over two years."

"I came this close to losing my kid, for God's sake. I need to give her what she needs and right now that's you. She's just a child, Dani. Can't you understand what this is like?"

Dani, frozen with a glacial anger at his words, replied, "Oh, yes, Detective Scarsdale, I understand perfectly." She picked up her ticket, turned, and left.

Scarsdale stood there, rocked by the obvious anger of her response. Too late, he realized the ineptness of his comment.

∞

Later that morning, he got a call from the county jail. Olsen wanted to talk to him. The county jail's interrogation room had a different layout from the interrogation rooms at the department—it had a one-way window which the department rooms lacked and manacle rings built into the table.

Scarsdale and Harris stood outside the window, observing Olsen. His handcuffs were tethered to the table.

"Sorry excuse for a human being," Harris said.

Scarsdale sighed. "Well, let's see what BS Olsen wants to spin today," he said as he opened the door to go in the room. For now, Harris would remain outside to watch Olsen's reactions. Scarsdale took a seat facing Olsen, laying a file folder down. "It's your dime. What's on your mind today?"

"I know who killed Ferguson. I mean, I don't know his name or nothing like that, but I seen him. I can pick him out of a lineup." He stared at Scarsdale with wide-open eyes. Scared eyes. "You'll tell the DA I helped you, won't ya? I mean, solving a murder ought to count for somethin, right?"

"Why should I? I have a witness who saw the man."

He hesitated, looking at Scarsdale, a confused look on his face. "Who?"

"Not your concern." Scarsdale stood up and turned the chair around so his chin rested on the back of it. "How could you pick him out of a line-up? Unless, of course, you were there when he murdered Ferguson, and you saw him without his mask."

Olsen swallowed hard. "Here's the deal—"

Scarsdale cut him off. "No, butt wipe, here's the deal. If you really know the guy, give me his name." Scarsdale slid a notepad across the table. "Otherwise, quit trying to jerk me around."

"All right," Olsen said in a frantic tone. "The dude used a fuckin knife big as a machete and a hatchet too."

"Like I said, give me his name."

Olsen looked at Scarsdale, his mouth agape. "Just like that?" He stared at Scarsdale through squinted eyes. "What guarantees do I got that you won't screw me over?"

Scarsdale grabbed the file and got up. "The hell with you. I'm out of here." He headed for the door.

Olsen shouted, "Wait a minute. I'll name everyone there that night *after* I gets a deal from the DA. I'll give ya names and where their trophies are located. Everything."

"Everything?"

"Everything." Olsen said, staring right at Scarsdale.

"Any jewelry, like bracelets in any of those trophies?" asked Scarsdale, sitting down. This creep had his attention now.

Olsen's voice quieted to almost a whisper. "Some jewelry, mostly pictures, DVD's, things like that."

"What about a bracelet?" Scarsdale pulled out a photograph Susan Crowell had given him. He slid it across the table. "Ever see that bracelet?"

Olsen picked up the photograph, examined it and slid it back to Scarsdale. "Yeah. But I don't buy or trade for none of that shit."

"Sure you don't. You have your own trophies, right?" Scarsdale sat on a corner of the table, facing Olsen and twirling a pen with his fingers to mask the quiver of his cop antennae. "Who had this bracelet? Tell me. Then—and—only then will I go to the DA."

Olsen sat back, holding his hands as close to his face as the tethered cuffs would allow. "I know who and I know where it is now—or was, but I'll talk *only* after I get my deal in writing."

Scarsdale wanted that bracelet. Whoever claimed it as a trophy was the killer of Amy Crowell. He needed to close that case and he needed to see the bracelet returned so Susan could get closure and learn who really killed Amy. And he needed anything else he could learn from Olsen about this bunch of pedophiles. He felt like Olsen was right on the verge. "I believe you. But the DA is gonna want a sign of your good faith. So tell me where the bracelet is located or I'm walking out that door."

"The fuckin' bracelet ain't goin' nowhere, man. You need to be chasing down the dude who hacked Fergie up. He's a big man. We call him the CEO. Wears a mask a lot. I seen him chop off Fergie's arm. He used a goddammed knife big as a machete."

"Yeah. Poor old Ferguson," Scarsdale said sarcastically before yawning. "The bracelet?"

"How come you ain't writing all this down?"

"Because your CEO didn't use a knife to cut off Fergie's arm. Try hatchet." Scarsdale stood up, gathering the picture and the file.

"Well, 'scuse me. I meant hatchet."

"Last time. Where's the bracelet?"

"And I'm tellin' *you* for the last time, get me my deal and I'll tell ya anything ya want to know." Olsen sat back, looking pleased with himself. "Or maybe I get a lawyer to do it."

"Whatever floats your boat, bedbug." He walked to the door.

"I ain't believin' this," Olsen said loudly. "So Fergie's life ain't worth as much as some fuckin' bracelet? That's bull-shit."

Scarsdale peered over his shoulder at Olsen. "You going to tell me the CEO's name?"

"I told ya." Olsen glared at him. "I don't know his damn name."

"Didn't think so." Scarsdale opened the door. "When you really want to talk, call me."

Olsen yelled at Scarsdale. "He's got a tattoo on his right forearm. A black and green one."

On the drive back to the department, Harris asked, "You think Olsen's screwing around about Ferguson's killer?"

"Maybe not. The old man living across the street saw four men leaving Ferguson's house that night. One was wearing a mask." He made a mental note to let the division's pedophile expert, Amanda Colbert, know the latest on the Ferguson murder.

❧❦❧

On the ride home, Scarsdale sorted through a myriad of ways to break the news to Shannon about Dani leaving. When

Scarsdale walked into his house around six o'clock, Mrs. Hargraves briefed him on Shannon's progress. Shannon had done very well playing with a couple of puzzles, her Barbie, and understood stories she read to her. Her memory and cognitive functions seemed normal. Another good day for his daughter.

He walked outside with her to explain the bad news he would be telling Shannon—Dani's departure—and that he expected her to act out. Mrs. Hargraves affirmed that Shannon indeed had spoken about Dani often and several times expressed a wish that Dani lived next door to them. She advised him to couch the revelation in positive terms so as to cushion the blow.

He paused at the front door before going inside, trying to think of how to break the news of Dani's departure, then strode into the living room with a big grin on his face albeit a forced one. A few times when he'd been a uniformed officer, he delivered bad news to parents and spouses. He'd felt sad to be the bearer of such news, standing there watching them break down into fits of sobbing, helpless to say or do anything that would be of any comfort.

Today, with Shannon, those old feelings resurfaced. But this time it wasn't strangers he had to tell; it was his own daughter. And he didn't feel sad; he felt sick to his stomach.

"What are you watching, sweetheart?" he asked her as he kissed her on the forehead.

"Shhh, Daddy" she answered, holding her finger up to her lips. "Scooby's in trouble."

He glanced at the TV—Scooby Doo. Sighing, he sat in the dark-blue upholstered chair next to the sofa and waited for the show to end. No sense ruining her day before he had to. He considered not telling her at all. She'd have that many more days of recovery time. She'd be stronger. Why would she have to know now anyway? he wondered. *If Dani comes back, where's the harm?* When he had told her about Charity's death, she'd flown into a tantrum and cried for a couple of days. She wouldn't even eat.

At that moment, the phone rang.

Suspecting it might be the department calling him out to a crime scene, he checked the caller ID. He relaxed. It was his mother.

"Hi, Mom. What's up?"

"Since you and Shannon can't come up here for Thanksgiving, your father and I have decided to bring Thanksgiving to you. Sarah and her family will be there, too. Unfortunately your brothers can't make it."

A huge grin stretched across his face. "Mom, that's great news. Shannon will love it."

He did a fist pump and mouthed the word *yes*! Problem solved.

"I thought as much. We figured having as much of the family together would boost Shannon's spirits. You don't have anything planned, do you?"

He peeked around the corner of the kitchen at Shannon, who was still glued to the TV. "Nope. Nothing at all." The weight of the world lifted off his shoulders. He wouldn't say anything to Shannon about Dani unless she asked.

"Good. Look for us Wednesday evening. And, son, don't worry about a thing. Between Sarah and me, we'll have everything we need. So do *not* run out and buy a bunch of stuff."

About fifteen minutes later, while he cooked dinner, Shannon ambled into the kitchen, dressed in a pair of pink pajamas and red socks. Her hair stuck out in all directions.

"Was that Dani on the phone? Is she going to be here Thursday?"

He smiled at her. "No, sweetheart. Dani won't be here Thursday."

Shannon stared at him in disbelief. "Why not?"

He squatted down in front of her. "She went to Germany to visit her parents. But—"

The corners of her mouth turned into a frown. A pinkish tinge formed on her eyes as they welled up. "Is she coming back?"

"Of course, she is." He hated to lie to his own daughter but this time was an exception.

She folded her arms across her chest then fell against him, crying. "Why did she leave?"

Time to change the subject, he reasoned. "What if I told you Grammie and PawPaw and Aunt Sarah and your cousins were coming here for Thanksgiving?"

Shannon's face brightened. "Grammie and PawPaw are coming?" She squealed in delight as he wiped the tears from her cheeks.

"That's right. We're having Thanksgiving right here. How's that sound?"

Shannon wrapped her arms tightly around his leg. Then she backed off. "Will Dani be here when Santa Claus comes?"

"Of course, she will." He didn't know whether Dani would ever be back and hated to lie again to Shannon, but her recovery was the highest priority. Later on, after Shannon was fully recovered, he'd sit her down and tell her the truth, whatever that turned out to be.

On Wednesday evening, after dinner, Shannon stood on the sofa, watching out the front window, in anticipation of her grandparents' arrival. The phone rang. She scrambled off the chair and picked it up just as Scarsdale walked up next to her.

"Hello."

A short period of silence ensued. He saw a smile cross her face.

"Grandma, guess what we're doing today?" A shorter pause. "Grammie and PawPaw are coming," she said excitedly.

A longer period of silence. Shannon cast a glance up at Scarsdale. "I was in the hospital. But I'm better now."

A brief silence.

"Okay. Here's Daddy. I love you, Grandma." She handed the phone to him. "Grandma wants to talk to you."

Wonderful. Charity's mother. Another Thanksgiving ruined by a call from them. "Hello, Marcy." His tone wasn't friendly. In fact, he bristled upon hearing her voice. From back when he was dating Charity, Marcy Piper had it in for him. He just wasn't good enough for her daughter. Then, when Charity married him over her vehement objections, Marcy refused to even speak to him. Luckily for him, he hardly ever saw her.

Her tone wasn't friendly either. "What happened to my granddaughter? Why was she in the hospital?"

"I'm fine. Thanks for asking. Shannon got sick. Now she's recuperating," he answered. "It's Thanksgiving. Can't we try to be somewhat civil today?"

"Sick from what? What did you do—or should I say fail to do for her?"

"Reyes Syndrome—and I didn't fail to do anything."

"I want a copy of the doctor's report."

"No way."

"You *will* get me a copy."

"You can *ask* from now till the cows come home. It's not going to happen."

"We'll see about that."

With Shannon sitting nearby, he didn't want to get into a war of words with her maternal grandmother. "So are you two having Thanksgiving—"

"We told her not to marry you. We warned her."

Scarsdale walked into the kitchen to get out of Shannon's earshot. "If Charity hadn't married me, you wouldn't have such a beautiful granddaughter, now, would you, Marcy?"

A short silence.

"You destroyed my daughter, but I'm going to take my granddaughter away from you before you ruin her, too."

Scarsdale felt the anger boiling up. He knew she liked finding someone's button and pushing as hard as she could. She had found his, and she pressed with all her might. *Don't let her bait you into saying something you'll regret.*

"I love you, too, Marcy. Have a nice day. Bye." He hung up. "They dropped the house on the wrong witch," he muttered.

This was the latest salvo in a war that had started when he'd asked Charity's father for permission to marry Charity. She wanted him to get her father's consent before she wedded. After Marcy browbeat her husband into rejecting Scarsdale's request, Scarsdale and Charity went with Plan B—a small wedding that her parents had refused to attend.

പ

On the Monday night following the Thanksgiving weekend, Scarsdale and Harris tailed Zarko as he drove straight from work to the Walnut Grove Apartments in Pflugerville.

A Canadian cold front had moved in during the afternoon, dropping the temperatures from the mid-sixties all the way down to the upper thirties after sunset. Typical Thanksgiving weather for Texas—warm one day and freezing the next.

Zarko parked facing Building Three. For the next hour, he sat in his truck.

"What's with this guy?" Scarsdale asked Harris. "Did he make us? I mean, who sits in his truck for a frickin hour?"

"Maybe he's waiting on someone?"

Scarsdale stared off into the darkness, his mind drifting. Dani didn't come back today—well, at least her office was still locked. He felt a little uneasy about her absence and Shannon had begun asking again—at breakfast today—when Dani was coming back. He was glad Doctor Tollerson cleared her to start back to kindergarten. It would help take her mind off the woman.

"Whose place is he eyeballing?" Harris asked.

"Good question," said Scarsdale, zipping up his fleece-lined jacket then blowing warm breath into his cupped hands. He'd forgotten to bring a pair of gloves.

"He's moving," Harris exclaimed.

Zarko went up the steps to the third floor, stopping in front of a darkened apartment. They watched him lean close to the door, like he was listening. He glanced around, as if making sure no one was watching, then he tried the doorknob.

"It's the second apartment on the left in that alcove. Number 312," Scarsdale said, peering through binoculars and hoping Zarko would break in so they could arrest him.

The office was closed, so he'd find out in the morning

who lived there. He watched Zarko place his ear against the door again then head back down the stairs to his truck.

"Let's find out what interested him so much about that apartment," Scarsdale said as he opened his door. He exited the car and walked straight to Zarko.

When Zarko saw him approaching, he stopped.

"Nice night, huh, Zarko? You know the drill. Hands on the hood," Scarsdale ordered.

Harris kept his flashlight shined on Zarko's face.

As he placed his hands on the hood of his truck, Zarko shot Scarsdale a hateful glance. "Don't you sonsabitches have something better to do than follow me around?"

"We enjoy following you around, shithead," Scarsdale said. After patting him down, Scarsdale yanked him back off the truck. "Give me your driver's license."

"What for?" Zarko asked.

Scarsdale smiled at him. "Sounds like he's refusing to identify himself. What do you think, partner?"

"Sure sounds like it." Harris said, pulling out his handcuffs. He kept the flashlight shining on Zarko's face, forcing Zarko to squint when he looked into the beam.

"This is bullshit. Fuckin harassment. You guys know exactly who I am."

"Not me," said Scarsdale. "To me, all you kiddie diddlers look alike."

Zarko held one hand up blocking the light from his eyes while reaching back for his wallet. He flipped his wallet open, removed his driver's license and handed it to Scarsdale.

Scarsdale noted the address. "This your correct address?"

Zarko sneered at him. "No, it's my grandmother's."

Scarsdale glanced at Harris who squeezed the handcuff. The sound of metal teeth clicking.

"It's mine," Zarko said, eyeing the handcuffs.

"Good. Now explain why you tried to break into that apartment up there" Scarsdale pointed up at the third floor of Building Three. Then he radioed the dispatcher, requesting a warrant check on Zarko.

"I was just goin' to see a friend."

"Who?" Harris asked.

"What difference does it make?" Zarko snapped.

"Well, asshole, you can tell us now or when we pull your ass out of that luxury suite at the county jail tomorrow," Harris said. "Of course, by then, we'll know who lives there and whether they even know you."

"It was a girl I met. Just checkin' to see if she was home. Is that a crime?"

"It won't be if you can tell me her name," Scarsdale said.

"I forgot her name. Is that a crime, too?"

Scarsdale started to hand the license back as Zarko held out his hand. Scarsdale dropped the license on the ground at Zarko's feet.

Zarko glanced at the license then sneered at Scarsdale before bending over to pick it up. "Asshole," he muttered.

They waited until Zarko got into his truck and drove off.

"He knows who lives there," Scarsdale said, watching the truck's taillights fade out in the distance. "I'll bet she's the blonde from Lasiter's closet."

⊱⊰

Scarsdale and Harris visited the Walnut Grove Apartments' office the next morning, asking for the name of the resident in apartment 312.

When the manager, Rick Loper, told them apartment 312 was leased to Dani Mueller, Scarsdale and Harris shared an astonished glance.

"Are you sure?" Scarsdale asked, hoping that Loper was wrong.

"Of course," Loper said as he opened the file folder and showed it to him. "But she left before Thanksgiving. Said she was going to visit her parents." He looked at Scarsdale with a quizzical expression. "Is there something I need to know about? Is she in some kind of trouble? This is an upscale complex, and the company wants to keep it that way."

"First of all, we're gathering information about a case, so I can't say any more about it."

"I understand," Loper said as he plopped the file on his desk.

"Second, don't disclose the fact that we asked for this information." Scarsdale closed his notebook. "A couple more questions. Did Ms. Mueller say when she'd be back?"

Loper furrowed his brows and squinted. "She works for you guys. You mean to tell me you don't know the answer already?"

"It's a big department. Everyone doesn't know everyone else. So…"

"She didn't say if she'd be back this year, but she did pay her rent up through January. And the other questions?"

Scarsdale pulled a photograph of Zarko out of his notebook and showed it to Loper. "Have you ever seen this man before?"

Loper studied the picture. "Yes, as a matter of fact I have," he said, nodding as he handed the photo back to Scarsdale. "He came in last Tuesday inquiring about a vacancy in Building 3. On the third floor, as a matter of fact."

"About what time was that?" Harris asked.

"Oh, I'd say…umm…just before dusk. Six or seven."

So, did you have a vacancy on three?" Scarsdale asked.

"And we did. Apartment 310. We showed it to him and he said he'd let us know."

"Does 310 have the same floor plan as 312, and where is it located?"

"Yes, it does." Loper picked up a map of the complex and pointed at apartment 310. "First one. Right here at the top of the stairs. Ms. Mueller lives in this one. An elderly couple live across from her."

Scarsdale and Harris walked back to the car.

"Zarko never wanted to rent that apartment," Scarsdale said. "He wanted to see the lay-out."

"Are you thinking what I'm thinking?" Harris asked.

"Yeah. Dani Mueller was the woman in Lasiter's closet. And Zarko wants to get rid of her."

"So what the hell was she doing in his closet ?"

Scarsdale recalled something Amanda had told him. "You remember that old man across the alley from Lasiter's? You thought the taillight sketch he drew fit a Mercedes?"

"Yeah."

"Well guess who sold her Mercedes recently."

Harris stopped and looked at Scarsdale before his eyes dropped to the pavement and his mouth tightened into a straight line.

For Scarsdale, if Dani was involved, it complicated things. Deep down, he hoped she had a plausible explanation. Like Harris said, she was too classy to be mixed up with the likes of Lasiter and Zarko. But if she was the one, he didn't want Shannon hanging out with her. After all, she *had* left town kind of suddenly. *If* she came back, they'd have a serious chat about Lasiter's murder.

CHAPTER 13

"There's more to doing good than hating evil."
~ *Anonymous*

When I saw my parents waiting at the baggage carousel of the Munich Airport, my heart swelled with a joy I hadn't felt in ages. My father towered over the crowd, his shaggy gray head scanning side to side for sight of me in that hulking, gentle way he had. I ran toward them and threw myself in my mother's arms. The Reverend Roland Engel beamed to have his two girls together at his side. I realized that we hadn't been together since Katarina's funeral, their only trip to the US, and drew my father into the embrace.

"It's so nice to have you home, Karla," Petra said in German.

I grimaced at the name Karla and caught a strange look from my mother. I smiled, hoping she wouldn't think any more of it. "It *is* good to be home, mother."

"How was your flight?" my father asked in German.

"It was good, Daddy," I said, wrapping my arms around his neck and kissing him on the cheek. It felt so right to have my father hug me. Stepping back, I gave both of them an apprising look. "Both of you look great." I glanced at the baggage carousel. "Oh, there's my suitcase."

I stepped toward the carousel but my father's long arm reached past me and grabbed it.

My pulse must have risen into the low hundreds as I prayed he wouldn't look at the ID tag on the suitcase handle. I never told them about my name change or what happened after they flew home. I hooked Daddy's arm and moved toward the exit. "C'mon let's go home."

❧

I unpacked my suitcase but before I could shove it under the bed, my mother came in. While I hung my jeans up in the closet, I glanced back to see her examining the ID tag on the suitcase handle.

"Who is Dani Mueller?"

I laughed, hoping to make a joke out of the name. "Oh, Dani Mueller is my secret name." I closed the bag and slid it under the bed.

My passport lay on the bed next to my purse. We both reached for it at the same time but she got it first. I saw her expression when she looked at the name under my photograph and the hurt in her eyes when she looked at me but before she could ask the question I knew was coming, my father strolled in the room. My mother hurriedly jammed my passport under the pillow.

He handed us each a stein with Spaten beer. Flashing a big grin, he held his stein up. "Welcome home, my beautiful daughter. Here's to the man who eliminated Katarina's murderer."

We tapped steins. "Thank you, Daddy. I'm glad to be home but I don't feel like a beautiful daughter right now." I didn't comment on the last part about his toast for whoever killed the man responsible for killing Katarina. I mean, what could I say…you're welcome?

I glanced at mother as I took a swallow of my beer. She sipped hers but looked away. I could see her eyes welling up. In that moment, I hated myself. She didn't understand the reason for the name change. How could she? I'd never told her what I'd done. I'd never told anyone. But Petra wasn't just my mother, she was also my best friend and I'd always shared everything with her. And Daddy…if he ever found out, I didn't know what he'd do.

On Tuesday afternoon, I strolled along Ludwigstrasse in Garmisch with Mother. The cold air felt good. There was a kind of sweetness in the air—a fresh mountain smell—that I realized I'd missed very much. The town hadn't grown much since I left to get married.

We shopped in silence, walking in and out of several shops. I knew a storm was brewing inside my mother's head over the name change. I tried to smooth things over by telling her about Shannon.

"I met this really sweet little girl back in Texas. Her name is Shannon. We became friends." I cast a quick glance at my mother. She continued to walk on, staring straight ahead. "Really good friends. Her daddy's a detective at the same place I work." *Or used to work?* I wondered.

She still wouldn't look at me. "Is his name Mueller?"

"No mother, his name is Scarsdale," I answered while searching through a rack of little girl's dresses. I wanted a gift for Shannon to make up for leaving without even saying good-bye. I'd acted selfishly. I'd run away. I'd mail the gifts to her if I decided to stay here. Then I remembered I'd never seen Shannon in a dress.

Chocolaterie Amelie had opened a store on Ludwigstrasse, a few doors away from where we shopped. I knew Scarsdale loved chocolate and figured he'd like some good German samples. If I went back, maybe it would help repair the scorched bridge between us.

After the chocolate shop, we searched through a few more stores before my mother pointed at a sidewalk café. The place had colorful paintings on the front of the building, much like many of the other restaurants in Garmisch.

"Let's get some lunch, Dani Mueller," Mother said, crossing the cobblestone street ahead of me.

"Sure. Let's eat something. Please don't address me as though I'm some stranger. I've been your daughter since I was born. My new name—nothing has changed that."

"My daughter is Karla Engel, not Dani Mueller."

She sat down at an outdoor table and dropped her shopping bags in the chair next to her.

I parked myself in the chair to her right and opened the menu.

She reached over and snatched the menu out of my hand. "Why did you change your name?" She sat there, arms folded across her chest, watching me, waiting for my answer.

"Okay, Mother, since you asked, I'll tell you why."

The waiter interrupted, asking for our order.

"Two coffees, please," I said. I looked across at Mother and reached for her hands but she pulled them off the table.

"*Nein.* You do not call us. You do not visit. Katarina is dead and yet you stay in America. And you have changed your name. Explain it to me, because I don't understand."

I took a deep breath and let it out. "I'm well aware Katarina is dead. I'm sorry I didn't call or come home sooner. But I live in Texas now. I have a job there—or I did."

Petra looked away.

I reached over and touched her arm. "Mother, please look at me."

When she did, I continued. "A few days after Burton, that animal who killed Katarina, was set free by a jury, he phoned me, laughing and bragging how much he enjoyed—" The tears welled up like a hot river. God, it was painful recounting that nightmare call. "He actually gloated and wanted me to know he'd *enjoyed* Katarina. He said he wore her bracelet so he could remember how—" I bit my lip hard until I could continue. "—how good she felt. In that moment, I lost it. I hunted him down while he was stalking another child. When I found him, I killed him." There, I'd said it and the storm of emotions I saw in my mother's face—shock, horror, and rage—felt like forgiveness, if not absolution.

I used my napkin to wipe my eyes. "Of course, I liked my birth name, but I had no choice, Mother. Burton's family harassed me day and night. Phone calls at all hours," I said, crying. "Flat tires. Damage to my car. Following me. If I hadn't changed my name and moved to Texas, Burton's family would have hurt me—or worse. They're as sick as he was and they know I killed him."

Mother got up and wrapped her arms around me. She didn't say anything. She didn't have to. She just held me tight.

I told her all about Lasiter, too. "I wanted to kill him a week ago. But I didn't. And now the man who actually killed *him* saw me there and is stalking me."

Mother pushed my shoulders back and looked at me. Then she brushed the tears from my cheeks. "Why didn't you tell me what happened earlier?"

"I didn't tell you sooner because I was afraid of what you'd think of me." I put my arms around her waist. "I'm so sorry, mother."

"Why didn't you just come home?"

"I didn't come home because I was scared they'd follow me and do something to you and Daddy."

"Instead, you changed your name?"

"Yes, I changed my name instead."

"But now you're home," she said, holding my face in her hands then kissing me on the forehead.

I hugged her. "Yes, Mother, I'm home now." *This was home. I felt safe here. Why should I ever go back?*

"Your father must never know what happened. He would freak out," she said, waving for the waiter.

That my mother would be willing to keep a secret from my father surprised me. "Right. He would freak out if he knew any of what I've done. When he picked up my luggage at the airport, I was terrified he'd see the ID tag."

Mother sat down when the waiter brought the coffee. "This girl, Shannon, what did you tell her?"

"I didn't. She was real sick. I don't want to say anything that would make her sick again." I took a swallow of coffee. I could see the wheels turning in my mother's head.

"Do you like this Scarsdale?"

"Yes, I like him but…I don't know. He lost his wife in October." I wasn't sure what I felt for him at this point. I wondered if I hadn't truly burned the bridge on Monday. I glanced across at my mother.

She looked at me with one eyebrow raised as though she knew something I didn't.

"What?"

She only smiled and shook her head. "This Shannon, she is young, *ya?*" Mom asked as she pushed her glasses further up on the bridge of her nose.

"Yes, Mom, she's about five years old," I said, stirring my coffee.

With an image of Shannon fresh in her mind, we hit the shops again.

"Now that you are home, you can change your name back to Karla," she said casually, removing a blue Dirndl dress and blouse from the children's dress rack.

"I still would have to go back to Texas and pack up my things. Changing my name back to Karla will have to wait. You understand, don't you?" I didn't know what I wanted to do. I felt happy to be home, but something tugged at me to go back to Austin.

She didn't answer me. "Would Shannon wear this?" she asked, holding it up.

"No, Mom. In Austin, they don't wear dresses much at all. Jeans or shorts." I picked up a Black Forest doll with a red rose apron an apple basket tucked in her arm. "Here. She would love this doll."

"And this?" Mom held up a child's edelweiss necklace. Three silver and bronze-colored edelweiss flowers on a silver chain. "This is pretty, don't you agree?"

I took the necklace from my mother and held it up. "Yes, very pretty." Shannon would love it, or at least I hoped she would. I wondered if she had any jewelry. I didn't recall seeing her with any. It would make a nice gift for Christmas but I wondered if all this gift buying was a waste of time.

As we strode up to the cashier, I saw a table with several music boxes. One in particular caught my eye—a German weather house music box. It was a miniature device in the shape of a German chalet that forecast the weather. It had two doors side by side. The left side had a girl, the right side a boy. The girl came out of the house when the weather was sunny and dry, while the boy came out to indicate rain. The tag on the bottom said it played "Edelweiss." It was identical to one

I'd had as a child. Although mine was still on my old dresser at my parents' house, it quit forecasting weather a long time ago. I wanted this one for Shannon. It was always good to know when the rain was going to fall in your life.

That night, I lay in bed, staring at the ceiling, debating what to do. A flurry of images—Shannon, Scarsdale, my apartment, Zarko, Parnell Burton, Amanda Colbert, my new car—flashed across my mind like a slide show. There were as many reasons to go back as to stay.

Two days later I sat on the stool in front of the mirror on my dresser, brushing my hair. My father strolled in and sat on the edge of my bed. I saw him in the mirror looking at me. He seemed as if he was choosing his words carefully. "What do you do in Austin?"

"I'm a crime analyst at the police department. I review crime reports about—"

"You're not a lawyer anymore?"

"Yes, I'm still a lawyer." I kept brushing my hair, my eyes glued to his reflection. "I'm just not practicing right now."

"Why not?" He bent down and slid the suitcase out.

"Because I'm not licensed in Texas, only California." I turned to face him. "What's the matter?"

My mother walked in and sat next to him, hooking her hand between his arm and his chest.

My heart thumped against my ribs as he lifted the ID tag up, sliding his finger over my name. Our eyes locked when he looked at me, still holding the tag. I'm sure they could hear my pulse pounding.

"I think you have something to tell me."

He said it in a calm way, making me think Mother had spilled the beans. She confirmed it when the corners of her mouth curled up slightly and she nodded at me.

I swallowed hard and decided to give him the shorthand version. "The man who murdered Katarina went free. He taunted me later, saying how much he enjoyed raping Katarina. When he started describing in detail what he did to her, I got so angry I hunted him down and killed him. Afterward his family stalked me day and night so I changed my name and—"

"So you ran away?" He didn't appear angry but the sadness resonated in his eyes.

I sat there for a moment, not sure what he thought. "Yes, sir, I ran away, but—"

"Why didn't you tell the police?"

"In America, once a man has been freed after a trial, he can't be tried again for that same crime. Not again, not ever. Burton could tell anyone, even the police, exactly what he did to Katarina and thumb his nose at them. There's nothing they could have done."

"I wish you had moved home where I could have protected you."

"I know you would have done what you could to protect me but I *couldn't* come home. You don't know how cruel that family is, what they're capable of doing. I changed my name because I didn't want them following me here and hurting you or Mother. Do you understand that? I love you both so much. I'd have nothing left if they did something to either of you."

"Are you going to stay here?"

I looked from him to my mother. "I don't know, Daddy. I have an apartment full of furniture and a new car. I'd have to go back to pack up and ship the car over." I took a big breath and exhaled. "The guys at the police department need me to help them. I can't really turn my back on them." I smiled. "Did Mother tell you about—"

"About that little Shannon. *Ja.*" He glanced at Mother before taking a deep breath, letting it out slowly. "You can do the same job with the police here, or practice law. Your family is here."

I scooted the stool over so I sat in front of both of them. "Yes, I could if they had an opening. If I wanted to practice law again, I'd have to get licensed in England first, then come here. I checked it out two years ago when I considered moving home. But that was before the Burton family came after me."

My mother spoke up. "Come. It's time to eat dinner." She

stood up and tugged at Daddy's arm until he stood up,too.

"Let's go eat."

He turned in my direction, reaching his hand out to me. "We love you. We will support whatever decision you make."

I took his hand and walked with them to the dinner table. "Thank you, but I'll think some more about whether to go back." I wished with all my heart I'd made better choices. I was the only child they had and I knew they'd be worried sick if I did go back to Texas now that they knew the whole story.

"I'm not happy about what you've done. But I understand why you had to do it. Nevertheless, it is wrong. Have you gone to Confession and Absolution?"

"Yes, I did go to Confession and Absolution later. A couple of times, actually."

On Saturday, while Daddy was at the church, Mother and I drove to the pedestrian shopping area near Am Kurpark. I pictured Father saying a lot of prayers for me. When we got home that afternoon, Mother asked me if I had decided.

"Not yet. I wish I could have it both ways…" I lowered my head. "Tell me what I should do."

"My dearest Karla." She grabbed my shoulders. "What does your heart tell you?" She peered into my eyes, searching for my answer.

"To go back."

She smiled. "Do you have feelings for this man, Scarsdale?"

I looked away, then down, before gazing at mother. "I don't love him, but, yes, I do have some feelings for him."

Monday, I began packing my suitcase for the return flight to Austin. I cast a quick glance at my father as he stood at the foot of my bed, twisting the curled ends of his white mustache. Whenever he worked on his mustache, I knew he was worried. And I knew this time it was me he worried about. "Promise you'll be careful."

I smiled at him, patting him on his cheek. "I promise I'll be careful." I wrapped my arms around his shoulders, hugging him tight. "Don't worry. I'll be okay.

"Call us every day. *Please.*"

I saw the sadness in his eyes. "I will."

☙❧

On the flight back, I looked out at the puffy clouds sailing by, still uncertain if going back to Texas was the right choice.

My last leg of my flight back landed at Austin-Bergstrom right around two o'clock in the afternoon. After retrieving my knife and pepper spray from the airport locker, I walked out of the airport and into the cool afternoon air of Austin. I sat back in the taxi and considered the realities of what I'd come back to. I wondered how Shannon was feeling. Was she still homebound? Or had she gone back to kindergarten? How was Scarsdale holding up?

I needed to check Parnell Burton's parole status. That was a priority. The Board had allowed me to protest his release the last time and I hoped I'd get the same courtesy this time. It wasn't unheard of for the Secretary of State's office to screw up the notification of pending parole.

And then there was Zarko. He wasn't likely to let this go. He'd want to settle the score and make certain I couldn't identify him as Lassiter's killer—and, most likely, as the man who killed Amy Crowell. This time I'd be ready. I looked at the knife in my purse. When he tried again, he'd pay dearly.

The taxi let me off right at the stairwell of my building. Standing at the bottom of the stairs, I pulled the knife from my purse, holding it close to my hip. I checked each landing as I slowly climbed the stairs, dragging the suitcase, and taking occasional glances behind me.

There was no sign of him in the bright light of day and I felt comfortable enough to retrieve my mail. As I walked past the apartment office, sorting the important stuff from the junk mail, Loper, my apartment manager, caught up with me.

"Welcome back. How was your trip?" he asked.

"Wonderful."

"The police were here asking questions about you."

I stopped and stared at Loper. "The police—who?"

"Two detectives. The big one asked when you were coming back."

"Jason Scarsdale?"

"Yep. That's him."

As far as I knew, I'd never told him where I lived—unless he got it from the personnel database. This could only mean one thing and the realization hit me like a shock wave.

"That's all he wanted? He didn't come all the way here just to ask when I'd be back." I stared at Loper with my hardest lawyer's gaze, willing him to tell me everything.

"Scarsdale didn't want me to say anything. But…they were working on a case. He showed me a photograph of a man, asking if I'd seen him before."

It had to be Zarko. "What about him?"

"The man had been here, inquiring about leasing the apartment next door to yours—while you were away."

Pictures of Zarko waiting by my door flashed through my mind. "Did you lease it to him?"

"Of course not."

Going up the stairs, all I could think about was the twin debacles at Lasiter's and Zarko's. Did Zarko tell the cops I was the one in the closet? Did Zarko's neighbor call the police after he yelled at me to get out of his yard?

I decided not to wait until tomorrow. I had Scarsdale's address. I'd use the gifts as a reason to go there. I had to find out what he knew about Zarko. About the closet fiasco. About my dumb idea of stalking Zarko. And I wanted to mend any rift between us.

੭৩੭৩

Mrs. Hargraves answered the door. "May I help you?"

"My name is Karla—I mean, Dani Mueller and—"

I didn't get to finish the sentence. Shannon's shrieks filled the room as she ran out the front door. "Dani, Dani. You came back."

Shannon pushed her way past the nanny. I squatted down just as Shannon leaped into my arms, almost bowling me over.

"I knew you'd come back." She hugged me around the neck, pressing her face tight against my cheek, and said, "I missed you, Dani. Promise me you won't go away again."

I hadn't expected such a fervent greeting. "I missed you too, sweetie." I didn't know what the future held, so I couldn't promise that I wouldn't leave again.

"I guess you two know each other," the nanny said, smiling. "Why don't you come in? Detective Scarsdale should be home any minute now."

Shannon wouldn't let go of my hand. She pulled me into her bedroom. "C'mon, I want to show you what Grammie and PawPaw got me."

"Let's wait 'til your daddy gets home." I reached into the bag and pulled out the doll. "I brought you something."

Shannon's eyes lit up when she saw it. She stood there fascinated with the colorful figure. "Apples?" she asked, carefully touching the apple basket.

"Yes and she's wearing the same kind of dress I wore when I was your age."

Shannon hugged the doll. "She's going to be Barbie's best friend in the whole world."

I heard the front door open. "I think your daddy's home."

Shannon rushed to the door, holding the doll by the arm and I followed her. "Daddy. Dani's here. Look what she brought me," she said, squealing in delight.

Scarsdale smiled at me then knelt down to examine the doll. "Very pretty. Did you thank her?" he asked.

As Shannon dashed toward me, Scarsdale and I locked eyes. "Hi," I said, giving him the warmest smile I could muster.

He gave me a steady gaze, the question in his eyes evident. *Okay, now what?*

Shannon threw her arms around my legs, making me look down. She looked up at me with a big wide smile. "Thank you."

"You're welcome, dear." Her dreamy brown eyes reminded me of Katarina and it made me glad just to see her smile. I watched her as she ran back to her father to retrieve the doll.

When I looked at him a second time he was all smiles, his eyes crinkling at the corners with real humor. He seemed to relax.

"You missed a great Thanksgiving dinner."

"Shannon said her grandparents came in for the big day."

He moved nearer to me, turning toward a bookcase. He placed his gun, holster, and handcuffs on the highest shelf. "We had a great time. Too bad you missed it." He cast a wary glance at me, though still smiling. "You were busy doing other things, I guess."

"What's that supposed to mean?" I asked.

He hesitated before scratching his nose while he stared at the floor, as if debating whether to respond. He peeled off his coat and draped it across the chair. "I hope your parents were doing well?" Then he came closer to me.

"Quite well, thank you for asking." For the first time we stood inches apart and I was drawn to his face. Rugged lines bore witness to a life deeply lived. A long crease across his forehead added to the life's map. Laugh lines set off his eyes which had a ring of green around the dark brown. They showed a hint of sadness. Not Brad Pitt by any measure but handsome in his own way. And he was a man I wanted to know better. I just wasn't sure I'd be able to.

"I'm glad you came back. How was your flight?"

"Nice, thank you." I raised my hand a few inches toward his face. I wanted to touch it, to feel his ruggedness with my fingers. But I stopped and let my hand drop to my side.

"You're welcome to stay for dinner, but I have to warn you, it's all leftovers."

"Thank you. Maybe another time. I have some unpacking to do."

Shannon grabbed my hand. "Please don't go."

"It's getting dark, and Zarko might be lurking nearby,"

Scarsdale said, as he looked squarely at me. He was searching for a reaction and I made sure he didn't get one.

"I heard you visited my apartment complex. Why?"

"Oh yeah. I was going to tell you about that." He walked a few steps away then turned to face me. "Harris and I followed Zarko over to your apartment. Watched him try your door. We couldn't figure out why he had so much interest in your apartment." He strolled toward the kitchen and I followed him. "You really should stay for dinner."

I pulled a quizzical look and played dumb. I certainly didn't want to bolster his suspicions about me. "Well, did you ever find out?"

He cast a quick over-the-shoulder glance at me. "Not yet." He opened the refrigerator. "I was kind of hoping you'd shed some light on that." He took out a large plate of wrapped turkey and set it on the counter, then paused to give me a closed-lipped smile.

"Why would *I* know what he was doing there?"

Jason looked at me intently. "I'll set a place for you," he said, opening a cabinet door and taking out three dinner plates. "We'll talk about him after dinner."

"Is that an invitation or an order?"

"An invitation, I assure you," he said and retrieved three sets of dinnerware from a drawer. He turned to face me. "And I apologize for sounding so cop-like. But I'm worried about him doing something to you." He gestured toward Shannon. "She really missed you. And if anything happened to you, she'd be very upset. I don't want to see her like that—ever again."

I managed a smile and refused to think about what he would ask concerning Zarko. "Then I'd be happy to eat leftovers."

Shannon yelled, "Yay!" She tugged at my hand. "Let's go set the table."

After dinner, Shannon went to her room to play with her new doll while Scarsdale and I sat at the dining room table sipping wine and chatting about her health and my trip. At precisely eight o'clock, Scarsdale put Shannon to bed.

He returned with his notepad, opening it to a blank page. "Can you think of any reason why Zarko would be stalking you?"

My heart beat like a hummingbird's wings. I shook my head. "No." I took a sip. "Maybe he mixed my apartment up with someone else's. That's possible." I sat back, crossing my legs. "Did you ask him?"

"He claimed he was looking for a woman he met, but didn't know her name. So, I'm just asking—does he know you? Work? Grocery store?"

I felt a coldness creep over me and an empty sense of isolation. Scarsdale knew more than he was letting on. Dammit. I never ever wanted it to come to this—a cat-and-mouse game between us. I didn't want to lie and I couldn't tell the truth. So I played dumb. "What's he look like?"

"He's in his late twenties, about five nine, a hundred and sixty pounds. Medium length curly brown hair." Scarsdale touched his cheek near the corner of his eye and traced a path down to the corner of his mouth. "He has a long scabbed-up scar from here all the way down to here."

A souvenir from me. My mind flashed back to that night.

Scarsdale watched me, waiting for an answer. "Ring any bells?"

"What?"

"His description? Does it ring any bells with you?"

"Yes. I saw his mug shot in the Lasiter file."

"He's hunting the woman who witnessed him murder Scott Lasiter. You don't know anything about that, do you?"

I looked at him, shrugged, and shook my head. "I knew about the woman from reading the police reports." We locked eyes. His look shook my resolve. "What? You think it was *me* in that closet?"

Even though I entered Lasiter's house with the intent to kill him, Scarsdale couldn't prove anything unless I admitted to it. And that wasn't going to happen.

But if Zarko implicated me, the best the prosecutors could

prove would be trespass. It's just a misdemeanor, but it would have a domino effect on my life.

My job at the police department would be gone. So would my law license. And that, coupled with Scarsdale finding out about Burton's death, would be the end of my relationship with Shannon and him. And I couldn't blame him. He had to protect Shannon. If the situation were reversed, it's what I would have done for Katarina.

But the prospect of never being able to visit Shannon again was a high price to pay. I had to find another avenue out of this mess. If I couldn't, I'd pack up and go home to Germany. For good, this time.

"Zarko isn't going to let up. He believes the woman in the closet lives there. So I'm thinking he followed the woman from Lasiter's house to your particular apartment. You're not rooming with another woman, are you?"

"No," I said, acting indignant. "Of course not. He's mistaken me for someone else. There's no other explanation."

"Once he sees your face, if he hasn't already, he'll be stalking you. As long as that woman is alive, in his mind, he's looking at going down for murder. And in his mind, that woman is you."

Scarsdale was correct. But Zarko wasn't alone in that belief. He believed it too or we wouldn't be having this cat-and-mouse chat. My stomach felt like it was twisted into knots. I should have listened to my parents and stayed there. "So what do I do? Move?"

"If you moved, he'd only follow you there."

Part of me wanted to thank Zarko for killing Lasiter. He'd saved me from a huge mistake. The other part wished I'd never let my rage over pedophiles go so far.

He leaned closer. His face was inches away again. "Talk to me, Dani. Tell me what's really going on. We can help each other."

I leaned back. "What could possibly be going on? Stop interrogating me."

He held his hands up. "I'm not, okay?" He wrote some

notes on the pad which I couldn't read. "Zarko was there for a reason. And it wasn't to sell Girl Scout cookies."

"That's enough." I jumped up, jabbing my finger on the table "You're accusing me of complicity in Lasiter's murder." I grabbed my purse and headed toward the front door.

"I didn't accuse you of anything."

I kept walking toward the door. I had to leave now. I had to be alone, before I came apart. I had to think this through.

"Wait a minute, Dani," he said. "Where are you going?"

I jerked the door open, not looking back. "Where do you think?"

When I got home, I grabbed Katarina's favorite pillow—the pale brown one with the seashell design—off the chair in my bedroom.

Slipping off the edge of the bed to the floor, both of my arms wrapped tightly around the pillow, I rocked back and forth, whispering a prayer I said every night when I was a child.

Later, with a glass of Grand Marnier in hand, I stood in the open air of my balcony, all sorts of thoughts crisscrossing my mind.

I nibbled on my fingernail when I wasn't taking a sip, debating whether I should tell Scarsdale the truth. I didn't want to spend any part of my life in a gray cinder block room the size of Lasiter's closet with a door to which someone else had the key.

If only I could have foreseen the price I'd pay for killing Burton and almost killing an innocent man, I'd have done it all differently.

My moral compass had spun out of control. But nothing would change what I had done. No amount of crying or begging or confessing.

My options were drying up faster than ice in August. If I told Scarsdale everything, if he was the straight arrow everyone called him, Shannon, our friendship, my job, my law license would all be gone.

CHAPTER 14

"Those who plot the destruction of others
often perish in the attempt." ~ *Thomas Moore*

At eleven thirty a.m. inmate Parnell James Burton finished the morning shift—his last one—in the unit kitchen at California's Pleasant Valley State Prison. The prison was located in central California in the town of Coalinga about two hundred miles south of Sacramento.

Parnell pranced into the dorm room he shared with thirty-five other inmates, doing a kind rhythmic dance, sliding his feet in a zippy moonwalk.

He scanned the room. The other inmates from his dorm were at chow. He peeled off the blue shirt with the gold lettering "CDC Prisoner" on the back. Taking a notebook brimming with news clippings, photos, and letters from his locker, he stretched out on his bunk. Today would be his last day inside.

Tonight he'd be guzzling down beer and sleeping on a nice thick mattress between fresh, clean, unstained sheets with a quilt on top and a soft feather pillow under his head. He'd leave the window open so he could smell the sweet fragrance of the pine trees, listen to the cars driving by, and hear the barking dogs. He'd feel the cool night air as it breezed over his face. No more guards and no Klaxon horns going off at three a.m., waking him to another day of slopping food on inmate trays—and best of all, no more lousy prison food.

Tonight he'd gobbled down hot, tender, tasty steaks done the way he liked—medium rare—and real chocolate ice cream swimming in a river of chocolate syrup. Yep, he thought, it's just a matter of hours now.

Flipping through the notebook, he stopped at a page with

a taped newspaper clipping, its edges frayed and curled at the corners. He'd read it so often over the past two years, he'd actually memorized it. The clipping described the brutal killing of his brother, Doyle Burton, in a wooded area of a Sacramento park over two years ago.

Parnell was an inch or two taller and six years younger than his brother. His handsome looks earned him the nickname of "Pretty Boy." After a couple of inmates ended up in the prison infirmary for calling him that, no one uttered it again—at least not within Parnell's earshot. That kind of crazy could get you a pass even in cell Block C.

One foot tapped against the other as he re-read a letter from his mother, Mattie. The letter, dated two years ago, stated that Karla Engel had closed her law practice, sold her house, and moved away. In the letter, Mattie told Parnell that Karla's address on the state bar website belonged to a private mailbox forwarding service.

Parnell closed the notebook when a correctional officer stopped at his bunk. "On your feet, Burton. Get dressed. I'll be back in a half hour to escort you to the parole office." The guard dropped a canvas bag on his bunk and pointed at Parnell's foot locker. "Be sure that foot locker is cleaned out."

Parnell glanced over at the officer, winked, and swung his legs onto the concrete floor. "Yes, sir, boss."

ᘓᕪᘓ

Dressed out in a pair of baggy jeans and a striped shirt that barely fit over his bulked arms, the ex-con stared straight ahead with a relaxed squint and a thin-lipped smile. With a hundred dollars and the canvas duffel bag draped over his shoulder, Parnell Burton walked out the main gate of Pleasant Valley State Prison, free on parole.

He stood alone on the sidewalk under the watchful eye of the guard high above in the brick tower. In front of him lay an asphalt parking lot and an assortment of cars and trucks. He glanced up at the bright blue sky, raising his hand over his brows to shield his eyes from the afternoon sun. A car horn beeped. A shiny, green, four-door sedan pulled up next to him.

The passenger window opened. "Hey, you, need a ride?" the female voice asked. He approached the open window, leaned down, and looked inside.

His mother Mattie sat in the driver's seat, a grin stretched across her face. Dressed in a pair of faded jeans and a red sweatshirt with an attached hood and a golden "49ers" logo on the front, Mattie reached over to hug Parnell as he got in. Her face was gaunt. Deep creases lined her forehead. Crow's feet crinkled around her eyes. Unbrushed, bleached-blonde hair with the brown roots showing barely covered her ears. A cigarette dangled from her lips.

He smiled back. "About time you showed up." He slammed the door as the car tires squealed and they accelerated down the road away from what had been Burton's home for the past six years.

Mattie gave him the once-over. "It's so good to see you out finally. You hungry?"

"Hell, yeah. I want a big ole steak smothered in mushrooms with one of those baked potatoes with everything. After that, gimme a gallon of chocolate ice cream, a bottle of chocolate syrup, and a spoon." He glanced at her. "Then I'm going to find that bitch who offed Doyle."

"The people I been asking don't know where she took off to. Like she up and vanished," she said, speeding onto Interstate 5, headed north.

"Bullshit. After we eat, take me by her old office. Somebody there knows where she fuckin' ran off to." He sighed as he scanned the pastures while they cruised down the highway toward Sacramento. "I missed this stuff."

"Parnell, what was Doyle doing out at them parks?"

He slammed his fist on the dashboard then turned very slowly toward her. His face reddened. "I told you—" He spoke in a soft tone that changed into a scream. "He didn't kill her *fuckin'* kid!" He turned away and stared out the window, soaking up the warm air washing over his face. After several seconds, he snorted. "He'd never do something like that."

Mattie chose her next words carefully. "I found things in his room, Parnell. Before he got himself arrested. I burned the stuff so the police wouldn't find them. I didn't want to say nothin' to you about it 'cause I knew how you and him was so close and all."

"What things?" he asked, casting a hard stare at her.

"He had naked pictures of little kids. They was—"

"Shut up."

She reached across the seat and patted his hand. "He was—"

"Shut up, goddammit!" he yelled, knocking her hand away. "I told you he'd *never* do shit like that. Just fuckin' shut up about it. I don't want to hear it."

Parnell's father had taken off soon after his third birthday. Doyle became his surrogate dad, teaching him how to play baseball, to shrug off pain in fights and football games, about girls, and all the stuff an inquiring young boy's mind wanted to know. Doyle had been his hero.

After a few minutes, Parnell pointed at a large sign for the Black Angus Restaurant. Under the words was a profile of a black cow.

"Pull in there."

Parnell ordered a sixteen-ounce T-bone, done medium rare. Not much of a conversationalist, he spent the wait time guzzling beer and gazing around the room, ogling a few of the waitresses. None of them objected; one or two even flirted with him.

When the steak arrived, he wasted no time wolfing it down, chasing every other bite with a big swallow of beer. He polished off one more beer before they left for home.

It was almost three 'o'clock when Mattie pulled the car into the driveway. The house had paint peeling off the exterior walls. Grass mixed with weeds grew in valiant patches in the surrounding hard packed dirt.

"Damn, this place needs a paint job," he said. "And some yard work. Why the hell didn't Phoenix paint the place?"

"He spends his time in San Francisco. Don't see him much."

When he got out of the car, Parnell scanned the neighborhood. He saw the North Laguna Creek Park entrance straight down the street. The houses on either side of his mom's place weren't in any better condition than hers. A couple homes were actually worse off—missing window screens and busted windows.

"Got any paint for this place, Mom?"

"No, or I'd have done it long ago."

"None of these lazy ass neighbors offered to do it for you?" He gave the neighbors' houses one last look before he headed for the front door.

"Nope. When Doyle was arrested…" Her voice trailed off.

"Well, screw them," Parnell said, walking up on the porch and into the house. "Get me the paint and I'll do it for ya this weekend. Get me a lawnmower too. I'll fix this place up."

A half hour later, she drove him down to Karla's old office. But no one there knew where she had gone. Karla hadn't told them and they hadn't asked. When he inquired about her former secretary, Ellen, all the women in the office would say was that Ellen had taken a job at a prosecutor's office in a nearby county.

When they got back to the house, he scooped a huge helping of chocolate ice cream into a large salad bowl and emptied a full bottle of Hershey's chocolate syrup over it. It took him less than fifteen minutes to clean the bowl.

That evening, he sat at the computer, flipping through online pages of the *Sacramento Bee* newspaper archives. Finally he found the story of Doyle's death. On the opposite page was a picture of a somber-faced Karla Engel walking out of the Sacramento County Courthouse. The caption under the photo read: "Grand Jury clears local lawyer in death of former defendant." The news account accompanying her picture stated that the dead man, Doyle Burton, had been recently acquitted in a jury trial for the brutal murder of the attorney's ten-year-old daughter. His body had been found by city workers in Reichmuth Park, bearing obvious signs of torture and mutilation. "You worthless cunt!" He sat there glowering at her picture. "You better hope I never find you."

That night, he lay between crisp white sheets with a fresh-smelling feather pillow under his head. The curtains waved as the cool breeze blew in and washed over him. He sucked in a deep breath. The citrusy smell of the Douglas fir trees replaced the nightly stink of pee, farts, and sweat. The branches scraping against the side of the house and the occasional yapping of a neighbor's dog took the place of loud snoring, crazy ass inmates banging away on their cell doors while yelling for a guard, and the buzzer that went off every friggin morning at precisely four o'clock.

Staring at the ceiling, he fantasized about what he'd do once he found Karla. His heart beat faster the more he thought about how he'd exact his revenge. His knife would be razor sharp. He'd start slow, beginning with her arms. Karla would scream but no one else would hear her.

CHAPTER 15

"It is not who is right, but what is right, that is important."
~ *Thomas Huxley*

Scarsdale went around to Amanda Colbert's cubicle to bring her up to speed about Ferguson and Olsen. Before he could say much, she held her finger to her lips, signaling him to silence.

She opened a drawer and pulled out a file. "Let's go get some coffee."

Amanda drove Scarsdale to the Denny's north of downtown Austin. After they ordered, Amanda removed a photograph from the file and slid it across the table to Scarsdale. "Recognize anybody?"

He studied the picture. "Yeah. Olsen and Zarko. The guy in the mask must be the one they call the CEO. And the other two guys?" He raised the picture closer. "Is that a tattoo on his arm?" Scarsdale rotated the photograph. "I can't make it out." He handed the picture back. "Olsen told me the guy who murdered Ferguson had a black and green tattoo on his right forearm and that—" He reached across and pointed to the right forearm. "—is his right forearm."

Amanda looked at it. "Sure looks like a tattoo." She pointed at the other two. "The skinny guy is Phillip Agosti and the weasel-looking dude is Rico Sanchez."

"Where did you get this?"

"The tooth fairy left it under my pillow."

Scarsdale snorted. "Seriously. I mean it looks like they posed. One big happy family."

"A snitch got it for me. Now's he's a dead snitch."

Scarsdale slid the picture back to her. "Ferguson?"

"And we have a winner," she said, slipping the photograph back in the folder. She looked around again then leaned closer to Scarsdale. "I wanted to get you out of the office because I didn't want to talk there. Somebody in the division is leaking information."

"Any idea who?"

"If I knew, I'd have busted his ass," she said, arching one eyebrow. "I suspect he's the head chicken hawk." She tapped the file folder. "The whole bunch of these freaks are part of an online porn ring. The head of the ring—the CEO dude, as you call him—I want to nail his ass."

Scarsdale saw it in her eyes—a fierce hatred brewing behind those mahogany orbs. "You really believe the CEO works for us?"

"Just a hunch. I don't have any proof. My snitch said he's tall. Nobody in that group has ever seen his face. He wears that mask when they meet. None of them even know his real name."

"How do you know we have a leak?"

"The last two times Sheila Zimmerman and I ran a paper on Sanchez, he sat outside on the front porch and asked us why it took so long to get there. He'd sanitized his place—a stack of *Good Housekeeping* magazines on the table. All the DVDs were of first-run legit movies. His laptop hard-drive sparkled, it was so clean."

"So who else knew you were running on him?"

"The usual suspects—Mitchell, Robertson, a few patrol officers, and Judge Boyd. Whoever else they told. The patrol officers didn't know until Sheila and I were parked in front of Sanchez's house."

"Maybe someone from another division listened in?" Scarsdale said, gulping down a mouthful of coffee.

"I don't know." She finished her coffee, dropped a five dollar bill on the table and got up.

"Other officers and even civilians wander around our cubicles all the time," he said as they marched out the door.

He snatched a quick look at a silent Amanda as she nibbled on her lip. "Mind if we make a stop at Ferguson's house?" she asked.

"Let's do it."

Amanda headed out of the Denny's parking lot. "One of my informants said Ferguson's trophies were still hidden in his house, including a notebook containing the codenames of other chicken hawks he ran with. Maybe the CEO's name is in there."

"I'd have figured whoever slaughtered Ferguson rummaged around, taking whatever was valuable."

"Probably tried to find it. Those deviants are ingenious when it comes to secreting their stashes. They know other freaks'll be searching for it, too."

After ducking under the yellow "Police Line. Do Not Cross" ribbon at Ferguson's house, the two detectives snapped on nitrile gloves and opened the door.

The scene they saw made them move cautiously through the entire house, checking to be sure no unexpected persons were there. The sofa rested on its back, the fabric bottom ripped out, seat cushions sliced open. Tables were overturned, books and knickknacks dumped on the floor. He nudged pieces of a busted up German beer stein and its silver-colored lid with his shoe.

Some kitchen drawers lay on their side on the floor, contents spilled out. Other drawers were teetering, yanked open as far as they'd go. Cabinet doors hung open. A red mixer lay adjacent to a cabinet door. The refrigerator had been pulled from its space. Scarsdale did his best to avoid stepping on shattered plates and cups.

He and Amanda checked the two bedrooms. Ferguson's bed rested on its side, the mattress and box spring leaning against the wall. The air conditioner vents had been pried from the walls. Dresser drawers hung open. Underwear and socks were strewn around the room.

"Someone beat us to it." Scarsdale sighed as he shoved a large box out of the way. He remembered how the house had looked when he and Harris first arrived following the frantic phone call by Ferguson's parole officer. Except for the body, everything had been neat and orderly.

Amanda snorted, "Maybe. Let's go one room at a time. The snitch said Ferguson hid his collection in one of the bedrooms."

"Let's start with the other room" Scarsdale said. "It looked like a studio."

"Sounds like a winner to me," Amanda agreed and started down the back hallway. She stopped at the doorway and noted the appearance.

The room had white walls bearing a lot of black scuffmarks. A single bulb hung down from an open ceiling light. There were only two pieces of furniture. A twin bed occupied the center of the room with the head of the bed up against the wall. The mattress was propped haphazardly and box spring lay against another wall, its thin covering, ripped away.

Like in the bedroom, the air conditioning duct had been removed.

A bulky old cathode-ray TV sat atop a combo VCR-DVD player in the corner on a wooden table. A camera-less tripod stood near the foot of the bed. The only window was covered with a blue sheet.

Scarsdale searched around the TV table. He picked up the TV to set it on the floor. "Light as a feather," he said, shaking it. Hearing a rattling sound, he set it back on the table. Using his pocket knife, he removed the back of the TV.

"Jackpot," he exclaimed, removing a stack of DVDs and photographs, handing them to Amanda.

"Hollowed out the TV," she said while examining the front and back of each DVD in the stack. "Yep. These were his trophies."

Then Scarsdale removed a small maroon-colored notebook, turning several pages. At the top of each page was "Pickleman GL." He waved the book in the air. "Here's the list of names." He thumbed through more pages, reading two names out loud. "Easy Boy gl. Daddyneeds1952."

"Let me see that," Amanda said.

She ran her finger down the list, reading off the names. "Pickleman was Ferguson. Easy Boy and Daddyneeds are two I haven't heard before. Rooster is one I never heard of either." She flipped the pages. "Half of these handles are new to me." She closed the book. "Means we have more of them to find. God's work is never done."

Scarsdale moved away from the TV, holding a large number of DVDs in each hand. "There's more in there. Find a box I can dump these in." He felt good. At least these kiddie porn films and photos would be out of circulation permanently.

When they finished, Amanda carried the box containing over seventy DVDs, twelve VHS tapes, and a stack of photographs. Most of the pictures were of children but there were three pictures that piqued Scarsdale's interest. One showed all five—Ferguson, Olsen, Zarko, Agosti, and Sanchez, posing together, arms draped over each other's shoulder, big happy grins on their faces.

"Humph. All five. Outstanding," Amanda said. "The CEO must have taken this picture."

"Either that or we have a new member."

❧❧

Two days after searching Ferguson's house, Scarsdale, Harris, and Amanda took the Ferguson photographs to Olsen at the county jail. Scarsdale went into the interrogation room while Amanda and Harris watched through the one-way window.

"Got my deal?" Olsen asked.

Scarsdale kept silent. He laid the three photographs on the table in front of Olsen. Olsen stiffened, the smile faded as he did a double-take. "You obviously recognize everyone. So tell me who they are," Scarsdale said. "Let's start with this one— the one with you and your asshole buddies."

"Don't know them," Olsen said.

Scarsdale shoved Olsen's chair tight against the table. "You don't recognize Fergie?"

"Okay," he said sharply, glaring at Scarsdale. "That's me. That dude is Ferguson and the other guys I don't know."

"You get your picture taken with people you don't know? Horseshit." He shoved Olsen's head forward. "Take another look, asshole." He let go. "Who are they?"

Olsen looked up at him. "I'm tellin' ya I don't know 'em."

"Who took the picture then?"

Olsen looked away. "I don't remember."

Scarsdale took a long, deep breath before exhaling slowly. "Maybe if I jerk your sorry ass out of that chair and knock the shit out of you, maybe then you'll remember."

Olsen rolled his eyes. "If I had my deal, I'd remember a lot of things."

He slid the next picture—one showing Olsen, Zarko and Ferguson—closer to Olsen. In this photo, Zarko's arm laid across Olsen's shoulders. "You know this guy?" Scarsdale pointed at Zarko.

"Nope."

Scarsdale leaned close to his face. "Here's how it's going down, you skinny little cockroach. When we nail Zarko and we will, I'm personally going to tell him you told me all about how he murdered Amy Crowell." Scarsdale stood up, picking up the photographs. He turned for the door but pivoted back to Olsen. "I almost forgot. We've got Ferguson's trophies and his black book with everyone's name in it. I'll probably slip up and tell them how you helped us find that book."

Olsen stared at him. "If I do tell ya, nobody finds out it was me who ratted on them."

"Agreed."

"Let me see the pictures again. Maybe I do know who those dudes are."

Scarsdale laid the photographs out.

Olsen pointed at Zarko. "I don't know his name." He looked up at Scarsdale. "For real, man. I don't know who he is. But I'll tell ya this—no one screws over him and walks, 'cept for the CEO. He's almost as friggin' mean as the CEO. See, me and Fergie, we're like passive G L's. G L's are—"

"Grown lizards. I know what the hell they are," Scarsdale said in a loud, sharp tone. "All I want are their frickin birth names." He glanced at the window, shaking his head as he clinched his mouth tight. The urge was almost over-powering. He wanted to pound Olsen's face into the table. If he ever caught Olsen near Shannon, they'd be doing Olsen's funeral.

Olsen jabbed his finger on Zarko's likeness in the picture. "This dude, when he gets pissed, he's a sadistic bastard." He looked at Scarsdale. "Unless the CEO is the one pissin' on him."

"Meaning what?" Scarsdale felt his heart beating faster. "He kills little girls when they don't do what he wants?"

"Yeah, that's it. If one of his girls resists or fights back, he goes nuts. Me and Ferguson didn't want nuthin' to do with that sonofabitch."

"Do you know of any girls who didn't do what he wanted recently?"

Olsen took a quick glance up at Scarsdale's hulking body. The detective had one hand on the back of Olsen's chair, the other rested on the table in front of him. "No, man. He don't talk much to any of us." He leaned away from Scarsdale and wouldn't look at him again.

"Has he ever mentioned the name Amy Crowell?"

Olsen's eyes were fixed on the table and he was shaking like a leaf in a windstorm. "I said, no, man."

Scarsdale knew Olsen was lying as well as scared. "Is Zarko the one who took Amy's bracelet?"

"If I had my deal—"

Scarsdale sat on the corner of the table. "This other dude. The one who wears a mask, tell me what you know about him."

"Like I told ya last time, he's the one who chopped off Fergie's arm. He didn't like to get his hands dirty so we did the videos and took the pictures. He sold them."

"And you don't know his name, where he works, lives, nothing?" Scarsdale said, leaning closer to Olsen's face.

Olsen shot Scarsdale a furtive glance. "Like I told ya, nobody knows his name. He's real underground about who he is."

"You see him on a regular basis? Does he live around here?"

Olsen stared at Scarsdale before looking at the one-way window.

Scarsdale saw Olsen swallow hard. Tiny beads of sweat formed on his forehead. He licked his lips.

"Well? Does he?" Scarsdale demanded.

"Call the jailer. I want to go back to my cell."

"Not until you answer my question."

"I don't fuckin' know," he yelled. "How many goddam times do I have to say it?"

Scarsdale got real close to Olsen's face.

Olsen stared straight ahead. His Adam's apple bounced up and down.

"Who killed Amy Crowell and where is her bracelet?"

Olsen shook his head. "You're the detective. Figure it out."

Scarsdale pulled back. "You've got that bracelet, don't you?"

Olsen frowned as he glared at Scarsdale. "Hell, no."

"Who then?" Scarsdale almost grabbed Olsen by the hair but remembered the cameras on each end of the room.

"Get me my deal and you'll know everything."

"You helped the CEO murder Ferguson, didn't you?"

Olsen bristled. "Fuck you. Fergie was my friend, I'd never hurt him."

"If you were really his friend, you'd want to see his killer off the street. I can't do that until I have a name." Scarsdale stood up. "Hell, if this CEO finds out I've been talking to you, maybe he'll come after you, since you and Ferguson were so damn close."

"Jailer!" Olsen yelled. "I'm ready. Jailer!"

⌘

The next day, Harris and Scarsdale sat in their car watching Zarko. Scarsdale showed the Ferguson group photo to Harris.

"Those pictures put Zarko right in the middle of this ring. I'm sure Zarko killed Lasiter. Maybe he killed Amy Crowell and pinned it on Lasiter," Scarsdale said. "I mean, I hate to think about the fact that we screwed up and arrested the wrong guy and now he's dead."

"How do we prove it was Zarko? I mean he sure won't admit it. Olsen's too damn scared," Harris said.

"We get the DA to cut him a deal. That's how."

"Good luck with that," Harris said.

Scarsdale chewed on his lower lip. "There might be another way." He rubbed his hand across his face. "But I'm not that desperate—yet."

Harris studied the photograph. "What? Break into Zarko's house?"

Scarsdale smiled but said nothing.

Harris stared at him. "Oh shit, that's what you're thinking, isn't it?" He studied Scarsdale's face. "If Zarko catches you in his house and complains to the chief, your ass'll be toast. Robertson and Winters will see to it."

"Just relax, will you? But the longer that sorry shit stays on the street…well, let's find him and show him some pictures."

☙❧

Scarsdale and Harris followed Zarko to a Starbuck's in northwest Austin. "We'll corner him when he comes out," Scarsdale said, checking his watch. One o'clock. The nanny should be picking Shannon up from kindergarten right about now.

It seemed like ages ago, that "bring your kid to work Friday," when Dani had suggested a girls' night some time to Shannon. At the time he'd smiled and said it sounded like a great idea. Of course, Shannon had extracted a promise on that. Tonight would have been the girls' night and when Dani proposed it to Shannon after the dinner of leftovers, his daughter had gone over the moon. But with Zarko stalking Dani and his own suspicions of her involvement in Lasiter's death, Scarsdale had reneged on his promise.

"Thinking about Shannon?" Harris asked.

"Yeah. She's pissed at me," he said, glancing at Harris. "I had promised her before Thanksgiving she could spend the night at Dani's. But with Zarko hanging around that apartment complex, no way. I cancelled it." A half-smile crossed his face as he watched the front door of Starbuck's. "She pouted so I put her in time-out until I got dinner ready. She refused to eat. Sat there the whole time with her arms folded, scowling at her plate."

Harris chuckled. "She hates you now, right?"

"Yep. Said she was going to live with Dani," he said, rubbing his eyes.

"She'll get over it."

Sitting there watching the front door of the coffee shop, he glanced at his personal cell, remembering the text messages Charity used to send when he was on a surveillance.

"Speak of the devil," said Harris. "There he is."

Zarko stood outside, looking around while he picked his teeth. He popped a cigarette out and lit up. After one long drag, he looked right at them then crossed the street, heading right for them.

"I think he made us," Harris said as both he and Scarsdale got out of the car.

"Like I give a damn."

The three of them met near Scarsdale's car.

"I'm warning you," Zarko said, jabbing his finger at Scarsdale.

"Go ahead, Zarko." Scarsdale stepped close so Zarko's finger touched his chest. "Warn me."

Zarko dropped his hand down, turned sideways, and glared at Scarsdale over his shoulder. "Quit following me around or—"

"Or what?" Scarsdale asked, getting in Zarko's face. "You going beat me up like you did Lasiter?"

"You got nothin on me," Zarko said, taking a short drag off his cigarette and blowing smoke out his nose. He flicked ashes on the ground in front of Scarsdale then took another drag off the cigarette, blowing smoke rings.

Scarsdale plopped the Ferguson photographs down on the hood of his car. "Recognize anyone?"

Zarko gazed down at the pictures. Scarsdale saw him fix his stare at one in particular—the one with all five of them together.

Scarsdale pointed at Olsen, Ferguson and Sanchez. "Three convicted pedophiles. And who do we have here? Damn, looks just like you, shithead. Of course, you don't have to say a word. This guy already said a lot," Scarsdale said, tapping Olsen's picture. He normally wouldn't break a promise not to disclose his sources, but promises to pedophiles didn't count.

Zarko took another glance then looked at Scarsdale. "Ain't me. Musta photoshopped it." He stepped back and spit on the asphalt pavement in front of Scarsdale. He ground it into the pavement with his boot while looking at Scarsdale. The left corner of Zarko's mouth curled up into a smirk.

"Oh, it's you, shithead. Stabbed and slabbed by one of your own," Scarsdale said.

"Prove it." Then he walked away.

"Count on it," Scarsdale said as he looked down at the fast drying sputum. *Would have been a good DNA specimen,* he thought.

An hour later, Scarsdale's cell phone buzzed. Lieutenant Mitchell. "What's up, L T?"

"There's a Travis County deputy sheriff in the lobby waiting for you."

"What's he want?"

"How the hell do I know? Get in here and find out."

Fifteen minutes later, Scarsdale strode into the lobby. "You looking for me?" he said to the deputy.

"Are you Jason Scarsdale?"

"Yeah, what's up?"

"I have some papers to serve on you," the deputy said, handing a brown manila envelope to Scarsdale. "Sign here."

Scarsdale walked back to his office carrying the thick envelope. He ripped it open and pulled a packet of papers out. It was a petition entitled "In The Interest of Shannon Kara Scarsdale." Charity's mother had filed a lawsuit against him seeking full custody of Shannon. He collapsed in his chair and read the first page. It alleged that Jake and Marcy Piper, the child's grandparents, sought custody of Shannon and that Shannon's present circumstances posed a danger to her physical health and emotional well-being. The petition asked for temporary orders granting immediate conservatorship to the Pipers. He slammed the papers down on his desk. "That bitch!" he yelled, not caring who heard him.

A minute later, Harris waltzed into Scarsdale's office. "Who's a bitch?"

He glared at Harris then handed him the papers. "Can you frickin believe this? That bitch wants to take Shannon away from me."

"Well, let's go, buddy. You're going to meet the premier family law attorney in Texas. Bring your checkbook because she ain't cheap."

Within fifteen minutes they were sitting in Alissa McGowan's office. She perused the petition. "There's several allegations here stating you neglected Shannon and endangered her. This affidavit is from a former babysitter stating that you administered aspirin to your daughter while she had a cold? And that was the reason Shannon developed Reyes Syndrome. Is that true?"

"Hell, no. She's the one who did that." Scarsdale detailed the facts from that Tuesday. "I put a Tylenol bottle in Shannon's backpack and told Fran to use that if necessary. When I picked Shannon up off her couch, she said she gave her a children's aspirin." He turned toward Harris. "Isn't that the way you remember it?"

"Yep." Harris nodded once. "Sounds pretty accurate."

"What about leaving her unattended at home while you went to a crime scene?"

"The last time I was called out, Charity was home."

"And this—during their visit for Charity's funeral, Shannon being sick and telling Marcy she hadn't eaten in a while?"

He shook his head slightly in disgust. "What a crock. Shannon had a little cold, some sniffles." He laid his arms on the desk. "If Shannon said that about not eating, it's probably because I was pre-occupied with funeral arrangements. But she always had food to eat. Always. Hell, my sister was there. She can verify that. My parents, too."

"Here she alleges you spanked Shannon too hard, leaving bruises on her buttocks and legs."

"One time, I told her if she didn't settle down, I'd spank her. But I never laid a hand on my daughter." He wagged his finger in the air. "Not one single time." He felt the blood rushing to his face. "How the hell would she know how Shannon lived? She only visited her twice."

"Okay. Cases like these are almost always about finger-pointing, he-said, she-said fights. They invariably come down to who has the most convincing witnesses," Alissa said. "A hearing is set in two weeks for temporary orders. I want both of you here Friday a week from now so I can prep you. I'll need to interview your current babysitter too. And—" Alissa said, staring straight at Scarsdale, "—bring Shannon and her medical file here Monday. Is 10 a.m. all right?"

Scarsdale nodded. "She's in kindergarten until one. How about two o'clock?"

"Two's fine. And get me anything you have on your former babysitter." She gave Scarsdale a business card. "Do you have any witnesses who can testify about your father-daughter relationship?"

He swallowed hard. Fear crept over him like fog rolling in. Looking across the desk at the attorney, he asked, "What are their chances of taking Shannon? Like I said, they don't have much history with her. They saw her two times. Once right after she was born and again at Charity's funeral. Wouldn't the judge consider that and the trauma of yanking her away from the only home she's ever known?" He felt his heart racing. He wiped sweaty palms on his trouser legs.

Alissa wrote some notes. "That's a point we'll explore. I doubt the judge will look favorably on Marcy if that's the extent of her history with Shannon. He'll weigh all the facts and decide based on the best interests of the child. We need clear and convincing evidence that persuades the judge you're the best choice. That babysitter will ding you, but if we can put on sufficient evidence showing she lied, painting a picture of you as a fit, capable, and caring father, then we have a good shot. So...witnesses?" Her pen hovered over the legal pad as she eyed him, waiting.

"My sister, Sarah. My parents." He gestured with his thumb in Harris's direction. "Harris and..."

"My wife, Mary," Harris said. "And Dani Mueller."

Scarsdale hesitated. *Crap, I don't want her to testify. If Marcy found out...*

Alissa raised her eyebrows. "Will this Dani be able to testify from her personal knowledge that you're a good father?"

"Shannon is really attached to her. She works at the department. But I don't know if she's willing. Maybe I should visit with her first," Scarsdale said. He and Harris stood up to leave. Was Dani still pissed at him over his implication that she was the woman in Lasiter's closet? She did cut her trip to Germany short so she could see Shannon. *How mad would she be if I don't use her? Mad enough to sabotage my chances?*

"She'd love to," said Harris. "Shannon and Dani are pals, according to what Shannon told me."

Scarsdale looked at Harris, wishing his partner had kept his mouth shut.

"So what about her?" Alissa asked. "I want everyone who can testify that you are a good father. So if she can say that then, yes, bring her. Plus I'll need any dirt you have on your witnesses. Marcy's attorney will check them out and I do *not* like nasty surprises. And, Mr. Scarsdale, one more thing. I can't guarantee you will prevail. You might lose Shannon. While I like your chances, cases like these aren't slam-dunks."

She stood up and offered a handshake.

As Harris and Scarsdale walked to the car, Harris put his arm around Scarsdale's shoulder. "I wish I had a dollar for every time she said that and her client won." He chuckled. "I'd be a friggin' millionaire."

Scarsdale was not amused. "She may not be able to say it but I damn sure will. There's no way in hell they're getting Shannon." He kicked an empty coke can that sailed into the air and flew over the top of two cars in the parking lot. "Whatever it takes." He propped his arms on the roof of the car, staring in Harris's direction. "Two times since she was born." He held two fingers up. "Just two frickin times in five years." He slapped both hands on the car's roof before opening the door. "Good for nothing bitch."

As they drove out of the parking lot, Harris spoke up. "So who are your witnesses besides Dani?"

Scarsdale chewed on his lower lip for a few seconds. "I don't know if Dani would be a good choice, now that I think about it." He glanced at Harris. "You know she might be the woman in Lasiter's closet, which makes me wonder what else she may have done. And if Marcy found out, she'd have a frickin field day with that information."

"So vet her. The word is she's from California. Run her through the databases. Want me to make some calls?"

"No. I'll do some discreet checking. Damn sure don't want her to find out. She's already super-pissed at me."

"Well, buddy, she'll make a good witness about how close you and Shannon are, so if she's clean, I strongly suggest you fall on your sword and make-up with her."

Scarsdale rubbed his chin. *What the hell she was doing in Lasiter's closet? If I pressed her about it, would she get more pissed? And if she did, what would she do about it?*

"Hell, I'll ask her myself," said Harris.

"No." He cast a quick glance at Harris. "I'll do it. But first I want to check her out."

"Go for it," Harris said, wagging his finger at Scarsdale as they pulled up to the police building. "The department already ran her criminal history," Harris said, walking away. "I gotta go see what Mitchell wants. Be right back."

Scarsdale phoned an agent he knew with the California Bureau of Investigation and Intelligence—Wilson Camp. He had met Camp at a conference on violent crimes in San Francisco a few years ago.

"What can you tell me about a female named Dani Mueller?" Scarsdale asked, spelling her last name. "She had a daughter named Katarina who died about three or four years ago."

"I vaguely remember that case. There was a Katarina murdered around that time but she was the daughter of a woman, last name of Engel. It was a really nasty killing as I recall. I think Sacramento PD cleared it with an arrest."

Scarsdale heard the pounding of a keyboard.

"Give me a minute. I'm looking the case up." Camp said. "Want me to call you back?"

"No, I'll hold."

A couple of minutes passed.

"Got it. Yeah, the mother was Karla Engel. A lawyer in Sacramento. Seems a few days after a jury acquitted the ex-con, he turned up dead. His name was Burton. Doyle Burton.

"How was Katarina Engel killed?"

"Bludgeoned to death. A number of stab wounds to the body. The crime scene photos are pretty brutal."

"And Burton? How did he die?"

"Hacked and stabbed to death. Even sliced off his pecker."

"I assume Engel—"

"The grand jury no-billed her. Then his family got on her ass. Forced her to move to Rockford, Illinois. As for Dani Mueller's driver's license...hmm, interesting."

"What?"

"Her and Engel's DL files are flagged. But both women are clean as far as a criminal history."

"Flagged? What's that mean?" Scarsdale asked.

"Not sure. Might mean Engel invoked the protections of the Safe at Home Act."

"Can I get copies of their DL photos?" Were Dani and Karla one and the same? If they were, their driver's licenses photos would prove it.

"I'll have to check with my chain of command first. If they approve, I'll put a rush on it."

Scarsdale sat at his desk, digesting what the agent had said as well as what he omitted. Personally he couldn't blame Dani—for avenging Katarina's killing. If he had been in her shoes, he would have done the same thing. But, regardless, she seemed to be a magnet for trouble—Zarko was after her and possibly these Burtons as well. He didn't need her dragging that baggage into Shannon's world. He phoned Alissa.

"I think we have enough witnesses without putting Dani on the stand."

"Jason, to win, I have to persuade this judge you're a great father. To do that, I need *all* the evidence and solid testimony favorable to our side I can acquire. I cannot and *will not* go in that courtroom with a barebones case. So let me ask you. Does Dani have a criminal history?"

He sighed. "No." He couldn't tell her about the closet suspicions since revealing matters from a pending investigation would violate the department's general orders forbidding such disclosure.

"Some kind of relationship difficulties with you?"

"Of course not."

"Then what's the problem?"

"I just thought we had enough with my sister, parents, and Shannon's nanny."

"Have Dani call me today."

❧❦❧

He stopped in Dani's doorway. She sat there with her back to the door. Talking to someone in German. *Maybe she's making plans to move back to Germany. That would solve everything.* He heard the word, *"Wiedersehen."* Scarsdale knew a total of three German words. *Wiedersehen* was one of them. When she hung up he walked in, right up behind her. "Hi, Dani."

She lurched forward and spun around. She looked like she'd seen a ghost. Her eyes quickly narrowed as she shot him a scathing look that seemed to bore a hole right through him. "You scared me. What do you want?"

"Sorry." His eyes darted around the room, as he tried to think of the right words. Finally they came to rest on her. "I'm really sorry about the other night. It's my job to check out every lead I get on a case. And I will do my job, no matter whose toes I step on. I hope you understand."

"And I hope you're satisfied that I had nothing to do with Lasiter's death."

He smiled. "I'll take your word for it." He had his suspicions but, for Shannon's sake and the custody hearing, he'd bite the bullet and give her the benefit of the doubt for now.

"I don't want you to take my word for it. Like I said, I want you to be satisfied that I had nothing to do with his murder."

He knew she had nothing to do with the actual killing but still had no answer whether she was the one in the closet, and if so, why was she there. "I'm satisfied you had nothing to do with his murder, okay?"

Harris and Alissa had backed him in a corner. He had to ask her to be a witness. *Maybe she'll decline. Maybe she'll be out of town that day.* "I have a favor to ask," he said into the silence that followed. "But if you can't do it for whatever reason, I'll understand."

"Speak," she said, folding her arms across her chest, staring at him, her jaw clenched tight.

"My former mother-in-law is suing for custody of Shannon. My attorney wants as many witnesses as I can muster to testify that I'm a good father to Shannon. But if you already have—"

"When is the hearing?" she asked, turning toward her desk.

"Right now, it's scheduled in two weeks."

He watched her flip her calendar open, checking dates. "If you already have plans—I heard you talking to your family in Germany. I've got some witnesses—"

"I'll think about it," Dani said, still looking at her calendar. "Is that it?" She turned around to face him. Her lips pressed together.

Scarsdale nodded then turned for the door. He felt a sense of relief. *Well, I asked. Sarah and the others will be enough anyway. Maybe I could get our priest to testify.*

As he walked out of her office, he wondered if Shannon would like to play some video games at that big new arcade on Highway 183. He'd heard their hot dogs were good and she loved hot dogs.

Suddenly he felt a tug on his arm.

"Wait a minute," Dani said.

He spun around and faced her. "What?"

She stopped a foot away from him. Her breath smelled like peppermint. "I'll do it."

His eyebrows arched up, making creases in his forehead. *Oh shit*! It took him a few seconds to speak. "Dani, if you have a trip planned or something on your calendar, please don't rearrange your schedule. I'd love to have you help me but not at the expense of you having to cancel some important event."

"Not a problem."

He gazed at her through squinted eyes. "Are you sure?"

"Positive," she said, her thumb and forefinger twisting a strand of hair by her ear.

Pulling Alissa's business card out of his pocket, he stared at it, hesitating, wondering if he should give it to her. *Maybe Marcy will come to her senses and call this stupid hearing off.*

He handed Dani the card. "Here's my attorney's number. She wanted you to call her today."

෴

Right after lunch, Scarsdale's office phone rang. Alissa McGowan's name and phone number showed on the screen.

"Mr. Scarsdale, I have some bad news."

"Give it to me." *She did it. She took her revenge. Dani screwed me over.*

"As you wish. Your in-laws claim that Charity called them the day before she died and said she was afraid of you and that she was leaving and taking Shannon home to them. According to your mother-in-law, Charity said you beat her up, leaving bruises on her body. Is any of that true? Their attorney plans to amend their petition to include those allegations."

"That's total *bullshit*," he yelled. "Charity wasn't afraid of anyone, most of all me. And I never hit her. Never! Besides if she was leaving, why was she still living with me the day she died?"

"The thing you have to realize is that smear campaigns are the type of tactics common in custody battles. Mole hills become mountains."

"So do bald-faced lies."

"Do you still have your phone bills from back then?"

"Yes, I think so."

"House phone and cell phones."

"I've got all of them."

"Bring me all of them."

"I'll get the 911 phone logs too."

"No, I'll get them along with a custodian's affidavit so they'll be in admissible form."

"Anything else?"

"Yes, I need to hire a private investigator to go up to your in-laws' town and snoop around. I need your permission to do that. There's a real good one up there named Sherry Kipper but she doesn't work cheap."

"Do it. Let me ask you something—can I recover my expenses if we win?

"Sure, unless Marcy's judgment-proof."

"So, any good news?"

"Yes. Dani will make a helluva great witness for you. I can't believe you wanted to pass her up."

How fucking wonderful. Once Marcy's lawyer questions Dani about her background and the Secretary of State flags. Dammit." He punched the wall. *I hope Shannon will like living in a foreign country.*

He needed a Plan B. Just like he and Charity had conjured up when her parents tried to put the screws to their wedding plans. Some place where they didn't honor US extradition requests. He had a lot of money in his savings account. Plus his retirement account and the insurance company's settlement of Charity's accident which he had planned to put into a trust for Shannon's college.

"At the temporary hearing, I expect the court will order a social study done. A social worker will visit your home. She'll take a tour of your home, spend time alone with Shannon, and interview you with and without Shannon present. That report plus what is presented to the judge in the hearing will form the basis for his decision. I'm not going to sugarcoat this. If your in-laws prevail at this level, it's going to be a really tough uphill fight for you to get Shannon back. Almost impossible."

CHAPTER 16

"Hot heads and cold hearts never solved anything."
~ *Anonymous*

Scarsdale lay there, listening to the ticking of his bedside clock while his eyes tracked the shifting shadows across the ceiling. Swinging his legs over the edge, he checked the time. One thirty in the morning. Rubbing his eyes, he headed out the door and down the hall toward Shannon's room. Peeking around the corner of the door, he saw her asleep, facing the door with her arm draped over the Bavarian doll.

Taking a deep breath, he pivoted around and headed to the kitchen. A glass of milk might help him sleep—sleep he needed since the custody hearing, after too many delays, would finally happen at ten o'clock today. As he sipped the milk, he leafed through some papers he left on the counter—his latest savings account statement and airline options for Samoa and Micronesia. Even though he vowed not to allow Marcy to take Shannon, doubts arose—would this be the right message to send Shannon? Would he be exchanging one bad situation for another? Would Shannon be able to adapt to a whole new culture? Would she tolerate not seeing her grandparents until she grew up? What would Shannon think of her father? What would his parents think?

∽∾∽

Scarsdale trudged into the courthouse, flashing his badge so he could bypass security. He stopped at the rear of a throng of people maneuvering to get an elevator. He checked to see where the four elevators were—one was stopped on floor three, another just arrived at the fifth floor and two seemed stuck on Eight. People elbowed their way closer to the doors—even he got jostled. A distinct odor of alcohol, mixed with cheap perfume and a trace of marihuana, made him sneeze a couple of times.

Looking around, Scarsdale didn't recognize anyone connected with his dreaded hearing. He leaned against the wall and let his thoughts drift. The events of the past five years flashed through his mind. The wedding Marcy refused to attend. Then Charity's funeral—the second time Marcy had seen Shannon since she was born—gushing over her granddaughter, telling Shannon how much she missed her.

Scarsdale stopped outside the big wooden courtroom doors. He stared at the brass door handles. *What will the judge decide*? His heart hammered against his chest. Taking a couple of deep breaths and swallowing hard, he pulled the courtroom doors open.

He sat at the large counsel table with Alissa while she perused a Southwestern Reporter and checked notes scribbled on a yellow pad. Across from him sat Charity's mother, Marcy, glaring at him with disdain. Her attorney, R. Dalton Wellington III, exchanged glances with Scarsdale and nodded politely. Wellington's side of the table looked like a law library—a stack of law books, more files, and a couple of legal pads with pens at the ready.

Behind Marcy sat an older female dressed in a blue pants suit, leafing through a file folder. Another woman, in designer jeans, sat near her. Alissa told Scarsdale they were Marcy's witnesses—one was a child psychologist and the other was a private investigator.

Mrs. Hargraves, Sarah, Harris, Mary, and Dani sat on the row behind Scarsdale. Mitchell, Shannon's kindergarten teacher, and Alissa's PI sat about ten feet apart on the benches behind them. He caught the profile of another person in the room, seated all the way in the back—Winters, his eyes like black dots, fixed on Scarsdale like a big cat stalking its prey.

Associate Judge Judith R. Kemper would be presiding. Alissa told him that in the majority of cases where the child was under the age of ten, Kemper denied the father custody. But those cases involved mother versus father. She said this would be a case of first impression for the judge and Alissa wouldn't venture so much as a guess as to what the outcome would be.

Scarsdale's thoughts drifted back to earlier that morning when he stood at his front door. Shannon ran to him, wanting a hug. He looked down at her, wondering if this would be the last day they would be together as a family. He didn't realize how scared he was until he saw his hands. They were shaking like leaves in a windstorm. The nightmarish thought raced through his mind. *Will the judge really take Shannon away from me?* That he might lose his reason for existing, for being alive, scared the hell out of him.

The two of them had bonded in the past month. He had done more with her in the past month than over the last five years—taking trips to SeaWorld and Fiesta, Texas, the beach at Port Aransas, bumper cars at the arcade, TV in the evening, and the two of them preparing dinner. He'd learned so much about her over the past few weeks that he hadn't known when Charity was alive. Like the other night, tucking her in bed, he gazed at her face. A single thought washed over him. *So this is what it's like to be a father.*

After the witnesses vacated the courtroom, Marcy took the stand. "Charity told me that he beat her up and used a rawhide strap on Shannon." Marcy glared at Scarsdale. "She was in tears over his—" Marcy pointed at Scarsdale. "—physical and verbal abuse of her and Shannon. She told me that she planned to leave him and bring Shannon to our home." Marcy wiped her eyes with a tissue. "She never got that chance." She went on to say that she feared for Shannon's safety if she continued to reside with "*him.*"

"Excuse me, but, for the record, exactly who is 'him'?" Judge Kemper asked Marcy.

Marcy gestured at Scarsdale. "You know—'*him.*'"

Judge Kemper smiled. "Let the record reflect that 'him' is the respondent, Mr. Scarsdale."

Marcy's attorney questioned her about the additional allegations of neglect, particularly the events around the funeral.

"When we took Shannon to lunch, she said she hadn't eaten since the day before."

On cross, Marcy admitted she couldn't recall for sure when Charity said he beat her or Shannon. She also admitted that, on the day of the funeral, she didn't actually see any welts on Shannon's legs. Marcy conceded under intense questioning from Alissa that maybe she misunderstood what Shannon said about not eating but added that Shannon appeared to be malnourished.

"Your honor, in light of Ms. Piper's new allegation regarding the child appearing malnourished, we plan to call her pediatrician to testify as a rebuttal witness."

The judge looked to Wellington. "Any objection?"

Wellington shut his eyes for a moment, like he wished Marcy had kept her mouth shut, then shook his head. "No, your honor."

Scarsdale rolled his eyes. He gripped the edge of the counsel table so hard his fingers turned white. Then banged the table with his fist. *Aggravated perjury is a felony, you lying bitch.* He saw Judge Kemper give him a hard stare.

Wellington's next witness was the psychologist, Doctor Jillian Acton. Her testimony was based upon her opinion that children in Shannon's age group fared better with a maternal figure than with a single father. She said maternal figures provided the emotional support and nurturing that Shannon needed. Because of this, she said, someone like Marcy Piper would surpass a father who was unresponsive to a young daughter's needs. She said police detectives, who work long hours and were subject to being called out to work during the night, tore at the heart of the family bond. She opined that Shannon would more likely prefer her maternal grandmother since Marcy would be more involved with her than Mr. Scarsdale.

Alissa framed her cross-examination question to Dr. Acton. "Assuming that Shannon would be better off living in the home of a female relative, Mr. Scarsdale's mother would be equally preferable. Wouldn't she?"

Dr. Acton answered, "I didn't mean to exclude Mrs. Scarsdale."

"Or even Mr. Scarsdale's sister?"

"Yes, of course." Dr. Acton sounded slightly irritated.

"And regarding his sister, Sarah, if she had children the same age as Shannon, she'd be even more preferable to either grandparent, wouldn't she?"

Dr. Acton cast an apologetic glance at Marcy and cleared her throat. "Certainly."

The former babysitter, Fran Tisdale, was the last performer in Marcy's menagerie of misinformation and deceit. Scarsdale's blood boiled when she laid the blame for the aspirin fiasco squarely at his feet.

He jumped when Dani tapped his elbow, handing him a note. When he unfolded it, it read "Stop looking like you're a whipped puppy." He glanced at Dani who shot him an angry glance before turning away.

Alissa called Dani followed by Harris to the stand. Dani testified about Shannon's unfaltering expressions of love for her father—both physical and verbal, adding that she never observed any bruising or other indicators of child abuse on Shannon.

Scarsdale smiled because Wellington got nowhere when he tried to trip Dani up by rephrasing her prior answers and asking trick questions. When Dani stepped off the stand, Wellington had exasperation written all over his face.

Alissa called Sarah to the stand. Sarah testified about staying at Scarsdale's house beginning the day after Charity was killed until well after the funeral.

"During your time there, did Shannon ever tell you she hadn't been fed?"

Sarah gave Marcy an angry glare. "No, she did not."

"Did you prepare meals during that time period for Shannon?" Alissa asked, turning to face Marcy and smiling.

"Yes, I prepared three meals a day each day I was there."

"And you were there for how long?" Alissa asked, still watching Marcy.

Alissa next offered to tender Shannon to testify as to who administered the aspirin. After a long session in sidebar between the judge and the two attorneys, Judge Kemper stated into the record that both sides agreed to the dismissal of the allegation that Scarsdale gave Shannon the aspirin.

At that point, Judge Kemper called a halt to any further testimony. She ordered Alissa to produce Shannon today so she could interview her in chambers alone. Then she ordered a social study on both households. She informed both Scarsdale and Marcy that she'd render a decision once she visited with Shannon and read the completed study.

Outside the courtroom, while Alissa and Wellington discussed issues away from their clients, Marcy approached Scarsdale, a snide grin on her face. "Make sure all of Shannon's clothes and toys are packed up for the trip. Shannon's going home with me. Loser."

He stood there for a full second, staring down at her. "You're just like a damn cow, bellowing and shitting."

Before he could say anything else, Sarah, Dani, and Harris pulled him away.

"C'mon, buddy. Let's get some lunch," Harris said, heading down the hall. Dani and Sarah, walking on each side of Scarsdale, gripped their hands tight around his forearms.

If any of Scarsdale's group had bothered to look back, they'd have seen Winters watching them.

಄ಞ಄

Zarko checked his watch as he walked past the concierge desk to the hotel's elevators. 4:15 p.m. Alone on the elevator, he pushed the button for the fourteenth floor. Getting off there, he strode to the stairwell door and, looking back to be sure he wasn't followed, darted down the steps, vaulting several at a time, to the next floor.

Once again checking to be sure he wasn't followed, he walked up to Room 1364 and, standing directly in front of the peephole as instructed, knocked on the door. After a few seconds, the door opened.

A spacious room with a two-seat sofa, a desk and chair, and a king-sized bed was revealed. The room smelled fresh, like the maid had sprayed Spring Boutique air freshener.

The door closed behind him. "Did you follow my instructions about checking for a tail?" a husky male voice asked.

"I didn't see anyone," Zarko said, turning to face him. He saw the ski mask covering the man's face.

"That's not what I asked you. Do I have to repeat it?" The man leaned closer to Zarko, eyeing the scar. "What happened to you?"

Zarko stepped back and swallowed, running his fingers down the scabbed up gash on his cheek. "Nothing. Happened at work."

"So, did you follow my instructions?"

"Yes, sir. I did exactly what you told me to do." Zarko knew what would happen if he said otherwise or confronted the man. Ferguson's carved up body was reminder enough.

The man slapped Zarko on the back of his head, hard enough to knock his head forward. "Good. Now what do you want? Make it quick," he said, checking his watch. "I need to be somewhere in half an hour."

"I got a problem that needs fixing," Zarko said as he peeked out the curtained-off window.

"The blonde-haired woman in Lasiter's house, right?" The man shoved Zarko away from the open window. "Keep the damn curtain closed."

Zarko saw a little more of the black and green tattoo when the CEO pulled the curtains closed but still couldn't make out the design. He moved away from the window and nodded. "Yes, sir."

"Do you know who she is?" the man asked, pouring some whiskey in a glass then handing it to Zarko.

Zarko shook his head. "Not by name. But she knows I

killed Lasiter. She was there." He took a long swallow of whiskey.

"So you followed her home," he said, placing a plastic red and white striped straw into his own glass before guiding the straw into the mask's opening for his mouth.

Zarko nodded, "Yes, sir." He belted down the last of his drink.

"Please tell me you didn't do something else dumb."

"No, of course not." He kept quiet about attacking Dani outside her apartment, hoping the CEO didn't know about it. The man seemed to know about everything else.

"And now you know where she lives and what she looks like. And she knows exactly who you are, too." He slowly traced his finger along the exposed metal parts of a holstered Glock 9mm lying on the desk, then looked at Zarko.

Zarko chewed on his lower lip as he watched him stroke the gun's grips. His skin tingled. He felt the hairs on the back of his neck stand up "How do you know that?"

The man started to take a sip then lowered the glass. "Tinker Bell told me. And I know about the detectives talking to you at her apartment. And by the way, dumbass, she works for the police. She's a crime analyst."

He swallowed hard. "So what do I do? She can identify me." Zarko felt the blood drain from his face when the man screwed a silencer into the barrel of his gun.

"Maybe we should fix it so there's nothing to identify."

Zarko backed away, his eyes wide open. A fearful expression on his face. "Are you going to—"

"Shoot you?" The man approached him, waving the gun slowly. "Hmmm, now there's an idea." He circled around Zarko, waving the gun. "I formed this little enterprise because there's a lot of money to be made in it. So long as we all adhere to the code of secrecy I set out. But when my associates keep screwing up—and I'm still quite upset about Ferguson. I hated that he forced me to kill him."

He pressed the gun against Zarko's forehead. "Put yourself in my shoes. I have a lot to lose should Scarsdale discover who I am. Money I earmarked for my retirement. My freedom. My reputation for being a peaceful and law-abiding citizen." He slid the gun down Zarko's face to his eye then over to the other eye. "I have two beautiful kids that I love very much. And it makes me very angry when an idiot like you threatens my relationship with them."

He jabbed the barrel against Zarko's nostril, pushing his head back. "So I ask you, what would you do if you were in my shoes?"

"I'll fix things. I'll kill her. Then you won't have anything to worry about," he said hurriedly. He raised his hand up to push the gun away.

The man lowered the gun. "Sure, idiot, kill her and have every cop in a hundred miles hunting for your dumb ass." He thumped Zarko on the head a few times with the barrel of the gun. "Hello. Anyone in there?" he asked. "Did you not hear me—I said she works for the police," the CEO said, dragging the gun barrel down the gash on Zarko's cheek.

"Don't do anything. Lay low for a while," the CEO said, now jabbing the gun barrel hard into Zarko's chest, making him stagger backward. "If you had stayed the hell away from her like I told you before, you wouldn't be in this bind. So don't compound your stupidity with another exhibition of mo-ronic behavior." The man wagged the gun in Zarko's face. "If you choose once again to disregard my advice and do some-thing stupid to her, if you so much as make her stub her little toe, you'll end up just like Ferguson. Understand?" He held out his hand. "Now I believe you have something for me."

Zarko reached inside his shirt and pulled a DVD out, handing it to the CEO.

The CEO smacked him on top of the head with it. "Stay away from her."

"Easy for you to say. You're not the one whose ass is on the—"

The man snapped his head around, giving Zarko a side-ways stare. "What was that?" Then he turned to face him. "You have something clever to say to me?"

Zarko's eyes widened at the gun barrel now pointed at him. He shrank back. "No, sir."

"Then we understand each other?"

"Yes, sir."

The CEO sucked up the last of his drink. "Police officers tend to be very protective of their own kind. This woman's every bit a member of their own kind. You get where I'm coming from?"

Zarko watched as the man poured himself another drink. "I get it. I'll leave the bitch alone."

Holding the bottle up, he looked at Zarko. "Want one for the road?"

"No, thank you."

Zarko grabbed the doorknob.

"I'm not finished with you."

Pivoting around slowly, Zarko looked at the man suspiciously. "What?"

"There's a little matter I want you to handle. At the county jail." He motioned for Zarko to come back. The man hung his arm around Zarko's shoulder then told him what he wanted done.

୧୭୧୭

The day after the hearing in family court, Scarsdale sat at his desk when Olsen's attorney, Manuel Fernandez, appeared at his cubicle. "Good afternoon, detective."

"What can I do for you, Mr. Fernandez?" he asked, closing the open case file.

"I represent Terry Wayne Olsen. He wants to make a deal but he's terrified of reprisals."

"Like from Tom Zarko?"

"No, another man. Someone he called the CEO."

"Well, until he's ready to talk, there's not much I can do," Scarsdale said returning to his paperwork.

"The US Marshals have a witness protection program. You could get the ball rolling with them. Once that's done, he'll tell you anything you want to know."

"And testify in court against Zarko and whoever the CEO guy is?"

"Yes, and anyone else involved."

Anyone else? That got Scarsdale's attention. "He'll snitch off the entire group?"

"Yes, all of them as well as the CEO. And the buyers. But, detective, it must be the federal program, not the state one." He handed Scarsdale his business card. "You can reach me at either of those numbers at the bottom."

Scarsdale typed up the supplementary report about Olsen's request and forwarded it to Mitchell.

A few minutes later, Mitchell stood at his cubicle. "Does the DA know about this?"

"Sorry. I forgot. I'll brief them right now." He cursed himself for being so absent-minded today. His mind was on Alissa's expected phone call. The judge was to make her decision earlier this morning.

"Let me know when you find out so I can forward this to Commander Robertson."

Scarsdale made two calls—to the DA's office and to the US Marshal's Office. A half hour later, Mitchell, Harris, and Scarsdale sat in Robertson's office.

"Do you really think the feds will approve this?" Robertson asked, adjusting his blue tie.

"I don't really know," Scarsdale said. "But it's certainly worth a try. If he'll net us the whole group, we have to ask."

"Okay. Do it," Robertson said. "Before you go, Scarsdale, I want to have a word with you."

Mitchell hesitated by the door. "Should I stay—"

Robertson waved dismissively at Mitchell. "I just need Scarsdale."

"Close the door and have a seat," Robertson said. He opened a file folder then looked at Scarsdale for a couple of seconds. "Tell me how this Lasiter case is progressing." Robertson reclined back in his chair, his elbows resting on the arms, staring at Scarsdale.

Scarsdale knew Robertson had some other reason for asking for a private briefing. "May I ask why? You get a copy of our reports. Everything is in there."

Robertson sat up, laying his arms on the desk. His brows narrowed. "You're right, I do. But I want to actually visit with you about something else." His tight-lipped expression shifted slowly into a thin smile. "I've been informed that you're dating Sex Crimes analyst, Dani Mueller. Is that correct?"

Scarsdale laughed. "Who told you that?"

"Answer my question. Is that true?"

"She and my daughter hit it off, so, yeah, we've spend some free time with her. But—"

Robertson rocked slowly back and forth. "You do remember the departmental general order about dating co-workers, don't you?"

"Yes, sir, but I'm not—"

"No buts. I have to admit I'm disappointed in you," he said, reclining back. "You're a professional. I thought you were smarter than that. You leave me with no choice. I have to report this to Commander Winters for whatever action he deems appropriate. Understand?" Robertson's lips curled into a faint smile.

Scarsdale's face flushed. "I'm *not* dating her. I never said I was. But I'm sure that omission won't matter to you. You've been gunning for me ever since that overtime appeal."

Robertson steepled his fingers. "Speaking of gunning for someone, I'm curious, detective. What satisfaction did you realize from telling my then wife that I screwed a woman in the backseat of my city car? How did that make you feel?"

Scarsdale looked at him quizzically. "You still believe I did that?"

"I *know* you did it."

"You're crazier than a shithouse mouse if you believe for a minute I'd do something like that—even to you."

Robertson walked around the desk and opened the door. "Depending on Commander Winters's decision, I want that Lasiter case cleared by the end of next week or I'll replace you. Now get out."

Later, Harris corralled Scarsdale in his cubicle. "What did he want with you?"

"He wants the Lasiter case solved by the end of next week. And he said he reported me to *Herr* Winters regarding my relationship with Dani." He rolled his eyes. "Like we really have a dating relationship."

"That's bullshit," Harris said.

Scarsdale turned to face him. "We close Lasiter or he'll replace me." He sat down at his desk, eyeing the stack of files. "We need to find out for sure whether Dani was the woman in the closet."

Harris sighed. "Any word from the Marshals?"

"Yeah, they'll mail me the paperwork but said it's not a slam-dunk that Olsen will qualify. He's got to provide them and us with a summary of his involvement, including the names of everyone else involved and their respective roles. Then the US Attorney's office has a number of added hoops for him to jump through."

His phone rang. Caller ID showed it to be Alissa McGowan.

He motioned for Harris to sit down.

"Congratulations, Jason. Judge Kemper ruled for you. But—"

Scarsdale's heart raced as he leaped up from his chair. "Great news! Thank you so much." He pumped his fist.

"Don't get too excited. You're definitely in the catbird seat but think of this hearing as a practice run for Marcy. Now she knows what her mistakes were and what our witnesses will say. It's not over yet. We still have the big trial to get past yet. The district judge could reverse that decision unless Marcy backs down."

"That'll never happen." Scarsdale's excitement faded. "Has the judge reversed those decisions before? Judge Kemper is her associate judge and Judge Marshall did delegate the case to her."

"Rarely do district judges overrule their magistrates, but it could happen."

A period of silence. He heard the rustling of papers.

"Now, Judge Kemper fashioned temporary orders. I mailed a copy to you. Marcy gets visitation one weekend a month restricted to one hundred miles of Austin unless you two mutually agree to other times and places."

"Mutually agree with her? Ha! That has about as much chance as a snowball in hell."

Alissa admonished him. "Jason, you have to be willing to compromise. After all, she is Shannon's grandmother. If you become intransigent, Marcy would have ammunition to add to her petition. Also, her attorney said she may seek grandparent access in a separate action."

He sighed. "Okay."

"Marcy's attorney asked me about a final settlement which includes visitation one weekend every other month, alternating Christmas holidays and one week in the summer. However, if you two don't come to some agreement, we gear up for the big trial. If we work something out, of course, there'll be no trial."

"If we agree, she can't take her out of the state, right?"

"Right."

"Okay, let's do it." Shannon needed to have contact with her grandparents, even if the grandmother was a bitch. It's what Charity would have wanted, he thought. "But I won't agree to any visitation out of state, under any circumstances. I don't trust her."

"I understand. How do you feel about her visiting Shannon at your home?

He sucked in a deep breath. "Okay."

"Good. He and I will draft the agreement for everybody's signature."

"I won't have to go back to court?"

"Not if we work this out. I'll be in touch," Alissa said.

Scarsdale leaned back in his chair, slowly swiveling it back and forth, clasping his hands together behind his head. A huge weight had been lifted off his shoulders.

"Feeling better now?" Harris asked.

"Yeah, I'm good. If I had a tail, I'd wag it." He leaned over and hi-fived Harris. "Shannon stays with me. Thanks to you and Mary—and Dani."

"Take Dani to lunch." Harris quickly held up his hands. "Oh wait, forget that. Robertson would have your ass."

"I'll go tell her how the custody hearing turned out. No harm in that."

His office phone rang. The caller ID showed "State of California."

"Hey, Scarsdale, Wilson Camp here. I'm faxing the DL photo of Karla Engel to you now. And I found out something else. Don't let anyone know what I'm about to tell you. It'd be my ass and I'm not kidding. Understand?"

"I won't say a word."

"Karla Engel and Dani Mueller are one and the same. Seems after the grand jury cleared her, Burton's family harassed the shit out of her. They were so bad she got a legal name change and hauled ass. If you want details about her daughter's murder and Burton's killing, call Detective Sam Goodnight at Sacramento PD."

"Thanks, Wilson. I owe you big time."

"What was that all about,' Harris asked.

Scarsdale sat there, thinking, while tapping the phone against his nose, his eyes in a faraway stare.

Harris waved his hand in front of Scarsdale's face. "Hey. You in there?" He slapped Scarsdale's arm. "Hey!"

Scarsdale blinked then looked at him. "Huh? Oh sorry. Just thinking about something." He punched in Detective Goodnight's number and waited as it rang. When Goodnight answered, Scarsdale introduced himself.

"I'm looking for information on an attorney from your city named Karla Engel. I understand you're familiar with her." The sound of the fax made him glance at it. Karla Engel's driver's license photo was coming through.

"Yep. She used to work for us as an analyst till she got her law license."

"Can you tell me what happened to her?" he asked, pulling the faxed photo off the tray. He stared at it for a few seconds then handed it to Harris.

"It's Dani. So?" Harris said.

Scarsdale held up a finger, asking Harris to wait. He heard Goodnight take a deep breath and let it out.

"Close to four years ago, her daughter's body turned up in a city park. Sexually assaulted and beaten really bad. The kid's face was totally unrecognizable. One of the worst cases I'd ever seen. Used DNA to ID the body. Anyway we arrested an ex-con named Doyle Burton but a jury let him go. A real classy guy. Been to prison twice for sex assault and burglary. A few days after his trial, some city workers found his body in another park. Butchered. Disemboweled. Bludgeoned with a bat. His pecker cut clean off."

"And this Karla did that?"

"Yeah, I think so."

"Ya'll arrest her?" Scarsdale asked.

"Nope. But the DA took her to a grand jury. They refused to indict her. If they had, no jury in this state would've convicted her except for maybe littering." Goodnight chuckled. "Officially I can't say Burton got what he deserved but personally—no one here lost any sleep over his demise. Anyway, after that, Burton's mother and her inbred kids terrorized the hell of her."

"So where is Karla Engel now?"

"Word is she's practicing law over near Chicago somewhere." A few seconds of silence. "Rockford, Illinois."

After hanging up, Scarsdale sat there, mum.

Harris slapped the picture with the back of his hand. "You had them fax a photo of Dani?"

Scarsdale pointed at it. "That's Karla Engel." He filled him in on what Goodnight said about Karla and Burton, then reached for the picture.

"Twin sisters?"

Scarsdale shook his head. "Nope. One and the same. She changed her name." Scarsdale briefed Harris on Agent Camp's information. Then he stuffed Dani's picture facedown at the very bottom of his lower drawer, under a thick stack of papers and folders. The same drawer where he always dumped stuff he had little interest in working.

He looked at Harris, took a deep breath and blew it out. "Dani's the woman in the closet."

Harris sat back, looking at Scarsdale like he just had an epiphany. He started to say something.

Scarsdale noticed the look. "Nope, I'm not telling anyone about what happened in California. She's been through hell but I can't risk letting her near Shannon."

"Why not?"

"First, Marcy'd have a field day if she ever found out. Second, with Zarko stalking Dani and if the Burtons find her…" He sighed. "I don't want Shannon caught in the middle." He whistled, shaking his head. "She has to tell us what happened at Lasiter's now. We're running out of time."

CHAPTER 17

"Malice drinks one-half of its own poison."
~ *Seneca*

I had enough experience as a lawyer to recognize a fishing expedition when I saw one. Robertson and Winters's smirky expressions said it all.

"Ms. Mueller, I understand that the prime suspect in the Lasiter murder, a man named Zarko, has been stalking you. Is that right?" Robertson asked.

Winters picked up Katarina's photograph. "Your daughter?"

"Yes, she—" I ignored Robertson's question, hoping he'd forget about it.

"Why would he be stalking you?" Robertson asked.

"Very pretty. Like her mother." Winters stared at her picture for a few seconds. "What's her name?"

"Thank you. It's Katarina," I answered without thinking.

"And what grade is Katarina in?"

"She passed away a few years ago." *You dummy, why did you tell him her name?*

Winters set the picture down. "I'm very sorry." He walked over to a map of Austin I had pinned up on the wall.

"I believe you were about to tell me about Zarko stalking you," Robertson asked.

I assumed he'd gotten that information from Scarsdale's reports. "I don't know if it meets the legal definition of stalking but, yes, I understand he's been observed hanging around my apartment."

Winters glanced at me over his shoulder. "And I suppose you have no clue how he found out where you live, do you?"

"Not really. Why are you asking?" I shifted my gaze from Robertson to Winters.

"This is very interesting. I never realized the number of thefts that happened in Austin." He tilted his head and leaned closer to the map. "Seems like the majority are across the river in south Austin."

"It would seem so. Look, I really need to finish this report for my boss." I hoped they'd take the hint.

"In your position, I'm certain you're familiar with Zarko's background, aren't you?" Robertson asked. He peered down at me and I didn't like his arrogant stance.

Winters turned around to face me, his arms folded across his chest.

"Yes, of course." They weren't going to take a hint. I'd need to be blunt.

"I'm wondering why he's stalking you," Robertson said.

I didn't like where this was headed. "Why don't you ask him? At a later time tell me. Then we'll both know."

A snide laugh from Robertson. "I understand you came here from California. Is that right?" he asked.

I knew enough from hearing the detectives discuss Robertson to realize his questions had some deeper purpose. Most of the detectives didn't like him and now I understood why. He was abrasive, at the very least.

Looking straight into his eyes I asked, "Commander, just what is it you're trying to find out?"

One corner of his mouth turned up in a half-smile. Nodding, he said, "You associate with my detectives. They've complimented you on your analytical skills. Obviously you are very good at what you do. So I thought it'd be worthwhile to meet you and get to know you better. Is that a problem for you?"

I felt my pulse race. "Nope, no problem. But I do have deadlines to meet and my boss doesn't like delays."

"I'll take care of Mr. Greenwood," Winters said.

Robertson sat while Winters, arms folded, leaned his back against the wall. This wouldn't be a short inquisition.

"I want to ask you about Detective Scarsdale. Has he ever asked you on a date?" Robertson asked.

"No, he hasn't. Why do you ask?"

Ah, now I see their game—they're after Jason.

Winters was next, ignoring my question.

"Did the two of you go out on a date a week or so ago?"

"No, there were three of us. Detective Scarsdale, his daughter, and me. We met at Chuck E. Cheese." I laughed.

"Mind sharing with us what it is you find so funny?" Winters asked.

"What sane man would take a woman on a date to Chuck E. Cheese?" I replied. "But please, answer my question. Why do you ask?"

"We're conducting an informal fact-gathering session," Winters replied. "I can make this formal if you wish." He shrugged. "It's up to you."

"Has he ever asked you out on a date?" Robertson asked.

"No. I would never have accepted if he had because that's a violation of department rules."

"But you did testify for him at a custody hearing. Did you meet with him to go over your testimony?" Winters asked.

"No, I went over it with his attorney."

They looked at each other. Winters then looked down, tugging at his nose. Robertson sat there, in silence.

"Okay, gentlemen, I assume we're done. I have to get this report finished."

"Have you two ever been to lunch together?" Winters asked.

"Just the two of us?"

Robertson nodded.

"Nope." My phone rang. The caller thought she'd dialed the criminal records section but I used the call to my advantage. "I understand. I'll be there in a few minutes." I picked up a thick file folder and moved toward the door. "Excuse me. My boss wants this file."

"I'm curious about your background," Robertson said. "I detect an accent. Where are you from?"

"Germany. Now if you gentlemen will excuse me, I have work to do."

"We don't hire foreign analysts without American accreditation. Where did you work before Austin?" Robertson asked.

I sighed. "California. Southern California. Now if you'll excuse me." I headed for the door.

"Which law enforcement agency did you work for?" Robertson asked.

I cast a quick glance over my shoulder, catching Robertson eyeing my backside. "Gentlemen, please, I must get this file to my boss. He has a meeting to attend and needs it now." I made my tone as no-nonsense as I could.

Winters smiled and chuckled like he knew I was lying, and then he nodded. "Okay. Do not discuss our meeting with anyone."

They walked outside my office then turned to face me.

One corner of Robertson's mouth curled up. "Perhaps we should continue this session in a more relaxed atmosphere. How does the Scholz Garten sound? Say around five today? Just the three of us," Robertson asked, leering at me. "It's a pleasant German-themed restaurant. They serve a variety of German beer. Maybe you'd feel more at ease there."

"Thank you, but no."

"Do you have some other favorite restaurant you frequent?" Robertson asked. "We could meet there. The Driskill Grill has a very nice Texas-themed restaurant and bar if that would be more to your liking."

I forced a smile, figuring what he was after. "I don't go to hotel bars for meetings. Thank you." I started to walk out but he blocked the door with his arm.

"You really should reconsider," Winters said.

"No," I answered. "Thank you." I enunciated each of the three words so there'd be no mistake. If I was going to bed with a man, it'd be one of my choosing, one I cared about.

"Hold on. I'm not finished," Winters said.

"Now what?" My tone would have frozen any reasonable man.

"I wanted to formally warn you of two things," Winters said. He held up his hand and tapped his forefinger to count off his points. "First, if Scarsdale asks you out on a date or to any social event, I expect you to notify me immediately. There will be severe consequences for failing to do so. Do you understand?"

I rolled my eyes and nodded. "And the second thing is…" I yawned. No point in trying to hide my contempt for either man.

"That applies to any other detectives, too," Robertson said.

"How about someone inviting me to Scholz Garten or Driskill Grill?"

Robertson's face almost turned purple with anger and he glowered at me. "That was for an official meeting. So don't get cute with me."

"No dating. I get it. Next?"

Robertson stepped closer to me, holding his finger up. It was a threatening gesture if ever I'd seen one.

"You're already on thin ice, Ms. Mueller. Don't push me."

Before I could respond, Winters jumped in. "Second, should you chose to disregard my warning and go on a date with him, be assured I'll have him suspended indefinitely and you'll be terminated. Is that clear?"

The lawyer in me couldn't let that pass. "Isn't that a bit extreme?"

"All my detectives will follow the rules to the letter or they'll be left to deal with the consequences." Robertson glanced from me to Winters. "Civilian violators aren't my problem."

Both men headed for my door. "I'll find out where you came from and whatever else is out there about you. Have a nice day, Ms. Mueller."

Robertson's snide words hung in the air like a bad smell and I was glad to see them go toward the elevator. I headed in the opposite direction but I looked over my shoulder and caught a glimpse of both men watching me as I turned the corner into my boss's office area. *What a pair of jerks.*

I'd already come to the realization that a dating relationship with Jason was dead in the water, thanks to his ex-mother-in-law. It would sting a little but I knew Jason would make the right choice for Shannon and his parent-child relationship. I'd had a couple of divorce cases involving children back in California and had counseled my clients to steer clear of any questionable involvements. And I was certainly a questionable involvement.

Pat Greenwood wasn't there so I hid out in his conference room, pretending to review old reports. I worried over Robertson's agenda. If he dug up my past and learned about Burton, I was certain he'd make sure I lost my job.

I got back to my office a few hours later, after missing lunch. There was a message on my phone from the chief's office telling me to come up to the seventh floor to meet with him at two o'clock. My watch showed 1:30. Maybe I was getting paranoid over Robertson but this was too coincidental.

Had he actually found out about Burton in the past few hours? Had he taken that information to the chief? He must have. I couldn't imagine another explanation. Every muscle in my body tightened like a bow string. Father was right. I should have stayed in Garmisch.

I'd made a royal mess of my life after Katarina was killed and it wasn't getting any better. After Burton, I had hoped I'd make a fresh start here. Then Lasiter was set free and I couldn't accept it, and look what a mess that had become. When I became friends with Scarsdale and Shannon, things seemed to be improving for me but my run of bad luck had no intention of letting up. How would it all end? Was I about to be fired? If so, Pat would have talked to me first. Should I resign so they wouldn't fire me?

If I was fired, I would go back to practicing law. Texas extended reciprocity to a certain class of California lawyers, of which I was one, so it would be back to the courtroom drama. I'd have to establish an internet presence with the Texas State

Bar which meant the Burtons might find me, if they were searching. My other option would be to wash my hands of all this departmental melodrama and go home to Germany. They seemed more intent here on screwing the rank and file than solving crimes. And I knew with that Winters-Robertson interrogation and my refusal to meet them after-hours, I was in their cross-hairs now.

When the elevator doors opened on seven, I trembled and my head pounded. I felt like throwing up. I promised myself I wouldn't give Robertson the satisfaction of seeing me upset and vowed not to even look in his direction.

Chief Nettleton's olive-skinned secretary, Tanya Spears, smiled at me. I had met her once at a department function a year ago. Her heavy purple eye shadow, red lipstick, and black eye liner reminded me of a call girl.

"Dani, go right in, they're expecting you." She had a funny squeaky voice but it didn't make me smile today.

Of course, it's *they*. I stopped as I grasped the doorknob. The chill I felt came from deep inside me.

She gestured with her head for me to go in.

I looked down at the doorknob again.

"Go on, Dani. They're waiting."

I backed away from the door. "Tanya, what is this all about?"

She smiled and shrugged at the same time, her grin sheepish.

If she's smiling, what is really going on? I wondered. "Tanya, tell me."

All I got was a smug look.

"You'll just have to go and find out." She had to open the door and push me in.

The chief sat tall in his big leather chair behind the empty expanse of his executive desk. I'd talked with him at some department function and had been surprised he was such a tall man, but his dark eyes peered at you from half-closed lids, like an alligator staring down his prey and you knew he was a force to be reckoned with. My stomach clenched when his salt and pepper mustache twitched and his mouth curled in a grin.

It's a good thing the chief had such a large office, complete with walnut bookshelves and the requisite ego wall to showcase awards and celebrity photos, because it was crowded. Two men and a woman sat in a recessed area on the other side of the bookcase. I couldn't see who they were but assumed the woman to be Emerald Fitzhenry from Human Resources. Of course, she'd be here. I didn't have a clue about the two men. Lieutenant Mitchell of Sex Crimes stood against the far wall with Amanda Colbert.

My boss, Pat Greenwood, smiled at me and gestured for me to sit in the chair next to him. The smile was a little reassuring so I sat and glanced back to see who belonged to the legs. Scarsdale and Harris. Scarsdale winked at me and Harris flashed a thumbs up. The woman sitting next to Harris was Ms. Fitzhenry.

In my peripheral vision, I saw Robertson sitting to Pat's left. We didn't make eye contact, but my heart started to hammer.

Why are we all here?

Tanya showed in two more people, a man and a woman with ID badges from the *Statesman* newspaper. They stood next to Mitchell. The man held a camera and the woman opened a black notebook. My heart nearly stopped, visions of the reporters who'd hounded me after Katarina's death reminding me just how juicy and newsworthy the truth would be to them.

Chief Nettleton spoke. "I believe we're ready now." He looked around the room and then pinned me with those alligator eyes. "Dani, each year the department recognizes a civilian employee for exemplary performance." He opened a folder and read from its contents. "You've been nominated by three detectives—" He gestured at Scarsdale, Harris, and Amanda, "—nominations which were approved by their supervisors and submitted to a committee, consisting of Commander Robertson and Pat Greenwood as well as Assistant Chief Dell Murphy. Unfortunately, Dell couldn't be here today due to other commitments. The committee evaluated twelve nominations and selected you as the finalist."

That's what all this was about? An award for me? I almost fainted with relief and cast a sideways glance at Pat. He was grinning. My face flushed.

Nettleton moved out from behind the desk, gesturing for me to stand next to him. It was photo op time and the guy with the camera moved in close. Nettleton handed me a crest shaped plaque of wood with my name etched on a brass plate. We stood side by side, each holding an edge of the award as the camera flashed. Nettleton's smile was better practiced than mine. I glanced over at Scarsdale and Harris. They were grinning like a pair of Cheshire cats. Amanda too.

The reporter approached when the cameraman stepped back. She asked the typical questions. "The chief filled us in on your job here. Can you tell me a little about your background? Like how long you've been a crime analyst, where else you worked? Your education and training. Things like that."

"I got much of my training here over the past two years. I took courses while I lived in California." I kept my responses to a bare minimum, omitting any history connected to my former name. I assumed the chief had already summarized the relevant parts to them anyway.

The woman cocked her head. "You have an accent. Where are you from?"

"Germany." I added to that in the hopes of cutting off further questions, "Texas is so much more like Germany than southern California."

She smiled. "So where in southern California did you live?"

"In the Los Angeles area."

That should give her a nice big rabbit trail to follow. There were close to forty different police agencies in the LA area. The reporter jotted notes and I shot a quick glance at Robertson. He was standing as close as he could, ear cocked, no doubt taking mental notes of his own.

CHAPTER 18

"One may smile, and smile, and be a villain."
~ *Shakespeare*

On Sunday morning, Robertson's cell phone rang. "Tell me what you found out, Captain Powers."

Powers worked as a captain at the San Francisco PD. He and Robertson had attended the FBI National Academy together.

Powers responded, "I ran your information through my usual contacts at Sacramento. "Nobody there ever heard of Dani Mueller. But there *was* an attorney named Karla Engel who lived in Sacramento and had a daughter named Katarina. The kid was brutally murdered about two or three years ago."

"Really?" Robertson said as his eyes darted round the room. "That sucks."

"There's more."

"Please, by all means, do continue."

"Karla Engel came from Germany. Married to an Air Force officer. They divorced about the time the daughter, Katarina, was born. Not long after her daughter was murdered, Karla Engel moved. If my math is right, that would be right about the time your Dani Mueller showed up."

"Humph. Where did Engel move to?"

"Rockford, Illinois. But when I called the number she left at State Bar, a receptionist at a woman's shelter in Chicago answered."

"Humph. A bogus number."

"Yep. She also set up a bogus law office there as well."

"A name change?"

"If she did, the court records are sealed tighter than a tick on a hound's back. But here's where it gets interesting. A few days after the man charged with killing her daughter—some ex-con named Doyle Burton—walked, he turned up dead. Engel was brought in but Sacramento PD didn't charge her and the grand jury no-billed her."

"You sure Karla Engel isn't still alive and well in Illinois and Dani Mueller just slipped by under the radar for years?"

"If Karla is alive and well, her name's no longer in the DL database. Plus Illinois has no record of her being issued a DL there."

"Anything on Mueller?"

"Yes and no. Seems Dani Mueller lived in Del Mar, California, down near LA. When I checked for a DL and criminal history on her, I got routed to the Secretary of State's office."

"Really? What's that mean?"

"Could mean the two women are actually one person. Apparently the State used their Klingon cloaking device to hide her. That'd explain the red herrings."

"Klingon cloaking device?"

"The Safe at Home Act." Powers went into some detail explaining how the Act worked.

"You did good, Captain. Thanks." He had what he wanted. Karla Engel, AKA Dani Mueller, was on the run from somebody. She'd killed a man vigilante style and walked away as Dani Mueller. Robertson sat there for a while, contemplating how to use this information to his advantage. The chief may not be so understanding about a vigilante killer in his ranks. Having been the one who uncovered that fact would be a valuable trump card that he'd play when it benefited him.

He heard the assistant chief, the number two official in the department, planned to retire soon. That position acted as the chief of police in Nettleton's absence. If he got that slot, he'd have rank over a few commanders and assistant chiefs to whom he owed payback. Being next in line to the chief had a nice ring to it. He salivated over the myriad of possibilities.

❧❦❧

Scarsdale leaned back in his desk chair, his feet resting on top of the desk. His fingers laced together behind his head. Eyes closed.

Harris plopped down in the guest chair. "Hey, what's up?"

Scarsdale didn't open his eyes as he answered, "I was just sitting here thinking about all the dumb things I've done in my life."

"Bet that kept you pretty busy."

Scarsdale opened his eyes, glancing at him before he flipped Harris the bird.

"Next Saturday Mary and I are throwing a pool party. Gonna have everyone over for BBQ. Except Robertson, of course. Bring Shannon."

Before Scarsdale answered, his phone rang. Travis County Jail showed on the caller screen.

"Now what," Scarsdale remarked, reaching over to pick up the phone.

"Detective Scarsdale, this is Sergeant Vincent. I'm the day shift jail supervisor. There's a note on Olsen's jail card to call you if anything happened. Olsen hung himself in his cell."

Scarsdale dropped his feet on the floor and sat bolt upright. "How the hell could he hang himself?" He closed his eyes, shook his head and grimaced.

"The report stated he hung himself from his shower stall using strips from his bed sheet," Vincent said.

"What the hell happened to spot checks every hour?"

"I just came on. Just letting you know what I was told."

Scarsdale slammed the phone down on its cradle. "Son of a bitch!" He sat there, staring straight ahead for a minute or two, chewing on his lower lip.

"Who hung themselves?" Harris asked.

"Olsen. Our last shot at clearing the Lasiter murder." He turned to face Harris. "Worthless jailers. Bet they never checked on him."

"Looks like we're fresh out of witnesses."

"Not quite," said Scarsdale. "We have one more."

"And just how do you think you're gonna get her to open up?"

"I don't have a clue." He massaged his chin, his thoughts drifting. "I'll figure something out."

"Not casting doubt on your persuasive abilities, but what if she still won't play ball?

"Then…" he shrugged. "We go to Plan B."

"Plan B as in breaking into Zarko's house? Uh-uh. There's no 'we' in Plan B, kemo sabe. I'm not getting my ass in a crack. Too close to retirement."

જ

Standing in the jail supervisor's office, Scarsdale inspected the county jailer's log. The night shift made the last check on Olsen's cell at six o'clock in the morning. The investigator's report indicated Olsen's body was discovered after shift change at eight. The jail visitor log showed none for Olsen in the past two days except his attorney. But he noticed Zarko's name down for another inmate—Rufus Short. That visit took place the day before. The jail sergeant said Short had been Olsen's cellmate until the prison bus hauled him away about 6 a.m. this morning.

Scarsdale asked the supervisor about Short. "Wouldn't the jailer have noticed Olsen when he got Short out for his bus ride?"

"Nope. Inmates like Short are pulled an hour before the bus departs for out-processing. And, as you can see from the log, Olsen was alive and well at five."

Scarsdale made a detour on his way back to the office. Parked across the street from Zarko's house, he sketched the area including the front and the neighbors' homes, noting vehicles, landmarks, and fences. Going down the alley, he stopped behind the house, sketching the back door area. He noted that the house across the alley appeared vacant and that each of the neighbors' homes on either side lacked line of sight to Zarko's back door.

ϾϿϾϿ

Back at the office, Scarsdale briefed Mitchell, Amanda, and Harris about his investigation into Olsen's apparent suicide. "Olsen didn't do it voluntarily. I think his former cellmate helped out. Zarko paid Olsen's cellmate a visit the day before. Now that cellmate just happens to be on his way back to Huntsville. Left just before Olsen's body was found."

"And you think Zarko set it all up?" Mitchell asked, reaching for his spitting cup.

Scarsdale popped four breath mints in his mouth, hoping they'd block the stench of Mitchell's tobacco, especially if he breathed through his mouth.

"Hell, yeah. Olsen agreed to make cases on every one of those pedophiles if he got a deal from the DA. And the US Marshal's Office approved his application for Witness Protection late yesterday. I'd have told Olsen this morning. Nobody commits suicide when they've got a deal like that cooking. Zarko made arrangements with Olsen's cellmate to do it and only somebody from this division had the intel. Whoever it was persuaded Zarko to set it up."

Mitchell scowled. "Shut the door." He looked from Harris all the way to Scarsdale. "We have a leak in the department. Robertson, Winters, and I tried unsuccessfully to pinpoint the source." He stared right at Scarsdale. "Robertson said he suspected Dani Mueller but he dropped the idea after getting new information about her." Mitchell spit in his cup. "Don't discuss this matter outside my office."

Scarsdale and Amanda locked eyes for an instant as all heads bobbed in unison.

"What information did Robertson discover?" asked Scarsdale, suspecting that Robertson found out about Dani's California past.

"Ask Robertson," Mitchell replied, spitting again. "Getting back to our problem, Robertson has decided to hold all reports from this division in his office until we find the source of the leak." He wiped his mouth with the back of his hand.

"That means no discussions with anybody outside this unit about our cases." He eyed each of the three detectives. "Any questions?"

Heads shook in unison.

He spit one more time while giving Scarsdale a hard stare. "Scarsdale, the clock is ticking on the Lasiter case. Think maybe I'll see an arrest in my lifetime?"

Scarsdale gave Mitchell a quick tight-lipped smile and nodded. He walked back to his cubicle, debating whether to tell Mitchell his suspicions about Dani being the woman in Lasiter's closet. Questions and doubts flowed like a river through his brain. She killed one pedophile, would she do it again? Why was Zarko stalking her unless she was the one in the closet? If he told Mitchell his suspicions and she wasn't the one, it would be a career killer for her. He'd give a year's wages to know what new information Robertson had uncovered on Dani? Did he find out about Burton and her daughter?

He walked past his cubicle, down the hall to Dani's office. One way or another, he'd get the answers he needed.

CHAPTER 19

It was around 1:30 when Jason walked in, closed the door, and took a seat in my office. We looked at each other in awkward silence before he finally spoke.

"I wanted to thank you for helping me in the custody hearing. The judge ruled that Shannon stays with me. Some kind of settlement may be worked out, allowing Marcy limited visitation. But I know she'll be watching my every move, just hoping I'll screw up so I've got to tread lightly."

He lowered his head and looked at the floor. I could tell this wasn't easy for him.

"That means I have to be very careful who Shannon…hangs around with. Does that make sense?"

"Absolutely. You mustn't do anything that might raise an issue about your suitability as a parent." I wanted to sound reassuring and casual but for some reason my heart was racing. It was clear by the stiff way he sat that there was more to this. "But that's not why you're here, is it?"

"No, it isn't." He leaned toward me, put his arms on his knees, and clasped his hands so tight the knuckles turned white. "I want to talk to you about something."

The way he stared at the floor, picking at his thumbnail, reminded me of a stymied schoolboy. I almost smiled but when he looked up at me his eyes were somber and a little wary.

Whatever this was about, it was difficult for him and in my head I vowed to grant any favor, any request as long as it wasn't about my past. "I know about Doyle Burton and what he did and about his family stalking you. And Karla Engel and the rabbit trail."

I don't believe it! I think my heart stopped. My breath certainly did. I just stared at him in astonishment. "How—" I swallowed hard and forced a breath. "May I ask how you found out?"

I'd prepared myself to keep my distance from Jason and his daughter so that his crazy ex-mother-in-law couldn't use a new relationship against him, but I'd never considered what a threat my past presented. It was supposed to be my secret.

"Information sharing between agencies."

So much for my anonymity under the Act. "Okay." I wondered if the Burtons would be as dedicated as Jason.

"I did some checking. Parnell Lewis Burton has a parole hearing coming up very soon. Were you aware of that?" he asked.

"I knew it was pending but I hadn't checked lately."

"I know about the grand jury action. And that's all I want to know about that. You've been through enough hell."

I could see the sympathy in his eyes.

"Let's talk about Lasiter. You tell me everything you saw and heard that night and I'll be equally honest with you. Do we have a deal?"

I let his offer sink in. There was no point in denying any-thing—yet. I nodded. "Yes, sure."

"This is what I know. I won't regurgitate what's in my reports. You already know that stuff. Fair enough?"

"Fair enough."

"You followed Lasiter to Dave's Bar that night while wearing a blonde wig. Later you parked your Mercedes in the alley behind Lasiter's house. And you traded it in for an Acura right after I asked you to do some searches for similar MOs. I assume Zarko followed you home from Lasiter's?"

"I guess so. Look, Jason, let's just cut to the chase, shall we?"

"Okay, tell me why you were in Lasiter's house?" He leaned back in the chair. For him the worst was over.

If I was serious about turning my messed up life around and escaping the best I could from this morass I'd put myself into, the choice was clear—tell enough of the truth to extricate myself in the least culpable manner possible. The rest I'd just have to live with and hope no one ever found out.

"I'm not sure if you'll understand, not being a mother." I got a cookie out of the nearest can and offered one to him.

"No," he said. "Thank you. Keep going."

I nibbled on the cookie and gave him a sanitized version of what happened. "Susan really wanted Amy's bracelet returned. I sensed her frustration. On a recess during the trial, she almost went up to Lasiter to ask for it back. After his trial ended, I wanted to find it for her. I understand exactly what having that bracelet meant to her. So I went into his house."

"How did you get in?"

"Lasiter left a spare key in the mailbox. When he and Zarko came in, I had to hide in the bedroom closet. I couldn't help but hear. I didn't know Zarko would end up killing him."

"How did you know it was Zarko?" He was in full cop mode now, crossing his legs into that right-angle position that guys do.

"I'd seen and heard Lasiter and Zarko at the bar. Besides, Lasiter called him by name—Tom. They got into a huge argument over Lasiter talking so much about Amy Crowell. Lasiter even accused Zarko of killing her."

"And what did Zarko say to that?"

"Just to shut up. He said the girl was dead and everyone was in the clear. But Lasiter wouldn't drop it. That's when the fight started."

"And you're positive Zarko killed him?" Jason asked.

"Positive." I reached for another cookie. "I recognized his voice then and when he confronted me outside my apartment."

That got his attention and he sat bolt upright. "Confronted you? When?"

"Right before I went to Germany." I didn't want to dig the hole any deeper so I skipped over the part about my midnight excursion to Zarko's house.

His face tightened. "Why didn't you tell me about that?"

"I don't know." I shrugged and looked away. "Maybe because I...I don't know." I sounded lame even to myself. I watched him take a deep breath and blow it out.

His next words came out softer. "Since he followed you home, it's safe to assume he followed you to my house."

Oh my God, I should have known that. "What do you want me to do?"

"Give me a written statement, detailing everything about your, uh...misadventure in Lasiter's house and the confrontation, as well as anything else about Zarko you *forgot* to tell me."

"If I admit to criminal trespassing, I'll lose my job and God knows what else. Then what? Jail? I don't think so." I sat back and thought a minute. "There's another way to do this."

His frown changed into a smile and he leaned closer until our faces were inches apart. A hint of men's cologne, like a mix of carnations and cloves, came off him. I liked it. "I'm all ears."

"Use me as a confidential informant to get a warrant. I've provided reliable information to you in the past." I could see the wheels turning in his head. Mind reading ability would be a nice trait to have right now.

"Good idea," he said. "So how do we do it?"

"I'll draft a statement, unsigned of course, for your case file. Use it to write the affidavit. The DA should have no problem approving it for a warrant."

It was the best solution I could come up with but I was left with a storm of new questions. Would he keep my secret? What did he think of me now? He couldn't let Shannon be alone with me.

This was more than a new relationship issue. Marcy would tear him apart in court and he'd be looking at supervised visitation at Marcy's house. Best to ignore all that for the moment.

"Zarko will eventually figure out I'm the source. I just don't want to be charged with an offense."

He thought it over, lips pressed together, eyes on the floor. "I don't know if that's a good idea. Right now, you're the only one who can tie him to Lasiter's death. Once Zarko realizes you talked to me, he'll triple his efforts to eliminate you."

⌘

Seven o'clock on Monday morning came fast. I grabbed a cup of coffee in the ground floor lounge and caught an empty elevator for the ride up. The elevator stopped on the first floor to take on a passenger—Robertson.

As soon as he saw me, he grinned—not one of those between people greeting each other but rather like a snarky arrogant one. I backed into the corner, keeping as much distance between us as I could get. My eyes locked on the floor indicator above the door. I wish I could say the ride up was uneventful, but such was not the case.

Robertson watched the floor numbers flash as we climbed. "You really should reconsider my request to meet me at the Driskill Grill after work. You help me, I help you." He glanced at me. "I can make it worth your while."

"Help you do what?"

"The three of us'll talk about it over drinks."

I turned to face him. "You expect me to go to some hotel with you and Commander Winters, have a few drinks, and then what? We adjourn to a room? I don't think so."

"Nothing like that. You help us with a problem. We return the favor."

I looked back at the floor lights over the elevator door. "No, thanks. I can handle any problems I might have."

"I'll bet Sacramento is nice this time of year," he said as the doors opened on four. He looked back at me, "Isn't that right, Karla?"

"Karla?" I managed a quizzical eyebrow lift.

He stood in the opening, keeping the elevator doors from closing. His smirk made my skin crawl. "How about Del Mar,

California or Rockford, Illinois? Ring any bells?" he asked before he turned and walked off.

CHAPTER 20

"To know what is right and not do it is the worst cowardice."
~ Confucius

ate Monday morning, Harris collapsed in the visitor
chair in Scarsdale's cubicle. "Let me read it," Harris
said, extending his hand.

A few minutes passed while Harris read Dani's statement.
Then he looked at Scarsdale.

"So she *was* the one in the closet." Harris spoke in a
hushed tone. "Let's get the warrant."

"No," Scarsdale said. "If Zarko takes this to trial, Dani
would have to testify, opening her to a criminal charge for
trespassing at the very minimum. Winters would insure she
lost her job. Besides, even though she claims to have been
there looking for the bracelet, my gut sense tells me there's
more to it than that. I suspect she went there to avenge Amy."

"What?" Harris asked. He stared at Scarsdale in disbelief.
"Start making sense, Jason."

"Okay. You already know what happened to her in California."

Harris nodded.

"Dani attended Lasiter's trial the day I testified, a fact she
admitted when she told me about the bracelet."

"So what? It was a public trial."

Scarsdale passed on that with a headshake. "Nicole said
she heard a commotion outside Lasiter's house that night. You
heard her when she said three or four minutes passed from the
time she heard the commotion until they went inside the house.
Dani had ample time to get out the back door before they came
in the front. Crime scene people and I both checked the back-

door. It had a sliding bolt lock that opened and closed without difficulty. She remained in that house for another reason, except that Zarko beat her to it."

"Now what?" Harris asked, massaging his chin.

"I got an email that Zarko was observed following a couple of little girls around at the park across from his work site three days ago." He handed Harris the email from Sheila Zimmerman, a Sex Crimes detective on loan to the Task Force. "I'm not waiting around for that bastard to kill another kid," he said, watching Harris read the email.

"Plan B?" Harris asked.

"Damn right. I won't involve you so you never heard me say a word, okay?"

"Fuck it," Harris said. "You need a look-out. Somebody to keep tabs on that asshole while you're—"

"Good. I'll do it as soon as he leaves to go play. Just make sure that asshole doesn't do another kid."

∾∙∾

The rented black sedan rolled up to the curb and parked in front of a gold-colored van. The driver sat there, taking a drag from the cigarette before holding it out the window and flicking the ashes. He checked the rearview mirror then adjusted the outside mirror so he could see the little blonde girl riding the bicycle, the pink one with the training wheels, down the sidewalk, toward a large tree.

He saw a silver-haired woman in her mid-fifties or so standing halfway between the house and the sidewalk, watching the girl like a hawk watching a field mouse. When the little girl rode closer to the tree, he heard the woman call to her.

"Shannon. That's far enough, honey. Ride back to me."

He picked up his cell phone from the console, opened the "camera" application and studied the photograph. Then he peered in the mirror at the little girl who was now riding toward him. He looked out the window as she came closer to his car. One corner of his mouth curled up.

"*Hola*, Shannon Scarsdale," he whispered. He took a long drag off his cigarette, flicked the ash out the window, and blew smoke rings while he watched Shannon ride past.

When the woman began walking in the direction of his car, he stuck the cigarette between his lips, drove to the end of the street, and hooked a right.

∽✺∽

Scarsdale sat in his SUV a block away from Zarko's house, waiting on Harris's call that Zarko had left the house. His watch showed 9:10 p.m. when his cell buzzed.

"I've got him southbound on Lamar Boulevard," Harris said. "Amanda is running parallel on a side street. We'll switch off so he doesn't make the tail."

"How the hell did Amanda find out?" Scarsdale asked.

"Relax. She wants this asshole as much or more than you do."

About 10:30, Scarsdale, dressed in black, crept down the alley and stopped at Zarko's back fence. He pulled a black knit ski mask down over his face and the nitrile gloves over his hands. Using his flashlight every few feet, he moved closer to the back door of the darkened house. The wood frame dwelling was one of those old Texas-style pier and beam structures built back in the fifties. The back door was half window.

He looked at the neighbors' houses to the north and south of Zarko's. Both places were dark. He tugged on the door but it didn't budge. Moving over to a low window, Scarsdale slid his fingers as far under the edge as he could and lifted. The window creaked as he slid it up. He leaned inside, listening and shining his light around the room. No growling dogs. A refrigerator sat off to the left. The kitchen counter ran along the wall from the refrigerator to the door. He hoisted one leg through the window followed by the rest of him.

Harris would call when Zarko headed home. If Harris didn't for whatever reason and he got caught, Robertson would make sure he got as long a prison sentence as possible. For house burglary, the range was five years to life. He knew cops in prison didn't fare well. It was a risk he had to take.

Leaving the window open, Scarsdale moved from room to room, beginning in the kitchen. He searched each drawer and shelf, thinking about the physical similarities between Lasiter and Zarko as well as Nicole's description of the man running from Lasiter's house.

When he opened the cabinet under the sink, he recoiled. "Holy shit." Several large cockroaches crawled up the walls of the cabinet. He checked the pantry closet next. Zarko had arranged the canned goods on one shelf with the veggies on one side and fruit on the other. Boxed items occupied the shelf below and glass containers filled the third shelf. The sight of such an orderly set-up irritated him. *How could someone as sick as Zarko be so damn anal?* Closing the door, he moved into the living room.

The room had wood floors with an oval rug covering a large area in the living room. A decent-looking sofa and chair. A fireplace with a wood mantle. Several magazines lay on the coffee table—*Good Housekeeping, Texas Highways,* and *Sports Illustrated.* He held each magazine up, shaking it but nothing fell out. There were two windows—one with a front yard view and the other out to the side of the house. Parting the blinds, he peered outside. No truck.

He lifted each seat cushion and checked under each piece of furniture, hoping to find Amy Crowell's gold bracelet or Zarko's stash of DVDs, pictures, and his black book.

Scarsdale knew anything he found would be inadmissible in court—the fruit of the poisonous tree. Unless he distorted the truth. Scarsdale preferred that term instead of "lied." He'd claim he found it in the trash, making it abandoned property and therefore admissible.

He opened the door to the closet, the one right next to the front door. Coats and jackets arranged with all facing on one direction. He went through each pocket. Nothing.

A few cardboard boxes sat on the floor. He dropped to his knees and eased his way under the coats. Just old clothes and a few knickknacks in the boxes. As he inched his way out to stand up, his cell phone snagged on a long coat and crashed to the floor. The battery cover and battery popped out. *Damn*. He reassembled the unit and snapped it back in his belt holder.

The flashlight beam reflected off a metal box on the top shelf. Jackpot? Adrenaline pumped through his veins. Using his pocketknife, Scarsdale jimmied the lock. He rummaged through the contents. A gold-colored bracelet. He looked inside for the initials "AC" but there weren't any. He shoved it in his pocket anyway, thinking it had to be a trophy that Zarko took off one of his little victims, and continued rifling the contents of the box. He found a pawn ticket for a bracelet at a Temple pawn shop—Stillhouse Pawn. He pocketed that too and then examined several photographs in the box.

One in particular caught his attention. A snapshot of the entire pedophile gang, similar to the one he'd found at Ferguson's. He stuffed the photo in his pocket then jammed the lid closed and put the box back.

He walked into the bedroom. The standard furniture: a bed made up, a nightstand with a lamp, and a dresser. He didn't find anything useful in the dresser or the nightstand. *What the hell? Does this bastard have a maid service? The place is too orderly*, he thought. Finding nothing under the bed, he turned his attention to the clothes closet.

Scarsdale shined the flashlight at the top shelf. Several cardboard boxes and two shoeboxes were lined up. Starting with the clothes, he noted the grouping—shirts hung with other shirts, trousers in their little group. On the floor, he saw shoes and boots lined up straight across like little soldiers at formation.

As he stuck his hand into a pocket of a shirt hanging up in the closet, he heard a car pull up in the front of the house. He sprinted to the front window, heard a car door slam and a police radio crackle. He peeked around the edge of the blinds. Police. *Son of a bitch* was the first thought in his mind as he raced to the kitchen window, hoping other officers weren't covering the back door. *Who called them?* He remembered his dropped cell phone. The phone powered off when the battery fell out. "Shit," he muttered as he closed the window.

After he exited the house, two flashlight beams shined in his direction. He heard nothing from either officer as he sprinted across the yard and vaulted over the three-foot high chain-link fence into the alley. Taking a quick glance back, he didn't see the flashlight beams anymore. At the end of the alley, Scarsdale hooked a right and shot down the sidewalk to his SUV. Driving away, he turned on his cell phone—one message. No time to listen to it. Besides, he knew who it was from.

☙❧

Scarsdale got home well after midnight. Mrs. Hargraves was drowsing on the living room sofa and got up when he woke her. She had put Shannon to bed around eight and when Scarsdale peeked in his daughter was sound asleep. He said goodnight to her, thanking her for staying so late. He walked her to her car and, as she pulled away, he called Harris. "My damn phone fell out of the holder and came apart. I forgot to turn it back on."

"Find anything?" Harris asked.

He emptied his pockets on the table. He gave the pawn ticket a closer inspection. "Nothing we can use." He'd never lied to his partner before but an ignorant Harris would be a safe Harris. There was no way of knowing yet if the patrol had seen him fleeing Zarko's house.

Scarsdale booted up his laptop, snapped on a pair of gloves while he watched the computer screen scroll through the litany of start-up windows. He got an envelope and slipped it in his printer. This late at night, he was pleased he'd left the printer running. The hellacious racket it made whenever he turned it on would wake Shannon. He walked over to the hallway and peered toward her bedroom door. All quiet.

He sat in front of the laptop, typed the address for his office, and printed an envelope. Dropping the pawn ticket inside, he peeled the paper ribbon off and sealed the envelope. Then he pasted a self-stick stamp on it. Tomorrow morning, he'd deposit it in the corner mailbox, guessing that it'd arrive on his desk the day after.

☙❧

Two days later, Scarsdale walked to his cubicle, sorting through his mail, hoping the envelope was in this batch. He wasn't disappointed. He sliced it open and removed the pawn ticket. Over the past two days, he'd checked the uniform patrol's incident log to make sure he hadn't been listed as a suspect for the break-in at Zarko's. Nothing on file. He breathed a sigh of relief—he had dodged the proverbial bullet.

He got the phone number for Temple police and asked to speak to the officer who handled the pawnshop detail. A few clicks and buzzes later, Detective Levine got the phone.

After Scarsdale introduced himself, he began, "I received an anonymous envelope containing a pawn ticket for the Stillhouse Pawn Shop for a bracelet. I think it may be connected to a murder case I'm working involving a pedophile. The ticket number is V651. Would it possible for you to eyeball the bracelet and call me back so I can run the description down to you?"

"I'll head over there right now," Levine replied. "What's your callback number?"

Scarsdale read off his direct number and hung up. Figuring he had time to update Harris about the "anonymous" envelope, he went to the man's cubicle. Not finding him, Scarsdale checked the Sign-in board. According to it, Harris had been summoned to Winters's office. Scarsdale returned to his desk and re-checked the incident log.

Still nothing more than the routine information—a neighbor called in, reporting that he saw a light moving around inside Zarko's house, believing that a burglar was there. Officers responded, heard a noise out back.

They searched the exterior but found no evidence of any forced entry, nor did they observe any suspicious persons in the vicinity. The officers cleared the scene about twenty minutes later. So why did Winters want Harris?

CHAPTER 21

"People will cease to commit atrocities
only when they cease to believe absurdities."
~ *Voltaire*

Sitting at a computer screen in his bedroom, Parnell munched on a peanut butter, pickle, and cheese sandwich as he hunted for clues to the whereabouts of Karla Engel. A bottle of beer sat near his keyboard. On the floor next to his chair sat an open box containing a single wedge of pepperoni pizza and several remnants of pizza, blanketed by several black houseflies.

Unable to find any trace of Engel, he targeted Karla's former secretary, Ellen Vrasil. One of the women at Karla's former law office had said Ellen now worked for a district attorney's office in another county. He checked each DA's office in California, beginning with Del Norte County in the far northwestern corner of the state.

Two days later, late at night, he hit pay dirt—Ellen Vrasil worked at the Madera County District Attorney's office. The next day, using a pre-paid cell phone, he called from the privacy of his truck. He felt confident he'd sound convincing since he'd had a lot of practice in the past six years manipulating guards and other prison employees.

"My name is Randy Ashburn. Ms. Engel represented me in a DUI case a few years back. She did fantastic job for me then—got me off," he said, chuckling. "But I—" He tried to sound nervous and embarrassed. "I, um, need her help again. A, uh, another DUI."

"I'm sorry, Mr. Ashburn, but she sold her practice to her partner, Chip Kellersmith, and moved away about a year or so ago. I notified all her clients. I guess I missed you," Ellen said.

"Yeah, I found that out when I went to her old office. Might you know where she's practicing now?"

"I don't think she still practices here. Check the State Bar website or call them if you don't—"

"Did she mention where she moved to?"

"Some city near Chicago. I'm sorry but I don't remember the name."

"Why did she move so far away?" Chicago was a big haystack to find a needle, he thought. "Could you have heard her wrong?"

"No, I distinctly recall her telling me some city in the Chicago area. As for why, I guess you didn't know but her daughter had been savagely murdered. She was very distraught over it."

"My God. How horrible. She's such a nice lady," Parnell said. "Why would anyone ever want to do something like that to hurt her? I guess some people are just animals." *She's gonna know hurt when I get my hands on her.*

"Yes, well, she was a very nice lady but I guess she needed to start over somewhere else. You should contact some other defense attorney. Have you considered the ones who took over her practice?"

"No. I want her. She's the best. Thanks."

Parnell heard her sigh.

"I don't know what to tell you. Maybe her old partner knows her new address."

"Yeah, maybe," he said before muttering, "Motherfucker."

"What did you just say?" Ellen asked.

"Nothing, nothing at all. Well, thank you anyway."

Parnell's next step was a search of the Illinois state bar website. Sure enough, he found her. Karla Engel, attorney at law. He copied the address. Then he brought up the Illinois driver's license screen. He figured he'd get her home address from it, but no driver's license was listed for her. So he punched in Karla's office phone number.

A woman answered, "Sunnybrook Women's Shelter. How may I help you?"

"I was trying to reach a certain number. I guess I dialed wrong." He recited the number.

"No, you dialed correct. Who are you trying to reach?"

"Never mind." He hung up. With one sweep of his thick arm, the papers on his desk flew into the air and floated to the floor. "You freakin' bitch," he yelled.

That night, he pried open the rear door at the Kellersmith Law Office. The office was located in a three-story renovated house on Eighth Street about two blocks from the Gordon D. Schaber Sacramento County Courthouse.

Once inside, he found Chip Kellersmith's office on the second floor. If Karla told anyone where she'd gone, Parnell figured it'd be her former partner. Spotting the computer monitor and keyboard he assumed it would be password-protected. Not having the time to fiddle with discovering the password, he searched each drawer of the mahogany-colored desk. He found a stack of five of Kellersmith's business cards paper clipped together.

One with the name Dani Mueller and a telephone number in Del Mar written on the back. Beneath it was scribbled an address with a post office box in Del Mar, California. Another card showed a Sybil Thompson with a Dallas phone number. A third card had Robyn Greenbriar and a St. Louis phone number. A fourth with Tanya Weathers in Montreal and a fifth named Eleanor Archer with a Ft. Lauderdale phone number.

"Damn, a 'ho in every city," he said, pocketing all five cards.

An hour later, at home, he Googled each name. The first four were duds and he was almost ready to quit for the night. He typed in the name of Dani Mueller and pressed the ENTER key. He yawned as the screen flickered before the Google list popped up. He sat there, yawning again, forcing his eyes to stay open as he scrolled down the list. The first listing he found showed the address and phone number belonged to a private mail drop in Del Mar. Two or three listings down, he struck gold. A newspaper article with a photograph of an Austin police crime analyst receiving an award for exceptional service. The caption underneath showed her name to be Dani Mueller, but he recognized the woman in the picture as Karla Engel. "Gotcha now, 'ho."

Two hours later, he heard a rapping noise. Turning toward the door he saw Mattie standing there with Phoenix Wilson and Bunny Burton.

Wearing a pair of designer jeans that appeared to have been painted on, Bunny sashayed into the room and dropped an envelope on his desk. "Happy Birthday, bro," she said before kissing him on the cheek.

"What's this?" he asked, picking it up and examining the envelope like it was some mysterious object. His years in prison had taught him to be wary.

"Your birthday present. Go ahead. Open it," Bunny said, standing in front of a wall mirror in his room. She moved her face from side to side, fluffed her bangs, then wiped a lipstick smudge away with her little finger.

He ripped the envelope open and pulled out a ticket. "Aw shit." He examined it more closely. "A bus ride to Austin."

Mattie picked up the litter of empty pizza boxes and balled up sandwich wrappers. "You can pay me back later."

"Want me to go with ya?" Phoenix asked, leaning against the doorframe, holding a driver's license in his hand.

Parnell snickered. "I can handle that bitch all by myself."

"Well, Doyle didn't fare so well." Phoenix walked over to Parnell and handed him a Texas driver's license. "You'll need this."

Bunny laughed as she continued to preen in the mirror. "Shit, Phoenix, if she yelled 'boo,' you'd cower behind Parnell."

Phoenix flipped her the bird. "Cocksucker."

Parnell checked out the license. His photo, height, and a San Antonio address. The license showed an alias: Peter Gilbert. Even the signature looked like one he'd written. "Good job, Phoenix."

"If you need me, you know where I'll be," he said, waving his hand over his shoulder.

Parnell stared straight ahead for a few seconds, relishing the thought of coming face to face with Karla or Dani or whatever friggin' name she was using—a meeting he'd waited over two years for. This time she'd be on the receiving end, screaming and begging. He jumped up from his chair and headed for the door.

Bunny spun around, "Hey, where ya goin?"

"Gotta get my knives all sharp."

Mattie handed him a smaller envelope as he went by.

He stopped to thumb through the contents: ten one-hundred dollar bills.

"Spendin' money," she said. "Bring me back that big pretty cuckoo clock she had in her office. You'll know it when you see it."

"Bring me something too," Bunny said.

❧❧❧

It was nearing seven in the evening on Wednesday when he stepped off the bus in Austin. Parnell took a taxi south on Interstate 35, headed for a hotel on the other side of the lake. He was glad he decided to wear a T-shirt and jeans. Now he fit right in with the locals.

His green duffel lay on the seat next to him. When the taxi drove west along Sixth Street, he eyed a mix of young and older people milling around the shops and bars. He even caught glimpses of a few college age women strolling along the sidewalk in shorts and skimpy tops. "Goddamn. Check out the 'hos," he said, twisting his body around so he could see out the rear window.

The taxi driver—an Indian—said nothing. As the cab drove over the Congress Avenue Bridge, Parnell saw a few paddleboats and a couple of canoes gliding along in the waters of Lady Bird Lake.

What really drew his attention was the throng of people

gathered on both sides of the Congress Avenue bridge. "What are they here for?"

"For the bats."

"Bats? What bats?"

"Every evening around dark, people come here to watch the bats fly out from under the bridge," said the cab driver.

Burton snorted. "Whatever."

Ten minutes later, he stood at the hotel registration desk filling out an information card. He handed it, the forged driver's license, and a credit card to the clerk.

"I have you down for a three-day stay with us, Mr. Gilbert," the clerk said. "Is that correct?"

"For now, yes." He'd stay as many days as it took to find Karla Engel and kill her. When he accomplished his goal, he'd check out and the hotel could charge whatever against the credit card. It didn't matter. He wasn't going to pay the bill anyway.

Up in his room, Burton set a photograph of Doyle and him on top of the TV. The picture showed the two brothers standing on each side of two field-dressed boar carcasses. He poured himself three fingers of Jack Daniels and stepped back to admire the picture. He, Doyle, and a friend of Doyle's had snuck onto a private hunting preserve, stalked a pack of feral hogs and killed two of them. Great days! He swirled the drink around before gulping down a mouthful.

Burton opened his notebook containing newspaper clippings from the *Sacramento Bee*, some photos and a few letters. Lying the notebook open on the shiny surface of the desk, he leafed through its contents, stopping at a photograph. He held the picture in front of him and sat back. At the bottom edge of the photograph was a name printed in heavy black letters: Karla Engel. "When I get my hands on you—"

Burton tossed the picture on the table, stood up, drink in hand and gazed out the window at the Austin skyline, then down at the joggers and bicyclists moving along the path that paralleled Lady Bird Lake.

The thought of being so close to killing Karla Engel made

him smile. He chugged down the rest of his drink and poured another one.

He sat back down and picked up the copy he'd made of the article from the *Austin American Statesman*. The photo showed a smiling Dani Mueller posing next to the Austin Police Chief, holding a plaque. About mid-way down, he read that she came to Austin from southern California.

"Southern California my ass," Parnell remarked.

He stepped over to his open suitcase. Reaching into the left side, he pulled out a large hunting knife—a Siberian skinner. It had a six-inch blade and a tan and brown stag handle.

He removed the skinner from its sheath and rotated it. His finger traced the edge of the shiny smooth blade, back and forth. He scraped the skinner across the back of his hand, shaving hairs away. "Better than a straight razor," he said.

Parnell saw his reflection in the wall-mounted mirror by the desk. His burr haircut made him look younger than his thirty-one years. He slid the sheathed skinner inside his left boot. He slipped the Smith & Wesson 9mm in the back of his waistband. He'd put it in the glove box for use later.

Satisfied with his image, he rummaged in the suitcase and drew out his prize. He inspected the leather business card case embossed with the Samsung logo. The crisp white cards for Pete Gilbert, Public Relations screamed legit. Phoenix did another nice piece of work, he thought.

Parnell's plan was to lay in wait for Dani at her place. But first he had to get her address. Around three-thirty the next afternoon, he parked his rental car in the lot across from the PD. Most of the employees parked there, or so he was told. At ten after four, he saw the woman he knew as Karla Engel walking across the lot to his left. She got into a silver Acura with paper buyer tags which told him she just purchased it. He followed her out onto the Interstate and drove north. He stayed in the right lane until the Highway 183 exit came up. A long line of traffic and an 18-wheeler prevented him from moving out of the exit lane.

As he sailed over the Interstate on the 183 flyover, Parnell slammed his fist against the steering wheel. "Motherfucker!"

He caught a glimpse out his passenger window of Dani's Acura speeding north on the Interstate while he drove out Highway 183, looking for the first exit.

He raced back to the PD parking lot, hoping to find some police clerk he could snow with his charm and good looks. About thirty minutes later, he spotted an excellent candidate—a Hispanic woman in her late twenties. He took a hard look at her when she passed by his car and muttered under his breath, "Not too bad. Bet you could suck chrome off a trailer hitch."

He watched her walk to a white Chevrolet sedan. He knew it would be a hit or miss gamble but he was primed and ready and wanted the address now. He fell in behind her when she drove away, hoping she'd pull into a bar. She stopped at red light so he pulled up on her right and looked over at her.

"Look at me, bitch. I'm smilin' at ya."

When she glanced in his direction, he gave her a big smile and flicked his eyebrows up several times—a signal that always worked back home. "You know you want me."

She grinned back.

He raised his hand to his face as if he was swigging down a beer and flicked his eyebrows up again.

She hesitated then smiled wide and nodded before waving for him to follow her.

Several minutes later, Parnell plopped down a ten spot and grabbed two perspiring bottles of Bud from the bartender. He took a seat next to her and held out his hand. "Pete Gilbert."

The woman shook Parnell's hand and introduced herself as Miranda Lopez.

"So what do you do for a living, Miranda?"

"I work at the police department in records but I'm taking the test for police cadet next week. If I pass all the tests and the interview, I'll be in the July seventeenth academy class."

"Really?" Parnell acted surprised but he really didn't give a shit. He wanted one thing and anyone who could get for him would be his best friend—for as long as it took to get it. "Well,

I'll just bet you'll make a helluva an officer." He raised his beer bottle up. "Here's to Austin's best cadet-to-be." They tapped bottles and swigged down some beer.

"So where do you work, Pete Gilbert?" she asked.

"Samsung. I'm a public relations specialist."

They made small talk before Parnell asked her to dance. Two country dances later, they waltzed back to their table.

Miranda giggled. "Buy me another beer."

After three more beers, Miranda stood up, a little wobbly and coaxed Parnell back out on the dance floor—this time for music with a faster beat. As she gyrated her hips to the beat, rubbing her body against his, she shot him an alluring look, parting her lips then flicking her eyebrows up.

He grabbed her around the waist and pulled her close when they walked back to the table. "Hey, wanna come back to my hotel room? Show ya my etchings," he whispered in her ear.

Miranda beamed. "Etchings? Does that bullshit line really work?"

He chuckled. "Sometimes."

They headed out to his car, their arms wrapped around each other's waist. Miranda's hand slid down to Parnell's butt and squeezed.

He laughed. "Damn, Miranda. You're hotter than desert sand at high noon. We're gonna have us some real fun, baby." He reached up and got a handful of her breast. "Let's go to your place instead."

The next evening, Miranda met Parnell at the same bar. After four beers—Reyes's magic number—and several dances later, Parnell figured the time was right to ask his questions. "Have you ever heard of a woman at the PD named Dani Mueller?"

"Oh yeah." Miranda looked at him. "Why? You want to get her in bed, too?" she asked before gulping down a mouthful of beer.

He laughed. "Hell, no. She's my second cousin, once removed. I'm lookin' for her address so I can pop in and surprise her. *Truer words*…Haven't seen her in God knows how long. And besides, you and me—" He grinned at her then leaned in close. "We got a good thing goin."

She turned her face away. "Is that why you picked me up?"

He pulled back, watching her. He rubbed the bridge of his nose then gazed into her dark brown eyes. "Sweetheart, if that's what you think of me then let's part company right now." He stood up and polished off his beer. "Have a nice night," he said, sporting a dejected expression, turning to leave.

"Wait a minute," she blurted out.

He kept walking but before he got to the door, she grabbed his arm. "Don't go." She toyed with a button on his shirt. "I'm sorry." She gazed up at his handsome face. "Forgive me?"

"I don't know. That hurt. I mean I really like you but a man's got his pride—"

"I can get you her address," Miranda offered. Burton seemed to hesitate and she took his hand. "C'mon, let's go back to my house."

❧❦❧

The alarm clock went off at five o'clock in the morning. Miranda sprang out of bed, showered, and got dressed.

Burton was dressed and waiting for her in the kitchen with a piping hot cup of coffee. She wrote her work number down on a sheet of notebook paper and handed it to him. "Call me after nine this morning."

He pulled her down on his lap. "All I want to do is surprise her. You come with me. We'll surprise her together unless you might get in trouble?" He kissed her. "Tell ya what. Get me her address and you and me, we'll go get ourselves a steak dinner tomorrow night then maybe a movie. This weekend I want to take you down to San Antonio. I'll make reservations at a hotel on the Riverwalk. How's that sound, honey?"

Her eyes sparkled. "Wonderful." She put her arm around his neck, gazing at him with starry eyes before kissing him. When she got off his lap he reached out a hand and stroked the inside of her thigh.

Miranda smiled wide and pushed his hand away. "That's enough for now."

He persisted.

She backed away, pushing at his hand again. "C'mon, stop it." She laughed. "If I don't leave now, I'll be late." She smiled and flicked her eyebrows up. "Then you won't get her address."

CHAPTER 22

"The obstacles of your past can become the gateways
that lead to new beginnings." ~ *Ralph Blum*

Sleep and stress fought with each other. Stress won. I lay
in the dark, wishing I could have a do-over—so many
things I'd have done differently. I tried to concentrate on
the lacy shadow of the tree outside my window instead of the
persistent image of Jason. I hadn't known him for very long
and yet I knew I cared about him already, and not just because
of Shannon.

Jason had to shield his daughter from me—I hated it but I
understood why.

I'd stay on my job—I loved it and I was a good crime analyst—but if my presence created an awkward working envi-
ronment for either of us, I'd transfer to another division, or do
something else. It was like being in the eye of the storm. The
price for the temporary loss of my moral compass was getting
steeper all the time and I suspected the final payment was
coming due. My heart raced with the realization that my life
and career here in Austin might be coming to an end.

I wasn't sleeping so I went in early, flipping my office
light on a few minutes after six. At least I wouldn't meet that
creepy Robertson on the elevator today. I sat back at my desk,
savoring my hot chocolate mocha and the blueberry pastry.
Starbuck's made the best mocha outside of Garmisch.

My phone rang, snapping me out of my delicious moment.

"Good morning, Karla. Oops, I meant Dani. I forget
which name you're going by. This is—"

"I know who it is. What do you want?"

"Watch your tone, young lady," Robertson warned. "As you realize by now, I'm sure, I know all about your California caper, a story I feel sure you don't want broadcast around the department. Having said that, I believe you should reconsider meeting us at the Driskill Grill."

"I'll give it some thought."

"Excellent. I'll expect your answer by nine o'clock. Have a nice day, Dani Engel. Darn it, there I go again. I meant Mueller."

Taking a sip of the mocha, I thought about his offer. When I called him back to tell him I'd meet him there when hell froze over, I wanted to honestly say I'd thought it over.

An icon on my desktop caught my eye—the shortcut to the Personnel database. I accessed it once in the past for an analysis my boss assigned to me.

I brought up the database with the home addresses and service time of officers. Robertson's departmental history stared back at me. It didn't tell me everything I wanted but it gave me enough. The internet was next. It held a treasure trove of information if you knew where to look. And I did. It took a couple hours but I found what I needed. Thank God for social networking sites.

I used a face search website that showed Robertson with an alias. An alias he created when he made his Facebook page: William V. Hansen, a private security consultant. Seemed Robertson, as Hansen, had a fling in Galveston. A woman named Elizabeth Haish filed a paternity suit against Hansen in Galveston County. The fact that he had a wife and two children here in Austin prompted him to settle with Elizabeth out of court. But his wife found out his lurid little secret and divorced him four months later.

I sat back, pleased with myself, and sipped the last of my chocolate mocha. When the Galveston district clerk's office opened at nine, I'd order copies of the entire file. Then Ms. Haish and I would have a little chat. I'd forego calling Robertson. Let him wonder.

The copies arrived around ten on my fax. Elizabeth Haish,

known as Lieutenant Elizabeth Haish-Burrows of the Galveston Police, seemed very pleasant to talk to after I explained my reason for calling.

"I'm so mad at myself for falling for his line of shit," Elizabeth, or Liz as she preferred to be called, told me. "He said he was divorced and traveled between his office in Austin and the one in Galveston. So stupid me, I fell for it. We kept seeing each other, whenever he'd arrive in town. I should have figured it out when he wouldn't take me home. Always to the Flagship Hotel. Told me his place was always a mess. That a nice girl like me deserved to be pampered. I'll admit they certainly did that at that hotel. When I came up pregnant, he sandbagged me with excuses why he couldn't marry me like he told me he wanted to do. Then he disappeared. I left messages but he never called back. So I hired a private investigator and had him followed. That's when I found out the rat was married with kids and who he really was. I blew up. You know the rest."

The faxes started rolling in from the Galveston District Clerk and from Liz herself. Nineteen pages total. This information would force Robertson's hand. It was comforting to know you had the trump card. But I wasn't naïve enough to believe he'd quit. Robertson was a very vindictive man. But at least he'd tread on eggshells until he found a new angle.

I emailed him.

> *Commander, I chatted with an old friend of yours—Lieutenant Haish-Burrows. She said to say hello to you and thanks for the support payments. If you'd care to discuss our chat, I'll be in my office for another hour. Then I have a meeting with the chief.*

I assumed he'd study the email, debate his choices, and then delete it. He'd elect to come down and try to bully his way out of this jam. Six or seven minutes later, I heard a rapping on my door.

"Come in."

He stood framed in the doorway with paper in his hand, which I assumed was my email. Slapping it with his free hand, he asked me, "What the hell is this?"

I knew my expression was one of smugness and that was fine with me. Like Americans say, digging up that information gave me a warm and fuzzy feeling. "What was that you said the last time you were here? Ah, yes, I'll find out about you." I picked up the faxed pages and pretended to read them. "She's a remarkable lady. Not happy at all with you, but at least you got a son out of the affair." I looked at him. "I'll bet you're so proud."

I couldn't see my face but my grin must have extended from ear to ear as his face turned a light shade of purple. Closing the door behind him, he cautioned me, 'Keep your voice down."

"Here's the deal, Commander, stop harassing Jason Scarsdale. No more threats about discipline for some insignificant rules infraction."

"What are you talking about?"

I chuckled. "You know exactly what I'm talking about." I pointed at Katarina's photograph. "If anyone finds out about my background—and I mean anyone—" I waved the faxes. "Your career is over." I paused to let it sink in. "So either agree or I'll go straight to the chief with this." I made an exaggerated show of looking at the clock. "In precisely eleven minutes."

He glared at me, which was about all he could do.

I glanced back at the clock. "Ten minutes now."

He gestured at the papers, smiling. "Let me see those papers."

I shook my head. "Nope." I pretended to read them again. "Let's see now. William V. Hansen settled the paternity action for twenty-five thousand dollars. Monthly support payments of four hundred a month." I smiled at him. "I'll bet that support is *not* being deducted from your paycheck, is it?"

He scowled at me.

I held up the Hansen photo from Facebook. "This is Hansen's photograph from Facebook. It's you. And of course, Elizabeth—" I smiled like I was sitting for a portrait. "She prefers to be called Liz. Liz said she'd be more than willing to drive up and meet with the chief if I needed her to do so. And your signature on this affidavit is notarized. The notary has a record of the ID you used to verify yourself as Hansen." Then I waved my copy of the birth certificate. "And your alias is on here too."

He massaged his chin as if pondering his dilemma and how best to extricate himself from it.

"Eight minutes to go which actually is three minutes. I wouldn't want to be late for that meeting. My way or the highway. What's it going to be?"

He nodded. "Agreed." He held out his hand for the papers. "You won't need those anymore."

I jerked them out of his reach. "*Au contraire*, Commander, you actually think I'd trust you to honor our agreement? I'll keep these documents in case you renege."

CHAPTER 23

"By perseverance the snail reached the ark."
~ *Charles Haddon Spurgeon*

Zarko sat in his truck, watching the front of Dani's apartment, wondering if the backfire alerted her. *Friggin' piece of shit truck*, he thought. If it wasn't the engine backfiring, it was the lousy clutch making the gears grind. He couldn't sneak up on a dead man with this crappy truck.

When he saw the blinds on the front window lift open, he knew someone was looking. Scarsdale's probably up there. Or some bitch cop staying with her. Figuring it'd be only a few minutes before the cops came storming into the parking lot, he fired up the engine of his old pickup. It backfired again.

"Shit."

He shoved the floor-mounted gearshift forward for first gear but the clutch was worn down. The gears made a loud grinding sound. "C'mon, you worthless piece of shit. Get in there." He kept forcing the shifter until it finally popped into place.

Hoping the CEO didn't find out he'd been at Dani's, Zarko considered how he could thwart Scarsdale's investigation. A believable alibi could blunt the impact of any DNA results. He'd claim that he'd cut himself while clearing broken glass and other debris away from Lasiter's head when he checked for a pulse. That wasn't a total lie—he did cut himself but not on glass. His fist struck Lasiter right in the teeth. And he did check for a pulse.

But what to do about that damn woman. He almost laughed, thinking how Scarsdale used her as a snitch. If he could only get rid of the bitch, if only that prick Lasiter hadn't said his name, Scarsdale would still be at square one. The friggin' cop had her locked up safer than gold at Ft. Knox. *Gotta be screwin'* her, he thought. After all, the CEO said Scarsdale and her hung out together. Driving south on Highway 183, he rested his head on his hand, propped up on the edge of the driver's window, and thought about Dani. He wondered if she had met or seen him before that night when Lasiter died. Her face didn't ring any bells.

As his finger traced the scar on his cheek, he recalled how she'd raked his face with that damn key. Liked to almost crushed his balls with her damn knee. His teeth clenched as he gripped the steering wheel so tight his fingers turned white, thinking about how she'd whipped his ass.

And that weekend before Thanksgiving. Someone had trashed his house and he bet it'd been that hooded dude he saw hide behind the hedge—or maybe it wasn't a dude at all, he thought, peering back in the direction of Dani's apartment—maybe it was her.

If he could just get her alone one more time, she'd pay. Damn straight she would. A corner of his mouth snaked its way up the side of his face. Getting rid of her would be the same as screwing over Scarsdale.

❧❧❧

Later Tuesday morning, Scarsdale got a call back from Detective Levine.

"I got a look at the bracelet. It's gold, fourteen carat, with an array of diamonds on each end and the initials 'AC' engraved on the inside," Levine said.

Scarsdale compared Levine's description with the one provided by Susan Crowell. A hands-on match. "It matches the one taken in our murder case. My partner and I can drive up this afternoon. Can you put a hold on it?"

"Consider it done."

Scarsdale grabbed the Crowell file and strode down to Mitchell's office. "Hey, Lieutenant, Harris and I are going up to Temple PD. I think we found the missing Crowell bracelet."

"Go!" Mitchell said.

Scarsdale paced like an expectant father, casting occasional glances at the wall clock, and peering over the entire set of cubicles as he waited for Harris to return from Winters's office.

When Harris did return, Scarsdale lured him out of the building.

"What did *Herr* Winters want?"

"To know if you and Dani were dating. That asshole believes the two of you are secretly meeting out of town and he wanted me to find out where." He walked on in silence before looking at Scarsdale. "You two aren't, are you?"

Scarsdale's face tightened. "Of course. In fact, we're on our way to Temple to meet her for dinner."

"Well, hell, give me a minute to run back to Winters's office and tell him his suspicions were right. Who knows? Maybe he'll want to go along."

"We've never been on a date and it's very doubtful we ever will."

"Never say never," Harris teased.

Neither man said anything after that. As they drove through Georgetown, Scarsdale cast a quick glance at Harris—his head laid back against the headrest, his mouth open wide, snoring.

Never say never. Would he and Dani ever go on a date? About the time the idea of a date intrigued him, Marcy's scowling face appeared. Like pouring a bucket of water on a small fire.

Alissa had asked Scarsdale to consider Marcy's visitation proposal: one weekend a month at his house. She and her husband would stay in the spare bedroom. If he got called out, she'd roam unsupervised all over his house, an idea he didn't relish. But Shannon would get more time with her maternal grandparents and maybe, just maybe, Marcy's henpecked hubby could keep her in check. Scarsdale dismissed that thought right away. He'd have to put a padlock on his bedroom door.

Thirty minutes later, Scarsdale saw the road sign indicating that they were now in Bell County and a half hour later they stood in the lobby of Temple Police Department. It had a spacious lobby, with lots of windows, unlike the one at Austin PD. *Not as reclusive and secretive as we are*, Scarsdale thought. They strolled up to a waist-high counter where a cute Hispanic female sat behind a thick window. Scarsdale figured the window was bullet-proof.

A few minutes later, an interior door opened and Detective Levine walked out to greet them. He looked stout as a fireplug with a receding hairline. Scarsdale guessed he was in his early thirties.

Dressed in a white shirt and tie, a Glock 9mm holstered on his right hip, and a badge clipped on his belt, Levine shook hands with both men.

"C'mon back to my area," Levine said.

The three men went through the security door, to the elevator, and up to the third floor. Levine's cubicle was green, a little larger than Scarsdale's, with a newer model flat-screen computer monitor—better than the one he had back in Austin. The cubicle had two guest chairs and a black reclining office chair on wheels. Scarsdale noted the ample cabinet and drawer space.

He elbowed Harris. "Helluva lot better set-up than we've got."

"You got that right."

"I assume you guys want to see the bracelet. So let's go," Levine said.

Scarsdale and Harris followed him down and out of the building to a dark blue sedan.

"I outrank you so I'll take the front seat," said Harris, moving between Scarsdale and the front door.

Scarsdale flipped him the bird as he opened the back door and slid inside. "Damn. This is plush," he said, inspecting the interior. "Cushioned armrests and headrests."

"I'm actually up for a new car next month," Levine said.

"A new one, huh?" Scarsdale said, running his hand

across the seat fabric. "Got any openings up here for two detectives?"

Levine laughed like he thought Scarsdale was joking.

Scarsdale tapped Harris on the shoulder. "He thinks I'm kidding."

Levine parked his plush car in front of the Stillhouse Pawn Shop. The three detectives went straight to the back counter where the shopkeeper, an overweight man wearing wire-rimmed spectacles, placed the bracelet on the counter. Scarsdale laid the picture of Amy's next to it. Picking the actual bracelet up, he turned it over and saw the initials "AC" engraved inside.

"Matches the picture and the description to a T," Scarsdale said.

"Okay," said Levine, looking right at the pawn shop owner. "I'll take that as evidence." He dropped the bracelet in a plastic bag, sealing same and handed it to Scarsdale. Levine signed off on the pawn shop release form. "You said you have a photo line-up to show him?" Levine asked. "And some questions?"

"Yes." Scarsdale laid a manila folder down on the countertop. It had six photographs of white males, all appearing about the same age, hair color and style, and clean-shaven. "Look at these photographs and tell me if you recognize the guy that pawned this bracelet."

The shopkeeper rested his thick arms on the glass and perused each picture. He kept glancing back at one certain photograph before looking at Scarsdale. He tapped Photo Number Five. "That one. He's the one."

The photo he had selected was of Tom Zarko. Scarsdale's pulse quickened. Almost two weeks since Lasiter's murder and now he considered Zarko a prime suspect in the killing of Amy Crowell. He had enough now to get an arrest warrant for Zarko for forgery and theft of the bracelet. Once he had been booked in jail, they'd get a DNA sample from him—one way or another.

Ripples of satisfaction rolled across his mind, balanced

against the realization he'd failed Scott Lasiter. Susan Crowell would have some closure when he showed her the bracelet, but it would have to stay in evidence until Zarko's cases were finally disposed of.

"What's the history with this bracelet? I mean was it part of a burglary or something like that?" the shop owner asked.

"Nope. A little girl was murdered and it was taken from her," Scarsdale said.

The owner stared at Scarsdale for a moment then shook his head in disbelief. "To kill a little girl over a piece of jewelry. I hope you catch that son of a bitch." He walked over to a file cabinet and retrieved a folder. He drew out a copy of a driver's license and handed it to Scarsdale. "I always make copies of the DL when I take a pawn from an out-of-towner."

Scarsdale looked at it—the driver's license had Lasiter's name and address but the photo belonged to Zarko. "He pasted his picture over top of Lasiter's." *Make that two forgery cases*, Scarsdale thought.

Then Scarsdale slid a pre-prepared statement in front of the owner with a few blanks that Scarsdale filled in. The statement indicated that the owner identified photograph number five as the person who pawned the bracelet, and included a brief description of the pawn transaction. On the drive back to Austin, Scarsdale called Susan Crowell on his cell. "Susan, we need to meet with you this afternoon."

"Certainly. May I ask what it's about?" Susan asked.

"We recovered a bracelet in Temple that matches the description of the one Amy wore that day."

A few seconds of silence. He heard her sniff. When she spoke, her voice cracked a little. "Does it have her initials inside?"

"Yes. A. C. and the diamonds too."

She thanked him profusely before he hung up.

"Good deal. She and her husband can now get some closure," Harris said.

"I can't imagine the nightmare her life's been since Amy was murdered. I hope..." He looked at Harris and let out a deep breath. "I hope she finds some peace now." He remembered Dani telling him about her recovery of Katarina's bracelet—how much it meant to her. He wondered what he'd feel if he were in her shoes.

He forced himself to think about Lasiter. Without looking at Harris, he said, "We got played and arrested the wrong man. And he paid the ultimate price for our fuck-up."

Harris sat there silent, peering at the cars and buildings flying by. Finally he spoke, "Everything we found, everything the witnesses said, pointed at Lasiter. Not one single person we talked to ever mentioned Zarko."

Scarsdale called the DA's office. Robert Fuller, the assistant DA who took over Coffield's caseload, answered the call. Fuller was a nine year veteran of the DA's office who gave detectives more leeway than a few of the other prosecutors.

Scarsdale expected Coffield to be the reviewer. "Where's Coffield?"

"Let's just say he decided the DA's Office didn't fit in with his career aspirations."

"So he got shit-canned?"

"No, not exactly, I'd say he got an offer he couldn't refuse."

Scarsdale briefed him on the Zarko case developments, beginning with the anonymous envelope containing the pawn ticket to the recovery of the bracelet and the identity switch by Zarko. Fuller agreed to prepare affidavits for three arrest warrants—forgery, theft, and Fraudulent Use of Identifying Information.

Then he called Mitchell to update him on the recovery of the bracelet. "The DA will have affidavits ready for pick-up. We'll arrest Zarko at his workplace and bring him in for a discussion about Lasiter's death and Amy Crowell's murder."

"Fine," Mitchell said, "I'll brief Robertson and Winters." Mitchell rolled his eyes. "He wants to be in the loop on all things Zarko, as does Winters."

❧❧❧

Scarsdale phoned Susan as soon as they parked at her building. She said she'd be waiting for them at the receptionist desk. She was waiting, her eyes bright and expectant when they entered. Scarsdale pulled the baggie containing the bracelet out of his pocket and handed it to her. She peered at it and her hand flew up to her mouth. Tears formed but she didn't cry. Nodding, she said, "Yes, that's her bracelet."

"Like I told you, we have to put it in evidence. As soon as the case is finished, I'll personally get it back to you," Scarsdale said.

"You said it was in Temple? Where exactly?"

"In a pawn shop," Scarsdale said.

"Did Lasiter pawn it before…" Her voice trailed off.

"No, a guy named Tom Zarko pawned it, using Lasiter's ID, after Lasiter died. We're picking up a warrant for him when we leave here."

∾∾∾

Walking along the narrow ledge on the third floor of the construction site, Zarko heard his cell phone buzz. He laid the steel rebar down and checked the caller ID but didn't recognize the number. He answered anyway. "Yeah."

"Yeah? Is that the way you answer my calls?" the husky male voice said.

Zarko stood there in silence, fuming. *Yeah motherfucker, it is. Whatcha gonna do about it?* He wished he had the guts to say that out loud.

"Answer my question, dipshit."

He seethed. "No, sir, it's not." Having to kowtow to that prick was a pain in the ass. He knew it. Ferguson had known it too but he made the mistake of trying to do something about it. Cost him his life.

"Good. I like obedience. Too bad Olsen didn't realize that. Trying to make a deal with the DA—tsk, tsk, tsk. Not smart. Not at all."

"I need to get these rebars over to the other side or I'll get in trouble. So what can I do for you, sir?" Zarko asked, through clenched teeth.

An audible sigh answered. "I call to save your ass and you say work is more important. You're an ungrateful shit, you know that, Zarko?"

The man was pushing Zarko's patience. He took a deep breath through his nose. "I'm sorry, sir."

"Scarsdale and Harris are on their way there to arrest you for forgery and theft. Do yourself and me a favor and get the hell out of town."

"I gotta get my stuff."

"Better hurry up. And there's one more thing I need you to do before you depart."

"And that is?"

"Grab Scarsdale's daughter. Drive her out to the lake—Bullick Hollow Road—then call me. I'll give you directions where to deliver her."

Silence.

"You need Scarsdale's address?" the CEO asked.

"I know where Scarsdale lives."

"I'll arrange to have an envelope with some travel cash for you after you drop her off."

Zarko hung up. A grin extended across his face. Stealing Scarsdale's kid really appealed to him. Beat the hell outta going after that damn woman. But he'd need a new ride.

Zarko climbed in his truck and sped off north toward Highway 183. He spotted a strip center and pulled into the lot, driving by a few cars before choosing a parking spot. He fished his gun from under the tattered seat and stuffed it in his waistband. He climbed out and strolled among the parked cars until he saw a middle-aged woman put her purse and a couple of plastic bags on the back seat of a blue Mazda sedan. She closed the door and moved toward the driver's door, keys in her hand.

Approaching from the rear, Zarko jammed the gun in her back. Jerking the keys out of her hand, he barked orders at her. "Don't say a fuckin' word. If you scream, I'll kill ya." He glanced around the lot. Not seeing anyone, he grabbed a handful of her hair and slammed her head into the side of a car parked next to hers. She let out a quick groan and fell to the ground, unconscious.

ɷ

Scarsdale and Harris picked up the warrants for Zarko's arrest and decided to switch cars—Harris's car needed gas and neither wanted to take the time now to do that. Driving Scarsdale's assigned Crown Victoria, they took off to hunt for Zarko.

Their first stop was his worksite.

"Where's Zarko?" Scarsdale asked, showing the foreman the warrant. "We're here to arrest him."

"Ya'll just missed him. He got a phone call, grabbed his jacket, and hauled ass. Maybe five, ten minutes ago."

Scarsdale and Harris looked at each other. "You know who called him?" Scarsdale asked.

The foreman shook his head, "Nope, can't say I do."

"Where did he go?"

"Beats me. When he hung up, he looked kind of wild-eyed. Like he was scared and pissed off at the same time. He ran out to his truck and tore out of the parking lot like his ass was on fire."

The ride to Zarko's house took just over ten minutes. No green truck and the front door was locked tight. Scarsdale and Harris sat in the car and waited for Zarko to return.

"Mitchell and Fuller knew about the warrants," Scarsdale said. "So did Robertson and Winters." He phoned Mitchell again. "Zarko left work in a big hurry right after he got a phone call. Somebody warned him we were coming."

"Let me check with Robertson and Winters. Where are you now?"

"Parked outside his house."

"Could be somebody overheard us discussing the case. Stay put until I call back."

Scarsdale pulled out his pocket notepad and flipped a few pages until he found what he wanted—Zarko's truck description and license plate number. He called communications and requested a look-out for the truck, giving the operator the arrest warrant number and charge so the officer could hold him until they arrived.

He also asked the operator to enter the information into TCIC and NCIC—the Texas Crime Information Center and its FBI counterpart, the National Crime Information Center. Officers anywhere would be able to check for warrants on Zarko if they stopped him for a traffic offense or under suspicious circumstances.

"Maybe he's hiding out at Ms. Lasiter's house," Harris said. "After all, she thinks he could do no wrong."

"Let's find out," Scarsdale said as he tapped in the number for Communications again on his cell. He asked dispatch to send a marked unit there, reading off the address from his notes.

Scarsdale's cell chirped. The screen showed Mitchell. "What did you find out?"

"Nothing yet. Keep looking for him," Mitchell said.

A half hour later, his cell went off.

"Hey, Detective, this is Spears. We cruised by that address a few times. No pick-up truck here. Maybe he skipped town?"

"I'd appreciate it if you guys stayed in the area. He may show later."

"Left town," Scarsdale said to Harris. Then he had an epiphany. He called the Pflugerville police, requesting a marked unit check the Oak Grove Apartments for a green Ford pick-up truck. He read off the license plate number. After hanging up, he cast a worried glance at Harris, "He'll want to even the score before he leaves town."

"You got a thing for her, don't you?" Harris teased.

Scarsdale adjusted his position on the seat. "I'd be lying if I said I didn't like her but Marcy'd have my ass if she ever found out about Dani's history." He'd spend his time with

Shannon and the memory of Charity. Maybe moving on wasn't in the cards. At least not right now.

"Well, Marcy won't be around here forever."

"Maybe not, but Robertson will be."

"As for Charity, you have to let her go."

Scarsdale heard bits and pieces of the Mazda theft broadcast over the radio as he talked about Dani. "She'd be perfect for Shannon. She loves kids and Shannon would fill that hole she has in her heart."

They watched an elderly man with a cane start across the street in front of them. "That's you, Harris, in ten years," Scarsdale joked.

"Hell, in ten years Mary and I will be traveling around the world." He stared into the distance for a few seconds. "There's a world cruise that sails all the way from Florida through the Canal and on for over a hundred days. Imagine being pampered for over a hundred—"

Scarsdale saw the blue Mazda turn the corner, heading toward them. He put his hand on Harris's shoulder as he watched the car pull to the curb, then make a U-turn. The driver was unmistakable. "Holy shit," he yelled. "It's Zarko. He's driving that stolen Mazda."

Scarsdale started the car, put in gear, and pulled away from the curb.

The old man heard the tires squealing and froze right in the middle of the street, forcing Scarsdale to a stop. He laid on the horn and Harris waved at the man to move. "Move. Get the hell out of the way." Scarsdale veered to the left, drove up over the curb around the old man. "Shit, Zarko made us. Took off right around the corner," he said as he raced down the street and turned left. No Mazda in sight. He slammed his fist down hard on the steering wheel. "Dammit!"

Harris was already on the phone to dispatch.

⌘

Zarko tore down two blocks and made a quick right, putting him on MOPAC. He headed for Highway 183 and Scarsdale's house, careful now to stay under the speed limit. He figured it would take another fifteen minutes to get there at this speed. He saw no sign in the rearview mirror that Scarsdale was in pursuit—*gotta love that old fart Mr. Davis and his afternoon constitutional.* Zarko grinned. For once he relished an order from the CEO. Payback was gonna be sweet. He had watched that house off and on enough times to know that Scarsdale's kid played outside during the afternoon.

⁊ᲷᲾ

Today was Marcy's first time alone with her granddaughter and in her son-in-law's house. She and Scarsdale agreed that she'd have this afternoon for visitation at his place. Once Mrs. Hargraves left, Marcy started exploring the house, beginning in the kitchen. She examined the food in the refrigerator for spoilage and the cabinet for unclean dishes—anything she could use to convince the judge she would be the better custodian for Shannon. Using the camera feature on her cell phone, she snapped pictures of a dried spot on the counter, a balled up napkin under the table and a thin layer of dust on top of a wood cabinet in the dining room.

Her inspection was interrupted by her granddaughter.

Shannon stood there, holding her bicycle helmet by the strap. "Grandma, want to see me ride my bike?" She pulled Marcy's hand in the direction of the front door.

"Sure. Why not?" She took one look around the living room as she followed Shannon outside. She'd finish her inspection later.

As Shannon wheeled her bike down the front walk toward the sidewalk, Marcy sat down on the concrete step. "Don't go far."

"I won't," Shannon said, strapping her helmet on. The bike had a pink frame with matching pink and yellow wheel paper and pink training wheels. "Look, Grandma."

Marcy flashed a smile, then looked down at her cell

phone. She typed in the email address for her attorney and attached the photographs she just took. Before she typed the message she caught a glimpse of Shannon riding down the sidewalk. They waved at each other before Marcy typed out her observations, embellishing the negatives. Her son-in-law may have won the battle but the war was far from over.

ෆ෩ෆ෩

Zarko parked one door down from Scarsdale's house. He watched Shannon ride her bicycle on the sidewalk about thirty or so feet from the front porch.

"Hello, little girl," he muttered.

There was a woman sitting on the front step. She wasn't the babysitter he'd seen so many times before. This one was older. She'd be easier to deal with if she created a problem.

Shannon pedaled closer to the Mazda.

Zarko glanced at the woman. Her eyes were glued to her cell phone as her fingers flew over the text keys.

Shannon rode past his car and Zarko saw his chance. He jumped out, ran around the back of the car, approaching Shannon from behind. He wrapped one arm around her chest, jerking her right off the pink bike. Shannon's scream, loud and high-pitched, shredded the silence.

Zarko clamped his hand tight over her mouth, but she twisted and squirmed, kicking wildly. She punched the air and landed a couple of sharp elbow jabs on Zarko's upper arm. He pressed her close to his body as he rounded the car. Yanking the driver's door open he tossed Shannon on the front seat.

"Hey! No! Let her alone," Marcy screamed as she ran toward the car. Zarko pulled out his gun and aimed at her. She ducked down, holding her hands up like a protective screen, begging him to let Shannon go. He jumped in and drove off, his little prize cowering and screaming on the front floorboard. In the rear view mirror he saw Marcy standing in the street, watching his car speed away.

Zarko took one last glance at the woman in the rear view

mirror and laughed out loud. Shannon screamed for her father. Her eyes were big with terror as tears streamed down her cheeks.

"Stop bawling, ya little brat." He shoved her down with his free hand. "Somebody wants to meet you."

CHAPTER 24

"I cannot think of any need in childhood
as strong as the need for a father's protection."
~ *Sigmund Freud*

Scarsdale and Harris scoured Zarko's neighborhood, but they knew he was long gone. It was unlikely he'd be back, but as cops they knew from experience that people like Zarko acted unpredictably. They'd have patrol keep an eye on Zarko's house.

Scarsdale's cell phone tweeted. The display showed Marcy's cell phone number. It was the last thing he needed and if she hadn't had Shannon for the day he wouldn't have answered. At least he could be assured the old witch hadn't given his daughter aspirin. He hit the answer button.

"What's up?" he asked, steeling himself for whatever chain jerk she'd contrived.

"*Jason, get home now!*" The panicked screech was anything but vintage Marcy and his gut clenched. "A man kidnapped Shannon. Hurry."

"What man?" he asked as he floored the accelerator. "Did you get a license number?"

"No. He took off before I could see it."

"What's up?" Harris asked.

"Somebody kidnapped Shannon. Call dispatch now."

He got home in less than ten minutes. Two patrol cars were parked across the street. One of the officers approached Scarsdale's car as it skidded to a stop in the driveway. He and Harris both bailed out of the car at the same time. Scarsdale saw Shannon's bike lying on its side on the sidewalk.

Scarsdale sprinted past the officer to face Marcy. As

much as he wanted to get in her face, it was far more urgent to get the information about the vehicle used, the description of the perp, and his last known direction out to area law enforcement as fast as possible.

He listened, forcing himself to calm down as the uniformed officer asked the questions and took down her answers. "What did he look like?"

"Maybe thirty. I'm not sure. About your height, with curly hair. I think he had a scar on his cheek. His clothes were dirty like he'd been working."

Scarsdale and Harris looked at each other. They said the name at the same time. "Zarko."

Shock held her sobs in check but tears ran down Marcy's cheeks. "He—he jumped out of his car and grabbed her off her bike. He was gone before I could get there. I—" She described the Mazda as best she could and pointed down the street. "He took off that way," she said, pointing north in the direction of Parmer Lane. "In a blue car." She wiped the tears from her eyes.

When the officer finished his interview of Marcy, he used his shoulder-mounted microphone to radio in the information for immediate broadcast and an Amber Alert.

Scarsdale wasted no time laying into her. "Why weren't you out there with her?" he asked, pointing toward the bicycle. "What the hell were you doing? Sitting on your ass, gabbing on your damn phone?"

She looked at him with a puzzled expression, tears streaming down her cheeks. "I was talking to my lawyer."

"Talking to your lawyer? So you weren't even watching her?" Scarsdale said, moving close to her face and waving a clenched fist, as the two officers watched in a kind of stunned silence. Marcy raised her hands to ward off any assault by Scarsdale while backing away.

"She was on her bicycle," Marcy said, nodding in the direction of the bike and inching her way closer to the two officers. "I just took my eyes off her for a minute." She looked at Scarsdale then the officers, as if searching for a friendly face.

"He pointed a gun at me."

Scarsdale pulled at his chin while he paced back and forth, cursing. He spun around, facing Marcy. His eyes blazed. "When I find her—if anything happens to her—if he—" He couldn't keep the menace from his eyes but he managed to choke down his threats. He turned his back to her and stood fixed like a statue, staring up the street in the direction Shannon's abductor had driven.

Harris put his hand on Scarsdale's shoulder. "It's gonna be okay, buddy."

One of the uniformed officers spoke. "We got the plate number. The car was stolen from a shopping center parking lot. Every officer for fifty miles will be looking for him."

"I'm so sorry, Jason," Marcy pleaded from behind him. "It was my fault."

Scarsdale stood there for a moment, staring into the distance, his mouth drawn into a tight, thin line. "No, it's not. It's mine. I should never have let you have visitation until I was present," he said to the empty street.

Scarsdale walked away while keying in Amanda Colbert's number on his cell. If anyone knew a pedophile's thought processes, it would be her. "Do you have any idea, any at all, where Zarko would go?" He was grabbing at straws but he couldn't just stand around, doing nothing to find his daughter.

"Just guessing, I'd say either Houston or Mexico. Why?"

"Because the bastard kidnapped my daughter," Scarsdale said, walking toward Shannon's tipped-over bike.

"Oh my God, Jason. Okay, I'll make some calls. See what I can find out."

The uniformed officer taking the report approached Scarsdale. "Detective, I need a recent photograph of Shannon.

Scarsdale looked at him before nodding. He knew why they wanted it—to identify her when or if she was found. "Yeah, I know." Scarsdale retrieved one from his wallet and gazed at her face. Would he ever see her again?

If Zarko hurts her, he's a dead son of a bitch. And no jury in the world will convict me, Scarsdale thought. He stood on the sidewalk, looking down at Shannon's abandoned bike then at the passing cars slowing down for the drivers to gawk. A passenger window rolled down and the occupant asked what happened.

Scarsdale glanced at Marcy who stood there, frozen in place in the middle of the yard, her fingers digging into her lower lip, her eyes jittery with panic. She said something to him but he couldn't hear it. Maybe he didn't want to.

Harris and the three officers stood nearby, talking and gesturing at the bike and the sidewalk.

Scarsdale's face distorted with anger and loathing because someone like Zarko had the audacity to hit back at him by snatching Shannon. That went beyond the threats he'd received from the human trash he had arrested. He wanted to beat Zarko into a bloody lifeless corpse.

He felt helpless, worthless to Shannon now. Images of her crying and screaming like she had when he'd told her that Mommy wasn't coming home again streamed like scenes from a horror movie across his mind. He'd give anything to hold Shannon in his arms now. He'd tell her everything would be all right and she would give him that giggle. He'd look into her soft brown eyes and brush back the wispy blonde hairs that were always curling around her beautiful face. His eyes flitted around the yard until they rested on Harris. He knew what he had to do. By the time Scarsdale cranked up his personal vehicle—a blue SUV, Harris had plopped down in the passenger seat.

"Where are we going?" Harris asked, buckling up. "Why not our car? There's no radio in here. No grill lights. Nothing."

Scarsdale patted his sidearm. "Got all I need and I'm going to Zarko's house." He looked at Harris. A cold dark hatred lay on the surface of Scarsdale's eyes. "Get out. I don't want you involved."

"No. We're partners and friends. Where you go, I go," Harris said, checking the magazine in his weapon.

"I'm not going to stand around here with my thumb up

my ass. There's got to be something in his place that'll tell us where he went with my daughter."

"You know if we go in there without a warrant, the case against Zarko flies right the window," Harris warned.

Scarsdale backed the SUV out then shoved the gearshift into Drive. The tires squealed. "Fuck the case. That son of a bitch's got my daughter and I'm going to find her." He stared straight ahead. "And when I do find that bastard, making a case on him won't matter. They'll be making one on me."

⚘⚘⚘

Zarko turned off Farm to Market Road 620. Shannon, curled into a ball on the front passenger floorboard, kept her frightened eyes glued on him.

"I want my daddy."

"Shut up!" He threw his jacket over Shannon's head. "Stop yer damn cryin' or I'll give you something to cry about, chicklet." About a mile down the lane, he stopped and backed the car into a clearing, behind a stand of cedar trees. Then he punched in a phone number on his cell.

"I got her. Where do you want me to take her?"

"Where are you now?" the husky voice said.

He started to say something witty but thought better of it. "About two miles down Comanche Trail. Maybe a mile or so from Bob Wentz Park."

"Drive toward Bob Wentz until you see a red sign with an arrow on the right side of the road. There's a gravel road off to the right. You'll pass a pale blue stone house on the right. Keep going up the hill. About a hundred yards farther up is a log home sitting back in the trees. Take her around back, knock four times. Wait ten seconds then ring the doorbell. Agosti will be there to take her. Think you can follow those directions?"

"Yeah, I got it. Then what? It won't take Scarsdale long to figure out it was me that snatched his kid. Does Agosti have the money you—"

"Shut up a minute."

A long moment of silence.

"Did you steal a Mazda? A blue one?"

"Yeah."

"Shit!" the CEO said.

"What's wrong?"

"It's got a LoJack tracker in it," the CEO said.

"Oh, yeah? How do you know?"

"My fairy fucking godmother told me. The woman you took it from turned in a stolen car report. They're searching for it now."

"I had no choice. Scarsdale knew my truck like the back of his hand." He watched, paralyzed, as a park ranger's car drove past.

A few seconds passed in silence.

"Drop off the kid and do yourself a big favor and drive it off into the lake. After you ditch the car, go to Bob Wentz Park Road. There's a gravel road that runs parallel to the Park. You know the one I'm talking about?"

"Yes."

"Go about a half-mile in and wait there. Somebody in a van will pick you up and take you to a safe house. Don't talk to anyone until he gets there," the CEO said. "Get going."

"How will I know who—"

Zarko heard the "click," then a dial tone.

After he did the door knocking ritual, he stood there, peering off into the thick woods that almost surrounded the house.

Agosti opened the screen door, eyeing Zarko before looking at a blindfolded Shannon.

Zarko saw the black eye and the swollen lip. "What happened to you? Mouth off at the CEO?"

Agosti cast a wary glance at Zarko before lowering his head and nodding. "Give her to me."

"Here ya go. Ya think you can handle her?"

Agosti gave Zarko a go-to-hell look as he reached for Shannon. "Oh, yeah."

Zarko laughed. "I'd hate to hear that she whipped your ass."

"Very funny," Agosti said, grabbing Shannon by the arm.

Zarko patted her on the head. "Told ya I'd take ya to your daddy, brat."

She screamed as loud as she could while trying to pull away from Agosti.

"Stop it, little girl. I ain't gonna hurt you." he soothed as he removed the blindfold.

Zarko looked at Agosti. "Gimme the friggin envelope."

Agosti looked at him like he was crazy. "What envelope?"

"The CEO told me you'd have an envelope for me when I delivered this little brat."

Agosti shook his head. "He didn't say anything about any envelope."

Zarko walked back to the Mazda, muttering a few expletives. Less than an hour later, Zarko leaned up against a tree just off the dirt road. He rubbed his sore leg muscles. He checked his watch as he heard the helicopter fly low overhead. He saw the words, AUSTIN POLICE, on the tail as it passed by, flying toward the spot where the Mazda went into the lake. Gazing down the road toward Bullick Hollow, he saw a brown van approaching.

The van pulled up next to him. The passenger window rolled down.

"Need a ride?" the driver asked, glowering at Zarko.

Zarko recognized him—Rico Sanchez. "Haven't seen you in a while, *muchacho*."

Sanchez didn't answer.

Zarko reached for the passenger door handle just as Sanchez leveled the pistol at him. Zarko saw the gun a second or two before Sanchez fired. Diving to the ground, Zarko pulled his own gun out. He heard the driver's door open. Looking under the van, he saw Sanchez's feet hit the ground then head toward the rear. Zarko fired a single shot, striking him in the left ankle.

Sanchez shrieked and fell to the ground.

Scrambling to his feet, Zarko ran around the front of the van. Sanchez lay on the gravel, clutching his leg, moaning.

"Not too bright, are ya, shithead?" Zarko sneered as he jammed his gun back in the waist of his jeans and flipped his shirt over it. "Shoulda looked underneath," he said, glancing in the direction of the park entrance. Nobody headed his way.

Sanchez stared up at him without saying a word, reaching, instead, for the pistol.

Zarko booted it away. He kicked Sanchez several times in the face with his steel-toed work boots. Then he removed the cushion off the driver's seat, placed it over Sanchez's face, holding it there until the man stopped struggling. Zarko rifled the dead man's pockets, taking all the cash and his cell phone. He dragged Sanchez's body into the woods and covered it with debris and leaves. "So long, asshole," he whispered, then he sprinted for the van.

As Zarko turned right from Bullick Hollow onto 620, Sanchez's cell phone buzzed. Zarko saw the display—Restricted. He pressed the green "Answer" button.

"I assume you got rid of him," the husky voice asked. "Did he give you any trouble?"

This time Zarko relished answering the CEO. "Yeah, I got rid of him. No trouble at all, you sorry motherfucker."

A few seconds of silence passed before the CEO spoke again. "Where are you going?"

Zarko hung up.

ଓଓଓ

"Stop crying, little girl," Agosti said.

He stood there, studying Shannon. He thought she was too young. Images of the little Amy Crowell girl came to mind. Amy had been older than this girl.

Agosti shuddered to think about it. But he knew the CEO was all about making money. He'd sell his own mother if there was money to be made, but he'd never get his hands dirty.

That's what Zarko and the rest of the group were for.

"What's your name?" he asked, bending over and stroking her hair.

She batted his hand away. "I want to go home. I want my daddy," she screamed through her tears, her eyes darting to the door.

"Well, that's not going to happen. Now please stop crying." He picked up a game controller for Nintendo and offered it to her. "Do you like to play games?" He installed a game cartridge. "This one is called Super Mario." He showed her how the game worked, then offered it to her again. "It's fun."

Still crying, Shannon backed away from him as he stepped toward her.

"Whatever," Agosti said, picking her up and placing her in a closet. "When you stop crying, you can come out."

An hour later, Agosti opened the closet door. Shannon sat on the floor with her legs drawn up to her chest, sobbing.

He held out his hand. "C'mon. Let's play with the Nintendo."

She didn't move, shaking her head. "No, I want my daddy."

"Well, life is full of disappointments." He snapped his fingers. "C'mon." He reached his arms out. When she shrank back, he reached down and picked her up.

Shannon screamed with all her might and tried to squirm free, pounding her little fists against his face, twisting, and kicking against his body.

"Stop it. I'm not going to hurt you. I promise." He carried her into the living room and half-sat, half-dropped her, on the couch. He picked up the game controller and tossed it on the chair near her when he heard the phone ring. Giving Shannon a quick glance, he walked around the corner, into the next room. Agosti checked the caller ID and saw the single word "Restricted," a word that signified fear.

"Sir?" he asked.

"You have the kid?"

"Yes, sir."

"Get her the hell out of that house now. Take her down to the lake, kill her, and dump her body in the water."

"I don't understand. You told me to keep her here until you came home."

"Get rid of her," the CEO shouted. "Wipe down anything she may have touched. And make damn sure nobody sees her."

Agosti hung up the phone. "C'mon, little girl, we're going to take a walk down to the lake. See the ducks," he said, walking back into the living room. He stopped, frozen in his tracks. The game controller lay on the floor.

No Shannon.

He stood there, a sick feeling coming over him as he scanned the room.

"C'mon, little girl, don't play games. Get over here." He waited a few seconds but still no Shannon. "I'll be very mad if I have to come find you. Don't make me mad."

He looked at the back door. The inner door stood open. Agosti racked his brain, wondering if he forgot to close it.

"No, no, no." He rushed toward it and saw Shannon disappearing into the woods.

"Holy shit," he yelled as he barreled out the screen door, across the yard into the woods. "Come back here," he screamed. He stopped inside the edge of the woods and listened. He heard the sound of twigs and branches snapping. Rushing into the woods, he caught up to Shannon as she scrambled up from a fall.

"Gotcha now, little girl," he said, slowing to a walk and moving closer to her. She backed up, her head pushing against a low branch that gave way, fear in her eyes and tears streaking down the slopes of her cheeks.

Agosti got close. He stooped down and just as he sprang at her, Shannon ducked down, pivoted, and ran. The branch whipped back, catching Agosti across the bridge of his nose. He staggered backward, grabbed for his nose, lost his footing, and fell on his rear. Touching his nose, he felt the wetness and saw the blood on his fingers. "Dammit."

Using a tree limb, he pulled himself up. Standing still,

Agosti heard only the gentle rustling of leaves. Looking in each direction, he saw only mesquite trees with their thorny limbs, low branches of the cedar trees, and patches of cactus.

Dragging his hand across his face, he scanned the trees, wondering which way she went. *Would searching for her now be futile?* he asked himself. Feeling his still swollen lip conjured up gory images of Ferguson after the CEO had finished with him. With a shudder, he waded deeper into the woods, ducking under cedar branches, cursing when mesquite thorns scratched and gashed his bare arms and face.

Agosti stopped by a rocky outcropping and checked his watch—two hours until sundown. He scanned the area. *Which frickin' way did she go?* He knew the consequences of crossing the CEO. Looking back toward the house, he could see part of the roof. Ahead, the woods only seemed to get thicker and thornier.

He cupped his hands around his mouth and shouted, "There's monsters in here, little girl. They'll eat you." He listened. Nothing. He ran his hand over his head, knocking small bits of debris from his hair. "Dammit, where is she?" he muttered. His eyes darted along the surrounding thickets. Nothing.

Screw it. She won't make it out of here anyhow. I'll tell him I drowned her just like he wanted. He'll never know any different. Agosti headed back to the house to wipe away any evidence that he or the girl were ever there.

❧❧❧

Shannon stopped behind a large tree and looked back, her little chest heaving. She was covered in dried leaves and twigs and her arms were scraped and bloodied by the falls she'd taken each time a root or stump caught her feet. She'd heard the man yelling about the monsters. *Do monsters live here? Are they chasing me?* Remembering her mother's voice telling her over and over, '*If a bad person comes after you, run away as fast as you can,*' she got up and scampered on as fast as her legs would take her.

She ran into a large clearing and stopped, out of breath. Looking behind her, she didn't see or hear anyone but she did hear music. The same kind of music her mommy and daddy danced to in the living room. She took off, running toward the sound. A few falls later, Shannon burst from the woods into the backyard of a big house. She saw a road on one side of the house. On the other side, a woman with a red and white checkered bandanna on her head and garden shears in her hand, clipped bushes. The music came from a radio resting on the ground beside her.

Shannon felt something cold and wet touch her elbow. A big black dog. Screaming, she ran for the road. As she neared the corner of the house, she heard the woman yell, "Hey, where are you going? Little girl, wait. Cisco, come here."

Shannon sensed the dog running next to her but she didn't look over. Too scared. When she tripped over a garden hose she found herself looking up into the eyes of the large dog. His coarse tongue lapped her face.

"Get back, Cisco," the red-bandana woman said as she pushed the dog out of the way. She helped Shannon up then brushed grass off her shirt and jeans.

Shannon tried to get away but the woman held her arm.

"It's okay, honey." The woman eyed Shannon, trying to place her. "I've never seen you around here before. Where do you live?" the woman asked, wiping dirt from Shannon's cheek with the back of her finger.

Shannon pointed toward the woods. "A bad man is after me."

"What?" The woman looked at the tree line. "It's okay now. Nobody's going to hurt you." The woman ushered her toward the house, casting occasional glances back at the woods. "What's your name?"

"Shannon." She looked over her shoulder at the woods as they walked to the house.

"Shannon, I'm Anna." The woman smiled at her. "You're safe now, sweetheart. Let's go inside and clean up the scrapes. My husband'll call the sheriff."

"I want to go home," Shannon said, still crying.

"I know, sweetheart." The woman gave a last look at the woods before closing the door behind her and turning the lock. "Let's get those scrapes cleaned up." She peeked around the corner. "Turner, call 911. Now!"

CHAPTER 25

"With foxes, we must play the fox." ~ *Thomas Fuller*

Zarko planned to drive the van west toward Llano and Mason using back roads where he'd be less likely to cross paths with big city cops or the Highway Patrol. He'd cross into Mexico at Amistad Lake near Del Rio and work his way down to Monterrey and then maybe to the coast, like Cancun. But first, he wanted his collection, his passport, and payback.

He drove past the street where his house was located. Scarsdale's Crown Vic was gone. He saw the dark blue SUV parked in the driveway of the house with a "For Sale" sign in the front yard but blew it off, thinking it belonged to a prospective buyer.

Zarko laughed at the thought of Scarsdale frantically searching the city for his daughter. "Now it's your turn to freak, shithead," he muttered.

Turning right at the next intersection, he drove parallel to his street. Another right took him up to the alley. No cop cars in sight.

Driving down the alley, he pulled into an open garage that belonged to a vacant house across from his backyard. Exiting the van, he looked both ways before racing across the alley, hopping the fence, and scurrying through his yard to the back door.

Once he got his stuff out of his house, he'd visit the CEO's storage unit and clean it out. He'd followed the man there after the hotel meeting and assumed the man kept his entire collection in there along with his list of buyers. Payback and dollar signs floated across Zarko's mind.

He couldn't go to the front door and risk being seen by the cops and he didn't have time to fiddle with the lock on the backdoor. Flipping his jacket back and pulling the gun from its makeshift holster inside his jeans, he smashed the butt against a single glass panel in the door. He knocked the remaining pieces out, reached through, and flipped the latch.

Ducking inside, he tucked the gun back between the belt and his jeans and headed for the fireplace. With one sweep of his arm, he sent the ornamental mugs and knickknacks, lining the mantle, crashing to the floor. Lifting up the top of the mantle, he peered inside: Four stacks of DVDs, a thick brown envelope full of pictures and cash, and his passport.

He stuffed the DVD's and the envelope into his jacket pocket. When he reached in to get the passport, he felt the hard barrel of a gun jam against the back of his head, driving his face into the mantle.

"You've got three seconds to tell me where my daughter is. One. Two."

He heard the "click" of the hammer being pulled back. "You ain't gonna shoot me. 'Cause if you do—" Zarko said as he turned to face Scarsdale. "—you'll never see your daughter again."

Scarsdale lowered the gun and holstered it.

Zarko pushed Scarsdale back just as Scarsdale's right fist landed square on Zarko's jaw, snapping his head back.

"I'll have your badge for this," Zarko snarled, massaging his jaw.

A split second later, a left hook connected with the side of Zarko's head, sending him to one knee. As he tried to clear his head, a knee caught him right under the chin, knocking him backward against the fireplace. He tasted his own blood as it trickled from his split lip.

Scarsdale grabbed a handful of Zarko's hair, yanked him to his feet, and pulled his head back. Then he grabbed Zarko's throat with his free hand and squeezed. "Where's my daughter?"

Zarko stared back at Scarsdale. "Fuck you."

When Scarsdale's cell phone chirped, Zarko saw Harris pull it out and answer it. He couldn't hear what was said on the phone because Harris moved well away from them. A few seconds later he saw Harris hand the phone to Scarsdale.

"It's Shannon," Harris said, glaring at Zarko.

Zarko felt the pain in the back of his head when Scarsdale shoved him against the fireplace. Taking the phone from Harris, he turned his back to Zarko.

He took a couple of steps toward Scarsdale, reaching under his jacket for the gun. "A reunion. How touching."

"Shannon?" Scarsdale asked before the phone touched his ear. "Where are you?"

Zarko saw Harris come up fast on his left side just as his legs came out from under him. Landing face-down on the floor, he felt Harris's knee on his neck as his left hand was pulled behind him. Then the cold metal of the handcuff ratcheting closed around his wrist was followed by the other wrist. Harris removed the gun from inside his belt.

"You're under arrest for aggravated kidnapping and forgery," Harris whispered in his ear.

"I'm gonna have both ya'll's badges for violating my civil rights," Zarko said, as Harris yanked him to his feet.

"Really? Shouldn't have resisted arrest and assaulted us, asshole," Harris said.

❧❧❧

The Travis County Sheriff's Office occupied a two story red brick building on Hudson Bend Road near Lake Travis. Scarsdale pulled into a visitor slot and sprint for the door. He and Harris were met by a deputy sheriff who walked them back to a patrol division office.

Scarsdale peered through the window to see Shannon nibbling on a chocolate bar and watching TV. A female deputy sat next to her. A box of tissues sat on the desk in front of Shannon. "Shannon," he shouted as he rushed through the door and headed for her.

Shannon squealed in delight when she saw him. "Daddy," she shrieked. She scrambled off the chair, dropping the candy bar on the floor and rushed toward Scarsdale with her arms extended.

He bent over and scooped her up, hugging her as she wrapped her legs around his waist and threw her arms around his neck, pressing her face tight against his.

"I knew you'd come. I knew it."

☙❧

When the two of them got home, Scarsdale had a pizza delivered—cheese, mushroom, and pepperoni—Shannon's favorite. He watched her for any signs of trauma, but other than a few scrapes and bruises where she'd fallen, she appeared to be in good shape. They spent the first part of the evening together on the sofa watching cartoons.

"Daddy, when is Dani coming over?" she asked, standing on the sofa and leaning against the back cushions.

"Where is Dani?" wasn't something he wanted to discuss tonight. So he changed the subject.

"Hey, how about you and me running away to Fiesta Texas to ride the Ferris wheel and the White Water Rapids and the bumper cars?" he asked. "And we'll go see Shamu later."

Shannon tilted her head back a little and peered down her nose at Scarsdale. A smile formed showing her white baby teeth. Her eyes lit up. "Really?"

He grinned. "Yes, really. We'll go there Friday. Get a hotel room right by the Park. We'll come home Sunday."

"Okay." She put her hand on his shoulder. "Can Dani go too?"

"I—I think Dani has other plans."

"What plans?"

"Hey, look, it's Scooby Doo." To tell her Dani wasn't ever coming over again would upset her. She'd endured enough trauma for a lifetime. Maybe, he thought, if Dani's name wasn't mentioned again, Shannon might forget her. But, while he may not mention her name around Shannon, he knew he couldn't get Dani out of his head, even if he really wanted to.

☙❧

The next morning, Scarsdale, Harris, and Amanda Colbert stood with Mitchell outside the interrogation room at the county jail. Tom Zarko sat at a gray metal table, his wrists cuffed through a large ring welded to the top of the table. An omnidirectional microphone sat in the middle of the table.

Scarsdale saw Zarko looking at the one-way window. He focused his view on the purplish bruise on Zarko's jaw and the swollen lower lip.

"You over there, Scarsdale? Hey, I just loved your little daughter," he said, before puckering his lips and blowing a kiss in the direction of the window. "Soft and so tender."

"That sorry bastard," Scarsdale said, heading for the interrogation room door.

Harris grabbed his arm and pulled him back. "I better go head to head with that mushroom. We'll have a real civil rights case to deal with if you go in there."

"Neither one of you will go in there. Amanda goes," Mitchell said, glaring at Zarko.

"Oh, goodie," Amanda said, cracking her knuckles as she studied Zarko.

"I don't know what happened to him but your report better be damn good," Mitchell said, glancing at Scarsdale. He looked at Harris. "You're going to write a supplement to his. I expect both reports on my desk by five today. Compare notes if you have to, but get it done. I don't want to be answering questions from a pair of FBI agents about his bullshit civil-rights case."

Scarsdale sucked in a deep breath through his nose as he watched Amanda walk in and sit down opposite Zarko.

She laid the bag with the bracelet on the table along with the pawn ticket and Lasiter's altered ID. Then she placed the composite drawing the police artist made from the Mazda owner's description, followed by the Lasiter DNA lab report.

"I'm Detective Colbert with the Austin police."

"Scarsdale's watchin' me through that window, ain't he?"

"Probably. So let's start with this—Detective Scarsdale's daughter is safely back with her father. Agosti is cooperating fully with us. So just sit there and behave."

His grin faded and the laugh lines around his eyes disappeared.

Standing at an angle at the window with his arms folded across his chest, Scarsdale watched Amanda flip through the reports, making little "aha" and "hmm" sounds, taking a moment to scribble a note or two on a yellow pad.

Then she eyed Zarko staring at the reports and the notepad, before focusing on Amy's bracelet. "You want a cup of coffee?"

He stared at her for a second or two. "You bullshittin' me? You'd really get me some coffee?"

"A hot cup, with cream and sugar too."

Scarsdale knew the head game she was playing with Zarko. Be nice, make him feel like a human being, and afford him a few creature comforts like coffee. It would show the judge that Zarko had been treated fairly, no rubber hose beatings, or other torture if the defense attorney attacked the interrogation and any resulting admissions.

"Hell, yeah. Milk if ya have it. I hate that powder shit."

Amanda glanced over her shoulder in the direction of the window. "Two cups of coffee, guys. One black. One with real milk."

Harris returned with two Styrofoam cups three-quarters full of coffee, the steamy vapor rising from the cup. He set the first cup down near Amanda. "Coffee with milk," he said, placing it on the table by Zarko's hands.

Amanda picked up her cup and took a sip. "Okay, bedbug, let's start with the Mazda carjacking. You left your truck parked a few spaces away. Plus the victim IDd you out of a photo line-up."

"Yeah, okay, not one of my better jobs," he said, peering

at her over the edge of the coffee cup. "I saw the chopper, so I guess ya'll know where the car is now."

"Divers found it. Tell me why you did it."

"Ya'll were lookin for me, and my crappy truck wouldn't have made it to the border, much less anywhere else.

"How did you know we were looking for you?"

"I got a call warnin' me ya'll were coming after me. So I took off. After I jacked that car, I went home to get the rest of my stuff and saw ya'll parked by my house. That Crown Vic had cop written all over it."

"Who called?"

"I don't know his name."

Amanda shrugged. "So let's talk about Lasiter. Why'd you two get into it. Because of Amy Crowell?"

Zarko leaned forward, tapping the table with his forefinger. "I didn't kill him. Shit. He was the only friend I had. That chick, the one in the closet? Scarsdale's snitch." He chuckled. "She lied her ass off." He sat back. "She's the one—"

"I'm like you. I hate it when someone lies to me or about me. So let me stop you right there. We have a DNA match and the samples came from different parts of his body and from broken items nearby, including the wall."

Scarsdale watched Zarko sip his coffee then chew on his lip as though he were weighing his options.

Amanda waved the bag containing the bracelet. "This bracelet belonged to a young girl named Amy Crowell. Her mother IDd it. You pawned this using Lasiter's forged ID. Dude, when you decide to commit crimes, you go through the Penal Code chapter by chapter," Amanda said.

"I didn't kill that girl."

"We'll get to the Amy Crowell killing later. Finish telling me why you killed Lasiter."

Zarko sipped more coffee as he stared at the bracelet. "Yeah, well, I better have me a lawyer."

Two days later, Zarko's court-appointed lawyer, Stan Houser, and Assistant DA Fuller met in Fuller's office to iron out the sticking points for a plea deal where Zarko would plead guilty to all the charged offenses after testifying against the man known as the CEO.

Houser dangled the fact that Zarko knew where the main man—the CEO—kept his stash, his records, and more. "Waive the death penalty. A twenty-year sentence and we have a deal."

"Fifty," Fuller replied. "Or I'll go for the needle for Amy Crowell and Lasiter.

Houser looked over at Zarko who nodded. "Okay."

Fuller hated making such a deal but it meant he'd have the CEO plus Susan Crowell, Shannon Scarsdale, and the others wouldn't have to relive their worst nightmares in front of a packed courtroom, and they would escape the ruthless hounding of the news reporters. Besides Agosti and Zarko would both be in prison for a lengthy period. And if police could seize the CEO's records, many more names would follow them to prison.

"All right, I'll draft the papers." Fuller took several forms from his drawer and filled in the blanks on each. After signing them, he slid them across the desk to Houser. "Give me concrete facts corroborating your client's statement, including exactly where the CEO hides his collection, the name of the bank where he deposits his profits and the names of the buyers he transacts with." Fuller flipped to a clean page on his legal pad, ready to write. "Let's start with who the CEO is."

"That character's identity is unknown. But he did see him and can pick him out of a line-up. As for the bank, my client wasn't privy to that information however…" He referred to his notes. "This CEO stores this garbage in a storage unit at M&M Storage, Number 23. Zarko followed him there after a meeting with him at the Camden Suites hotel."

"Is that when Zarko saw his face?"

"Yes. When the man walked to the storage unit and when he left."

"And what did he see this CEO do at the storage unit?" Fuller asked.

"He watched him put a DVD, containing pornographic material, and his ski mask inside the storage unit."

"For clarification, Zarko saw him without the mask and can ID him in a line-up and in open court?"

"Yes."

"To be sure his information is fresh, when did Zarko see him go to the storage unit?"

"Three days ago. He said the unit has a large number of boxes stored inside," Houser said. "As for the names of the bidders, he doesn't know because the guy keeps his dealings private. Zarko and the others, whoever's still left, got the videos and pictures then gave them to him to sell. They get a small percentage of the profits. Since the CEO kept the sales amounts secret, none of them were privy to the actual amount earned. Now, my client will also testify to witnessing this man murder a guy named Clay Ferguson. I'm sure Agosti told you plenty about Ferguson."

ᏣᏍᏣ

Lieutenant Mitchell kept the development close to his chest. His warning to Scarsdale and Harris to move fast was issued with a throatier growl harsher than his usual bark. The threat of a department leak had hit him at the core. Until they had hard evidence, Zarko's plea deal went no farther than the three of them. Armed with a copy of Zarko's signed affidavit, Scarsdale and Harris met with Jim Stemple, the owner of M&M Storage to identify the leaseholder of Unit 23.

He opened a file drawer and pulled a folder out. The tab indicated "Number 23." He showed Scarsdale and Harris the signed lease contract. The lessee's name was Burt Hotchkins.

Harris and Scarsdale looked at each other.

"Describe Hotchkins." Harris said.

"He's a white dude, maybe in his early forties, short brown hair. A husky guy. Blue eyes. He wears a long-sleeved shirt all the time. Except this one time in August. It was over a hundred degrees that day. He comes here in short-sleeves." Stemple patted his right forearm. "He's got a tattoo of a black and green scorpion right here."

The two detectives nodded at each other. "Sounds like our man," Harris said.

"I'll tell ya' somethin'," Stemple said, "One day, I walked past twenty-three when he was looking in a box. I stopped to say hello. Just trying to be neighborly, you know. Anyhow he got really paranoid, closing up that box like he was afraid I'd see super-secret stuff. That's when I heard it."

"Heard what," Scarsdale asked.

"A police radio. Saw it lying on top of one of the other boxes."

"How do you know it was a police radio?" Harris asked.

"I was close enough to see the words 'Austin PD' on the front of it."

"Then what happened?" Scarsdale asked.

"Well, he turned it off in a big hurry then got real shitty. Told me to leave." Stemple tapped himself on the chest with his thumb. "Me. I had half a mind to tell him to get his crap out of my facility."

Later that afternoon, Scarsdale and Harris met Jim Stemple at the department. They showed him a fat book with photographs of all APD officers and employees. Stemple flipped to the second page. He recoiled and pointed at one picture. "That's him."

"You sure?" asked Scarsdale.

"Damn sure am. That's Hotchkins." He looked straight into Scarsdale's eyes and held the gaze. "So he's a cop? What's in those boxes?"

"Can't say who he is and, as for what's in those boxes, we'll be coming out later with a search warrant."

"You don't need any warrant. I'll open it myself."

Scarsdale smiled and shook his head. "Have to go by the rules, Mr. Stemple. Appreciate the offer, though. There are two things I would like you to do for us. First, don't mention your meetings with us to anyone. Second, I'd like you to make an important phone call."

While Amanda kept surveillance on the unit, Scarsdale got a search warrant.

That evening, Scarsdale, Harris, Mitchell, and Assistant Chief Dell Murphy joined Amanda and several uniformed officers at strategic locations at M&M Storage. Each detective had line of sight on Unit 23.

From Scarsdale's vantage point, he saw Stemple walking toward the Unit with the lessee. Stemple was a natural. He'd lured the renter of unit 23 with a tale of vandalism like a seasoned spider. Scarsdale keyed his microphone button.

"Guys, here he comes."

Scarsdale saw Stemple stop in front of the targeted unit, gesturing, and talking to the CEO before walking away. The CEO looked around as if checking for spying eyes. After unlocking it, he jerked the door up and, taking one last look around, entered the unit.

Scarsdale saw him raise a tarp, exposing a stack of boxes. He opened one box, seeming to peer inside. He repeated it for each box. Moving to a table, the CEO opened a laptop and typed on the keyboard.

"We got him. Let's go," Scarsdale said into the microphone.

Amanda and Scarsdale sprinted in first, followed by Harris and the others, each with their weapon trained on the CEO.

"Get on the ground now," shouted Scarsdale.

The CEO stood up, his eyes darting from the two seasoned detectives to the uniforms that followed them. He grabbed the laptop and flung it against the wall of the unit. Scarsdale, Harris and Amanda grabbed him and threw him to the ground before he could do any more damage. Scarsdale dropped his knee on the back of the man's neck, pinning him to the ground.

Harris twisted his arms behind his back and cuffed him. Scarsdale slid the right shirt sleeve up the arm. "Nice scorpion tattoo, *Commander* Winters," he said, jerking him to his feet.

Amanda read him his rights as Scarsdale stuffed a copy of the search warrant into his shirt pocket. "Okay, Chester the molester, let's see what you've got in here."

Scarsdale found the black ski mask under a box. Holding

it up, he grinned at Winters. "Been out trick or treating, ass-hole?"

Winters kept quiet.

Amanda boxed up the laptop. "Give me all the computer items you find. The lab guys will search the drives for his buyers' names."

Scarsdale and Harris searched inside the boxes. Two boxes tucked way back in a far corner had several three-ring binders filled with photographs. Another box had stacks of DVDs, some thumb drives and an external hard drive. He showed one binder to Murphy who looked at Winters in disgust.

"Be sure to get his badge, ID, and weapon," Murphy said as he turned and walked away.

"You're arresting me?" Winters said. "Dell, what's going on? Is this some kind of sick joke?"

Murphy answered Winters's question with his middle finger flashed over his shoulder as he headed out of the unit.

Scarsdale snapped the binder shut. "You're under arrest for the murder of Clay Ferguson, the possession and promotion of child pornography, and the aggravated kidnapping of my daughter." He nodded at the two smiling officers. "He's all yours."

☙❧

Lying in bed that night, Scarsdale stuck the bookmark between the pages and closed *Single Fathers Raising Daughters*. The clock showed a few minutes after one. It had been a long day, but a very fruitful one. He wondered what the chief's reaction had been when he listened to Winters' secret recordings, especially the one with Robertson.

Not really sleepy, he folded his arms behind his head and stared up at the ceiling.

Images of Dani flitted past his eyes—that day in the break room when he came back from leave, when she'd appeared at his cubicle with the Ferguson analysis, when she'd watched over Shannon at the departmental kid's party.

Closing his eyes he could see her face, her warm smile, those honey-brown eyes that seemed to search deep inside his soul, and the way she always toyed with a lock of her hair. He felt something for her but couldn't make sense of it.

Then Shannon's voice broke the silence. "Daddy, I'm scared," she whimpered.

He half-rolled to the left and saw her standing in the doorway in her Donald Duck pajamas, bathed in the light from the hallway, the Bavarian doll pinned tight against her chest.

He lifted the bed covers. "C'mon, princess. Crawl in."

Shannon rolled on her side, facing him, laying her hand on his arm. A few minutes later, she shook his arm. "Daddy, is Dani mad at me?"

He put his arm around her. "Not at all, sweetheart. Why would you think that?"

"'Cause she doesn't come here anymore."

"She works real hard. Maybe she's tired and not in the mood for company."

"She's never ever coming back, is she?" Shannon asked.

"I don't know. Maybe she will. Let's talk about it tomorrow, okay?" He rolled over, facing the opposite wall.

Shannon laid the doll between them, pulling the covers up around its neck. "Goodnight, Daddy."

CHAPTER 26

"Before you embark on a journey of revenge,
dig two graves." ~ *Confucius*

Patience and cash were running out for Parnell. He had to find Dani soon. It was 9:30 a.m. when he punched in Miranda's phone number. "Hey, baby. It's Pete."

"Hey, you. I've been waiting for you to call."

"Just wonderin' if you got Dani Mueller's address."

"Yes," she said with a hint of reservation in her words. "Please don't tell anyone I gave it to you. We're not supposed to—"

"I understand, sweetheart. By the way, I reserved a room for us this weekend at one of the fanciest hotels on the Riverwalk, just like I said I would. They have a jazz band there. Tell me you like jazz," Parnell said, sitting on the edge of the hotel bed, sliding the Siberian Skinner across the whetstone.

"I've never listened to it before but I always wanted to. Ready to write?" Miranda asked.

When she finished reciting Dani's home address, she asked Parnell when he planned to pick her up tonight for the dinner and movie.

"I'll give you a call this afternoon," he said. "Right now, I have to drive down to San Antonio. While I'm there, I'll reserve our hotel room."

"I thought you said you already did that?"

"Uh-uh. I said I was going to do that."

◈◈◈

At one o'clock Parnell sat at the hotel bar nursing a whiskey and seven while he envisioned how he'd torture Karla.

Around three o'clock, he bounced up the three flights of steps to Apartment 312. He glanced around. Not seeing any-one, he stuck the two lock picks in the keyhole. One minute. He had to give the door a hard shove before it opened. Inside, a hint of cinnamon in the air.

Parnell wanted that knife and the bracelet so he started with the bathroom. He dumped the contents from the dirty clothes hamper on the floor. Picking up a pair of panties, he held them against his nose. "Ahhh, sweet."

Each of the three drawers in the bathroom cabinet got yanked out and tossed on the floor. He swept the towels and bed sheets off the shelves in the linen closet. Finding nothing he wanted, he looked toward the bedroom.

He picked Dani's jewelry box off her dresser and turned it upside down. Using his boot, he sorted through the contents until he saw a bracelet fitting the description Mattie gave him of the one Doyle wore before he died.

Now he wanted the knife used to kill his brother. Parnell jerked all five drawers out of her dresser, one at a time and turned each one upside down, pouring their contents out on the carpet. "Where's that fuckin knife?" Tossing each drawer aside like a piece of trash, he went to her bed and lifted the mattress up, checked underneath and let it fall while turning his attention to the nightstand.

He pulled the single drawer out and rummaged through the contents. Then he flung the wood drawer across the room. Its contents scattered over the bed and the floor.

"Goddammit," he yelled, kicking at the nightstand with the bottom of his boot, sending it crashing against the wall. The lamp fell off and shattered. The table toppled over, reveal-ing a white box.

He stood there in a kind of stunned silence, staring at the box for a few seconds. "Goddamn, what the hell is this?" he said, speaking just above a whisper. Squatting down he ripped the top off the box and reached inside, pulling out her diary.

Inside he found entries she made about his brother taunting her, using Katarina's stolen bracelet as bait. He read the details of their confrontation. "You lyin' cocksucker," he said, heaving the book against the wall after reading the part about how she killed Doyle.

Newspaper clippings spilled from the book and fluttered down like snowflakes. He saw the headline on one that landed near him—Doyle's trial and murder. Another clipping told of her daughter's murder. Yet another summarized Karla's interview with the police and her appearance before the grand jury. He ripped up each of them and tossed them like confetti at her bed.

Parnell walked into the living room and saw the big ornate cuckoo clock resting on the fireplace mantle. It showed 4:30. He figured she'd get home around five or five-thirty. Once he was finished with her, he'd take that clock—the one Mattie wanted—and her Acura. An ex-con friend ran a chop shop in Sacramento and would split the profits from the sale of the car's parts.

Parnell took two beers from the fridge and plopped down in her recliner. That's when he saw the knife, jammed between the seat cushion and the arm. He held it up, twisting side to side. After polishing off the first, he tossed the bottle on the living room carpet. When he finished the second beer, he flung it against the wall and watched it bounce off and roll to a stop on the sofa cushion. Hearing footsteps approaching from outside, Parnell looked out the peephole, saw Dani and slipped inside the closet next to the front door. He stuffed her knife in his waistband and drew the Skinner out of its sheath.

೧೨೧೨

I threw my shoulder against my front door, pushing it open. After four tries to close it, I shoved the door against the frame and fastened the chain lock. *I have to get this fixed—now.*

I went straight to the kitchen phone to call the manager. Once that was done, I intended to pour myself a celebratory

Grand Marnier for putting Robertson on the ropes. Only I never made it to the phone. The two empty beer bottles on my living room floor, and the cuckoo clock sitting on the recliner told me something was very wrong here. Upon hearing a noise behind me, I turned toward the front door and saw him.

He stood there, a cold stare and a snarky smile. Light glinted off the edges of the knife he held. Parnell, Doyle Burton's brother. He was bigger than Doyle with an even worse temper. I remembered him, dressed in prison coveralls, a deputy seated next to him. He had been subpoenaed to testify for Doyle.

"Been a while, you fuckin' cunt."

My heart almost stopped beating. Nausea rose from my stomach. I spun and ran for the kitchen counter, wanting to reach a butcher knife but he caught me and jerked me back. I rammed my elbow into his face as hard as I could. A popping sound was followed by a grunt.

He spun me around so we stood face to face. The awful smell of his breath—the beer and whatever else—almost gagged me. A trail of bright red blood trickled from his nose over his upper lip. He wiped it off with the back of his hand.

I raked his face with my fingernails, peeling skin off his cheeks. Tiny beads of blood like miniature oil wells spouted up from the scratches. Too bad I missed his eyes. When he let go of me and grabbed for his face, I lunged again for the butcher knife. That's when I felt it—a hard blow to the side of my face. A momentary flash of white light followed by excruciating pain shot through my head. While I struggled to clear my brain, his hands gripped my throat like a vise. He bent me backward against the counter. His hands gripped my throat and squeezed. I couldn't breathe. My fingers clawed at his fingers. The room began spinning. My vision blurred then everything went black.

❧❧❧

Scarsdale pecked out the last of his investigative summaries on the computer keyboard. He had promised Shannon he'd take her to the six o'clock showing this evening of The Chronicles of Narnia: The Lion, The Witch and The Wardrobe. It was a long film so he wanted to make the early show. He didn't want to keep her up too late.

Miranda Lopez poked her head around the corner. "Detective Scarsdale?"

He glanced at her and continued typing. "That's me. What do you need?"

"I met this guy and we…"

He looked at her.

She bowed her head and clasped her hands so tightly Scarsdale saw her fingers turn white. "He wanted Dani Mueller's home address. I knew she worked with you and—"

"What guy?" The first name that popped into his mind was Parnell Burton.

"He said his name was Pete Gilbert. He said he'd call me this afternoon to finalize our date and—"

"What did he want her address for?" Scarsdale asked. His cop instincts told him something wasn't right with this picture.

Miranda swallowed hard and looked around. "She's his second cousin."

"Oh shit." He pointed to the guest chair in his cubicle. "She's from Germany. She doesn't have any relatives in the States." Scarsdale took a deep breath and let it out. "Tell me you didn't give it to him."

She stared at him with wet eyes then nodded. "He said he worked for Samsung as a public relations specialist. I mean he seemed so…" Miranda said, her voice trailing off.

He brought up the California parole website and scrolled down the list of parolees, hoping he wouldn't see Burton's name. Mid-way down the third list, he saw it—Parnell James Burton. Paroled 7 days ago. "Son of a bitch!" He moved the computer monitor around so Miranda could see the photograph. "Is this the man?"

Her eyes almost bugged out of her head when she saw Parnell Burton's picture. When she looked at Scarsdale, he saw the realization in her eyes that she'd been used. Miranda's mouth fell open then her hand went to her mouth.

"Oh my God," she murmured, "I hope he—"

"Stay put," he said.

Her police career was toast but he dismissed the thought as he trotted down the hall to Dani's office. The door was locked. He saw no light coming from under the door. Sprinting back to his office, he picked up his cell phone and dialed her home number. After several rings, he pressed the "END CALL" button. *Maybe she's at the pool or getting her mail*, he thought before yelling for Harris. They headed for the Crown Vic.

☙❧

My vision was still fuzzy when I came to. I shook my head to clear the cobwebs. That's when I discovered Burton had tied me to a chair in the kitchen. My hands were tied so tight behind the back of the chair that the bindings cut into my wrists. Twisting my arms back and forth made the cord only cut deeper. Looking around, I spotted a ball of Number 18 twine and a roll of duct tape on the counter.

He paraded around my apartment like he owned it, guzzling another beer, the long shiny knife in his right hand and the butt of a gun protruding from his waistband.

"What do you want?" I asked, as if I didn't already know.

He let out a hideous laugh then came toward me. Stopping directly in front of me, he leaned down, his face just inches from mine. "What do I want? You really have to ask me that?"

He grabbed my chin and jerked my head back so we were eye to eye. "I'll tell ya want I want. You and me, we're gonna have us a little party. Except it won't be so much fun for you." He laughed again as he waved the knife back and forth inches from my face. "There's no tree in here to tie you to so I improvised. Now you're gonna know how Doyle felt when you cut him up." He held the knife up. "I think it's only right that you die by the same knife you killed my brother with."

Then he stood up, gulped the last of the beer before slinging it against the wall behind me. The bottle exploded and made me jump.

"So what am I supposed to call you?" he asked, pacing around the chair. "Karla or Dani. How about bitch—or 'ho?"

He smacked me in the back of the head with the butt of the knife. "You were fuckin' that DA, weren't ya? The two of you framed Doyle, didn't ya?" He stopped in front of me again. "Well, hoochie mama, you screwed your last man."

He pulled Katarina's bracelet out of his pants pocket and dangled it. "Bunny's gonna *love* wearing this." He walked over to the cuckoo clock and tapped the point of the knife on the edge of it. "And this is gonna look good in my mom's living room." He glanced back at me. "Kinda dress the place up." He scanned the room. "But I don't know what to bring back for Phoenix. Got any of them fancy dresses?" He picked up the photograph of Katarina and me on the beach, looked at it then busted it across his knee. Then he disappeared into my bedroom.

A minute or so later, he walked out carrying my diary, waving the book in the air. "I read this piece of crap, you lyin bitch." He hit me on the head with it. "That shit about when you killed Doyle."

He tossed the book across the living room, then raised the knife slashed my upper arm.

I bit my lip to keep from screaming. No reason to give him the satisfaction that he'd hurt me. Blood coursed down my arm and dripped into a puddle on the floor.

"He wasn't doin nuthin. You jumped him from behind. Cut him up bad. All that crap about him killing your kid was bullshit." He gestured wildly with my knife. "That jury said he didn't do it." He jabbed the point of the knife against my cheek, an inch or so under my eye. "Maybe you did it," he whispered.

I pulled and pushed against the wrist bindings. "He slaughtered my daughter and got away with it. He even phoned me and told me all about it. How he raped her before he beat her with a baseball bat. Before he strangled her," I screamed at him. "Yeah, I killed him and I'd do it all again."

Parnell backhanded me across the face, snapping my head to the side. "Shut up, ya hear me? My brother never did that. You beat him with that bat and sliced him up like he was a piece of meat." He yanked my head back by the hair, pressing the knife against my throat. "Isn't that right, bitch?" He let go, shoving my head forward. "Well, I read that doctor's report. I know what you did." His tone softened, becoming little more than a whisper. "You're gonna die like he did. Slow and pain-ful."

"It was *his* bat. The same bat he used to club my daughter. The one he was getting ready to use on another child. Yes, I stabbed him so many times I lost count. He was a pedophile, a sick freak, preying on little kids."

Parnell slapped me across the face, splitting my lip.

I tasted my own blood.

"No he wasn't," he screamed. He dragged the blade the length of my face, from my temple down to my jaw. "When they find you, nobody's gonna recognize you."

"You're a coward, just like your brother."

He leaned close and whispered again, "First I'm gonna skin you. Then gut ya like field-dressing a deer." He stood up, waving the blade in a circular motion. "But I'm gonna keep you alive so you can feel each slice."

He circled me, jabbing the point of the blade into my hands and arms. Tiny red dots of blood popped up.

"You and your brother like it when your victim can't fight back, don't you?"

I saw the silvery tip of my knife coming at me when Par-nell lunged.

"I told you to shut up!"

I twisted away from the path of the knife as best I could but not enough. The first twinge felt like a needle prick then I felt the blade sink deep inside. It felt so cold, like death's fin-gertips had touched me. The pain tore through me.

When I opened my eyes, I saw the silvery blade dripping red blood. Each breath felt harder to draw in. The pain was too much. I screamed. Then his fist came at me like a torpedo.

❦

Parnell's fist struck Dani just under the side of her jaw. Her head bounced off the back of the chair and came to rest on her chest. Blood oozed out of the corner of her mouth. Her eyes were shut.

He grabbed another beer from the refrigerator, popped the top, and took a long gulp. After a minute or two, he lifted her chin up with the top of the bottle. Then let go. Her head dropped to her chest.

"Shit." He paced back and forth, chugging the beer before tossing the empty bottle in the sink. "Fuck me!" he yelled, running his hands over his head as he circled the chair.

❦

Scarsdale told Harris on the ride over that Parnell Burton had been paroled and was in town. Both men vaulted up the steps. When they reached the top, Scarsdale saw Dani's door partly open. Holding his Glock in both hands, he hugged the wall, inching closer to the door. Harris slid along the wall behind him. When he got to her door, he listened. A man he assumed was Parnell Burton screamed a string of profanities, ending with, "Wake up, bitch."

In a whisper, Scarsdale described the floor plan of the apartment based on what he had seen in the manager's office.

Burton's voice rang out. "Goddammit! Wake up. You ain't as hurt as bad as you're gonna be."

Furniture screeched across bare floor. It had to be the kitchen but Scarsdale couldn't be sure. If Burton was trying to wake her, Dani was still alive but probably hurt bad.

Taking shallow breaths, he carefully pushed on the door. It opened a few inches. The security chain made a snapping noise. He paused and listened but only heard the sound of cars passing by on the street. Parnell must have heard the chain snap and was waiting for them. He signaled to Harris that, on the count of three, he'd force his way in.

On three, he raised his foot and kicked the door with everything he had. The chain snapped and the door crashed against the wall. Aiming his weapon straight ahead he rushed in first. He saw Parnell standing behind Dani, holding her by the hair, a gun pressed to her temple. Parnell's eyes looked like cold black marbles.

"Drop the gun. Now!" Scarsdale ordered, sliding himself to the right of the doorway to make way for Harris. With Burton using Dani as a shield, Scarsdale didn't have a clear field of fire.

But Burton did. In one quick movement, he swung the gun around. A bullet tore right through Scarsdale's upper arm.

Scarsdale staggered backward against the front window frame before dropping to a knee. His left arm burned like someone jabbed a hot soldering iron into it before going numb. He slapped his hand over the wound. Blood oozed from between his fingers.

Harris charged in.

Scarsdale heard a second shot and saw Harris go down.

Harris yelped, dropping his gun, as he grabbed for his thigh with both hands. "Sonofabitch!"

Burton aimed his gun back at Scarsdale, firing two more shots while screaming profanities.

Scarsdale saw Burton walking toward him, the barrel of the gun pointed at his head. Raising the Glock, he squeezed the trigger. The bullet ripped a hole in Burton's gut.

The man stood there, stock-still, his eyes widening in disbelief as he looked down to see blood pouring out of the wound.

Scarsdale's second shot hit Burton above the left eye.

Burton staggered backward and collapsed.

Scarsdale waited a few seconds with his gun trained on Burton before moving toward him, his weapon pointed at the man's head. His left arm throbbed and blood dripped off his fingertips like a leaky faucet.

He kicked Parnell's gun back toward the door. Then he knelt down and felt for a pulse. None. Holstering his gun, Scarsdale hurried over to Harris. Taking his belt off, he fastened it around the thigh in tourniquet-fashion.

"I got it," Harris said, grabbing the end of the belt. "Check Dani."

His numb arm dangling at his side, Scarsdale rushed over to an unconscious Dani. Her right eye and lip were swollen. Angry red bruises circled her throat. Pressing his fingers against her neck, he found a pulse. Scarsdale grabbed the knife off the counter and sliced the cord binding her arms. He lifted Dani out of the chair and laid her on the floor.

Grabbing a kitchen towel, he pressed it against the stab wound on her side, holding it in place with his knee. He saw a red and purplish contusion on her jaw and wondered if Parnell broke it. He peered inside her open mouth but couldn't see anything obstructing the airway. Using his coat sleeve as a sponge, he mopped the blood from around her mouth. Then he managed to call 911.

ⱷⱾⱻ

When the ER doctor emerged from Dani's exam room, he briefed Scarsdale on the extent of her injuries. The abdominal wound wasn't as bad as it had first appeared. The blade had gone through layers of muscle, the wound requiring several stitches. No organs had been penetrated.

Her lower mandible had a hairline fracture that didn't require stabilization but she'd be on a liquid diet and minimal talking. The doctor had sedated her because of the painful nature of the jaw fracture. The wound on her arm required several stiches. The remaining wounds were superficial and would heal over the next few days. As for Harris, the doctor told Scarsdale the bullet struck the femur, shattering it. Harris would have a permanent limp when he got back on his feet.

Scarsdale's wound required a few stitches. The bullet had passed through the flesh of his arm. He wondered how Shannon would react when she saw the bandaging.

Scarsdale, Amanda, and a gimpy Harris visited Dani each of the three days she was hospitalized. When the doctor released her, Scarsdale drove her back to her apartment.

She didn't say much during the ride, spending the time gazing out the side window, seemingly lost in thought.

He glanced over at her a few times, noticing the yellowish-red bruising around her face and neck. He knew she was still in some pain and wanted to say something to cheer her up, but decided not to intrude on her thoughts. She was probably trying to make sense of what happened.

"Here's home," he said, keeping his tone upbeat.

A disheveled Dani Mueller paused in the doorway of her trashed-out apartment for a minute or so. She wrapped her arms across her chest, hugging herself, seemingly hesitant about going inside.

He gazed at her, wishing he could wipe away the terror and hopelessness written on her face.

She didn't resist when he wrapped his right arm around her shoulders, pulling her close. She leaned her head against his chest.

"He has a step-brother and a sister. When they hear about what happened, they'll come after me. His mom may come with them."

Her whole body shook.

"They won't get near you. We'll move you to another complex."

She turned around to face him. "Wherever I move, they'll find me. Germany is my only option. Nobody else needs to get hurt because of me." She touched his bandaged arm. "Look what happened to you—and to Sean. And Zarko—what he did to Shannon." She wept. "It's tearing me up inside."

"What happened wasn't your fault. Winters had it in for me, so Zarko did what he ordered him to do. Let me get you a tissue."

"I'm all right," she said, wiping her eyes with the heel of her hands.

"Let's grab a few of your things. You can stay in the spare bedroom at my house until you heal up."

"No, thank you," she said. "I'll be okay. I have to call the movers, the airline, and my parents," she said, standing in the middle of the living room, a grim look on her face as she surveyed the damaged apartment.

Using his good arm, he pulled her into a long gentle hug, careful not to press against her left side or her sore jaw. When he let go, he let his eyes soak up her features: the curly locks of her uncombed hair, the smooth curve of her cheeks, the Cupid's bow lips, her satiny smooth skin, and her honey-brown eyes, now red-rimmed and tormented.

"I really wish you'd change your mind and stay," he said, following her into the bedroom.

"I can't." She turned, looked right into his eyes, and reached her hand up, letting her fingers caress the rugged lines of his face.

"Shannon asks about you every day, when you're coming over. She thinks you're mad at her," he said, his mind racing to think of more reasons to convince her to stay.

Her words came out so soft he had to lean closer to hear. "Everything about me, my past mistakes, it's out there for everyone to read about. Once Marcy finds out about me, once she discovers I spent time with Shannon, she'll haul you back into court." Holding her side, she bent down and picked up her diary, set it on the nightstand, and walked back into the living room. "I wish with all my heart things had been different, but—" She stared at the bloody stain on the carpet for a few seconds before gazing into his eyes. "I'm very sorry. It's all my…" Her voice trailed off.

He saw the tears streaming down her cheeks, her lip quivering. He lifted his finger to brush a tear away. "That's crazy," Scarsdale exclaimed, not knowing what else to say.

She sniffed then wiped at her nose with a tissue. "It's the truth," she said, her voice cracking. "None of this would have happened if I had moved home after my divorce." She walked over to the front door and held it open.

"Dani, it doesn't have to be like this." His eyes peered into hers. He didn't want her to leave but he didn't know any way to stop her.

"Please don't make this any harder for either of us." She sniffed again and raised her head high. "I care a lot about you, Jason. And I love Shannon to death but—" She wiped her eyes, flashed her eyebrows up, and forced a smile. "Tell her I'll write to her." She pulled his head over and kissed him on the cheek. "Now please go."

"Dani—"

She put her finger up to his lips. "Please?"

He walked out and she closed the door. This time it shut securely.

He stood outside her door for almost a minute, questioning whether he had done the right thing by keeping Shannon away from her; wondering if he was letting a good woman slip away.

✄◑✄◑

Scarsdale strolled along the beach at Port Aransas, carrying his running shoes, watching Shannon chase seagulls along the shoreline. It had been four weeks since her ordeal and she seemed happy and content.

The ebb and flow of the cool Gulf water was soothing. It lapped at his bare feet as seagulls called, some gliding, and some hovering. A few waltzing on the sand shadowed him.

Dani was gone, leaving him with an emptiness he hadn't expected. He thought of several things he had wanted to say to her, to ask her, of places he wanted to take her.

His life had changed completely and it felt like the other shoe had dropped, taking him full circle from Charity's death to a truly new start. He had even stopped wearing his wedding ring.

Sean Harris took medical retirement. He and Mary bought

a log cabin up in Colorado near a river well stocked with trout. Harris insisted he and Shannon come up there.

After the contents of the Winters-Robertson tape recording became known to the chief, Robertson resigned in lieu of termination and left Austin for a position with a private investigation firm in Boston.

Mitchell succeeded Robertson as Commander of the Violent Crimes Division. Amanda Colbert made lieutenant and took over as head of Sex Crimes. It would be her job to appoint his new partner. Winters pled out to six concurrent life sentences in state court and awaited trial in US District Court for multiple counts of interstate distribution of child pornography and income tax evasion.

Marcy had made the big gesture, sending Scarsdale a letter, apologizing for being such a wicked mother-in-law. She stated that, like everyone else, she made a lot of mistakes and asked for his forgiveness. She promised to be a better grandmother to Shannon. She closed with the hope that Scarsdale would move on with his life and find happiness again. What else could she possibly have done? His attorney, Alissa, had already sent him a copy of the judge's order dismissing the custody suit with prejudice, meaning Marcy wouldn't be able to re-open it.

A few feet away, Shannon played in the shallows, laughing and splashing water on her father. He pretended to chase after her, scooping and tossing handfuls of saltwater on her. A man walking his dog walked toward them and Shannon paused, alert and wary before she scampered to her father's side. Scarsdale rested his hand on her head. Her hair felt warm and silky beneath his hand. He'd learned she was a fighter and she'd proven herself to be brave, but her caution pleased him.

He shook his head in awe that he had ever considered eating his pistol. His wry smile faded as Dani's image filled his head. The same image that popped up every night since she'd left three weeks ago. He imagined her strolling along some cobble-stoned Garmisch street, checking out the shops, maybe sitting at an outdoor café with friends, sipping a Spaten. He wondered what she was doing right now. If she'd found a job and with whom. Had her wounds healed? Was she happy? Would he ever see her again? It was this last question that haunted him.

He thought about what she meant to him, to Shannon, to both of them. For a week or so after she left, he tried to convince himself it didn't matter, but he couldn't. He'd seen a future with her.

He wondered if she'd felt the same. *Why did I let her go? What the hell is wrong with me?* In that instant, he unclipped his cell and punched in a phone number. *Why not?* he thought, waiting for someone to answer.

കൈൻ

On Sunday afternoon, three weeks and one day after I left Austin, I sat at my parent's kitchen table, holding the pink envelope bearing my name and address. The return address showed Shannon C. Scarsdale, Austin, Texas. I opened it and removed the letter.

It had been written on lined notebook paper and was dated a week ago. I knew the uneven blocky handwriting was Shannon's and read the letter as mother prepared dinner.

Dear Dani,

> *I wish you would come back. I miss you a lot. Daddy misses you too. He doesn't say it but I know he does. I named my doll after you so you would always be close to me. Daddy said dinner is ready so I have to go now. I love you, Dani*

> *Shannon*

I felt my eyes well up. "I love you, too, Shannon—and your daddy," I whispered in English. I remembered how good it felt when he held me close.

"What did you say?" Petra asked, turning to look at me. "Why are you crying?"

I held up the letter before folding it. "It's from Shannon. I said I missed her, too." My side still felt sore so I took my time getting up before heading for the door.

"Where are you going? Dinner will be ready soon."

"I'm going for a walk. Don't worry, I'll be back in time for dinner."

I sensed my mother's eyes tracking me across the living room and out the door.

While I strolled past the homes on Danielstrasse, I wondered what Jason and Shannon were doing right now. It would be mid-morning back in Austin. Maybe they just finished up breakfast. I unfolded Shannon's letter and read it again.

I felt like the rope in a tug-of-war. A big part of me wanted to go back to Texas. I really felt the pull of Jason and Shannon but, except for ten short years with Katarina, my time in America had been one disaster after another. I wanted a family but would they really want me? Maybe after enough time passed so the Burtons forgot about me, I'd think about returning.

But for now at least, Garmisch was home. My father had arranged an interview for a crime analyst position with the Bavarian State Criminal Police Office in Munich. If I got the job, the commute wouldn't take much longer than it did in Austin.

∽∾∽∾

The following Monday, Scarsdale walked towards Gate 6 at the Austin-Bergstrom Airport, holding the boarding passes the attendant had given him and towing a dark green Samsonite behind him.

"Daddy, do you think Dani will be happy to see us?" Shannon asked, pulling a small blue suitcase as they headed down the concourse.

"I hope so."

"Do you think Dani will take me up on the mountains?"

He gazed down at her, smiling. "I'll bet she will if you ask her."

As they walked past Gate 8, Shannon's head turned as a little boy and his mother moved past them in the opposite direction.

He glanced over his shoulder at the two before looking down at Shannon. "You okay?"

"Will Dani come home with us?" she asked, still staring at the boy and his mother.

He gazed at his daughter when she looked up at him, the question laying right on the surface of her coffee-brown eyes. It was the same haunting question he asked himself over and over since he made the trip reservations. "I don't know, princess, but we're going to invite her."

THE END

About the Author

Alan Brenham is the pseudonym for Alan Behr, an American author and attorney. He served as a law enforcement officer before earning a law degree and has worked as a prosecutor and a criminal defense attorney. He has traveled to several countries in Europe, the Middle East, Alaska, and almost every island in the Caribbean. While on assignment with US Army, he lived in Berlin, Germany. Brenham and his wife, Lillian, currently live in Texas.